HELEN ASHTON

William and Dorothy

COLLINS
14 ST JAMES'S PLACE LONDON

FIRST PUBLISHED 1938
THIS EDITION 1974

ISBN 0 00 221930 1

PRINTED IN GREAT BRITAIN
COLLINS CLEAR-TYPE PRESS : LONDON AND GLASGOW

AUTHOR'S NOTE

THE FIRST idea of this book was given to me by my sister, Katharine Davies, when we were collaborating in, *I Had a Sister* (Lovat Dickson. 1937). It was she who suggested that Dorothy Wordsworth should be made the heroine of this novel. I could not have written it without constant reference to the life of Dorothy Wordsworth by Professor Ernest de Selincourt; or without the kind permission of MacMillan & Company to quote and paraphrase very freely from Dorothy Wordsworth's adorable journals. All the descriptions of scenery in chapters II.-IX. are hers and much of the narrative is as far as possible in her own words. The conversations are based, wherever possible, on the Wordsworth family letters. I append a short list of those books through which my quotations may be most readily traced to their original sources. As regards the places where the Wordsworths lived, I wish to thank Lady Pinney for a sight of Racedown House and its relics; Mrs. Bell, formerly Lady Beaumont and mother of the present Sir George Beaumont, for permission to see Coleorton Hall and the winter garden laid out by William Wordsworth; and Mrs. Wakefield, of Keswick, for taking me to Greta Hall and Applethwaite. My friend, Phyllis Bentley, gave me much of the information about old Halifax and showed me what is left of the town that Dorothy knew. The National Trust have preserved to our use Dove Cottage and the little house at Nether Stowey in which the Coleridges lived, very much as Dorothy saw them in her lifetime.

COLERIDGE, S. T. C. *Anima Poetae.* 1895. *Table Talk.* 1886. *Biographia Literaria.* 1891.

DE QUINCEY. *Recollections of the Lakes and of the Lake Poets.* 1863.

De Selincourt, E. *Dorothy Wordsworth.* 1933. *The Early Letters of William and Dorothy Wordsworth.* 1932. *The Middle Years.* 1935. Two vols.

Griggs, E. L. and G. E. *Letters of Hartley Coleridge.* 1936.

Grigg, E. L. *Hartley Coleridge; His Life and Work.* 1929.

Hazlitt, W. *On My First Acquaintance with English Poets.* (In Collected Essays.)

Knight. *Memorials of Coleorton.* Two vols. 1887. *Letters of the Wordsworth Family.* Three vols. 1907.

Lamb, C. *Essays of Elia;* and *Eliana.* 1869.

Lucas, E. V. *Life of Charles Lamb.* Two vols. *Letters of Charles and Mary Lamb.* Three vols. 1935.

Legouis, A. *William Wordsworth and Annette Vallon.* 1922.

Lockhart, J. G. *Life of Sir Walter Scott.* Seven vols. 1837-8.

Maclean, C. M. *Dorothy Wordsworth; The Early Years.* 1932.

Pinney, H. and Bergen, E. *Racedown and the Wordsworths.* 1932.

Rawnsley, H. R. *Literary Associations of the Lake District.* Two vols. 1894.

Sandford. *Mrs. Thomas Poole and His Friends.* Two vols. 1888.

Sackville-West, E. *A Flame in Sunlight; De Quincey.* 1936.

Wordsworth, D. *Recollections of a Tour made in Scotland* (A.D. 1803). 1874. *Journals of Dorothy Wordsworth* (ed. Knight). Two vols. 1910.

Wordsworth, W. *Collected Poems.* Ed. 1893, with Miss Fenwick's notes.

I

1

THE TIME was a June evening, breathless and overcast, with thunder behind the hills; the year 1797. George the Third was on the throne, not yet out of his wits, and England was at war with the new French Republic. The place was a valley on the borders of Dorset and Devon, a green and quiet meadow beside a wandering brook, set about with fairy rushes; daffodils grew there in the springtime and the trees were bowed by gales from the sea. In this landscape a young man and woman were walking arm in arm.

He was a gaunt, raw-boned, rustic fellow, like a North-country Don Quixote, with large hands and feet, of which he was very conscious in company, and something of a roll or lounge in his gait; his gawky limbs were displayed in a brown fustian jacket and striped pantaloons, all old and shabby, for he was very poor. He had an uncommonly plain face, with a high narrow forehead, oppressed by thought, a bold Roman nose, furrowed cheeks, thick red-brown hair and a most fiery eye; but there was a convulsive inclination to laughter about his mouth, a good deal at variance, they say, with the solemn and stately expression of his other features. The girl who paced beside him, with the same ungraceful rapid walk, was a small and slender creature, in a skimpy gown of India calico; her light curls were turned in under an old hat of Dunstable straw, which she had tied under her chin with a black ribbon. They fell about a thin eager face, tanned by sun and wind to an Egyptian brown. She had a pair of grey eyes, not soft, but wildly startling in their ardour and intelligence. All her gestures were nervous and quick ; she had a thin hand, a light foot, a softly stammering voice, a glance at once innocent and eager. Her name was Dorothy Wordsworth. She was twenty-five years old, a girl with a fire in her heart and the young man with her was her elder brother William. He wrote poetry, which was admired by nobody yet save his sister and he was expecting a visit from a fellow-poet, Samuel Taylor Coleridge. This stranger was coming over from Nether Stowey, in Somerset, where he lived with his wife and child, and at that time Dorothy had never seen him.

She said to her brother, shaking him impatiently by the arm, "I do wish you would tell me what the man is like." They had few visitors in their rustic poverty and this unknown friend had long occupied her thoughts; but William was in one of his silent moods and would only grumble, "I've told you before. One can't describe him; a strange fellow, a great talker, a fine preacher, an odd fish; a madman, perhaps, a genius, at any rate. You won't be able to get him out of your head, once you've seen him." There was a mixture of clear gushing accents in his voice, a deep guttural intonation, a northern burr like the crust on wine; his sister had a touch of it, too, caught in their Cumberland childhood, as she demanded, "Well, what has he done so far?" William admitted, "Nothing much. He has written some verses, preached a sermon or two in the Unitarian chapels and edited a paper in Bristol; but that's finished." It did not sound much to her, but William persisted, "He has it all before him. Every one who meets him sees this fire in him, he is like a torch to set other men alight. I feel I can do anything when I am with him. He has a great future." His sister gave him an eager doubtful look and asked a woman's question, "What does he look like?" but got an absent answer, "He has the brow of an angel and the mouth of a beast." It startled her and she made a soft questioning sound; her brother laughed harshly and told her, "Well, he says so himself." Then he urged her, "Look, your eyes are better than mine. Is there not some one at the gate?" She strained her eyes obediently. William flung off her arm and began running in his own ungainly fashion up the rough sloping pasture, shouting and waving his hat. She followed him a little way, then stopped and stood gazing, checked by a vague foreboding which she could not name.

A stranger had come into the meadow and into her life, a young and eager being who leapt over the gate and bounded down the pathless field at an angle towards them. He met her brother half-way down the slope. They greeted each other gaily, turned and came back towards her, laughing and talking together at a great rate. She stood where she was with her hands crossed on her breast in an unconscious childish gesture, oddly sacrificial. They both smiled upon her as they came up to her. William said, "This is my dear, dear sister" and pulled her forward. She surrendered her hand to the stranger's grasp and raised her eyes to his face.

We have her own word for it that she thought him very plain at first ; that is, for about three minutes. A girl's fancy is quickly caught or baffled; and here was a big heavy young man, in dusty black clothes, with a loose white neckcloth like a preacher. He had a pale flabby face and the loose wide mouth of the orator, he could not breathe through his nose and his thick sensual lips were commonly parted to disclose blackened irregular teeth. He had long rough untidy hair, raven-black, hanging about a broad and shining forehead and full grey eyes, shaded by heavy brows. It was a face which a stranger might admire or pity and a woman love too easily; a countenance which her destiny would oblige her to learn by heart. She did not know that yet, but she perceived at once that here was a being of a different order from the rest of her brother's acquaintances. She was a simple girl and country-bred; while she stammered a greeting to him and smiled at him from under her old straw hat, her first fear was that she had not got a fine enough dinner for him. She and William rarely ate meat; they lived on bread and butter, eggs from the farm, the potatoes and vegetables which William raised in the garden and Cheshire cheese, of which William was inordinately fond. Sometimes they got a hare or a rabbit, but this stranger might expect better fare and it was very important to please him, because he might help William to get a foot inside some publisher's door. Her mind was full of housekeeping thoughts as she climbed the hill beside her two immortals. The stranger, for his part, had expected a pretty woman. At first he thought his friend's sister rather ordinary, and planned to tell his wife as much; but then he caught the sidelong gleam of those wild grey eyes and changed his mind, admitting that if he had expected to see an ordinary woman he would have thought her pretty. She was a burning girl, as variable as a candle in a wind. He found her manner simple, ardent and impressive; he liked the way she hung on her brother's words and ran to pick the clumsy fellow up before he stumbled on an awkward subject. It was obvious that she thought the sky itself hardly tall enough for her William to walk under.

2

They approached Racedown House, which hung on the hill-side above them, a flat-fronted elegant Georgian residence in three stories, built of red and purple bricks burnt on the estate and at that time partly stuccoed against the driving south-west gales coming up from the Channel. It had a walled kitchen garden and a square of flint and stone farm-buildings, much older than itself, on the north-east and was altogether quite imposing; the stranger flung up his fine eloquent hands and protested to William, "You did not tell me that you lived in such a great house." Dorothy laughed out loud at that and said, "We are only the caretakers; we live in a corner of it, like mice in the wainscoting." William shrugged his shoulders clumsily and said, in his harsh fashion, "A rich merchant's folly, no more. Old Mr. Pinney has made money in the West India sugar trade and cannot be content to live in Bristol any longer, he must set up for a country gentleman. He has built this great place in a corner of the county where there is nothing to do; his neighbours will not know him and in the winter there is not even a passable road to it. Some day he means to retire and live here, but meanwhile he cannot find a tenant who will pay him any rent for the property. His sons come here from time to time, to shoot the covers, or ride to hounds, or go coursing hares on the hills, but nobody wants to live here all the year round. He is glad enough, I dare say, to have us keep the house warm for him."

Dorothy blushed for her brother's awkward fashion of admitting his obligations, she struggled with her stammer and protested, "B-but we are very glad to be here and it was very good of the Pinneys to lend us the house." William would not let it go at that; he insisted on making the situation clear, for at this stage of his existence he suspected that every one was criticising his poverty and lack of occupation. He scowled and twisted his clumsy hands about as he burst out, "It costs them nothing. Old Mr. Pinney did not even know we were here at first. Basil Montague, who is my friend, was young John Frederick's tutor at Cambridge and asked him to lend us the place; he did not tell his father and the old man was uncommonly vexed when he found that we were living in his precious house rent-free. His sons persuaded him to let us stay until another tenant could be found, but we should be sent packing to-morrow if it suited the old man to get rid of us." Dorothy did not know how to quiet him and was grateful to their guest for saying heartily, "Well, at least you are very well housed." She plucked up courage to explain, "It is a beautiful house, I think. I shall never love any place so well as I love Racedown, it is the first home that William and I have had together."

They approached the house and a small boy came running up to them, Mr. Montague's little boy Basil, who lived with them; he attached himself to Dorothy and peeped from behind them at the stranger, shyly smiling. They went in and showed the visitor all over the house. Miss Wordsworth was touchingly delighted with it. She did the honours as eagerly as a bride and indeed the place was charming, though of course absurdly large for them. At that date it had two parlours, one on either side of the hall, and four excellent bed-chambers above, besides attics and offices. Their common parlour was the prettiest little room that could be, with very neat furniture, a large bookcase on each side of the fire, a marble chimneypiece, a bath-stove and an oilcloth for the floor. It had besides other elegancies, such as a cracked gilt pierglass, a reading-stand, and Miss Pinney's own pianoforte, sadly jangled and out of tune after ten winters near the sea, but Miss Wordsworth could not play a note; she said, with a laugh, "I have no elegant accomplishments." The other parlour was rather larger, had a good carpet, sideboards in the recesses on either side of the fire and upon the whole a smart appearance; but they did not like it half so well as their little breakfast room, so there she set down her visitor to talk to William, while she busied herself with getting the dinner on the table. It should have been ready by five, but their visitor had delayed them.

She could have wished it a better one, when all was set on, but by that time her young men were so deep in an argument upon subject and metre that they hardly noticed what was put before them. It enchanted her to see how William had relaxed and warmed in the stranger's presence, for he was usually jerky, uncertain and watchful with every one but her. Immediately the meal was finished he dragged the manuscript of his new poem, *The Ruined Cottage*, out of his desk; a mournful tale of war and a betrayed woman, a common theme with him at that time, but he had his own reason for brooding upon it. As she carried the white Wedgwood plates and dishes into the kitchen she heard his harsh chanting voice already declaiming fragments of verse in the parlour. The stranger, too, had had a manuscript of his own in his knapsack, it appeared. When she carried the tea-tray into the parlour later on he had it out already. After tea he read out an act and a half of a dreary young man's tragedy called *Osorio*, waving an eloquent hand, while her brother sprawled on the cracked black-leather sofa. She sat in the window-seat, listening to the fiery pair and darning stockings as long as the light lasted. William produced a tragedy of his own, very long and gloomy, called *The Borderers*, with a romantic argumentative villain in it, straight from the German; such villains were then in the height of fashion.

Their voices went on and on, while a thrush sang its own evening song in the apple-boughs outside and the smell of the night-scented stocks came in like the breath of Paradise. William had not been able to smell anything in the garden all that summer, because he had been ill and very unhappy, but on this evening he suddenly asked, "What smells so sweet under the window?" He did not stay for an answer, but went on reading. The poem was a very melancholy one, called *Guilt and Sorrow*, but his sister thought that his voice sounded more cheerful than it had done for months. She smiled as she listened and let her idle hands fall in her lap. She would not light the candles yet, for fear of interrupting her two young poets. William's stockings must wait.

3

Next morning, while William was digging the potatoes, she was sent to take their guest up through the oaks and hazels to the green earthwork on the top of Pilsdown Pen. They sat down there together, under a stunted thorn, which leant away from the sea, as all the trees did in that country; they looked south under the sun to the empty green vale of Marshwood and the sea-sparkle between the intersecting hills and almost at once he burst out, "You must tell me who you are and where you come from and how it is that I find you hidden away in Dorset, like a primrose in a ditch."

She had not been looking at him; she had been lost in her thoughts, hearing the furze-pods popping in the hot sun, breathing the cocoanut scent of the gorse mixed with sea-salt, idly pulling up thyme and crowsfoot out of the turf. She started when he spoke to her, blushed up to her forehead and was angry with herself for her own shyness. She did not know what to say to him, or how to set him talking yet; she wished that William were with them. She was always tongue-tied with young men, they frightened her and when she was frightened she knew that she stammered badly. All that she could find to say sounded to her dull and stupid. "Oh! we are very simple people, there is no story about us. We come from the north, from Cockermouth in Cumberland. My father was an attorney there, agent to Sir John Lowther and my mother's parents kept a draper's shop in Penrith. They are all dead now and William and I live together." She sat blushing and paling under his brilliant gaze as he smiled upon her and encouraged her, "William says that you were bred among mountains."

She corrected him in an innocent literal fashion. "Oh! the mountains are not very close to Cockermouth. It is a little market town in an open green valley. Our house was right on the street, but it had a great garden behind, running down to the river. You could walk up and down our terrace and see the castle reflected in the salmon-pool. The Derwent is a fine river for salmon, you can see them jumping in the evening, or lying under the bridge waiting to run up on the next flood. The boys used to bathe in the lasher below the mill, in summer, when the yellow ragwort came out in the fields; and we had a hedge in the garden, of roses and privet, where they used to hunt for birds' nests. William showed me a sparrow's nest there once, when I was very little. I recollect that I was afraid to go near it. That is really the very first thing that I can remember." She found that she had been talking for quite a long time and her stammer came back. She struggled with it and said, "But William remembers Cockermouth better than I do, I was only six when my mother died. He was her favourite son and grieved for her sadly. I can just remember her pale face as she lay dying. After that I was taken away to Halifax in Yorkshire and brought up by a dear cousin of hers. I always called her Aunt Threlkeld."

He said vaguely, "Halifax? Is not that a very dreary ugly town? and Yorkshire a wretched cold country? I am sure I have always been told so." She denied that hotly. "Oh! no; it is a fine town, full of people and full of trade; but so is all the West Riding. The men work the looms and the women card and spin, even the children are busy, there is not a beggar nor an idle person to be seen. Why, there is scarcely a hill but you will find a spring of water and a coalpit on the highest part of it. The hills run this way and that, and the houses are scattered and spread all over the moors, and at every house you will see a tenter and on every tenter a piece of cloth drying. It is a fine sight on a fair day, to see all the white cloths reflecting the sun. There is nothing like it here in the South." She was quite breathless with vexation, so he laughed and said kindly, "Well, I see I must not speak ill of Halifax." She persisted, "Oh! Halifax is not to be equalled in England"; then recollected herself, blushed and stammered and pleaded, "Well, it may be a cold country, but I think the people there have the warmest hearts in the world."

Seeing him inclined to listen further, she plucked up courage and told him about her childhood in the north. He drew out of her all sort of forgotten tales about playing behind the counter of Aunt Threlkeld's milliner's shop, or going to service on Sundays at the Northgate End Chapel in the fields near the Calder Beck, how she used to dangle her feet in a square pew in the gallery, hear the clerk line out the psalms and watch the Reverend John Relph thump his red velvet cushion in the high pulpit till the dust flew out. You could see it whirling about in the slant of sunshine that came through the gallery windows. A great treat had been to go down with Uncle Sam Threlkeld to the open market called the Piece Hall, where lengths of cloth hung down from the arcaded galleries, and the buyers and sellers came and went between the carts and horses on the greasy cobblestones, and there was always a sour smell of newly-dyed cloth and a clatter of clogs on the stones. She laughed and confessed, "I could talk all day long about Halifax" and sighed, "I wish that I had never been forced to leave it, but my father died when I was sixteen and I had to go back to my grandparents in Penrith. That seemed to me very dull. In Yorkshire my aunt had a houseful of young nephews and nieces, it was a cheerful home, full of good talk and kindness; but at Penrith my grandparents were so harsh and so untender that I felt like a stranger. They were old folk and very strict, they thought book-learning a waste of time for a girl. My grandmother wanted to turn me into a notable housekeeper and she kept me all the time sitting and sewing. I was not allowed to walk out except on Sundays. It was like being in prison to me." And she gave him a wild and desperate look at the very thought of it, flinging out her arms as if people were crowding about her. It quite startled him for the moment, she looked so wild and strange. She saw that and checked herself, for she was always afraid of her own wild temper, the fire in her heart which flamed up so readily.

She said, "Well, I must have been a sore trial to my grandmother. She thought me careless and absent-minded and so I dare say I was and too fierce for her to tame. I have a very quick temper, you know; the boys are all good in our family, but I was always a termagant." She said this so quaintly that she made him laugh, then sighed, "But we could none of us behave well enough to please the old people. They were not fit to bring up children. We were found fault with every hour of the day, my grandparents never spoke to us except to scold us and the servants were encouraged to be insolent to us because we were poor. However, I must not think of it now. My grandfather and my grandmother are both in their graves, poor souls! and we have escaped. I have long forgiven them what they did to me. Only I cannot bear to think how unkindly they treated my brothers. Why, at the beginning of the very first summer they were all three left at school for a whole week after the holidays had begun, just because they had not

he came here, after living alone in London. I have had to make him a whole new set of shirts and you know they say there are twenty thousand stitches in a shirt. Besides, I take down all William's poetry as he composes it and afterwards I copy it out. He cannot bear to take pen in hand unless he is obliged. He lets his verses fall and I come behind and gather them up." He said, "I see you are a very useful person"; and she blushed and laughed and turned the dough again; she said, "Well, I cannot bear to be idle. We are both of us poor, you know, and I must see to everything myself. Besides, Basil keeps me busy, as you see. He is a dear little boy, and we are glad to have him. His mother is dead and his father cannot well do with him in chambers in London. We have grown very fond of the child but when he came to us first he was extremely petted and ready to cry at the least little thing. William could not endure the sound, it interrupted his work. So I have had to teach Basil manners." Coleridge said with approval, "He is the best behaved child I ever saw, never fretful or discontented. I see you know how to manage children." She told him, "I learnt the way of it when I was living with my uncle, Canon Cookson, and his wife in Norfolk. They had a nursery full of babies and I loved them and looked after them."

He burst out, "Ah! you must see my Hartley, my infant philosopher. He is the most wonderful child in the world"; then smiled at himself and said, "All parents think that, I know, but he is really an exquisite creature. He is just nine months old." She stood smiling at him, wondering innocently what the child of such a man would be like, a fairy boy, she fancied, bright as a dewdrop, too good for this world and ready to slip out of it at the touch of adversity; but as she lost herself in such thoughts it occurred to her that she knew nothing of his wife. He spoke of her so little that she had not even begun to guess what kind of a woman he would love. The thought made her colour up and tremble; she turned her back on him hurriedly and went to see whether her oven was ready. The blast which rushed out at her was excuse enough for her hot cheeks. She raked out the ashes, caught up the loaves from the table and pushed them in. When she had clanged the door to she was able to return composedly to the table, wiping her hands on her apron and boasting cheerfully, "William will eat no bread that is not of my baking, he says there is no bread like mine."

Her guest did not laugh at her innocent vanity, but said warmly, "William is a lucky fellow. I envy him." She turned her flushed cheek aside and confessed, "Our aunts and uncles think it is a sad wild scheme for us to live together. They wanted William to go into the church, or study law, but he has no bent for either. He cares for nothing but poetry. We two have always planned to have a cottage together, where he could write and I could wash and cook and mend for him. It is a desperate struggle to make ends meet, for we have but seventy or eighty pounds a year to live upon. It was left us by William's friend, poor Raisley Calvert ; he was a poet who died young and he bequeathed this to William. My father's money is all kept from us; that is Sir John Lowther's fault. He owed my father nearly five thousand pounds in wages when he died and we children cannot get it paid. We brought a lawsuit against Sir John, but we cannot get justice."

She was a passionate girl and could spit fire like a wet candle when she was vexed; she burst out, "Some day we shall bring that wicked man to book" with so much violence that her companion was quite startled. He said consolingly, "I know what it is to be desperate for money. Last year, when my paper failed, I could not tell where to turn. I used to write begging letters by the hour to any one who could help me, while my Sara watched my face working and wanted to know what was the matter; but I could not tell her. Poor thing! she cannot understand why I do not make my fortune; she believes in me as devoutly as you do in your brother. She thinks too well of me, I fear." He laughed with an odd irritable affection and said impatiently, "Well, we should have starved, or gone to a debtors' prison, if it had not been for my good friend Tom Poole. I cannot tell you what his kindness has been. He has taken us to live near him at Nether Stowey, he has done everything for us."

There was a rueful note in his admission, which he excused by saying, with a short sulky laugh, "The trouble is, Tom cannot be content to be your friend, he must be your saviour. He goes clod-hopping over your feelings. I cannot choke down the bread of charity very easily." She raised her head and answered proudly, "Well, I have eaten a deal of it and will eat more and be grateful, too, if only I can keep a roof over William's head until he has done his work." He cried out, "I honour you for it, he is happy to have such a sister"; but she only shook her head and said, "William is not happy. I am often very anxious about him. He was in great trouble when he came here and I have done all that I could to comfort and establish him, but sometimes I think he needs more help than I can give." He assured her, "William does not think so. He says that he owes you everything, that you have saved him to himself," but he could not reassure her. She said, "I cannot satisfy William. He has a strange unhappy nature, and I am too much like him to change it. He is unlike other men. Do you not feel it?" She raised her eyes to his and their light confused him; he said, in a tone between jest and earnest, "Yes, William is an odd fellow, he strides on so far before you that he dwindles in the distance. I can tell you I feel myself a very little man beside him." Then, as she continued to gaze imploringly at him, he smiled kindly and seriously upon her and said, "You are right to believe in William. I don't know why I say so, but I think that one day he will do something great."

At that she gave him a glance of timid, yet most exquisite gratitude and a long sigh, as if her heart had been relieved from a burden. She said calmly, "Then you must be his friend. We will think what can be done, you shall help him to get away from here. He must not be buried all his life in these valleys. There is something great in William and it must have its way with him." He caught fire from her: he took her hand in his and promised, "I will do all I can for your brother."

He kept his promise, saying that evening, as they sat in the parlour, "Well, to-morrow I must go home again, but this is not to be a long farewell. You must visit Nether Stowey. I must have you there with me, now that we have found each other we cannot be parted. Come immediately; come with me to-morrow." He was all fire and enthusiasm, as she fancied he might be over anything new. William said doubtfully, "I have a great deal of work still to do on my tragedy," but his friend overbore him. "You will work the better for the change of scene. You can write with us, in the lime-tree bower you will not be interrupted. Poole is constantly talking of you, he admired you immensely when he met you in Bristol. He thinks you the greatest man he ever knew." William reddened, grinned frightfully and twisted his big hands about, but he was obviously flattered. "Oh! you must certainly come," persisted Coleridge. "We cannot do without you; and your exquisite sister, we must have her too." He turned his brilliant eyes and smile upon Dorothy, who sat by the window, using the last of the faded light to patch one of William's old shirts. She coloured deeply under that bright compelling glance and bent down over the work on her knee, then found that she had run the needle into her hand. William said, in brotherly surprise, "You will not have room for Dorothy?" His friend insisted, "But indeed we shall. The party would not be complete without her. The cottage is not very big to be sure, but Sara will manage somehow. We shall be very snug, a nest of singing birds crammed in edgeful." His eager voice softened to a pleading note as he urged her, "You will come too, I hope." She drew out the thread with a hand which was not altogether steady and murmured, "Yes, I will come."

He said cheerfully, "Then that is all settled. I shall go back to-morrow and make everything ready. You must arrange to leave Basil with your maid while you are away. Next week I shall come and fetch you. The roads are execrable, I fear, but it is only forty miles up hill and down dale and I can borrow Tom Poole's horse; it is tolerably quiet and I am not a bad whip, I assure you." He made the large boastful gestures of one who is in fact not much at home with horses and said, "We shall be a cheerful party. There are the good Pooles, and Charles Lloyd, who boards with us; the oddest fellow, a Quaker, a bit of a poet, a quarrelsome man, but you will like him. And my old schoolfellow, Charles Lamb, is coming down for a fortnight's holiday. Poor soul, he needs it sadly, I fear; he has been through a sea of troubles lately. He loved a pretty country girl, the sweetest yellow-haired blue-eyed beauty and they were not allowed to marry. Charles was out of his mind about her. You know how these things can break a young man's heart."

He sighed and Dorothy wondered, with a sharp innocent prick of jealousy, whether he was thinking of the unknown wife of whom he had spoken to her that afternoon. William sat hunched ungracefully in his chair, with drooping eyelids and set lips and his most impenetrable look, while their friend ran on, in his musical voice, "Poor Charles, he has a sister too; you must meet her, but not yet. She is the dearest and best of women. Charles calls her sister and friend. They are like the pair of you, two minds with but a single thought, he hardly knows how to go on living without her. It is a dreadful story. Mary is shut away in a mad-house. Last summer, in a fit of madness, she killed their mother."

Dorothy uttered a soft shocked murmur and he turned to her, as she sat in shadow against the sunset window. "Oh! it was the most tragic business. He rushed in and found her standing over her mother, knife in hand. He blames himself bitterly that he did not get the doctor for her in time. She had had some symptoms of the trouble before, I fear it runs in the family. He says she used to walk past the hospital of Bedlam and look at the two statues of raving and moping madness on the gates, and say that she feared to end her days there. Charles would starve sooner than let her be shut up in such a place. He knows too well how the poor mad folk are starved and chained up and beaten. He has promised that he will look after her all her life. He has a foolish old father on his hands, who cannot bear the sight of poor Mary, but when the old man dies, as he soon must, she is to come home and live with Charles. They hope to spend the rest of their days together, he is everything to her. You can understand that." He spoke to William, but he looked at Dorothy, who clasped her hands in her lap and said in her soft fervent voice, "Yes, I can understand it."

He nodded his head and told her confidently, "I am certain you will love Charles. He is the quaintest, liveliest little fellow, almost a cripple, with his lame leg and his big head, but very active. He will stammer dreadfully at first, but not when he gets to know you. He and I were charity boys at Christ's Hospital together. When I saw him first he was quite a little boy, very proud of his blue gown and leather belt and yellow stockings. He is my very oldest friend. I believe the silly fellow believes that one of these days I shall do something to set the Thames on fire." And he concluded with a laugh at his own sentiment, "He teases me as he teases every one. He calls me Col and says I talk too much and very likely I do." She started and sighed at that and turned away; she had caught herself thinking that she would like that light melodious voice to go on sounding in her ears for ever.

5

Next morning he left them, rambling on to the last moment about his plans for making them visit him and promising to come back and fetch them both immediately. William borrowed a horse from Joseph Gill, the bailiff at the home farm, and started to ride a little way with him. Dorothy was glad to see her brother so cheerful. She packed him off with a list of purchases to be made in Crewkerne and a last injunction not to forget to fetch their letters from the post. In their rural solitude such matters were important, though William was always cross when you asked him to do shopping. It was a fine glittering morning, with high clouds driving in from the sea; the two young men set out in great spirits, waving her farewell from the gate.

When the dust cloud had died down she felt very low. The sun had gone in and a cold wind had sprung up, she knew not whence; the house seemed dreadfully vacant and quiet without them, and the sight of their empty plates and broken egg-shells in the dining-room did not cheer her. However, she employed herself briskly in clearing the table and washing up the plates; after that she put the drawers in order in William's bedroom and laid by his clothes, which he always scattered here, there and everywhere. Then it was time to give Basil his lessons and his dinner and take him out walking. These occupations kept the fiery girl busy all the morning and most of the afternoon: she was determined not to fret because their guest was gone, or because William had ridden further than he meant and did not come home in time for dinner. But as the afternoon wore into evening and tea-time passed, she became anxious, for the wind was rising, clapping doors and whining through keyholes and driving the smoke down the chimney. It promised a stormy night. She was restless and could settle to nothing, her mind was full of fears about her darling. Basil was in bed and she walked up and down the parlour, stopping often to peer through the unshuttered windows, until it grew so dark that they reflected nothing but her own face. At last she heard the farm dog barking and the sound of hoofs on the road; presently the gate opened and shut and there were footsteps in the gravel outside. She ran out and opened the door and heard her brother's voice. He came in and flung off his old Cumberland plaid and put his arms round her; his mouth and breath were very cold when he kissed her. He was very silent and tired out, but gentle, friendly and loving to her. She made tea for him and they sat a little by the fire, not talking much and very soon they went to bed. She thought, "He will talk to me in the morning."

Next day, however, he was in one of his sullen irritable moods, a familiar reaction which she had dreaded, but more than half-expected, after the pleasant conversation of the last few days. He kept away from her all day, went a long walk by himself on the tops of the hills, came back and shut himself up in the parlour with his French and Italian books and would hardly answer when she spoke to him. His sister knew this mood well enough. William could be very trying at times and when he was sulky he was like Basil, best left alone, he would come out quite good-humoured in the end. She would not permit herself to compare him with the bright bewildering guest who had just departed. William was her own dear brother, she understood him and she would not change him.

At night she had her reward. The child had been put to bed and she sat alone in the parlour, in the twilight, for once with her busy hands folded before her, feeling a little sad, when William came to the open window and put in his head. She could not see his face, but she heard him say, in the rough schoolboy tone which he often affected, "Come out here, Dolly; I've something to show you." The nickname and phrase both came straight from their common childhood and had a kind of sulky appeal in them which could always touch her. She rose immediately and joined him at the hall door. The wind had blown itself out and fallen quiet at sunset; there were a few faint misty stars overhead, but no moon, the night was warm and still. He took her by the elbow and led her without speaking to the orchard; stood still under the great plum-tree and pointed and muttered, "Look there." In the dewy grass by the hedge she made out a wavering green illumination, a light which throbbed like a little burning heart. She fell on her knees and breathed, "A glow-worm; oh! William, how perfect." She heard his harsh voice continuing above her, "I found it last night, quite by chance, in the hedge, when I was riding home through the storm to you.

I picked it up and laid it on a leaf and carried it back in my hand. It went on shining all the way, only more faintly, and I laid it down safely by itself here under the plum-tree and left it for you to see." He added with his rough abashed laugh, "All day I've wondered if it would shine for you to-night. I knew you'd never seen one." She could not speak for tears, which brimmed up and made the green light dazzle. In the dark and quiet night he knelt beside her and touched her hand and said, "They shine for love."

II

I

THEIR friend did not return that week, nor yet the next; Dorothy had leisure to learn that such bright spirits commonly disappoint the inexperienced by scattering casual hopes which they afterwards forget to fulfil. William, who was, she guessed, very much disappointed himself, told her roughly, "It's my belief the fellow never meant to come back at all." She knew by that how much he had counted upon this stranger. However, before the end of the month he suddenly arrived, glorious as ever and unconscious of any offence. He stayed a couple of days, turned the house upside down, rushed off again and finally reappeared with a one-horse chaise, waving his hands about and urging her to put on her hat and come with him to Nether Stowey. He gave them an hour to pack in, then swept them off up hill and down dale, through the cider country and across the green and silver flats of Sedgemoor, where the sleepy muddy streams wound through meadows dotted with grazing sheep. There the gentle wind murmured all day long through waving reeds, and the villages, with their tall church towers, floated like rafts on a sea of summer grasses. Nether Stowey turned out to be a winding village street, in the lee of the wooded Quantocks. Its gardens that month were gay with roses, pinks and lupins, white lilies and grey lavender, and Sweet William, which she loved for its name and its homely cottage smell. The bees were very busy in the tall steeples of the pink and red and yellow hollyhocks, crimson valerian hung out of all the stone walls and there was a pleasant noise of water running in the gutter beside the street.

The Coleridges had a dwelling which was little more than a cottage, a low square building, dark and noisy, with all its windows looking on the street. It had two low parlours, one on either side of a flagged entry and a kitchen behind. Its four poky attic bedrooms opened inconveniently out of each other and smelt of mice, but Dorothy's was a little better than the others, because it belonged to Charles Lloyd, who paid for his board and lodging and had conveniently gone back to his Quaker parents in Birmingham for a visit. Mrs. Coleridge proved to be a helpless pretty round-faced creature, as pink and white as a daisy in her skimpy striped gingham gown, with its round neck and short sleeves, which revealed her plump creamy dimpled neck and arms. She tried in vain to look like an experienced married woman in a useless little muslin apron and a frilled mob cap, but the house was in a dreadful muddle, according to North-country standards. She was much taken up with her baby, but seemed proud of her young husband and deeply in love with him.

She did not find much to say to her husband's guests. She bade them welcome with a pretty flutter, but somehow succeeded in giving Dorothy the impression that they were a good deal in her way. The cottage was certainly small and crowded, you could not blame her for being a little lukewarm over their arrival. The baby was an exquisite creature, with his mother's delicate features and his father's god-like brow. He had been, they said, an eight-months' child and he was still very small. He gazed upon them all with a fathomless look of unearthly wisdom and then smiled and made sweet babbling musical noises. His father was enchanted with him, carried him in his arms, tossed him up, tried to conceal his affection by grumbling, "The women say he is like me, but that is no great compliment, for indeed I have seen handsomer babies in my lifetime." Then he hung over the infant, entranced by its solemn gaze, and murmured, "I should not wonder if he knows more about the immortality of the soul than we do." The young mother looked on jealously while Dorothy held little Hartley in her arms; William gazed upon him gravely, as a big dog looks at a puppy. Presently Mrs. Coleridge gave them dinner, very late. They had eggs and bacon, green peas and young potatoes out of the garden, raspberries and clotted cream, to which their host was immoderately partial; he fairly cleaned out the dish, talking all the while.

2

When dinner was over he took them out into the garden behind the house. It was a long narrow strip of ground, with raspberry canes and currant bushes among the roses, a few gnarled trees of cider apples, and a clipped arbour of limes, full of murmuring bees and smelling sweet as honey. The beds, however, were dreadfully overrun with weeds; evidently the poet had not worked there so hard or so successfully as he pretended. William struggled with his convulsive grin, as he stared about him and quoted a North-country proverb, "A man of words and not of deeds, is like a garden full of weeds." Their friend blushed and smiled and excused himself quaintly, "What right have I to decide whether a rose or a thistle has the better right to existence?" a heresy which caused William to shake his head. Then they all went down past the stinking tan-pits and through the back way into Mr. Poole's garden.

He came to meet them, rubbing his hands in welcome, and shaking the two strangers by the hand as if he would never let them go, while he beamed upon them and repeated in his broad Somerset burr, "Come in, come in and take us as we be." She liked Tom Poole from the very first. He was the kind of man that she could always understand, a hook-nosed, thick-set fellow in his early thirties, with a red shining face the colour of raw beef, abrupt and outspoken, but shrewd, sturdy and uncommonly sensible in all that he said. He was rustic in his appearance and provincial in his speech, with a harsh voice spoilt by snuff-taking and a surly manner which did not long conceal from her the kindness and simplicity of his nature. He was noisy and aggressive at first in his methods; she got the impression that, like William, he was on the defensive with strangers because he was sensitive about his own shortcomings. He took refuge in clownishness because he fancied that it suited with those republican opinions, which had made him unpopular with his neighbours. Certainly he and William bristled at each other to begin with like two strange dogs. Perhaps, too, he had expected Dorothy to be some sort of a fine lady, for he began, with a bow and a clumsy scrape, "Reckon we'd best go indoors, Miss Wordsworth, and sit in the parlour with my old mother. We generally sits in the jasmine arbour of an evening, but I know you ladies doesn't care for the stink of the tan-pits." He called it *harbour*, whether by accident or design she did not know. She laughed and protested, "I shall never notice the tan-pits, Mr. Poole."

It was a kindly untruth, for the smell was extremely penetrating and quite drowned the scent of the jasmine; however, the tanner was mollified, took her by the elbow and led her down the path, grumbling, "Well, when my cousins from Over Stowey come to spend the day they scream at the very idea of sitting out in my *harbour*. They swear they can't smell anything there but hides. They're all growing very fine ladies now, especially my Cousin Charlotte; they should remember what they comes from, say I, and not turn up their noses at the pits. Money don't smell and that's a fact." Dorothy laughed and said, "I am not a fine lady, I hope." He squeezed her bare elbow in his warm hand and told her, "That you're not," with what was evidently approval, but continued to develop his grievance against his cousins, when they were all four settled in the jasmine bower. "Stupid creatures, but it's all my uncle's fault. Nowadays when a man retires they call him a gentleman, no matter how poor he is; and his sons and daughters get gilded notions and fancy they ought to be fine ladies and gentlemen in their turn. Up at Over Stowey my uncle's girls all want to marry gentlemen and the boys intend to be apothecaries, or attorneys, or poor curates like my Cousin John. My uncle would have thought it a step backwards if he'd bred his boys to a trade and his girls to housekeeping."

He stared at William, who sat there looking down his nose, awkward and unapproachable, and said, "But I dare say you don't agree with me, Mr. Wordsworth." William, to his sister's despair, unfolded his long legs, stretched himself and grunted, "Well, my grandparents were in the haberdashery trade, but my father was an attorney and so is my elder brother; and I went to college myself and meant to go into the church, only I changed my mind." It was just the kind of thing he was always saying, graceless, sulky and stiff. Dorothy knew that he only did it because he was gauche and shy; he wanted to impress strangers and did not know how to set about it. He was dreadfully conscious of his country clothes and accent; he carried his stubborn, unmarketable genius about with him like a sack of stones and did not know where to set it down. In company he was always clownish and vulgar, like a young farmer ill at ease in his Sunday clothes, and seemed to have no idea of how to set about making friends with strangers. She supposed that it came from being brought up an unwanted child in other folks' houses, a poor scholar, a poor relation, with no acknowledged place or work as yet in the world. He was always at his worst with some one like Tom Poole, boisterous, tactless and encouraging; he shrank back into his shell and turned as prickly as a hedgehog. Dorothy clasped her hands in despair. The tanner screwed up his face into countless indignant wrinkles, pushed out his lips, snorted and blew like a porpoise.

He grumbled, in his broad Somerset accent, "Well, I never had no college education. I'm not a shining scholar like our friend here, or his brother-in-law, Mr. Southey, who won all the prizes at Oxford. You mustn't expect me to have any book-learning. All the reading I've done I've had to scratch for myself. My old dad wouldn't let me go off to Tiverton grammar school, he said a tanner didn't need to fiddle with books. He wouldn't even keep accounts. He used to say, I owe no man anything, the pits are full and there's money in the stocking, what more do you want. He turned up his nose at scholars, did my old dad."

William looked down his own long Wordsworth nose and said nothing. Coleridge laughed his pleasant laugh and said, to smooth things over. "Well, it is true, we scholars are all poor creatures." Tom Poole gazed at him reproachfully; he said, "Nay, I never meant that. Why, learning is a grand thing, the best thing in the world, I wish I'd had more of it. I envy you gentlemen the chances you've had. All I say is, I'm a tanner and proud of it. If ever I have a son, I'll train him up for the business, but I'll give him plenty of schooling too. I think education is the most important thing in life to a man, and I can't see why a tradesman shouldn't be as well informed as anybody. I don't believe you can educate a man above his station." He gazed imploringly at them all. Dorothy felt quite sorry for him, he looked so puzzled and bewildered. She smiled at him and comforted him in her soft stammer, "I am sure you love learning, Mr. Poole." He cheered up quickly and said, "Well, I had many a quarrel with my old dad about it; that's all I know. But I stuck to my books. I taught myself to read Latin and such and learnt French from a refugee priest." He gazed round upon them, looking foolish and eager, like a clumsy dog. She said gently, "Well, I honour you for it." He sighed and repeated, "Ah! I'd have liked the chance to go to school and college"; but William merely grunted, "Cambridge was never any good to me. I only learnt to waste time and money there."

He nursed his elbows morosely and stretched himself yawning on his uncomfortable green bench, while Tom Poole rambled on to Dorothy, "Well, you don't want to hear me grumble about my cousins, but they do vex me and I suppose I vexes them. I go stuffing my republican notions down their throats at tea-parties and talking about public affairs instead of silly gossip. I don't see why folks can't take opposite sides in politics without quarrelling, do you?" She smiled at him very kindly, she could realise how unmanageable he might be at a village tea-party. He told her proudly and innocently, "They think me a very dangerous person down here, stirring up the workers to make trouble and lending them seditious books, like Tom Paine's *Rights of Man.*" He sank his voice to an absurdly mysterious whisper as he assured her, "At one time the Government used to open my letters in the post," and looked so owlish that she found it difficult not to laugh in his round red face.

He mopped his brow, scattered a fresh cloud of snuff over himself as he stuffed his nose and ran on, "Well, it makes me wild, you know, to hear a silly woman like my Cousin Charlotte, who never opens a book, squawking about the dreadful revolution, and that horrid Paris; saying, You must keep poor people down, or they'll get ideas above their station ; those agitators who persuaded the sailors at Spithead to mutiny ought to be stood up against a wall and shot. That's what she said to me the other day. I answered, Sailors, and soldiers too, won't be blind instruments any longer, they want to know what they're fighting about. She went on about how it was our duty to go to war with France because they cut off their King's head and I told her I reckoned every English soldier killed in such an unjust war was as much of a martyr as Louis Seize. She thought that shocking and declared I ought to be shut up in Taunton jail. She's very patriotic, is my Cousin Charlotte and all for going to war; she doesn't know what war is like, or she wouldn't sit at home and talk of it so calmly. Not that I hold with chopping off heads, but that's the French way; they can't do things quietly and decently. When the revolution comes here it'll be a different business, I hope."

At that William unfolded himself and broke out in his harsh voice, "Mr. Poole, you don't know what you're talking about." His sister started and bit her lip till the blood came. Their host had blundered upon the worst subject possible, a thing which William could not discuss quietly at any time. She tried to interrupt, but was betrayed by her stammer and could not speak quickly. Their friend said, "Wordsworth has been in France more than once. He was in Paris when the revolution began; he speaks with more authority than the rest of us," but he did not mend matters. Tom Poole cried out with staring eyes, "What, you were there, sir? You can tell me what it was like?" with his ignorant blundering enthusiasm, babbling, "I'd have given my head to see what you've seen; tell me how it all went." William had the sick white face which his sister knew only too well, he looked as green as if he were going to faint, in the shadow of the jasmine leaves. He said in his most disagreeable tone, "What do you want me to tell you? I can remember it all well enough; too well, God knows. They were pulling women out of prison and cutting them to pieces on the pavement under your window; they were hanging men on the ropes across the streets, instead of lanterns; they were beating drums and ringing the bells backwards and carrying heads and hearts about the city on pikes. They had just recently found out how quickly they could kill people with the guillotine and they were standing round it counting heads and yelling for more entertainment. The whole city had gone mad, the people had turned into wild beasts. The streets were full of untrained, undrilled boys marching away to the war, singing the Marseillaise; it was a new tune then and at night you could not sleep, because of the rumble of carts, taking the corpses to the quicklime pits. No need to talk of that. I ran away from it, I hadn't the pluck to stay there. You may see it here yet, if you and your friends talk loud enough." He got up and walked out of the arbour, leaving Tom Poole choking.

She exchanged an imploring glance with Coleridge, who jumped to his feet and ran out into the sunshine after William. She laid her hand on the tanner's arm and raised her luminous grey eyes to his; she said, "Oh! you must forgive him, you must not mind him. He cannot bear to talk of it, you do not know how much he suffered. When first he came back he could not sleep at night for thinking of it all, or if he slept he used to wake up screaming. I have often gone to him and comforted him when he did not know where he was or what he was saying." The good fellow mumbled, "Well, I am sorry I spoke of it. I did not think I should set him off like that, but it is my way to say what I think." She gave him a trembling smile and murmured, "I am afraid it is William's way too," and after a moment he burst out, "Well, you are a good creature; there is no quarrelling with you, at any rate. You are not like my Cousin Charlotte, who never did a hand's turn in her life and thinks that poor folk are fit for nothing but to work all their days or go to prison." And he patted her hand in an absurd brotherly fashion, "I am a stupid fellow, I know that well enough. I can't tell how to talk to clever folk like Mr. Coleridge and your brother. I'd best leave them to their own arguments and learn what I can from listening to them."

The look on his face touched her as he continued, "It'll be a great thing for our friend to have you and your brother here for a while. I'm as fond of him as I can be, but of course he ain't interested in my simple notions and that little wife of his may be sweet enough and pretty enough, but she can't talk to him about books and poetry and such. He has a fire in him. He needs a man of his own size, to measure his mind against. I've been thinking that lately. I think about him a good deal, you know, one way and another." She said, "I am sure you think nothing but what is good and kind. He says you have done everything to help him." He burst out with a shamefaced fervour, "I can't tell you what I feel about that young man. He's everything I'd like to be and never could; he's going to do something uncommonly fine, one of these days. It's as if he were a sort of young brother to me, I want him to have all the chances nobody never gave me. I hate to see him wasting his time on what's of no consequence, upon my soul I do! I can't bear to watch him scribbling for the papers, preaching a sermon, talking of turning himself into a minister in some chapel, worrying himself to death over making ends meet, trying to live by digging his garden, when he don't hardly know one end of a spade from the other. He's fit for bigger things than that, Miss Wordsworth." She said, "I think he is," most fervently and he looked sharply at her and said, "You feel it too; don't you? Just as I dare say you feel the same about that brother of yours; queer creatures, both of 'em, not the same as the rest of us. They need room to grow in and time, too, like young oak trees. We must see that they get it." He rubbed the top of his head and grumbled, "Can't get the folks around here to see it, though. I've had no end of trouble over our young friend. He came down here first with that brother-in-law of his, Robert Southey, who talked a lot of clever Oxford nonsense about being an atheist and frightened the whole lot of them with his revolutionary ideas. It's taking them a long time to find out that Mr. Coleridge is the most devout and peaceful creature ever born, much too good for them. They fancy he must be tarred with the same brush as myself and young Bob Southey. They're a very prejudiced narrow-minded lot and Cousin Charlotte is the worst."

At this she laughed in his face. He gave her a shy grin which somehow pleased her very well, sighed and said, "Ah! there was only one of my cousins that was ever any good to me and that was my cousin Penelope. She was a sweet pretty creature and could sing like a nightingale. I used to write verses to her when I was a lad." He pasued and sighed over some unknown recollection and his harsh red face looked for the moment quite bewildered, as if he could not understand why the world was such a difficult place to live in. Then he collected himself, took some more snuff and said, "Ah! well, Penelope's married and gone away, God bless her; and I've no use for the rest of them, but Charlotte is the worst of the family. I'm glad you ain't the same sort of girl as Charlotte." She burst out laughing at him, he looked so comical and mischievous as he sat there, with his hands on his knees, which were wide apart, and his head bent sideways squinting at her. He laughed too, then jumped up and shook himself and said, "But why do we sit here? Come into the house, Miss Wordsworth, and see my old mother. I'll show you my books and the copy of the Barberini vase that the Wedgwoods made for me and the lock of George Washington's hair that an American lady gave me; it is one of my precious treasures. And I am very sorry I said anything to vex that brother of yours, but he must not mind me; nobody minds Tom Poole."

3

So she went into the tannery house and talked for a while with his mother, a delicate withered old woman, with a tremulous movement of hand and head and a constant look of pride and love for her son. She could speak of nothing but him and held Dorothy by the sleeve to assure her, "Tom is the best boy in the world. No one can tell you what a good son he has been to me since his father died. You must not believe all the stories they tell in the village about his wicked notions, how he wants to take away all our money and give it to the poor, and pull down the church about the parson's ears, and teach the soldiers and sailors to mutiny, and bring the French over to burn us in our beds. Tom would never do any such thing, there is nobody has a better heart than Tom." Dorothy could well believe it.

Presently Tom said to her, wrinkling up his face into the kindest possible smile, "Now you would like to go and look for that brother of yours." So she said good-bye to them both and went back past the tanpits into the Coleridges' garden, but if she had hoped in her heart to find their friend with him she did not do so. William was sitting by himself in the lime-tree bower, with his elbows on the green wooden table and his head in his hands. She went up to him and sat beside him. At first he did not move, he only sat there perfectly rigid, digging his clenched fists into his eyes as if to drive some sight away; but presently he shifted a little and let one hand fall on the table and she took it in her own. They sat so for a while, then she ventured, "Cannot you forget such things, William?" and as he did not answer, "It is five years since all that happened to you."

He moved his hand as if he wished to shake hers away, but she would not release him; he said bitterly, "Yes, five years is a long time. Why should I still torment myself by thinking of that autumn? Most men would have forgotten it by now, would they not? Why should I blame myself perpetually for a boy's folly?" His sister did not dare to look at him, but she murmured unwillingly, "I did not know you thought of her so much, or so often. It is so long since we spoke of her." As she felt his hand clench itself in an agony of resistance beneath her fingers she added the soft single word, "Annette."

He repeated it with a kind of groan, "Annette . . . Annette," and then burst out at her, "Do you want me to forget that I loved a woman and betrayed her and left her to bear her child alone, because I was too much of a coward to stay with her? Do you think that desertion and disgrace are easy to put out of one's mind?" He gave his short harsh laugh and complained. "Some men would find it easy. I do not. Well, that is my misfortune, but time may cure it yet. In another five years, if the war goes on so long, I shall hardly remember that there is such a woman in the world as Annette Vallon." And he added, under his breath, "I suppose she calls herself that still. I never gave her the right to any other name."

His sister began to stammer out all the old excuses which she had long treasured in her mind for him, "B-but you could not help yourself, William, you could not go back then to marry her. The war had begun, you had no money, you could not bring her or the child to England. The whole family were against you. No one would help you. It was quite impossible." She indeed had been the only one who at that time had not turned against William, when he had wanted to marry his mistress, a penniless Frenchwoman, a Roman Catholic older than himself, a woman out of an enemy country, in wartime. She understood now, better than she had done then, what difficulties had stood in his way; but she persisted proudly, "You could never do anything ignoble, William. When peace comes, you will go back to her. She will be waiting for you and you will be married and you will bring both of them to England, to me." William only sat staring at the ground, with his fixed impenetrable look and said, under his breath, as if he were speaking to himself and not to her, "I have not had a letter now for a very long time. I do not know whether she gets my letters, or even the money that I send to Blois. For all I know, she may have forgotten me."

His sister cried out at that, "How could she ever forget you? Her lover, the father of her child?" He did not answer and after a moment she murmured, "Imagine, neither you nor I have ever seen Caroline and she is nearly five years old." She felt him move impatiently, as if he could not bear to be questioned longer, but she could not refrain from the cry of her heart, "Oh! I wonder so much whether she is like you!" He said then harshly, "If Caroline is like me she will make an ugly woman. She had better try to grow like her mother." His sister had often asked him jealously what that unknown Frenchwoman had been like, but he had only turned away and muttered, "Little . . . dark . . . lively . . . always laughing." It had not sounded at all the right thing for William's wife. His sister sat there in the arbour, recollecting all that past shame and misery and the colour ran up her brown face. William put his head on his clenched fists and muttered, "But you do not understand how I feel about her now. It is like a fire in my heart, always burning and tormenting me, when I remember that time. I cannot be rid of it, but I do not love her now. I do not want to go back and marry her. I wish the war might go on for ever, so that I need not see her again." That startled Dorothy and she drew back quickly. Her brother muttered, "No, you can't understand; you can only despise me, as I despise myself continually."

She bit her lip till the blood came and stared at the ground; then she stammered passionately, "D-do n-not speak to me so. I could never despise you. I cannot always understand you, but you could never do anything that would drive me from you." At that he took her hand in his clumsy grip and muttered, "I could not endure my life if I had not you to help me." She said, and meant it truly, "That is all I care for." They sat together in the lime-tree bower, side by side, not speaking; presently their friend came and fetched them in.

They stayed a fortnight in the cottage in the village street. The July weather continued gloriously fine. They walked on the smooth airy ridge of the Quantocks and saw the wide landscape dissolved in sunshine below them; at night the moon came up out of the marshes like a haystack on fire. When it was too hot to walk out they sat in Poole's arbour, ate bread and cheese, drank the rough sweet cider called Taunton ale and talked of politics and poetry. After the first few days he and William got on better, though Dorothy fancied that they would never be great friends, any more than she could fancy herself growing really intimate with Sara Coleridge. The two women had very little in common, once they had done talking about the baby or the dinner. Mrs. Coleridge thought Nether Stowey a dull stupid place and was always wishing herself back in her native town of Bristol. She would run on to Dorothy in her flat sweet peevish voice, "Was you ever in Bristol, Miss Wordsworth? My sister Edith and me was born and bred there. Bristol is a fine town, I can tell you; there is always something lively going on in Bristol, what with the soldiers drilling on the Downs, and the band playing, and all the fine ladies and gentlemen going to the Pump Room to take the waters, or running in and out of the shops and the circulating libraries. Edith and me had a milliner's shop, you know, after my poor father failed in his business and all the quality used to come to us for new bonnets to wear at the races, or scarves and feathers to dress their heads for the Assembly Rooms. Everybody wore feathers then, and did their hair in curls, but I hear that is quite gone out now; they are all taking to caps and turbans. My sister Edith writes to me that a poke bonnet is quite the thing; but Lord! what use have I for fashions here?

In Nether Stowey you may go out into the street twenty times a day and see nothing but a pig going to market, or a shepherd driving lambs to the butcher's, or maybe the doctor's gig waiting for him to go out on his rounds. Why, I must go into Bridgwater by the carrier's cart if I want so much as new roses for my slippers, or a ribbon for my cap! I was never in such a stupid place in my life. I hardly went out at all last winter, for there are no pavements even in the village and in wet weather the lanes are so muddy that you cannot walk in them. I had to stop at home all day long and mind the baby. I am sure if I had known that we should not be able to afford anything better than this I should never have married Mr. Coleridge."

Dorothy gazed upon her in sad amazement, but she did not perceive it and ran on in the same flute-like, complaining accents, "People should look at these things beforehand, but I suppose if they did they would not marry at all. I am sure there was no need for me to have Mr. Coleridge, for there was a very fine young man, a mercer in our street, whose father was in a good way of business and I am sure he would have offered for me if he had not been told that I was already promised. It was my brother-in-law, Mr. Southey, who arranged the match, you know. He told Mr. Coleridge that people would take it very ill if we did not marry after all the talk that there had been about us, and my sister Edith scolded him and declared that he had behaved very badly by me. So it was all made up between us and we were married at St. Mary Redcliffe, but I am sure I would never have agreed to it if I had thought that I was to come and live in Nether Stowey." She smoothed down her ruffled muslin apron and sighed, "Do you not think these poets are sad unpractical creatures when it comes to making money and paying their bills and so forth? I dare say your brother is just the same."

Dorothy protested indignantly, "William always pays his bills," for this was a matter in which the North-country brother and sister had been most strictly brought up. Mrs.

Coleridge only sighed, "Well, I meant no offence, I am sure. Only I thought your brother might be just such another as Mr. Coleridge, getting up in the middle of the night to write poetry and making a muddle of his affairs and setting people by the ears with his odd notions; and if he were I should be very sorry for you. I know I often wish I had not chosen a poet. Just imagine, he wanted me to go to America with him, when we were married first. There were to be twelve of us together and we were to live on the banks of some river. I cannot remember the name of it, only it was a very odd Indian name and the gentlemen liked the sound of it. We were to grow everything we ate and the women were to look after the children and make all the clothes and do the cooking; but nobody was to work more than three hours a day and everybody was to have his own opinions about religion and politics and so forth. I am sure it would have been very uncomfortable, I am very glad it came to nothing. So we came here instead and Mr. Southey left my poor sister at the church door and went off to Spain, which I thought was very ill-done of him; however, he is home again now. I hear everything is right between them and they are to live in Bristol. She sent me a very pretty morning cap from there the other day; I will lend it to you to copy, for it doesn't suit me at all."

Then with much greater animation she would exclaim, "My dear, that old Dunstable straw hat of yours is not at all what they are wearing this year. I wish you would let me alter it for you. It is only a matter of turning it up at the back and putting in a new ribbon, or a bunch of flowers, or a feather. Edith tells me a coquelicot feather will be worn very much next winter; coquelicot colour is to be all the rage. You must let me try my hand on it." Dorothy could only laugh and say, "I fear you must think me very old-fashioned. This hat is three years old. I have worn nothing on my head but a sun-bonnet all this summer. There was nobody to see me at Racedown but the pigs and chickens. William never knows what I have on from one year's end to another;" and Mrs.

Coleridge would lament, "Yes, these poets are sad, absent-minded creatures."

She was always ready to chat about frocks and ribbons; but when the men talked about poetry and so forth she pouted, opened light blue eyes and complained, "I know you don't want to listen to me; I'm not clever enough for you." Tom Poole laughed at her, loudly and cheerfully. William usually stared and went on with what he was saying, but even he was sometimes teased into watching her with an odd resentful fascinated look, as if she charmed and disturbed him in spite of himself. Her husband laughed at her and told her not to worry her pretty head about politics, or poetry either; but at times she seemed to vex him beyond patience and then he would turn round and tell her sharply to hold her tongue. She could deal with that easily enough. She had a thousand ways of smiling, teasing, weeping and relenting, with which to revenge herself. She knew how to shed large tears that left her lashes bright, she could scratch and play as gracefully as a young kitten. Their quarrels were public enough; she often seemed to anger him on purpose, then ran out and slammed the door in his face. So far he had not failed to follow eagerly. They were a demonstrative pair; he was very fond and proud, could not let her pass his chair without catching at her fluttering pink skirt or the hem of her apron. Sometimes he would take her captive by one finger and fondle her hand as he talked to the others, keeping her standing beside him, with downcast fluttering lashes and mounting colour. She would turn her plump white neck sideways with a nestling, birdlike motion and glance at the strangers in smiling satisfaction. You could not quarrel with such innocent defiance. She had after all a right to flaunt their happiness a little, only Dorothy found, after a time, that she could hardly bear to watch it.

At night she could not get to sleep because her stifling attic was next to theirs. The low-ceilinged bedroom, with its single square window down by the floor, seemed to store up all the heat of the long summer day. She used to lie wide awake, tossing and turning to find a cool place in the feather bed, while a quiet square of moonlight shifted across the boards and an overblown rose tapped at the pane. She could not choose but hear the two voices murmuring together on the other side of the wall. They seemed to talk to each other very late. She could not tell what they said, but she could catch the shrill complaint, the woman's laugh stifled as soon as raised, the man's deep murmuring protest, long-continued and urgent; and sometimes a whimper from the half-awakened child. She used to bury her head in her pillow to shut out the sounds, until their voices blended in a soft and drowsy murmur and finally died away. After that everything was quiet and she could sleep, if she chose.

5

At the beginning of the second week, when William and she came back one evening from what they always called a *wander* by themselves among the hanging oak-woods, there was a black-clad young man in the parlour talking to Sara about her husband's schooldays; a shy silent fellow, who stammered, blinked and smiled very sweetly—Charles Lamb, of whom they had heard, just come down by coach from London. He had only a week's holiday from the East India House and they were to show him everything in that country, but at the very beginning a sadly unfortunate thing occurred. Dear Sara, bustling about in her incapable fashion preparing the baby's pap, accidentally upset a skillet of boiling milk over her husband's foot and scalded him so dreadfully that he could not walk for days. The lime-tree bower became his prison, while his three guests walked together on the tops of the hills.

The stranger proved an admirable walker. For all his black dusty London clothes, thin shoes and lame leg, he could go as fast and as far as any of them. He would screw up his face and protest that he was a mere Cockney, but she suspected that he did this to tease William, who was always very solemn about his love for the country. William took it all quite seriously and could not tell what the little man would be at; but when he was alone with Dorothy Mr. Lamb would talk quite charmingly about his childhood in Hertfordshire, and holidays at a farm called Mackery End. Usually Tom Poole went with them. He knew the country like the palm of his own hand and was full of stories about woodcock and wild red deer, badger, otter and fox. He could talk very well, too, about the history of the neighbourhood. He could tell tales which had come down from his great-grandfather's time, about Monmouth's rebellion, staff officers watching the battle of Sedgemoor from the tower of Weston Zoyland church, men hanging in the gatehouse of Cothelstone Manor, Taunton Castle full of prisoners groaning in their straw and Judge Jefferies on the bench, roaring his way through the Bloody Assize. Nearer in time he had tales of bread riots and rick burning, hanging and transportation, which filled him with high indignation, and a long rambling story, which he told to every one in the same words, more or less, about how he had witnessed the execution of the charcoal-burner, John Walford, on the hill above the village.

"Poor John, I knew him well. When I was a boy he taught me to tickle trout and set snares for woodcock and find plover's eggs. There was no harm in him, but he was wild and got into bad company. There was a girl he should have married, Ann Rice, a fine clever lass. She would have kept him straight if any one could, but his mother came between them and after that John took to bad courses. He fell in with another woman, a poor degraded thing, and was forced to marry her against his will, so in the end it came to throat-cutting. I heard him ask for his old sweetheart as he stood under the gallows and the cry went round, Is Ann Rice here? She was found and dragged up to the cart and as she knelt on the straw he bent down his head over her shoulder. They talked together for nearly ten minutes, while we all stood silent and staring; then he bent down his head and tried to kiss her. I heard the officer who was by say, You had better not; it can be of no use. Poor John snatched her hand and kissed it, as she was drawn back and I saw the tears roll down his cheeks for the first time. He struggled with himself for a minute or two, then he wiped his face and said, I am ready now. They read him the usual prayers and I heard him join in the Lord's Prayer and the Creed. After that he stood upon a board put across the cart and the rope was tied round his neck. He made a speech to the people, said that he was guilty and begged for forgiveness; I dare say he had learnt it off by heart. The crowd were so quiet that you could hear every word and afterwards the birds twittering in the woods. Then the hangman cracked his whip and started the cart and John was turned off." Honest Tom gazed round on all their intent faces, sighed and said, "I never want to see such a thing again. Poor John! he did not deserve to come to such a bad end."

Nobody spoke for a minute or two, then William stretched himself and said, in his harsh voice, "By God! I'd like to write a poem about that." Tom Poole looked rather taken aback. He retorted, "Ah! it is but a tale to you. If you had known poor John you might feel differently"; then collected himself and sighed, "Well, perhaps a thing like that should be written down and made known. Poor folk have nobody to speak for them or pity them. I wish some of you writing gentlemen would take a true story now and then and work upon it, but no! you're all for knights and ladies and tales of chivalry. Nobody would read a poem about a charcoal-burner, or a pedlar, or a shepherd." William at this became very thoughtful and said, "I am not so sure. If that is true, it is a thing that must be altered," and Coleridge said, with a cheerful laugh, "Perhaps you are the man to alter it." Of course he was not serious, he was always advising William to begin an epic, or another tragedy, something in the grand style. The little clerk from London, Charles Lamb, only watched and smiled and listened, while they talked. He had written a few sonnets himself and they were just going to be published in a small volume, together with a few more by Coleridge and Charles Lloyd, but he did not think much of his own contribution. He said that his writing days were over. "I have p-put all that behind me," he assured them, in his gentle stammering voice, when they questioned him, "and b-burnt my little foolish journal. I have other work in the world now. I am wedded to the fortunes of my sister and my poor old father."

Coleridge asked him about this sister one day, in Dorothy's hearing, but he only looked exceedingly sad and said, turning away his face, "She is quite well, but I fear she must not come to live with us for a great while yet. It would hurt her, and hurt my father, for them to be together; besides, people will gossip, you know, whatever pains one takes against it and I fear the story will not be forgotten for a long while." Coleridge burst out, "Why should she not come here and live with us?" disregarding his wife's startled angry look, but the little man shook his head and sighed, "Dear Col, it would be too exciting for her. She is perpetually on the brink of madness and you would make her dance within an inch of the precipice. She must be with duller fancies and cooler intellects."

He concluded with his melancholy smile, "I know a young man of this description, who has suited her these twenty years and may live to do so still, if we are one day restored to each other." Coleridge assured him heartily, "I am sure she will recover"; and he admitted, "She keeps serene and cheerful. I walk over to see her every Sunday. To have her recover in half a year from such an illness is a great mercy." He seemed, however, sadly melancholy about his old father. They were living together in a brown cottage in Pentonville, near the Angel Tavern, and Dorothy's heart ached to hear him describe, in his uncomplaining fashion, how he came home at night, worn out with his day's work at the East India House and was set down at once to cards with this old father. "He will not let me enjoy a meal in peace, or sit down to read a book, or write a letter, for he says, 'If you won't play with me you might as well not come home at all.'" The only peace he got, he said, was when a former schoolfellow, Sam Le Grice, dropped in to play cribbage with the doting old man. "Do you remember Le Grice in the old days at Christ's Hospital? He was a dear comical fellow always. He was very good to me last winter. I have known him to play at cards, meal times excepted, all day long, in long days too, to save me from being teased by the old man, when I was not able to bear it." And he turned away his face with the tormented smile upon it and muttered, "God bless him for it."

Dorothy could hardly bear to listen to Charles, or to think of him going back at the end of his short holiday, to be shut up again between four walls, in the hot stony desert of August London. He assured her that he was a true Cockney, never happy for long away from his pavements, but for all that she fancied that he went off very reluctantly to catch the coach at Bridgwater. He wrote them all a charming letter from London, feared that he had been too shy and silent when he was with them and said, "it was kind of you all to endure me as you did!" He had left his greatcoat behind and asked them to send it after him; she felt that he wished he could have left himself behind too.

6

She did not, however, have leisure to regret him long, for that very week, out of a clear sky, it was suddenly decided that she and William were to come and live in Somerset. It was all done inside two days. Tom Poole managed it for them in his own tempestuous overbearing fashion. There was a house called Alfoxton, or Alfoxden, three miles from Nether Stowey and not two miles from the sea. They had often looked down upon it from the hills. It was long, white and low, of a classical simplicity and stood in a deer park; it had a walled garden and meadows sloped before it towards the sea. Behind it rose hills shaggy with oak woods and hollies; in a wander by themselves she and William found out a waterfall in a cool damp dell, clothed with ferns and green leathery fronds of hart's-tongue, as loud as any in their native hills. At first it seemed to them absurd to think of living in a mansion with a large park and seventy head of deer. They only hoped to rent a cottage near it, but Tom Poole, who knew everybody's business, swore that old Lady St. Aubyn, who owned the place, detested it. She never came there and the bailiff, John Bartholomew, at the home farm, would be glad to have the place occupied at a caretaking rent. He marched the brother and sister over to the farm, in his own masterful fashion; and before they had made up their minds in the matter, or quite understood what was happening, they had been bustled into taking the place for a year, for twenty-three pounds. Dorothy feeling still a little dazed, murmured, "Well, it is not very expensive, certainly"; and William, with his convulsive grin, reminded her, "We had no deer at Racedown." She was rather nervous about the whole affair, but William seemed so anxious to live at Alfoxden that she could not disappoint him. She had not seen him so pleased about anything for years. She vowed in her own heart that she would scrub floors and cook dinners every day, if it would make William happy. She wrote to the Pinneys at Bristol and told them that she and William would not be going back to Racedown, and arranged to send for Basil Montagu. William, as usual, left everything to her. She did not think that he ought to be worried about practical matters, that was her business. William had better things to think about.

Their friend Coleridge, of course, was enchanted with the plan and made a thousand absurd suggestions for their comfort. Mrs. Coleridge said, in her whining voice, "Oh! my dear, how will you manage in that great house, with only some cottage woman to help you with the cleaning? You will never get through the work. To be sure you would have had to go away soon, for Mr. Lloyd is coming back and will want his room again, but we could have found you some lodging in the village. I wish it may not all turn out a sad mistake. When Mr. Poole and Mr. Coleridge get a notion into their heads there is no stopping them." She brightened up considerably when the actual date was fixed and said that now she would be able to get on with her washing. It was done once a month in those days by all good housekeepers, and it was a great undertaking, for all the water had to be drawn from the well and heated in the copper and a woman got in to help from the village. Mrs. Coleridge made a great work about it, with all the baby clothes, and said, "I wish I could have invited you to stay longer," in such a half-hearted manner that Dorothy perfectly understood her intention to be rid of her visitors before washing-day.

III

I

THEY moved into Alfoxden on July the fourteenth, 1797, a date which Mr. Poole considered memorable, because it was the ninth anniversary of the fall of the Bastille. Next morning Dorothy's housekeeping was interrupted by Mrs. Coleridge, hot and breathless, begging to be relieved of a most unwelcome guest, who had been planted upon her by her husband's enthusiasm, right in the middle of the washing. Dorothy knew all about him and her heart sank when his name was pronounced; he was John Thelwall, the Patriot, or Citizen Thelwall, as he preferred to be called, and he had spent most of the last year in jail, because of his revolutionary opinions. She felt sure that William and he would quarrel and so they did at sight. William had long outgrown his revolutionary phase. The citizen proved to be an honest, violent, excitable man, tactless and blundering; she herself could not but pity him when he bared his forehead to the cool air blowing in from the sea, stared about him as if he had never been in such a fine house before and sighed, "This is a better place than Newgate." Their friend suggested, with his bright Olympian air, "It would be a fine place to talk treason in, Citizen," but the agitator shook his head and complained, "It's a place to make a man forget that treason is necessary. I should do no more work for poor folk if I lived in a house like this." She felt for the moment a touch of shame, because she and William had found such a happy solitude. It was dreadful to see the little tailor glance over his shoulder and burst out, "They will catch me again, you know; they will shut me up in Newgate and this time I shan't get out so easily. I shall likely die in prison, it's not a healthy place for a man of my years." For all that, neither she nor William liked him much and it was a relief when he went away; even Tom Poole's hospitality had found its limit, and he had refused to find a cottage for Citizen Thelwall in Nether Stowey.

After he had gone all the gossip broke out afresh. Perhaps Cousin Charlotte had something to do with it. First of all Dorothy found that the village people looked at her oddly, then they began to be as rude as they dared; she could not understand it, but Mrs. Coleridge was only too glad to enlighten her. "They think you are French spies brought over by Mr. Poole. They have been following your brother about and listening to him and to my husband behind hedges for three weeks. The innkeeper told them your brother was only a poet, who wanted to put Nether Stowey into a book, but that was not enough to satisfy them. Now that the French have invaded Switzerland everybody is in a sad taking, they think Bony and his warriors will be coming here next, to murder us all in our beds. And your brother is always watching the sea, so of course they think he is looking out for the invasion, though some people say perhaps he is only in league with smugglers." This made Dorothy laugh and Mrs. Coleridge drew up her chin out of its lawn frill and reproved her, " It is all very well to laugh, but he may yet find himself in trouble. They say there is not much harm in my husband, for all his wild talk, because he is such a whirlbrain, he says whatever comes uppermost; but your brother never says a word, he is the dark traitor." And she added, with a kitten's delight in scratching, "They cannot make you out at all. They think you are the strangest pair, living in that great house by yourselves, doing your own housework, tramping about the hills at all hours of the day or night as if you were poachers, and never going to church. They say all Mr. Poole's friends are queer folk and they can none of them understand how the little boy comes to be with you." She sank her voice to a confidential whisper and made her eyes as round as a kitten's while she murmured, "They know you call him by a different name, but of course they think he must be your brother's child, or even yours." She gave a shrill spiteful little giggle at Dorothy's startled look, put her pretty head on one side, fingered a curl and whispered, "They all say Basil is very like you."

Dorothy stared at her dumbfounded and suddenly thought, "Why, I never understood it before; she hates our being here, she is jealous of the pair of us." While she pondered this development Mrs. Coleridge ran on, "I assure you I told them not to talk so wickedly and said they should all be ashamed of themselves, but really I am not surprised, for you know how village folk will talk and wonder over what they do not understand. It is all very shocking, to be sure." Dorothy was so angry that she could not speak; her stammer tripped her up and she choked on the word, "Disgusting . . ." She looked down at her own hands and found them shaking with rage. Mrs. Coleridge surveyed her confusion with enjoyment, gave a high shrill laugh and consoled her, "I contradicted it, of course; that was only friendly. I would have done that for you even if I had been sure that it was true." The fiery girl burst out, "How can you talk so? Of course it is not true," with so much virginal fury that the plump petted little woman drew back and whimpered, "Well, you need not be angry with me. After all, I know nothing about you. Your brother may have had half a dozen sons and daughters without benefit of clergy, for all I know; though to be sure you might not have been told of it either. A brother does not tell his sister everything." There was not much love lost between her and William at any time. Dorothy opened her mouth for a protest, but was struck dumb by the inopportune recollection of Caroline, William's French daughter in Blois, the child whom she had never seen. She gazed in helpless silence at her adversary, who returned a hard and smiling stare; then she stammered fiercely, "B-Basil is no relation of ours." She was so angry that she felt quite sick. She was shaking all over. Mrs. Coleridge tossed her head and shrugged her shoulders; she said, "Well, I thought it only friendly to tell you what people are saying." Dorothy struggled to collect her feelings and was presently able to reply, "I think such gossip is better not repeated." This did not please Mrs. Coleridge, but it did silence her.

2

Presently Dorothy said that she must go back to Alfoxden. Her friend Coleridge had come in by that time and he offered to walk back with her through the holly wood, but Mrs. Coleridge would not let him. She said, "I want you to chop some wood for me"; and when he seemed reluctant pouted and complained, "I cannot possibly dress your dinner, if I do not have some kindlings. The box is quite empty and you know Mr. Poole's gardener will never do anything for me." So her immortal had to employ himself with chopping sticks and the angry Dorothy walked back through the wood alone. Mrs. Coleridge was always ready with some such excuse, it was becoming quite clear that she resented the time that her husband spent with the Wordsworths. He walked to them almost every day, or they to him, and they would accompany each other back and forth; often they drank tea with the Pooles or at some neighbour's fireside. All through the autumn he spent more time with them than he did in his own house. He and William would argue together by the hour about poetry and philosophy. The two young men and the young woman walked together in the crisp October weather on the tops of the brown hills or in the great holly wood, the largest in England. Mrs. Coleridge could not come with them on such long walks; she was already at work again carrying her second child. She sat indoors a great deal, looking pinched and shivering, hugged herself over a smoky fire of Sedgemoor peat and complained to every one of the cold. The parlour was very draughty, though her husband had stuffed up the ill-fitting doors and windows with green list for her. She had no shoes except her thin kid slippers, would not wear ploughboy's boots as Dorothy did and could not be persuaded to quit the village; the most she would do was to clink up and down the garden path in pattens when the sun was out, or go round to tea with old Mrs. Poole. She was not brought up to a country life.

They had all three been a great wander together one stormy afternoon, over the top of the ridge and down by the coombe, through a dripping sea of last year's straw-coloured bracken. The hills were running with peaty water and when they got back to the village they were all wet through; Dorothy's skirt was soaked to the knees and her old duffle-grey cloak was clinging to her. Sara Coleridge appeared at the door of the parlour and screeched in dismay as they came trooping in, stamping their wet boots and shaking the rain from their coats in the narrow flagged entry. She spread out her arms to defend Mr. Poole's new red carpet from William's muddy boots and gaiters, lamenting, "Why, you must be wet to the skin! How can you go out in such dreadful weather I thought you were all lost on the hills." She looked pinched and sulky. She crossed her bare arms over the bosom of her low-necked blue gown and drew back fretfully from the shower of drops which William was scattering about him as he shook out his North-country shepherd's plaid. She attacked her husband, shuddering; "How can you be so foolish as to go tramping about the country as if you were a ploughboy, in such shocking weather? You know you suffer most dreadfully from rheumatism when you go out in the rain. Last winter you were always complaining of your aches and pains. I suppose I shall have all the trouble of nursing you through one of your attacks again and you will start dosing yourself with that dreadful Kendal Black Drop. Mr. Poole says laudanum is very bad for you. I am certain you take too much of it, it is foolish to be always dosing yourself with doctor's stuff. You must go up and change your clothes at once; it is sitting in a wet coat and breeches that does all the mischief, but you will never take proper care of yourself. You are as helpless as a baby when it comes to practical matters."

She poured all this out to her husband in a fretful complaining whine, ignoring his friends. Dorothy stared, bewildered by so much inhospitality; William turned aside and rubbed his bony hands to warm them. He said to his sister, "I think you and I had better go home." Mrs. Coleridge did not contradict him; she stood there defending her carpet and her gown, and her husband laughed at her. He only sounded gay and scornful as he maintained, "You need not trouble yourself over me, there is no need for me to change my clothes. I shall do perfectly well once I can get to the fire." He did not look as if any mortal ill could touch him, standing under the lamp in his dripping garments, with his black hair plastered down by the rain on his white forehead and his eyes glittering in his pale vivid face. Dorothy had never seen any one like him. She felt her heart beating fast in her throat as she looked from husband to wife. They were staring at each other as if they were old enemies and ready to join battle; she did not know how the plump little sulky woman could stand there with such obstinacy, denying her husband warmth and shelter. She put out her hand to keep him off and exclaimed, "Don't come near me in those wet clothes. If you won't change them you must go and dry them in the kitchen."

He drew back and the smile faded from his lips; he told her sharply, "Well, think of your guests, at least; don't keep them standing here in the cold. Here's William needs a dish of tea as soon as you can make it and Dorothy is half-drowned. Take her to our bedroom and lend her a gown and a pair of dry shoes." He could assume an air of authority when he chose, though this was but seldom and he did it now; Sara retreated reluctantly from her post in the doorway, while Dorothy protested in her soft stammer, "B-but I never catch cold." He laughed at her with the same bright look which his wife had rejected and took her carelessly by the arm. She felt the touch of his fingers run through her like a consuming fire. He said nothing, but pushed her into the parlour, as if she had been a little girl, ignoring her protest. The winding staircase went up out of one corner and she found herself climbing it meekly, leaving dark footmarks on the carpet, with Sara behind her. As they went up she heard the two young men tramping off together to the warm and cheerful kitchen. They were laughing together and their hobnailed boots were grinding on the flags. She would much rather have gone with them than into the Coleridges' bedroom.

It had no fireplace and the winter damp was sweating off the walls; it struck as cold as a well after the heat of the stuffy little parlour. Dorothy shuddered as she stood in the steam of her own wet clothes, averting her eyes from the evidences of their cramped and intimate life together. Mrs. Coleridge was a dreadfully untidy woman and her husband not much better; the place was in a sad nursery muddle, with the baby's clothes and theirs lying about on the floor, his coats and her dresses hanging on a row of pegs behind the door, his country boots and her coloured kid slippers in a row beneath the bed, which had their pillows at the head and Hartley's cradle at the foot. She could not bear to look about her. Mrs. Coleridge stood helplessly by the door, murmuring, "I don't know what I can lend you, I'm sure. You're such a little creature; we are much about the same height, to be sure, but I should make two of you. Besides, I have so few clothes. I haven't had a new dress since I married. All my gowns are worn out." She gave a disgusted twitch to a faded cotton frock hanging behind the door and fell to lamenting her own grievances. She never lost sight of them for long. "But where's the use of my buying new gowns, even if I had the money for them. I have lost my shape completely since Hartley was born, you would never suppose that once I had as neat a waist as any girl in Bristol. Now here I am at work again and I suppose I shall soon be such a size that none of my gowns will fit me any longer."

She had quite forgotten Dorothy's needs as she ran on, "Well, I must go to Bristol soon, money or no money; I cannot be buried here the whole of the winter. I must have some clothes to my back, even if I am not fit to be seen and there are a score of things wanted for baby. My husband will have to find the money somehow, even if he borrows it from Mr. Poole again. I knew we should be poor at first, but I never thought we should be in such straits as this. Scribbling won't pay our bills and how we are to feed and clothe two children I don't know. It's my opinion that a man ought not to get married if he cannot keep his wife and family in comfort; do you not think so yourself?" Dorothy had let her old grey cloak slip from her and it lay in a wet heap on the boards. She dragged up her soaked cashmere gown over her head and heard Mrs. Coleridge complaining, "Every one told me he would do something splendid." She emerged from the muffling folds and said energetically, "One of these days he will, I am sure of it." She had spoken more fervently than she knew; Mrs. Coleridge gave her a spiteful glance and said, "Oh! I know you and your brother are always encouraging him to waste his time on poetry, instead of looking about for some useful work to do. You think nothing else matters but making verses." Dorothy said, "Nothing else does matter, for him or for William."

Mrs. Coleridge shrugged her plump shoulders and turned away; Dorothy burst out passionately, "How can you treat him so? I should have thought . . . I should have thought . . . you would have been proud . . . proud . . ." Her stammer overcame her, as it always did when she was deeply moved. Mrs. Coleridge turned round again, with her pretty common face all screwed up into a frown. She retorted, "What business is that of yours? I'll thank you not to interfere between us. I've had enough of you and that brother of yours, coming here and upsetting things. If you knew all I have to bear, miss, you'd not talk so." Dorothy coloured up to her forehead at the sudden venom of the attack and stood helpless, struggling to check an anger so fervent that it must have swept this insignificant little creature away. Mrs. Coleridge rummaged crossly among the torn and faded garments behind the door, plucked out a shapeless old red cashmere morning gown and tossed it on the bed, exclaiming, "Here, take this, if you must have something to put on your back. It's the only one that won't trail on the ground. And find yourself a pair of shoes, any pair except my new red ones; I don't want those stretched. You've got very large feet, haven't you? for such a little woman; I suppose it comes from all this walking. You'll excuse me staying up here any longer, I hope; I must go down and see what those men are doing."

She flounced out and banged the door. Dorothy was left to strip the wet stockings from her cold feet, drag on a dry pair, and pin herself into the red gown; it proved to be the oldest that Sara had and it did not suit her. She combed out her wet brown hair before the glass which daily reflected husband and wife. It showed her nothing but a pair of dark exhausted eyes in a face faded and pale as ashes; she was never one to look long in her glass for love of anything that she saw there, but on this night she gazed forlornly at the image between the candles and found herself wishing, passionately and hopelessly, that she could change herself into quite another sort of woman. She could not foresee any happiness for the one in the mirror.

It was a struggle to go downstairs in that old gown and drink Sara Coleridge's tea, to choke down her hot resentment, and pretend that nothing had gone wrong between them; none the easier because the little woman herself had already got over her temper. She never was angry with you for very long, though it was not so much that she repented of her scratches as that she forgot she had ever inflicted them. She was too stupid and guileless to bear malice and was apparently surprised that any one could resent her pinpricks. On this occasion she was already quite composed; after a few grave looks and short replies from Dorothy she suddenly laughed, quite sweetly and childishly, and burst out, "Oh! my dear Miss Wordsworth, now you are angry with me. She is quite out of humour with me," said she, beaming round at her husband and William, "because of something sharp that I said to her upstairs. But you must not mind me," she urged, laying her plump hand on Dorothy's knee and looking very plaintive. "If you only knew how ill I feel you would excuse me, I am sure"; then wandered off into a long story of her bodily inconveniences, which caused the inexperienced Dorothy to blush a little. Observing this, Mrs. Coleridge tossed her head, laughed and said with matronly condescension, "Oh! my dear, you will learn all this for yourself in good time, no doubt. Wait till you have a husband of your own to plague you and one baby teething and another on the way; then you'll find out that love isn't all wedding cake and marriage bells; no, nor all sonnets and verses neither."

Dorothy answered hastily, though in rather a shaken tone, "Oh! I shall never marry." Mrs. Coleridge tittered and protested; "What, do you mean to stop at home all your days and look after this brother of yours, for fear some other woman should get him?"

William scowled at the fire; his friend said, in his warm, eager voice, "Oh! somebody will come riding along and take her away from William, to be sure." William turned his head quickly, as if something had startled him, and said, "I could never let Dorothy go." Mrs. Coleridge stared from one to the other, laughing her silly fretful laugh, and Dorothy thought again, "Yes, she hates me."

3

The winter was not so severe, on that warm and sheltered west-country coast, as it had been in Dorothy's childhood in the north; it did not seem absurd to have their friend come bursting in, one November afternoon, and invite them to walk off with him for two days or three days to Minehead and Lynton. They started off gaily on the eight-mile stretch to Watchet, where they meant to sleep. William tramped straight ahead with his hands behind him and his eyes on the ground, as he always walked, keeping up a great pace; Coleridge continually crossed their way, shifting from one side of the footpath to the other, an odd movement and characteristic of him. She did not at that time realise that it betrayed a natural uncertainty of purpose. He seemed unable to keep on in a straight line; however, he went very fast and covered a lot of ground and she followed at their heels like a little dog.

It was a mild pleasant cloudy afternoon; the sea was calm and of a sober grey, streaked by the clouds passing over it. When they sat down to rest on a stile beside the road above Watchet she could see the purple moors inland looking like far motionless clouds themselves. All the capes and islands lay clear to seaward, under the declining invisible sun. The far Welsh mountains were capped by a range of cloud, she thought that she had never seen such a union of earth and sea and sky. All about her on the hillside were miles of grass, withered and yellow and shaking in the wind, but glittering with gossamer threads, which caught the light. She sat on the step of the stile with her arms about her knees. Her old straw hat had slipped off the back of her head and hung by its ribbons between her shoulders, her soft hair was uncovered. She did not know that she had a faint child-like smile on her upturned face as she sat gazing at the wide prospect. William, who never cared where he flung himself down, lay sprawling on the turf at her feet, with his big limbs all abroad; their friend sat on the bar of the stile above them, with the wind fluttering his black hair. They were all three perfectly happy, they had the fire of youth and poetry in their hearts. William folded his arms behind his head and remarked thoughtfully, "You can hear the sound of the sea distinctly now on the tops of the hills. We could never do that in summer. It's because the leaves are all off the trees, I suppose." She said eagerly, "And there are no birds singing, no insects humming; they make a kind of noiseless noise that lives in the summer air. There is nothing now but the dead sound of the sheepbells in the coombe." They were silent and it came floating up to them, exquisitely soothing. For a long time nobody spoke.

Then the two young men went back to an argument which had beguiled their walk, an old battle between them about what was, or was not, a proper subject for a poem. Her friend considered that you must always choose a high romantic theme, and for his part he favoured something fantastic, unearthly; but William maintained that you could impart a poetic interest to ordinary life and nature. He was always planning to write poems about cottagers and shepherds and such poor folk; he said that no subject ought to be neglected because it was unpoetical at first sight and he went about setting down the simple and fervent language which the common people used. The two young men were always discussing this point and striking fire out of each other, but she did not always listen to them, because they said the same thing many times over. She sat wrapped in her old cloak, looking at the scarlet cups of the moss on the bank beside her, thinking them more proper than acorns for fairy cups and idly noticing the locks of wool, spangled with moisture and stained with ruddle, which the sheep had rubbed off and left sticking to the round wood. When she listened again they were teasing each other about what kind of a poem each would write about the harbour of Watchet, lying under the headland below them, and a ship sailing out of it on a great voyage. William had settled himself comfortably against the bank, with one knee crossed over the other, and his arms under his head. He grinned affectionately up at their friend, whose bright eyes had begun to sparkle with excitement over some notion which was taking shape in his brain. William screwed up his face, looking teasing and comical. He said, "You will spoil it all with your foolish fantastic notions about ghosts and spirits."

Their friend leant forward and urged, "No, but listen, man; this is the way I should do it. There was a ship; there was a ship," said he, fixing William with his glittering eye. "She sailed southwards on a merry voyage, but there was a man on board her who had done some great evil to his fellows and so all came to no good. They were caught in the ice-pack, maybe, or becalmed on some tropic ocean. They prayed for rain and none came. All the crew dropped down dead and my old navigator was left alone among the rotting corpses." He seemed delighted with his notion; but William, unmoved, said, "Ah! you've been reading Shelvocke's voyages, I see and you mean to sail her round the Horn. I was reading a proper mariner's tale the other day myself, of how a ship was nearly cast away in those waters. Icebergs came drifting by, as tall as the mast and as green as emeralds. You heard them growling in the fog and a great bird, an albatross, floated overhead like an angel, or came on deck to be fed. Maybe your fellow's crime was that he killed an albatross. Sailors say that brings bad luck, sure as fate."

Dorothy listened with all her ears. Their friend said, "That's a pretty notion"; and became thoughtful, but William teased him, "Ah! you won't be able to handle it. You'll spoil it with a lot of your supernatural nonsense, make the ship sail by magic without wind or tide, most likely; or get the dead men up to work the ropes. You know nothing about such matters; you want my brother John to give you some advice, he can spin rare yarns by the hour about his voyages. Now if I were writing this ballad I should make that sailor of yours a proper old sea-dog, with a tarry pigtail and a ragged patched blue coat, a sturdy beggar such as you see on the roads hereabouts, as long and lank and brown as the ribbed sea-sand, with a wooden leg, maybe, and a bundle on his back and a birdcage tied up in a handkerchief. And he should tell his tale to some stranger in a tavern, over a noggin of rum, or at a village wedding, all in very simple words, such as poor folk use, and say he never had any luck in this world after he killed the albatross."

Their friend laughed and said, "We must write it together, I see. It shall be a ballad done by all three of us and we will sell it to the *Monthly Magazine* and get five pounds to pay for our holiday. And we will call it the *Rime of the Ancient Mariner*." William grumbled, "Too many cooks spoil the broth; we should never get as much as five shillings for it." He wanted to know why the ancient mariner could not simply be called *The Old Sailor*; he always liked everything plain, did William. Dorothy gazed from one to other entranced; William said, with the loving smile which he always had for her, "She listens like a three-year child; you have quite bewitched her." Their friend smiled too; he said, "You must tell us the end of it, my dear; how is it to be finished?" She coloured up to her forehead, but said bravely, "I should like him to repent of killing the innocent bird, and to be forgiven and come back safe home to his own country." William grumbled, "Girls have all soft hearts; she'll spoil your poem for you." They all got up and went on cheerfully past the cell of the holy hermit St. Decuman and down the hill to Watchet. Next day they went on between the moorland and the sea, through Dunster to Minehead, and so to Porlock and Lynton; and home again by the Exe valley. They were not away more than a week, but Mrs. Coleridge cried and complained as if she had been left alone for a month. That rather spoilt Dorothy's pleasure; however, it was the finest wander that she and William had ever had. She would not admit to herself why this was so, but she knew that deep in her heart she would remember it all her life.

4

A little before Christmas their friend came out with one of his sudden plans; he proposed that they should go up to London, with an introduction from him, and offer William's tragedy to the manager of Covent Garden Theatre. So they drove up by coach, a chilly business in the December weather when they could only afford outside places; spent three weeks in London and found it a dreary smoky rainy place after the west-country. They went to see Charles Lamb in his lodgings in Pentonville, but did not meet his unknown sister, who was just then shut up in the Hoxton madhouse, with a recurrence of her disorder. They dined with Mrs. Coleridge's brother-in-law, Robert Southey, who proved to be a dull good bookish young man, without any fire in him, handsome enough in a black-haired, eagle-nosed fashion, but very stiff and condescending in his manners. He had a way of tilting his head and peering down at you which really came from being short-sighted, but looked as if he meant to patronise you. He and William took an immediate dislike to each other; Dorothy could see that William thought him a coxcomb and a pedant and that he thought William a boor. She had no notion then how much she would come to like him in later years, nor guess how much shyness his chilling air concealed. His wife Edith was very like her sister Sara, but less pretty and with a good deal more sense. Both husband and wife did their best to be polite to the two uncouth strangers. Robert Southey arranged an interview with the manager of Covent Garden, who kept the play three weeks, but in the end it was returned, with the curt verdict, "Impossible that this should succeed." They could go home again, they had wasted their money.

William was very stiff, as always, when things went wrong for him. He persisted that he had never had the smallest expectation of getting his tragedy performed; the stage was in a poor way, he would wait a few years until public taste had improved and then perhaps try again, for the moment he was only interested in writing lyrics. Dorothy knew better than to force her sympathy upon him. William could never bear a hand laid on a wound. They drove home again, over the frozen waste of Salisbury Plain and were back at their own fireside for Christmas Day. It was Dorothy's birthday and she was twenty-five, she thought it something of a landmark in many ways. She and William sat cosily together beside their fire of blazing logs, and heard the owls hooting in the Alfoxden woods. They reminded William of the owls at Hawkshead, when he was a boy, how he used to imitate their hooting through his closed hands and make the birds answer him with long halloos and screams and loud redoubled echoes. It pleased her to hear him talk of those days. He said that some day he would write a long poem about his own childhood and put in the owls.

The only sad thing about that pleasant Christmas was that their friend was not with them. While they were in London he had gone up to the north, to Shrewsbury. The Unitarian chapel there lacked a minister and he was dallying with the idea of applying for the post. When one of his religious fits was upon him he could preach a magnificent sermon, but Dorothy could hardly fancy him dwindling into a minister; however, as Mrs. Coleridge said, in that way he could at least provide for his wife and children. Dorothy missed him very much, but on the other hand his wife was much more ready to be friendly when he was away. She was now beginning to lose her shape and did not care to be seen about the village, but, like other women in her case, though looking worse she felt better and liked the company of another young woman. She was always asking Dorothy over to listen to her chatter of clothes and babies and to be teased by hearing the loving phrases in her husband's letters. It was a kind office which Dorothy would have evaded if she could, but her conscience was a tender one and it obliged her to walk through the holly wood, two or three times a week and endure an hour in the cottage in the village street. William grumbled about it and said, "Why do you trouble yourself to go? It is of no use; that woman will never like you." He always hated her to give her time to any one but him.

Soon after they came back from London he had begged her to keep a journal. "It will be very useful to me," he was pleased to declare, "if you make careful notes of the weather day by day, and the flowers as they come out, and everything of that nature; only you must try and write a better hand than you do, or I shall not be able to read it." So she bought an exercise-book at the village shop and began in her sprawling sloping widely-spaced hand to set down all that she saw. At first it was difficult, for she had never kept a journal before and she did not know what William wanted her to say. She sat down after tea in the parlour, when she had brightened the fire and drawn the curtains, opened her mahogany desk and mended her quill briskly, but after that she had to confess, "I can think of nothing to put down. It has been a most uninteresting day; I only walked to the farm for eggs with Basil and on the way back picked up sticks and fir-apples in the wood." But William, drawing down his long lip and putting on a schoolmaster's air, insisted firmly, "I am not going to think of things for you to say. You must describe your walk. I should like you to form the habit of noting down something that you have seen every day; it will train your observation and your memory." And he returned to his book, which was *Tristram Shandy*. So Dorothy bit the top of her quill, dipped it obediently in the ink and wrote doubtfully, "The green paths down the hillsides are channels for streams. The young wheat is streaked by silver lines of water running between the ridges, the sheep are gathered together on the slopes. After the wet, dark days, the country seems more populous. It peoples itself in the sunbeams."

She paused and gazed at this sentence doubtfully, feeling sure that William would not approve of the repetition; but she did not want to have an erasure on the first page, so she let it go and went on, more cheerfully, "The garden, mimic of spring, is gay with flowers. The purple-starred hepaticæ spreads itself in the sun, and the clustering snowdrops put forth their white heads, at first upright, ribbed with green, and like a rosebud when completely opened, hanging their heads downwards but slowly lengthening their slender stems." She could not think of any other flowers to put in, so she finished with the wood behind the house. "The slanting woods of an unvarying brown showing the light through the thin network of their upper boughs. Upon the highest ridge of that round hill covered with planted oaks, the shafts of the trees show in the light like the columns of a ruin." That is the way that Dorothy Wordsworth's Alfoxden journal begins.

She showed it to William, who frowned over it and said there was too much repetition. She must learn to turn her sentences better and not leave out all the verbs from mere idleness. He did not think a snowdrop at all like a rose in shape, though he appreciated the Grecian colonnade of her hilltop grove; but no doubt in time she would do better, for a first attempt it might pass. So she thankfully closed the inkpot, sanded the book, wiped her quill-pen and put all away. She made him some more tea, which he always liked to drink late at night. After that he read her a poem of his own about an old huntsman and then they went to bed.

On the next day she recorded the scarlet cups of the moss, how they were more proper than acorns for fairy goblets; and on the day after, as she walked to Holford, the ivy twisting round the oaks like bristled serpents. It became an enchanting game for them both. William scrutinised each entry and sometimes broke a promise and suggested something of his own; he made her put in a moon rainbow and said that some day he would use it for a lyric. So after that she put in everything that pleased him, besides some things which she chose to preserve for her own recollection. She thought that she would like to read the book again when William was a famous poet and she was quite an old woman.

They had some wild weather at the beginning of February; they could not walk at all on the hilltops for some days, but had to shelter in the woods. There they had cover at all times and could pick up great armfuls of the rotten boughs blown down by the wind. The oak-trees roared overhead and the ground seemed in motion with the multitudes of dancing leaves, which made a rustling sound, distinct from that of the trees; she put it all down for William in her journal, and she did so faithfully. When a whirlblast came from behind the hill the hailstones danced among the withered leaves, but she and William were safe and snug in the undergrove of hollies, which was green all the year round. They sat close together under one cloak and divided their shelter with a herd of donkeys, which pastured in quietness under the trees, undisturbed by the storm. William wrote some lines for her about the dead leaves and hailstones and said that he thought he should like to write a poem about asses and their queer tricks and habits. He was amused by the way they turned their long ears about and the hard dry seesaw of their horrible braying; he swore that he felt quite a liking for a creature which was often so dreadfully abused.

5

He was working very hard all that winter, composing and planning according to his new theory, that nothing in common life was unpoetical. He had done a poem about an *Idiot Boy*, from a story Tom Poole had told him, and several about cottagers and their ways, besides a lyric about a caged thrush, which he had heard singing in a London street and another, which made his sister weep, about a shepherd whose flock had been sold, one by one, to buy his children bread. Dorothy and William had met this gaunt creature weeping on the highway, with a lamb in his arms, going to market and he had told them mournfully that it was the last of all his flock. Dorothy could hardly read the poem for crying. All these lyrics William was to complete as fast as possible, and they were to be offered to Mr. Cottle, the publisher, of Bristol, together with some of Coleridge's verses and with the ballad of the *Ancient Mariner*. Their friend had gone on with it by himself in the end and it was almost finished. It had worked out much longer than had been expected and William thought it foolish and exaggerated, but Dorothy found it strangely beautiful and exciting, though of course she felt that William must know best, when it came to discussing what was, or was not, a good poem.

She did hope the book would succeed; William would be so dreadfully disappointed otherwise. He was working altogether too hard. He had always suffered greatly from headaches, the scholar's malady; when the bad weather kept him indoors he sometimes made himself quite ill with his writing, he sat up late at night and could not sleep. She wished that the fine weather would come and that their friend would return; they got on ill without him. The winter seemed as if it would never end, and William did not seem very happy in his own mind about his *Idiot Boy* poem. She thought that he always wrote most easily when he could compose out of doors. He liked best to be able to walk up and down a straight gravel path, or in some place where the swing of his verse and his march met with no interruption. In this he was unlike her friend, who liked to compose walking over uneven ground, or breaking through the straggling branches of a coppice wood. She sometimes thought that this summed up the whole difference between them.

Their bright wanderer came back to them before the fine weather did, rushing home suddenly from the north, very full of himself and of a strange and handsome offer which had been made to him. He did not mean to be a Unitarian minister now, not he, though indeed he had preached very well at Shrewsbury and might have had the chapel there, he believed, if he had chosen; but there was something better on foot. It was all owing to Tom Poole, once again. The tanner had introduced him to some people named Wedgwood, china manufacturers at a place called Etruria, near Burslem in Staffordshire. There were two brothers, sons of the old Josiah Wedgwood who had founded the firm, the irascible old master-potter who used to hobble round the works and smash all faulty pieces with his crutch, swearing, "That's not good enough for Josiah Wedgwood." His elder son, Josiah the second, was just such another enthusiast, always experimenting with glazes and firing and modelling. He would talk by the hour, said Coleridge, about his blue and grey and yellow jasper-ware, his urns and bowls of black Egyptian basalt, his red and black Etruscan vases, with Mr. Flaxman's designs upon them, copied from the antique. It was fascinating to listen to him. But there was another brother, Tom, a wasted hectic creature, who suffered agonies from asthma. He had been a patient of Tom Poole's friend, Dr. Beddoes, at the hot wells in Bristol, where Dr. Beddoes and his young assistant, Humphry Davy, had been treating him in an experimental chamber filled with strange gases, but they had not done Tom any good. His asthma was just as bad as ever and some day it would kill him. He was a queer fellow, Tom, he dabbled in chemistry and had a notion that you could make pictures of people's profiles by casting their shadows upon paper soaked in nitrate of silver; but this method of his, which he called photography, was laughed at by everybody. It was clear that Tom Wedgwood had been enchanted by Coleridge and had sat fascinated, with a flush of excitement in his thin cheeks, while that marvellous web of talk was spun about him. The Wedgwood brothers were rich and charitable, ready to befriend a young and struggling genius. They had a number of such pensioners already and Tom had persuaded his brother to offer Coleridge a pension of a hundred and fifty pounds a year, without any conditions, so that he might be free to live and write as he chose.

It was like a fairy tale. Coleridge could babble of nothing but the Wedgwoods, their kindness and generosity, and all the fine things that he would do to reward and justify their bounty. He had accepted the offer as soon as he heard of it, all in a moment, while he was tying up one of his shoes. William stared at his friend doubtfully and offered few and grudging congratulations ; but Dorothy was delighted. The tears came into her eyes when she heard her friend say, with a sudden drop into humility, "It is an exquisite relief. I have been almost out of my mind sometimes to think how I could contrive to feed my wife and children." Mrs. Coleridge, though quite vague as to how or why they were all to be so much more comfortable than before, thought it no more than her husband's due. She said, "I dare say they will never miss it, they are so very rich. Now we shall be able to move into a better house and pay the butcher and the baker what we owe them and perhaps I shall be allowed to order myself a new gown sometimes without being scolded. I am sick and tired of all this pinching and scraping. I am sure I can use every penny of the money. It is not so very much, after all; I think they might have made it two hundred while they were about it."

6

Early in March something happened to vex the Wordsworths greatly. Lady St. Aubyn, the owner of Alfoxden, sent them word that they could not stay in the house after the end of July. Their year's agreement would finish then and she had found another tenant for the place. It was a shock to brother and sister and still more so when Farmer Bartholomew, the bailiff, let out the reason. Lady St. Aubyn did not think they were sufficiently respectable people to live in her house. "She's wholly took against you," he said gloomily. "She's a very determined woman, is Lady St. Aubyn." Mrs. Coleridge, said, with sparkling eyes of malice, "Well, I told you how it would be, they think you are very queer people"; and her husband groaned, "It is that cursed business about poor Thelwall over again. I blame myself for bringing him to you." Tom Poole was very angry indeed and said that he should write a strong letter to the old lady. "I will assure her that Citizen Thelwall did not go to Alfoxden by your invitation. I will tell her that you are most respectable people and have an uncle who is Canon of Windsor." This fact had already impressed the honest tanner himself considerably; and he was sure that it would silence Lady St. Aubyn, but William said unhappily, "That cock won't fight. My Uncle Cookson will never tell her anything good of me." He was sure that the Canon had not yet forgotten or forgiven the French business about Annette. The whole family had washed their hands of William after that. It was all very annoying. There did not seem to be any other house to be let at a reasonable rent in the neighbourhood and though Tom Poole faithfully wrote his letter and advanced all his arguments, even down to the Canon of Windsor, he got no answer; the Wordsworths would have to move at midsummer. Dorothy felt that she could not bear to think of it and she tried to put it all out of her mind. There were still four months for her to be happy in; after that she would go back to everyday life.

The spring came slowly up that way and about the middle of March there was a great fall of snow, which the neighbours told her was very rare in that part of the world. It came in the night and when she went to the farm next morning in her clogs, to fetch eggs, the sun shone bright and clear. There was a deep stillness in the thickest part of the wood, undisturbed except by the occasional dropping of snow from the holly boughs. She heard no other sound but that of the water and the slender notes of a redbreast, which sang at intervals on the outskirts of the southern side of the grove. There the bright green moss was bare at the roots of the trees and the little birds were upon it. The whole appearance of the wood she thought enchanting and each tree, taken singly, was beautiful. The branches of the hollies were pendant with their white burden, but still showed their bright red berries and their glossy green leaves; the bare branches of the oaks were thickened with the snow. It was a wood of enchantment and she walked in it and drank the sparkling air and was happy all by herself, with no one to trouble her. William was writing hard and would not be disturbed; he had begun an enormous poem, which he said would take him several years to write, a moral epic, addressed to his friend and called *The Recluse*. He would put into it all his views of Man, Nature and Society and some account of himself. He had already composed some ten or twelve hundred lines of this poem and he was perfectly happy sitting in the library, by a roaring fire, hammering out verses; he did not want any company. She had not taken Basil with her, for fear the drifts should be too deep for him, but had left him throwing snowballs on the lawn and making a snowman with coals for eyes. Their friend was away, he had gone over to a lonely farmhouse, between Porlock and Lynton, because he said he could not get any writing done at home, for Sara's chatter. Dorothy had the snowy woods to herself.

When he came back the snow had all melted away. He descended upon them one mild evening, on his way home from Porlock, having turned aside out of his road to bring them a poem which he had made for them while he was away, a strange unearthly fragment about the Emperor of China, some of the loveliest words ever written. "*In Xanadu did Khubla Khan a stately pleasure house ordain . . .*" That was the beginning of it, as he recited it to them, standing before their fire in the steam of his damp clothes. She did not know what it meant nor did he. He said to her, "I wrote it in a dream. I had been taking my Kendal Black Drop, to drive the pain out of my joints. I had been walking all morning in the rain, and the fire and the laudanum together sent me into a kind of stupor. I had not slept much the night before and must have dozed for about three hours, but all the time I was making poetry in my dreams. I must have composed between two and three hundred lines. When I awoke I seemed to remember the whole of it perfectly clearly and I took pen, ink and paper and wrote down what you have there; but at that moment I was unfortunately called out by a person on business from Porlock, and detained by him above an hour and when I came back I could not recall my vision. It had all passed away, like ripples on the surface of a stream when you throw a stone into it; there was only a vague and dim recollection left." She stared from his smiling face to the paper in her hand and said slowly, "I cannot bear to think of it. This is the most beautiful poem that I have ever read." He caught fire from her and asked her, "Do you think that?" very eagerly. Then the light in his face died away and he knit his dark brows and sighed, "Well, there will never be any more of it; I have forgotten my dream."

William studied the poem again for himself and shook his head doubtfully; he said, "There is not much sense in that,

I do not know how you could finish it." Their friend laughed, in his pleasant way and said, "Oh! there is never much sense in my head, you know. I ramble from one thing to another, I do not finish anything." She saw his great light eyes turned upon her brother with impatient affection and marvelled at the power in that hasty glance; she understood that there was something god-like in this man, some quality that even William could not match, and thought, "We are right to believe in him; he is great, already." She found him most strangely excited that night, wild and unlike himself. Sometimes he did not seem to understand what they said to him, he stared and rambled a little in his talk, almost as if he had a fever upon him, and complained that his head was full of opium still. She said that she would walk through the wood with him and see him as far as Nether Stowey. She did not like to think of him being out there alone. He said that he would be glad of her company but William would not go with them. He was cold, his head ached, and he wanted to sit by the fire. So she wrapped herself in her old duffle-grey cloak and went with her friend.

The night was cloudy, but not dark, they could see to walk under the trees in the grove. They went through the low damp dell by the waterfall, where they could hear the leathery green hart's-tongue ferns rustling in the dark against the dripping rocks. Presently the moon came out and at once the shadows of the oaks blackened, and their lines became more strongly marked; the withered leaves were coloured with a deeper yellow and a brighter gloss spotted the hollies. In the distance they heard a dog howling, a strange uncouth sound, prolonged and melancholy. Her friend raised his head and muttered irritably, "What ails the beast?" and she said hurriedly, "It is the miller's dog; I often hear it complaining so when it is tied up at night. It barks at the murmur of the village stream." He said, "It sounds very wretched and afraid," and walked on beside her, plunged in some melancholy stupor. The sea was making a loud noise behind them, as if disturbed, but the wind was silent; only when they came to the clearing and looked up at the great oak-tree, whose crooked arm pointed upwards to the moon, she saw that the sole remaining leaf there was dancing round and round like a rag blown by the wind, in some faint moving air above them. Her friend took her by the arm and pointed to it with a wild distracted stare, saying, "Does it not look as if it were alive?"

She was startled by his manner and peered anxiously at him through the gloom, but she could only make out the pale gleam of his brow and the deep sockets of the eyes beneath it, black and without expression, like holes in a skull. He went on muttering to himself, in his new strange preoccupied manner, as if he were talking to himself and not to her. "I began a poem a little while ago, about this very clearing. I had been reading old chronicles, about warlocks and witches and fancied a pale yellow-haired lady, kneeling where the moonlight falls under the oak, very richly clad. It would be frightful to see her there, you know, pretending to pray, a witch disguised, with a small dull eye like a snake." He passed his hand over his brow, as if he did not know where he was and said, with an effort to speak steadily, "I never finished it. I am not industrious like William. My desk is full of such fragments, though this, to be sure, was better than most." She did not know what to say to him, but murmured reproachfully, "Why must you think of evil in a place like this?"

He burst out with a violence which alarmed her, "But there is evil everywhere, don't you know that yet? don't you fear it?" Then he checked himself and said in a mournful way, "No; you're innocent yet, you don't know what the world can do to you. William knows better; he has seen evil triumph, he knows that nothing is safe. I ought to have a girl like you in my fable, or one like my poor foolish Sara, an innocent powerless creature, too simple to guess the spell that evil chance can put upon her. Innocence has no power, it only lives to be betrayed and corrupted. You'll find that out soon enough." She shrank back a little and he stared at her fixedly, pushing forward his head; she got the feeling that he could not really see her. Then he suddenly began to laugh, a harsh jangled laugh which echoed dreadfully in the leafless wood. It started two night-birds from the great tree above them and afterwards an owl uttered a sudden quavering hoot quite close at hand. The double echo startled the man at her side, and he trembled from head to foot and stared round him for a moment, bewildered. Then he turned and ran from her. She heard him going for a long way, breaking through the branches of the midnight wood. He sounded lost and frantic as if he were trying to break his way out of prison.

7

After the snow had melted the spring came in quickly. There was a thick mist from the sea in the early mornings, but after it had moved quietly away up the coombe the dewy lawn sparkled in the sun. Dorothy had never seen the warm west-country in bud before and her friend, who had been bred up in a Devon parsonage, laughed at her delight. All through April there was a multitude of primroses, dog-violets, periwinkle and stitchwort in the lanes. Cowslips powdered the meadows; the cottage gardens were gay with brown velvet wallflowers, forget-me-nots and blue and white hyacinths; the cider-orchards were clotted with pink and white blossom. It became warm enough to sit out in the little flagged court before the house. Basil and she gathered great baskets of primroses in the wood; William allowed them to leave their books and give the first fine days to idleness, so they all went down for a picnic to the shore. The lapwings tumbled and twisted in their ecstatic flight above the newly-ploughed fields, the garden was full of fat newly-hatched thrushes scrambling about after the old birds to be fed. There were lambs in the coombe with thick legs, large heads and black staring eyes; Basil loved to run races with them. The village girls made a holiday show on the hills with their pink and blue print petticoats, the whole countryside was gay. She could not bear to think that at midsummer she must pack and leave it.

Their friend seemed only just to have taken this in. He went about all the time proclaiming that he would never be able to endure Nether Stowey without them, he said that he would go wherever they did. One night he came bursting in with a fine new plan of his own. "We must all spend the winter in Germany and learn the language. We will go to some small town first and board with a respectable family until we can understand their tongue and then we will move on to one of the university towns and study philosophy. You will not be a farthing poorer than you are here. Living is very cheap and you will soon be able to add to your incomes, for you will both be able to do translation from the German. It is the most profitable kind of literary labour nowadays. Every one is wild to read their philosophy, but few people have the leisure or the energy to learn such a crabbed language. Cottle would employ all three of us; you can do such work, my dear, as well as William can."

He turned his glowing eyes upon her as she dallied with the romantic prospect. She murmured, "There is the journey to be paid for," but her friend mocked prudence. "Why, Cottle will give you twenty or thirty pounds for William's share in the Lyrical Ballads and that will pay for the journey, or we will beg our fares from the kind Wedgwoods and pay them back later." William objected, "There is your wife to consider and the children too," but he would not be checked; he waved his hands about and said airily, "Oh! Sara will be quite strong again by August or September. We can find a furnished house and hire a nurse-girl, if they will not take the children in any lodging. I suppose there are cows in Germany, as well as in other countries. I shall tell Sara not to be foolish." He was so boastful about it that Dorothy felt certain he was afraid of his wife's tantrums and objections, but there was that in his look and air which compelled her to yield. All her being turned towards him, like a weed bending and waving in a strong stream. When he fixed his eyes upon her and urged her, "You will come; say you will come. We cannot do without you, Dorothy"; he pronounced her name in such a tone that it set all her nerves quivering, like the strings of a harp swept by a gentle yet accomplished hand. She could not resist his entreaty; she sighed a "Yes," as faint and dying as the sound of the harp strings falling into silence. William moved awkwardly in his chair, crossed his legs, cleared his throat, stared at her as if awaking out of a dream and mumbled, "Well, we will think of it. You shall talk to your wife about it and tell us how she takes it." Dorothy added, with her soft stammer, "It would be delightful. I should like it, I believe, above all things. I have always wanted to go to Germany."

Mrs. Coleridge fell into strong hysterics at the thought of taking her children into what she supposed to be a savage country. She wept and fainted and terrified the household; she was very near her time and there was no arguing with her. She worked herself up into a sad state. Her husband reported ruefully that he could not go on talking about his plan to her, he would have to leave it alone until after the baby was born. Perhaps she would be more reasonable then. He could not bear to see the shapeless, helpless creature with her face distorted with crying and he did not talk to her any longer about Germany; but he had not forgotten his plan for all that. He was always harking back to it in conversation with William and Dorothy, like an obstinate child bent upon a promised treat, saying, "Next winter when we are in Germany we will do this or that. It will be delightful, we shall all be very happy together," and repeating what he had said upon their first acquaintance, "We must never be parted; we are three persons and one soul."

Sara's second child was born that May. It was another boy and his father, who liked odd names, called him Berkeley, after the philosopher. He said that both his sons were now called after philosophers and Mrs. Coleridge, who knew nothing about such matters, was nevertheless well pleased to have her son called after a bishop. She thought that very respectable. Dorothy and William walked over one day to Nether Stowey, to see the new arrival, and Dorothy was taken up to visit Sara in the bedroom. The young mother was rosy and cheerful, she had come through her trouble quite easily, though she had a thousand complaints to make about her sufferings. She sat up in bed with her hair curling under her muslin cap and the baby in her arms, as proud as a cat with one kitten. She was quite wrapped up in the baby, had no eyes for his father when he stole up to look at them, only wanted to be left alone to cuddle the child. He was very proud and fond, his fatherhood was one of the simpler aspects of his nature. With the child in his arms, held carefully if a little gingerly, he seemed much like any other young husband of twenty-five years in the same case, proud, smiling, conscious, very much absorbed. He held out the baby for Dorothy to see with no thought but the common one, "Do you think he is like me? or like his mother?"

She put out her hand and touched the child's warm downy head. She felt the mysterious fountain of new life pulsating strongly between the sutures of the egg-shell skull and suddenly she was overcome by a frightful pang of jealous hatred, which blazed up like a flame in her heart. She detested the soft complacent woman and her child and could have wished them every ill, because they stood between her and the man who smiled at her with so much careless kindness. She stood burning and shaking all over, terrified by the violence of her own feelings. She made her escape as soon as she could and ran down to William, but now she knew what ailed her, a common sickness and all too easily named. She had slipped into love unconsciously, just when she thought herself quite safe, with their friendship and his marriage to protect her; now she was head over ears and might get out as best she could.

At the end of the week Coleridge came up ruefully one morning and complained that there was no place for him at home. The house was entirely given up to nursery affairs, he could not work with the baby thrust into his arms, a napkin airing on his knee and Hartley stumbling and laughing about the floor. He insisted that they should come with him for a wander. They might go to Cheddar, it would only take a day or two. There was an underground river there, which flowed through caverns measureless to man, like the river in his poem. He had seen it the year before and could not rest now till he had shown it to William and Dorothy. The Mendips were honeycombed by stalactite caves, he said, but only the outer chambers were known. Shepherds had climbed down the swallet-holes a little way sometimes, after lost lambs, and heard water running far underground, and the miners had penetrated the Roman lead mines. It was a savage and enchanted country and deserved a poet. William was interested immediately and said, "Yes, we will come; there is no reason why we should not." He loved seeing new places; he was really more interested in places than in people, it was one of the differences between him and his sister. She astonished herself and the two men by stammering at the same moment that she could not manage it, but William stared at her in so much surprise, and her friend with so much disappointment, that she was not able to hold to that sudden alarmed withdrawal.

They set out next day across the marshes, steering a course by Glastonbury Tor, which rose like a beacon to guide them among the lines of waving willows and the silver pattern of the dikes. They came to the hills and stared up at the limestone bastions and escarpments of the gorge; they saw the clear river breaking forth from underground, full-grown and bright as crystal, strong enough to turn a mill; they fed the swans which floated above their own reflections upon the bishop's moat at Wells. It should have been a charming wander, and the two young men were merry enough, but it was not a happy time for Dorothy. There was a soft fever burning in her, smouldering and consuming her, she was blindly, desperately in love. She could not put back the clock for herself, she feared her future; she did not know what was to become of her, but she knew as clearly as if she had been told that nothing would ever be the same again for her, once she had left Alfoxden. She had been utterly happy there, for the first time in her life and that sweet careless time was coming to an end. She had begun to feel that in some way these two men, whom she loved so dearly, would tear her heart in two between them. One night she suddenly astonished William by imploring him, "Do not let us go to Germany; or at least let us two go by ourselves"; but William only gave her his owlish stare and wanted her reasons, which of course she could not state. She said lamely that she fancied Mrs. Coleridge did not like the plan. William stuck out his long lip and said that he was not going to alter his plans for a silly woman like Mrs. Coleridge, so his sister had to give way and hold her tongue.

8

There was trouble about the German plan again as soon as they got back to Nether Stowey. Mrs. Coleridge had persuaded herself that it had long been abandoned; when she found that it was not she fell into lamentations, as she had done before. The method had worked admirably then and she naturally supposed that it would work again, but though she upset the baby into screaming fits she did not this time get her way with her husband. She was stupidly bewildered when after all her weeping and wailing he declared that if she would not come to Germany he would go without her. He was like a child bent on a promised treat. He had actually persuaded the kind Wedgwoods to pay for the journey for all three of them and he would not listen to argument or reason. Neither would Mrs. Coleridge. Poor Tom Poole, rubbing the top of his head perplexedly and rashly sympathising first with one side, then with the other, presently found that he had involved himself in looking after Mrs. Coleridge and her two babies. They were to stop in his Nether Stowey cottage for the winter, which was not at all what poor Tom had bargained for, but an old bachelor must be at every one's service.

Dorothy was very much startled when she heard this. She remained quite silent while her friend explained triumphantly how well matters had been arranged and what a much more delightful time they would now have in Germany, moving from place to place as the wind blew and doing just what they chose. She went over next morning to Nether Stowey and was not surprised to find Mrs. Coleridge very chilly. "I wish you may enjoy yourselves," said she, with a toss of her curl-papers, "going off to get frostbitten in a place where it snows all winter and the people eat raw ham and you cannot speak a word of the language. I should dislike it exceedingly. I should not dream of taking the children there." She rocked her baby in her arms and said to it, spitefully, "Did they think I would take you to freeze in a nasty foreign city and be bitten by fleas and all manner of vermin, and catch a fever and die. No, never . . . never . . ." and hugged the little creature ostentatiously, turning her shoulder to Dorothy and saying over it, "I should have thought you would be ashamed to suggest such a thing, when you pretend to be so fond of children. I know you put this crazy notion into my poor husband's head; or if it was not you, it was that brother of yours."

Dorothy controlled her temper as best she could and answered civilly, "Indeed I think he put it into ours; William and he have made up their minds that they ought to learn German." Mrs. Coleridge sniffed and exclaimed, "German, indeed! it's my notion they think of nothing but amusing themselves. I don't hold with all this gadding about. When once a man is married, he should settle down and look after his family, say I. Well, he can go if he likes; I shall not budge, if he asks me ever so often. A mother should stay at home and mind her children." She got red about the nose and watery about the eyes; she whimpered unhappily, "Time was, he'd not have left me alone all winter in a stupid place like this, with nothing to divert me and not a soul to speak to, while he went gallivanting all over Europe with a couple of people who are no better than strangers, when all's said and done. The truth is, men are all the same. Once they've got what they want out of you, they go on to the next girl they see. You'll find that out for yourself, all in good time."

She dumped the baby down in its cradle, planted herself in front of Dorothy, who had risen from her chair in some distress and more resentment and stared her up and down; then said spitefully, "Well, much good may it do you, taking another woman's husband away from her. I shall get him back at the end of the winter, I suppose and time enough, too. I shall do very well without him. What do I want with him here? I've got my hands full enough, haven't I? I'd as lief be left in peace for a few months. I don't care how long he stays away." Dorothy could find no reply. Mrs. Coleridge, as if ashamed of her outburst, rocked the cradle violently with her foot. The baby burst out into a wail and she dropped on her knees beside it, exclaiming passionately, "No, I'll not leave you, my precious darling. You don't care if I'm old and ugly, you'll still love me even if your father leaves me." She wept over it, then sobbed and dried her tears and moaned forlornly, "They say it isn't lucky to cry on a baby's face." Then she got up again and said with a hard stare, "You'll excuse my asking you to go. I've a great deal to do this morning and I can't stand here talking." Dorothy was obliged to leave her. She repeated the conversation to William, who said gloomily, "I cannot think how Coleridge ever came to marry that woman. She is the wrong wife for him, ignorant and stupid, she will never make him happy."

9

After that much of Dorothy's pleasure in their preparations was gone, but she hardened her heart and did everything that William wished. He left all the arrangements to her. She packed Basil Montagu back to his father in London. That briefless barrister still owed them a good deal of money for the child's board and lodging and teaching. She did not think that he could afford to send his son to Germany and she fancied that their pupil had now reached an age when he ought to be more with other children.

Mr. Cottle the publisher came over from Bristol at the end of May for a visit, to arrange about William's poems. He had already published one volume for Coleridge and now offered to make up another with four of his poems on supernatural subjects and nineteen of William's village lyrics. "It will be a basket of our best fish, cleaned and gutted," said Coleridge cheerfully. The Wordsworths were delighted and at the bottom of their innocent hearts greatly surprised that any one would look at William's queer poems. They did not bargain at all with Mr. Cottle; he got the copyright for thirty pounds, which had been his first offer. He was an amiable, enthusiastic, rather unbusinesslike young man, who had wooed the thankless muse himself in some very limping verses and was unwisely ready to encourage other men's experiments. He had already dropped some money over Coleridge's earlier poems and over his bankrupt newspaper, *The Watchman*; he said that he would print five hundred copies of the *Lyrical Ballads* and if the edition went off well he would reprint. He was a little doubtful about the *Idiot Boy* and so was William; but he took it in the end and the *Ancient Mariner* too, though William had his fears about that and thought it might damn the volume. Dorothy was quite sure that the *Lyrical Ballads* would sell rapidly and make a great deal of money and fame for its authors.

At the very end of their time at Alfoxden, when they were almost too busy to attend to him, they had one other visitor, a strange wild dark-haired youth, whose name was William Hazlitt. Nobody knew then that he had any future; he was just a gawky boy who had walked all the way from Shropshire to visit Coleridge. His father was the Unitarian minister of a place with a queer name, Wem, near Shrewsbury. He had come tramping down through the endless orchards of the Severn valley, by Worcester and Tewkesbury and Gloucester, between the smooth ramparts of Cotswold and the blue mountains of Wales, with a knapsack on his back and a book in each pocket, repeating poetry from milestone to milestone to charm away the long road. It was his first venture from home and he had enjoyed himself enormously, shaping a course from one cathedral city to another through the light sweet summer showers. lounging at his ease in inn parlours, deliberating happily between a rabbit smothered in onions or a dish of veal cutlets for his supper, like a seasoned traveller, and sitting up half the night to drop youthful tears on the romantic pages of *Paul and Virginia* or *Clarissa Harlowe*; such were his innocent youthful dissipations.

This odd quarrelsome creature, fervent and enthusiastic, won Dorothy's heart immediately by his overflowing admiration of her friend. Coleridge attracted many such innocent and fervid natures to his eloquent discourse, as flies are attracted to honey, or bees in swarming time to the sound of a brass pan. He had captured the young Hazlitt with a single sermon, when he went north to Shrewsbury. The boy had sat spellbound in the chapel, and afterwards in his father's parlour, listening to that astounding flow of oratory over a dinner of Welsh mutton and turnips. At his time of life, such an impression may be lasting. He talked of it to Dorothy with stumbling excitement, all through the first evening, after Coleridge had planted him at Alfoxden and gone home; Mrs. Coleridge had refused to take in the young stranger, but Dorothy was more indulgent. William was away for the night, gone to Bristol to see Mr. Cottle and she could please herself by listening as long as she chose to the boy's babble of Coleridge's wonderful visit. Afterwards she read him some of her brother's poems in her soft stammering voice and then put him to sleep in the old room which they gave to such stray visitors. It had blue hangings and the walls were covered with round-faced family portraits of the time of George the First; it looked out into the amphitheatre of the shaggy coombe and when he woke in the morning he would hear the stags calling in the woods.

Next day, when William came home, they strolled out and sat on a fallen ash tree in the deer park. Coleridge came and read aloud William's new poem of *Betty Foy* in his sonorous and musical accents, which perhaps made the verse seem more melodious than it actually was, while the queer boy sat entranced and open-mouthed. Later they took him down to Tom Poole's, where they sat in the jasmine arbour, with the bees murmuring round them, drank flip and talked of everything in heaven and earth. He stayed for quite a long visit and they took him for all their favourite walks. After he had gone Mrs. Coleridge made William grin broadly, saying, in her silly way, "Did Mr. Hazlitt not offer for your sister? We all thought he was going to, he seemed so devoted to her. To be sure, he is younger than she is, but his father is quite comfortably off; it would not be at all a bad match." William repeated this as a huge joke and was surprised to find how extremely angry his sister was about it; but even after it had been denied Mrs. Coleridge still affected to believe it and said, "Well, it would have done very nicely."

After that the bubble of time swelled and swelled until it was ready to burst. They cleaned down the house and set it all in order; they dismissed their little servant girl from the village, who wept at parting with Dorothy and said she would have gone with her to the world's end. They walked on the hills and to the shore and in the holly wood for the last time together. There was an evening when they stayed out quite late to hear the nightingales sing. The sky was overspread with one continuous cloud at first and they could only see the full moon moving above it, whitening the cloud. The air was like milk on their lips and the dew sticky like cobwebs on their faces. There was not light enough even to cast their shadows before them; but there must have been a wind moving somewhere, for before they came to the edge of the woods the clouds parted abruptly and left the full moon sailing in glory, in the centre of a black blue vault, followed by a multitude of stars, small, sharp and bright. When they turned and looked back the lawns were bleached by the bright soft light as if they were covered with hoar frost. The broad white sea looked full and swollen to the very brim; the bay was clear as glass, the moonlight lay upon it and the shadow of the moon. They entered the wood and lingered on the mossy bridge in the coombe. They heard the hidden brook singing its quiet tune, as it did all night long to the sleeping woods, but over that they heard the nightingales. The balmy night was full of their song, from every thicket they answered and provoked one another with musical murmurs, ecstatic warbling melodies and long sweet single notes, intolerably poignant. William said under his breath, "I never heard so many. They sing as if they were drunk!" and Dorothy held her breath for delight and wonder.

Her friend was leaning beside her on the cool stone parapet of the bridge. He murmured in her ear, "Why do we call it a melancholy song? They sing like that because they are merry; the night is not long enough for them to tell all their love in." His own voice was low and full of feeling. She turned her head to look at him and saw his eyes glitter in the moonlight; they were fixed on her with a strange look of entreaty. She turned her head away. In the moonlit bushes close at hand she saw the bright eye of a nightingale glisten through the leaves. It filled its throat and sang with piercing ecstasy. There was an intolerable pain and pleasure in that moment; she knew that she would remember it all her life long. The bird sang as if its heart would break; but then the cloud swept back over the moon, the shadows of the trees on the ground became indistinct and confused, the bright reflected glitter faded from the hollies and all the nightingales fell silent. The enchanted moment had been stretched to its uttermost and was broken.

William lifted his elbows from the bridge, shifted his feet

and said in his harsh voice, "Haven't we loitered long enough? It's three miles and more through the wood to your house; your wife will be looking for you by this time." His sister knew from the way he spoke that he could not bear that sweet music any longer. William was not like her, he was afraid of too much beauty. He had endured passion once and did not mean to endure it again; he wanted to be left in peace for the rest of his life, but she had all her suffering yet to do. She did not speak. Their friend shrugged his shoulders and said ruefully, "*The words of Mercury are harsh after the songs of Apollo*. Well, I suppose you are right; it is late enough and Sara will think I have deserted her. I shall see you to-morrow." He went away from them through the darkened wood towards his home and they heard his footsteps rustling through the deep bed of last year's leaves. The moon came out as he went and all the nightingales burst out once more into music, like a thousand airy harps; she thought they sang in mockery.

10

After that her time ran away like sand tumbling down in an hour glass; she could not catch or count it. William and she paid their farewell visits, packed their boxes, locked up Alfoxden and came away; she had a strange feeling, as the door closed upon them, that she would never cross that threshold again. They spent a few days with the Coleridges, a polite necessity which pleased no one but their host. They said good-bye to Tom Poole and she had an uncomfortable fear that they had taken his dearest friend away from him; she did not yet understand that for Coleridge a new face would always be more interesting than an old one. He would teach her that later. They went to Bristol to stay with William's publisher. He had a house in Wine Street, in the heart of the city, not a stone's throw from the river; its windows looked down upon the swarming deafening bustle of the High Cross, where four streets met. Bristol seemed a terribly noisy place to her. It was at that time the second city in the kingdom. The gabled half-timbered houses were crammed together as tight as they would stand; the pavements were encumbered with casks and bales, so that you could hardly walk along them. The dusty streets reeked of raw wool, green hides, and tobacco; of wine and hops and Jamaica rum; of boiling tar, brine, river mud, and stinking fish from the wharves. Clustered masts poked up between the houses, the lapping oily green water reflected the tavern lights at night; there were sailors everywhere, swaggering up and down with gold rings in their ears. At night she could not sleep for the smells and the heat and the screaming, fighting and singing in the stifling alleys.

Mr. Cottle amiably took them for a walk on the Downs, to watch the troops drilling to fight the French, and for a row down the river. They went to see the blue glass in the windows of St. Mary Redcliffe. He said cheerfully, "This is the church where our friend Coleridge married Miss Fricker"; but she had remembered that before, well enough. They visited the Pinneys at their fine house in Great George Street, were kindly received and talked of Racedown, but she was not happy in Bristol. She was glad enough when William came in one evening, looking white and wild, as he always did when he could not sleep at night, and burst out, "I cannot endure this town any longer. Cottle will not listen to reason about the poems; I have done all I can to them, he must print them now as they stand. You and I will go away from here into Wales, until it is time for us to sail for Germany." She astonished herself and him by flinging her arms about him and bursting into tears, sobbing, "It is so hateful here." He grinned and twisted his face about and patted her shoulder. He was quite kind, as he always was when she was in trouble, she did not need to tell him why she was unhappy.

So next day they crossed the Severn ferry and walked ten miles further to Tintern Abbey, between the low red cliffs and hanging woods of the Wye valley. The next morning they walked right up by Monmouth to Goodrich Castle and slept there, came down-stream again and took boat to Bristol. William made up a poem on *Tintern Abbey* as they walked along; he finished it and committed it to paper after they got back, sitting in Mr. Cottle's parlour in Wine Street, over the shop. It was a beautiful wander, Dorothy thought, and a beautiful poem; but William said that she only liked it because there were some lines in it addressed to her. He did not think very much of it himself and only let it go into the *Lyrical Ballads* because Mr. Cottle complained that the volume would be too slender without it.

Their friend joined them again, in tearing spirits, having escaped from his wife and family, with his mind set upon foreign travel. When she saw his face again and heard his voice she understood that she was lost. She had tried night and day not to think of him, but he had never been out of her thoughts all the time; she had ached for him continually and now that she had him back again she was perfectly and completely happy. It was no use, she could not do without him. She would go where he said, do what he chose, offend every one for him, even William. He did not know it yet, but when they were in Germany together she would make him understand what he had done to her, she would show him the fire in her heart. Meanwhile they three were together again as they had been at the beginning and ready to start on their travels; they were as happy as the day was long. They left Bristol at the end of August, going up to London together, by wagon and coach and postchaise and some part of the way on foot, to save their money. The journey was charmingly pleasant. They were admitted into the presence chamber at Blenheim and saw the University at Oxford, which the two young men compared with their own University of Cambridge, to the disadvantage of the former. They spent a fortnight in London and then took coach for Yarmouth. On Sunday morning, September 16th, 1798, at eleven o'clock, they set sail for Hamburg. This was the first time that Dorothy Wordsworth went out of England into foreign parts.

IV

I

It was her first voyage and she had looked forward to it enormously, but little guessed that she would be sea-sick all the way. The men were cheerful enough and found company which amused them; but she was the only woman on board and she lay wretchedly tossing in the dark creaking cabin, sick, shivering and forlorn, while the ship floundered among the short choppy waves of the North Sea. For forty-eight hours she listened to the water streaming and gurgling past, the crash of waves on deck and the wind whistling in the shrouds. She heard the men talking and singing in the cabin next door, and sometimes clinking plates and glasses. She smelt cooking, tobacco-smoke, tar and sea-water on wet wood and wished herself dead many times. She did not stagger on deck until the Tuesday morning, when they were in smooth water at the mouth of the Elbe.

The air revived her then, she was able to sit in the sun, watch the light creep across the deck-planks and blink at the flat green Holstein shore, where red cattle were feeding in the saltings and all the windmills were turning in a fresh autumn breeze behind the long black Cuxhaven dyke. Every one else was on deck and William and her friend came to her at once and were very kind. William, to be sure, gave her a frightful sympathetic grin and said, in his brotherly fashion, "You look quite frog-coloured still," which was not consoling; but he fetched her some ship's biscuit and a glass of brandy and water and after that she felt better. Her friend sat by her for a long time, telling her of the voyage and of a bird which he had seen, far from land, riding the crests of the green waves.

It took them two days to work up the river against the yeasty current which came pouring down out of Germany.

At night they anchored off slimy grey mudbanks. In the afternoon of the second day they made out the red brick spires of Altona in the thickening forest of masts ahead. The packet anchored among the crowded shipping; they took a boat and were rowed through the canals, between gabled warehouses and under bridges to the landing-stage. William left his sister and his friend to mind the luggage while he went to look for lodgings. They sat for an hour beside the lapping green oily water, with the sea-gulls wheeling and crying overhead. She was enchanted by her first sight of a foreign city. Her wide eyes roved all ways, taking in the crazy timbered houses, with their peaked crow-stepped gables, carved beams and projecting upper stories. She was charmed by the strange foreign crowd pushing and jostling about her; the clean well-dressed Dutch women, in black velvet jackets and immense skirts, with straw bonnets as big as umbrellas and shaped like oyster shells; the housewives of the town, chaffering round the fish-stalls, in coloured gowns of all fashions, hatless, with their fair hair plaited round their heads; the servant girls, in coloured skirts and jackets, and crimped white caps; the fruit-women walking along proudly with their baskets perched on white turbans. The men were not so gaily dressed, but yet they were not like an English crowd, for she saw soldiers everywhere in red coats and immense cocked hats; peasants in baggy Dutch trousers and round caps; lean-waisted elegant officers swaggering along in tight belts and long coats, taking the middle of the pavement. All the men, she said, seemed to have china pipes in their mouths. She was ready to think Hamburg a fine and merry city; she thought that she would soon fill her journal for William.

After about an hour they saw him reappear. Two porters carried their luggage upon a sort of wheelbarrow and they were conducted through ill-paved stinking streets to the inn where he had found them a lodging. She tried not to think it a poor place, since it was the best they could afford, but her heart sank when she had climbed to her room, at the top of the house. The carpetless brown painted floor had just been washed, but this had only spread the dirt about; dinner was over and they could get nothing to eat but cold veal and some badly-pickled cucumbers. However, they consoled themselves with a bottle of good wine, at one mark forty, which William solemnly put down in his account book; and then they went out to see the sights as English travellers like to do.

2

They spent twelve days altogether in Hamburg and she filled her journal conscientiously with all that she saw. The city did not please her quite so well as it had done at first; she found the narrow streets hot, dirty and evil-smelling in the close September weather. When she and William tried an afternoon walk among the shady avenues and pleasant suburbs outside the walls it irked them to have to come back inside the gates by half-past six, but after that time there was no admittance into the city. She had no word of German and William had less than he had imagined. He was cheated by the jovial greasy landlord of four guineas and a baker tried to charge him double for fresh rolls; the very porters would have overcharged him for carrying his luggage to the post-house, so he had to carry the boxes himself in a shower of rain. William hated to be over-reached in money matters and he decided that the Hamburgers were all greedy and dishonest. Dorothy was shocked by finding the shops open and people at work on Sundays, or driving out to the beer gardens and theatres in the evening. The inhabitants seemed sober and prosperous, and there were not many beggars, but she was astonished to see a man beating a decent elderly woman under her window, with nobody interfering. Once when William and she were walking in the town, they saw a surly fellow driving a poor Jew forwards with foul language, and hitting him with a stick. The Jew hurried meekly forward with bent head, he made no effort to defend himself. The soldiers lounging at the drawbridge looked on with what seemed to her a cold unfeeling cruelty and laughed as she clutched at William's arm; a man standing by said to her in broken English, "The Jews have no right to reign in the city of Hamburg." This seemed to her extraordinary and she would have hung back and protested, but William took her by the arm and hurried her away. He did not seem at all surprised, but then he had seen more brutality in the world than she had done.

They did not see nearly as much of their friend as they had expected to do and perhaps this was why Hamburg did not please her, but she consoled herself by thinking that when they were alone together in some little University town it would be different. In Hambug he was here, there and everywhere, using his letters of introduction and visiting people who were interested in the young English writer. He had already made a certain name for himself in his own country, but to find himself admired in this strange city had perhaps turned his head a little. He left the Wordsworths a good deal alone in their uncomfortable inn. However, he did take them one afternoon to dine with a certain Herr Klopstock, a rich merchant whose brother was the famous poet.

It was a great occasion and Dorothy and William both felt young and insignificant; William got very red about the ears, blushed, cracked his knuckles, twisted his feet about and was very uncomfortable in his tight best coat. They dined in a long room over the warehouse. It was hung with gilt leather and had a balcony which gave upon the glittering water. Here they all sat round a long table and struggled with a huge meal of unfamiliar dishes, soup, stewed veal, sausages with sauercraut, oysters with spinach, and an endless variety of dessert. Frau Klopstock, at the head of the table, ladled out great platefuls of rich and spicy food and a barelegged peasant girl carried them round. Dorothy could not eat half of what they hospitably pressed upon her. The merchant Klopstock was polite and kind, he spoke good careful English and his wife and daughter smiled wordlessly at the English strangers. The poet proved to be a lively wrinkled old man, who still wore the velvet coat and knee-breeches, folded stock and embroidered waistcoat which had been the fashion in his youth. He had a puckered wasted face under a huge *toupet*, a high hill of powdered horse-hair sloping back from his forehead. He had his second wife with him, a flaxen pink-faced young woman in a very low gown, vain and disagreeable in her manners and very cool to Dorothy. The old poet carried on an animated monologue; their friend Coleridge talked well and freely, as he always did, and evidently impressed the Germans; William got out an occasional stumbling reply. They sat on the balcony for a long time, ate cream cakes and drank coffee, and watched the ships coming and going; there was a great glare from the low sun on the water. Dorothy found the occasion pleasant but very exhausting and went home at seven with a strong headache; but she put the whole affair down in her diary next morning where it still stands, because William said, with his broad grin, that some day she would be glad to tell her grandchildren, or his, that she had once dined with the great Klopstock, the father of German poetry.

Almost immediately after that dinner they found themselves alone in Hamburg. Their friend had dashed off quite suddenly to Ratzeburg, without making any plans for rejoining them; he always did things in a hurry. They told him at parting that they would go on to Goslar, in the Harz, as they had arranged and begin to learn the language there; the place was said to be cheap and pretty and they would join him, or he could join them, as soon as he had done with the Ratzeburg professors. They could not help feeling a little forlorn after he left them. Dorothy reflected, with a flare of resentment, "His wife need not have been so jealous of our coming, if this is all that we are to see of him"; but then she blamed herself for her own ingratitude and considered, "It should be quite enough for me, to be abroad for the first time, and to be with William." Nevertheless, she longed to be out of Hamburg, where everything had gone wrong for her and she guessed that William felt much the same. Two days later they set out, with six other passengers, at five in the evening, in the diligence for Goslar.

They travelled all through one sleepless moonlit night and most of the next two days, jolting and shaken, aching in every bone, over the dreary Lüneburger Heide. The ramshackle draughty wagon lumbered through the deep sand of the ill-made road. They saw nothing but the sand blowing in the autumn wind, the heated air shimmering at midday over the immense barren plain, sometimes a flock of sheep grazing. She was sick and ill much of the way, from the dreadful jolting of the wagon. On the evening of the second day they came to Brunswick. She thought it an old silent dull-looking town, with none of the bustle and gaiety of Hamburg. She and William walked about the streets to stretch themselves a little and peeped into the gardens of the duke's white palace, but found it too late to go inside. Next morning early they took their places in the diligence and drove on to Goslar; it was Saturday, October the sixth, 1798. There they might sit down and look about them and perhaps wonder a little why they had come.

3

Goslar was a page from a fairy-tale which she did not know, a dark forbidding secret town of winding cobbled alleys, where the houses went up by six or seven projecting stories to crow-stepped gables, topped by a carved pinnacle or a stork's nest. The timbers of these romantic houses were blackened with age, and carved into cherubs and trumpeters, crowned angels, flowers and fruit and stag's heads; their windows were filled with green rounds of bottle glass and intricate leaded tracery. In the middle of the town was a market-place, and a fountain which would drop with icicles all winter long.

There was a richly carved and ornamented Town Hall and a guildhouse for the cloth-workers, set upon arches; a dilapidated cathedral, with its pointed arches and clustered pillars all falling into ruin; the remains of a palace, where the Emperor had once held court. The place lay at the foot of small insignificant hills, clothed with pointed firs, and all about it stretched the dreary plain, a melancholy landscape under a dun-coloured sky. There were ramparts round the town, a great girdle of walls and towers, with pointed lead or copper roofs like witches' hats and many weathercocks all pointing steadily into the bitter east wind blowing from Russia. The gates of the town were shut every night at half-past six and after that there was no way to go in or out. The people were all wrapped up against the weather, which had suddenly turned dreadfully cold. The peasant women, with great baskets on their shoulders, held the corners of their shawls against their mouths, the men had fur coats or cloaks hugged round their shoulders, even the donkeys stood with their backs to the wind.

At first it was all rather amusing to the English brother and sister. They found very cheap lodgings with a Frau Dippermaier, who kept a draper's shop in the Breite Strasse, between the market and the town gate. They enjoyed the queer foreign food, bitter rye-bread and sausages, cabbage soup and pickled herrings; there was not much meat to be got, but there was plenty of goat's milk cheese, which William liked, and spiced gingerbread and coffee. They bought German books and studied the language; they practised their conversation on Frau Dippermaier and her five flaxen-haired, snub-nosed children and on the apprentice, who came up to sit with them in the evenings, but they did not get on very fast. They knew nobody else to speak to outside the house. William used to go down in the evenings sometimes to the Achtermannturm, a great round tower on the ramparts which had lately been turned into a beer-hall. He could sit there under the painted ceiling in a pleasant fume of smoke, drinking a mug of beer or a pot of coffee, listening to the students in their coloured caps singing folk-songs, and watching the fat burghers smoking their china pipes; but he could not take his sister there and he did not get to know any one who could be brought home to talk to her. They waited from day to day, expecting their friend to come to them, but he did not even write to them from Ratzeburg; by the middle of October they had got as far as saying to each other that perhaps they had better try to join him, when suddenly the weather broke and they found themselves imprisoned for the winter.

They had not understood that this would be so. Nobody could move out of the town for four or five months. The winter was the coldest that had been known in Goslar for a century. All the streets were choked with snow, it slid from the roofs with a soft crunching sound and heaped itself in the corners. The double windows had been pasted up for the winter and now they were frozen over with patterns like ferns. The Dippermaier children used to heat copper coins and burn peep-holes with them, so as to look out at the soft whirling flakes. Their mother told them, "Mother Hölle is at work up above, plucking her geese for feather beds," and indeed the snow looked just like a storm of feathers. There was a queer white reflected light on the ceiling, mixed with the rosy glow from the great china stove. They stuffed it with armfuls of pinewood and it roared and crackled delightfully. There was a galloping horse from the Brunswick coat of arms on the black iron fire-door and they got quite fond of him; William even wrote a poem about him, but when they left the parlour they had to wrap themselves up in greatcoats, for the air stung like cold iron. Poor William had not even a fireplace in his bedroom, which was over an archway; the servant girl, standing with her arms akimbo and a broad grin on her sunburnt flat face, used to tell him cheerfully that some morning she would find him frozen to death in his bed.

He used to walk on the ramparts every day, in a calfskin coat and bonnet such as the peasants used, staring over the black-and-white landscape of the frozen plain and hammering out verses to himself. When the weather was not too severe Dorothy would go with him, wrapped in a sheepskin coat, and tramp up and down with him for an hour or more. Sometimes they walked in a little garden behind the cathedral, with the powdery snow rising up like smoke behind their feet. There was very little sun and there were a great many storms; often she could not get out of the house for several days together and this told on her spirits very much. She missed her friend sadly and thought of him continually; she began to imagine that one of them had done something to offend him. A woman in love yields to such fancies very readily and she could not keep the idea out of her head.

William was hard at work and seemed happier than she had expected. He had enlarged the scope of his great poem. He was now going to divide it into two parts, the first, which he would call *The Prelude*, should give an account of his own youth, explaining who he was and by what experience and training he had been fitted to serve the Muses; the second part which he would call *The Recluse*, should expound his philosophy and have for its principal subject the sensations and opinions of a poet living in retirement. All this he explained at considerable length and very solemnly to his sister, his only listener. It should be, said William, a huge Gothic cathedral of a poem, at which he would labour all his life long; he could see it all clearly before him; even such minor pieces as he might from time to time compose should be like little cells, oratories and sepulchral recesses about the main building. Dorothy had no doubt at all that he could do it. He told her that she could be of the greatest possible help to him if she would remember all that she could of their common childhood and this delighted her. They talked together by the hour of England, walking on the ramparts in the cloud of their own breath, or sitting beside the roaring stove. The truth was that they were both excessively homesick. It was a pleasure to both of them to slip back into memories of their northern winters.

William talked of his schooldays at Hawkshead and she of her girlhood in Halifax. The snow reminded her of a true story which her Aunt Threlkeld used to relate, about a little girl called Lucy Gray, who went out to meet her father by Sterne Mill Bridge and was lost in a snowstorm. They traced her footmarks down the steep hill, and through the broken hawthorn hedge by the long stone wall, across the field until they came to the bridge; and followed them into the middle of the plank, "*but further there were none.*" Such had always been the words with which Aunt Threlkeld concluded her story and they came back to Dorothy's lips unbidden, though she had not thought of that story for years. She said to her brother, "When I was quite a child I used to cry about Lucy. I heard the wind wailing round the house, like a child crying for its mother, and fancied that she was not drowned but lost, and still wandering about in the storm." William saw something in this story which took him captive. He wrote it out then and there, sitting between his two candles, with his long serious horse-face bent down over the paper and that strange swell about his mouth which always appeared when he was most moved. She sat by the stove, knitted a stocking for him and watched his hand beating out the measure on the table. When he was in that sweet mood, placid, absorbed and utterly dependent upon her, she could persuade herself that she needed no other companion.

He worked very hard all through December. The fire of poetry was burning brightly within him. He could have written five times as much, he said, if he had not been prevented by a nervous uneasiness and pain about the heart which came upon him after long sitting at his desk, but he had no books and so must write to employ his mind. She wished that he could have had Coleridge with him, to talk over the plans for the great epic, for no one else, not even she, could strike such bright sparks from William as he did, but she wished in vain. Just before Christmas they did receive a letter, but it was only a light careless account of the pleasant life which Coleridge led in Ratzeburg, where he had been figuring away, he boasted, among barons, counts and countesses skating on the frozen lake. She had a jealous picture of him, vividly flushed and handsome, gliding hand in hand through the many-coloured crowd with a plump and pretty young Gräfin or Baronin, blue-eyed and yellow-haired and adoring, much like his own Sara. It was an absurd fancy, but it had great power to vex poor Dorothy in her solitude. She would have liked to show him that she could skate herself as well as any German girl. She had learnt the pretty art long ago, at Halifax, in her childhood, among the frozen Yorkshire moors, but all that she could do was to dash off a schoolgirl letter, all about William, and how well he skated, in his own powerful and ungraceful fashion. She told her friend vexedly, "A race with William upon his native lakes would leave to the heart and the imagination something more dear and valuable than the gay sight of ladies and countesses whirling along the lake at Ratzeburg."

She wanted to show him what he was missing, while he wasted his time in such elegant and worthless society, so she copied for him some lines which her brother had lately written, about skating on Esthwaite in a winter sunset when he was a boy, lovely lines in which the precipices rang to the tune of steel and crystal and the flying skater saw the world go spinning past him as he checked his flight. Her sore heart swelled with pride and pleasure as she traced the words and she could not forbear to enclose two other fragments, one about nutting in the autumn woods, the other a night-piece of a boy rowing among mountains fearfully, in a stolen boat; no one but William could have written them. She hoped against hope that they might decoy her faithless friend to come to her; and she slipped in a message at the end, saying that he must come with them to the north of England, in summer, and explore his native mountains with William. "And I would follow at your heels," wrote poor Dorothy, "and hear your dear voices again."

She had just set that down when she heard William's foot on the stair. She pushed the paper into a book, hastily, with one of her burning blushes; she did not want her brother to read what she had written. He came in with a sprinkling of snow on his shoulders, dry as powder; he had been walking by moonlight on the ramparts in his fur gown and black fur cap, in which she fancied that he looked like a prince of Muscovy. He had on that shining and exalted look which he wore when he had been tramping up and down in the bitter cold, unconscious of his surroundings, beating out his verse to the tune of his own measured footfall on the frozen ground. At such times he neither knew nor cared what she was doing, only his eyes and mouth took on a faintly peevish puckered look when he saw that she was using the table at which he commonly sat when he was writing. She got up hastily, saying, "I have finished, William, if you want the pen and ink." He did not trouble to thank her. He hung the fur cap and coat up behind the door, shaking the dry snow from them; that done, he moved in his abstracted way towards the table and sat down.

There were several papers of hers lying there before him. He pushed them impatiently out of his way and took up the quill pen; it was still wet from her writing. It was only when he noted this that he said vaguely, "Were you copying something?" She was able to sweep the papers out of his way and tell him hurriedly, "I was sending your last verses to Coleridge; the nutting poem and the skater and the boat." Her brother nodded; he said, "Yes, I'd like him to see those," and added, as he dipped his pen, "Tell the fellow to keep anything of mine that you send him. In travelling, you know, we might easily lose a copy and then we should be glad to have his." She waited for any other message, but there was none. William had already begun to set down in haste whatever it was that had come to him as he walked on the ramparts of Goslar, under the icy moon. She murmured, below her breath, "I am afraid we shall not see him now before the spring. I doubt he does not mean to come here after all." There was all the sadness of her forsaken heart in the fall of her voice on the words; but William scratched busily away with his squeaking quill, only muttered, "I never thought he would; you cannot count on him." The words dropped into the silence of the firelit room like an epitaph.

She put his message in at the end of the letter, later in the evening, but she did not dare to read what she had written before. She dashed down "Farewell, God bless you, dear Coleridge, our very dear friend"; in the corner of the sheet, folded it, sealed it and sent it away. Next day she would have given worlds to recall it, but it was too late.

4

Christmas should have been charming and she tried to think it so. She was twenty-seven on Christmas Day. The market was full of little fir trees, every family bought one, trimmed it up with candles, gilt gingerbread and red apples, and sang hymns round it with grave deliberate tunes; she had never heard of any of these customs in England. They all sat round the stove downstairs on Christmas night and ate gingerbread men with currant eyes and the servant girl told the children fairy tales. She came from the Harz mountains and could go on for hours about the witches dancing on top of the Brocken and the dwarfs digging gold in the mines. William enjoyed these innocent and charming recitals as much as the children did; it became a custom to go down every night and hear them. William would cram his mouth with gingerbread and twist his lantern jaws into their widest grin over the comical adventures of the miller's youngest son, or the boy who could not shiver or shake. He liked the friendly animals too; the birds who gathered up the corn for the perplexed prince, the grateful wolf who licked his hand in the forest, the clever fox who told him the answer to the princess's riddle. These were charming tales; but there were others which Dorothy did not like so well, sinister stories about the green-haired water-nymph who dragged travellers under water, or about the witch with the red eyes and the long nose who lived in the gingerbread house in the forest, roasted the wood-cutter's children for her supper, turned young maidens into nightingales and young handsome swaggering princes into stone.

Such stories made her shiver; and there were others which weighed down her heart with a load of sorrow. They were not children's stories at all, they were meant for her. "*Es waren zwei Königskinder* . . ." there were once a brother and sister who loved each other dearly, but their parents were dead and they had lost their kingdom. They wandered hand in hand through the enchanted wood of the world; the brother drank of a brook which turned him into a hunted roebuck, or an evil spell turned him into a swan, with a golden crown on its head. He had to fly about the world for seven long years while his sister spun nettles into flax, to weave the shirt which would disenchant him. The true princess was forced to stain her skin Egyptian-brown with walnut juice and wash dishes in the kitchen, or herd geese in the meadow, while her lover slept with a false bride and could not hear her crying under his window. Of course when Ilse told these tales to the children they all had a happy ending. The true knight climbed the glass mountain, the false bride could not wear the magic slipper, the prince awoke from his drugged sleep and knew the voice of his true love. She had a dress embroidered with sun, moon and stars, so fine that it would go through her wedding-ring, they were married and lived happily ever after. That was well enough for children to believe, but when you grew up you know better. Sometimes the enchanted roebuck was torn to pieces by the hounds, or the swan with the golden crown fell to the hunter's arrow; sometimes the prince was drugged so deep by the false bride that his true love could not make him hear her; sometimes the princess grew old on the glass hill because no knight came by who could climb it. Life was not so easy as the fairy tales made out.

She had no word for a long time from their friend. She

tormented herself daily to remember what she had written to him and fell from a hot fit into a cold one twenty times a week, while she pondered what he had made of her letter and humiliated herself with fancying that it had betrayed her longing for him too plainly. Life had not yet tamed her fierce spirit and she could not bear to think that he might pity her; but when he did answer in the end, it was nothing but a careless letter, praising William's verses and vaguely speaking of meeting in the spring. She chose to read into it a certain withdrawal not expressed in words and writhed at her own unhappy fancies of what he might think of her.

After the New Year she fell ill of a sickness which the people of the house said came from Russia. She had an aching in all her bones, fever, and a sore throat and chest; she lay in her bed in her small room, with the door open to get what warmth she could from the sitting-room stove and shivered and shook. All one night she was light-headed and said she knew not what. William was an angel and distracted about her, he waited on her hand and foot, but she had a delusion that he was going away. She cried and clung to him and implored him not to desert her; she said that no one loved her except this brother of hers. All this she only remembered vaguely afterwards, she dared not think what else she might have said. William was very much affected. He sat beside her, held her hand tight in his long bony fingers and covered her up with the blankets when she threw them off; he repeated over and over again that he would not leave her. Frau Dippermaier stood by the bed and remarked with gloomy satisfaction that young people often died of this sickness; it was called the influenza, or some such name, and it came from Russia on the east wind. People sickened and died from it in a few days, bubbling in their chests as if they were drowning; you could not do anything for them.

Dorothy, however, did not die of the influenza, though she felt so weak and wretched, after the fever left her, that she cried by the hour and wished herself dead; but William had apparently persuaded himself that she might, for when she got better she found that he had written three or four sad little poems about a girl who died young. He had used the name of Lucy because it was in his head since her story of the child who had been lost in the snow, and it was an easy name to fit into his simple jogging metre. One poem even pretended to be about a lover who came riding home by moonlight and fancied that his love was dead, but it was really all about Dorothy. He said to her, in his shamefaced fashion, "I wrote it when you were ill; a strange fit of passion came over me, I fancied that you were going to die and leave me"; and then he took her hand and put it to his cheek, with one of his odd rare gestures, which were almost those of a lover. He said, "You must never leave me. We will stay together all our lives. I could not live without you."

William was a great comfort, and when she got up he watched over her continually, making her sit by the stove and counting her mouthfuls while she ate. They talked a great deal of their childhood, reminding each other of the house by the Derwent, and the garden running down to the water. William said, "Let us find a cottage somewhere in the mountains and live in it together." She laughed weakly and said, "We need a gingerbread house or a charcoal-burner's hut; that is how all the fairy-tales begin," but she soon found that William did not mean her to laugh. He was quite serious about his plan, and he worked it all out penny by penny, explaining just what he wanted. At first she was languid, with the fatigue of convalescence, but as she recovered she took fire from him. They sat together by the stove, with the wind whistling through the key-hole, and settled everything that they would like to have in the cottage, from the clock on the mantelpiece to the patchwork quilts on the beds and the honeysuckle which they would plant over the porch. She began to feel as if it were a real place, already waiting for them somewhere whenever the snow weather would let them go out and look for it. William said, "As soon as we can travel we'll leave this town. It was a mistake ever to come here. We have made no friends and learnt no German; we have not been happy. I did not realise until I came overseas how much I loved my own country. I wish we had stayed at home." She forbore to remind him who had persuaded them into Germany and then deserted them; she would not speak of him. All the pain and passion of her feeling for her friend seemed to have been burnt out of her by the fever of her sickness. She felt clean and empty and was content to be no more than a child again with William.

5

Presently, quite suddenly, the winter was past and gone. The snow ran melting everywhere, the wet green moss under the drooping branches of the fir-trees was green as emeralds. It was so bright that it made their eyes ache after being so long accustomed to the snow. They were too impatient to wait for settled weather and as soon as the roads were fairly open they sent away their packages and started from the town on foot. After their dark imprisonment it was delightful to be walking among the mountains, though the ways were bad and they were often ankle-deep in water and clay. All her airy spirits awoke and sang to be on a wander again with William; she stared about her with delight. William, to be sure, laughed at these gentle pine-clad slopes, castled crags and tiny waterfalls, running grey with melted snow; he said they were as much like mountains as a kitten was like a tiger; but then, he had seen the Alps and been over the Simplon pass with his friend Jones, when he was at college. Dorothy, who had never yet seen a real snow mountain, was charmed by the tame romantic valleys of the Harz. The peasant women striding along, in their full-coloured skirts, with bundles on their backs, stared at the queer gawky English pair, strolling along, idle and unencumbered, with their faces raised to the bright sky, at a time when all honest folk were busy working.

They thought Dorothy mad to be walking alone with a man.

Brother and sister wandered through the Harz mountains and on to the Thuringian forests, perhaps to Weimar and Eisenach and Erfurt; but nobody knows just where they went, except that they did not see their friend until April, when they spent two days with him in the little university town of Göttingen. He looked as handsome and vaguely noble as ever, but he had grown his hair an inch longer and put on some weight; he looked pale and flabby beside her lean bony brother. Dorothy thought him somewhat spoilt by the adulation of the university circle, where he had been much admired. He had developed a gracious turn of the head and a wave of the hand which did not altogether please her. She preferred William's gawky simplicity. She had had a moment of panic when she saw him, lest the fire in her heart should blaze up again and consume her; she was not sorry to find him a little dashed and changed from the bright being who had lived in her solitary recollections all that winter. She found that she could talk to him quite steadily and cheerfully, with only the least little touch of resentment for his long neglect.

There were a few awkward moments just at the beginning. Then William and she, quite bewildered, found themselves accepting the blame for their long separation. Their friend said repeatedly, "I thought we three were to have spent the whole winter together. I have been very lonely and wanted you. Why did you not come to me?" He did not stay for her answer, which might have been an indignant one, but went on talking of all that he had done and read and learnt. In the middle he dropped out a sad piece of news. His little second son, Berkeley, the summer's child, had only lived nine months, he had sickened and died of a consumption after being inoculated for the smallpox. When Dorothy heard that she was shocked and silenced; she had a dreadful momentary superstition that she had done some evil to the child in that moment when she touched its head and wished it ill. She trembled, turned pale and looked silently at her friend, who sighed, in his beautiful melancholy voice, "Oh! this sad, sad, sad scene-shifter, Death."

He seemed quite sincere in these regrets, but complained that his wife was always writing and begging him to go home to Nether Stowey, which he refused to do. When they asked him his plans he was, as always, hopelessly indefinite. He professed a wish to live near them, said, "I could not endure Nether Stowey without you," but rambled on, "I cannot earn money away from London and I have no opportunity to go there. No one buys books nowadays except rich folk with great libraries and what can I write that would please a rich man? Then what suits Sara does not suit me and what suits me does not suit her; we being each what we are, I do not know where we can both be happy. My friends don't make the society that will satisfy a young and pretty woman. I think we should live in a town, or near one; but I must have a house with a garden and a study big enough for me to be out of the noise of women and children; that is absolutely necessary for me." He turned from one to the other with his old helplessly vague smile and said, "You must find me a house to live in quite near you. I leave it to you. I am sure I shall like whatever you choose." Dorothy felt certain that Sara would not and hoped that the plan might come to nothing.

They heard from him that the *Lyrical Ballads* had been a sad failure. There was no more money to come to them from that affair, indeed the first edition of five hundred copies had hardly been disposed of. William said in his tactless outspoken fashion, "I always knew nobody would swallow your poem about the ancient mariner"; but in this he was wrong. Mr. Cottle said that quite a number of copies had been sold, absurdly, to seafaring men who heard of this piece and thought the book was a collection of sea-shanties. However, through this and other ventures Mr. Cottle had been obliged to go out of the publishing business altogether and he had handed over their copyright, with several other worthless assets, to the firm of Longman, who had bought his business. Coleridge was very much vexed with his brother-in-law, Robert Southey, who had given the book a bad review and found it destitute of all merit; this vexed Dorothy, but William pretended not to mind. He said, in his lofty way, "I care nothing for the praise of any professional writer, except as it may help me to pudding; I published the poems for money, and money alone." His sister knew that he was disappointed, but William would never confess a wound; he pretended to have forgotten all about the *Lyrical Ballads* and to be interested in nothing but his enormous poem, *The Prelude*. He said that he must go back to the north of England, sit down there and write about his childhood; and Dorothy was willing enough. So they left their friend in Göttingen and went home.

6

The Wordsworths had some relations who lived in the North-country, people called Hutchinson, twice cross-related by marriage in the previous generation. William's most respectable uncle, Canon Cookson of Windsor, and the Hutchinsons' uncle, William Monkhouse, had married two sisters, Anne and Dorothy Cowper, and on the strength of this the young Wordsworths and Hutchinsons had always called each other cousins. The Hutchinsons were a big rambling family, there had been ten of them. Old Mr. Hutchinson had been in the tobacco business and connected with the famous snuff-mills at Kendal, but he had lost money and died poor. His children had been scattered about and brought up by various relations, just like the young Wordsworths, who were well able to pity them for it. William and the eldest girl, Mary, were the same age and had been to the same school, Dame Birkett's, at Penrith; it was said in the family that they had learnt their letters off the same copy of the *Spectator*. There was also a family legend that they had once exchanged grass-rings, when very small, and vowed to marry each other when they grew up; but William always denied this hotly when he was teased about it. Later on Dorothy had made particular friends with Mary and Peggy, who had been her chief consolation when she was living with her crabbed old grandparents in her teens at Penrith. On winter evenings these three girls used to compare grievances and lament the misfortune of losing their parents and being thrown upon the mercy of ill-natured relatives. They used to steal out to each other's houses and gossip together over the kitchen fire, as girls will, or prolong the moment of parting by pacing arm in arm, up one street and down another, by moonlight or starshine.

In the summer when William came down from Cambridge, he used to walk with them along the wooded banks of the Eamont, or climb the mouldering stair to the crumbling red walls of Brougham Castle and sit all afternoon upon a turret, hearing the wild flowers and grasses whisper in the summer wind. In those days he had seemed very fond of Mary and she had been a kind of second sister to him; nobody thought of anything more. After that he went away to France and got himself into all his trouble with Annette Vallon, and when he came home again, Dorothy invited Mary to come and stay with them at Racedown, but it was not like the old days any more. William had been stiff and shy with Mary and she had seemed a little afraid of him. She had clung to Dorothy's side, and William, though he was cheerful at times and more like his old self, yet seemed to prefer to leave the two girls together. He had actually rushed off to Bristol, in the very middle of Mary's visit, with Basil's father, to visit the Pinneys and Mary had been quite hurt about it. So that it was something of a surprise to Dorothy, as they sat in their London lodging, to hear William say suddenly, "When we go north I should like to go first to Sockburn and see the Hutchinsons." However, she was only too willing; so they set out together.

Sockburn was a grazing farm, between Darlington and Northallerton, where Tom Hutchinson, the best of the brothers, lived with his brother George and his sisters Mary, Sara and

Joanna. Poor little Peggy, who had been Dorothy's own favourite, had died young of consumption. Dorothy had spent a month at Sockburn, three years earlier, but William had never seen it and she longed to show it to him. It was a great square of farm-buildings like a fortified place, set in a meadow scattered over with sheep and green as emerald, washed nearly round by the noble stream of Tees. They got a rare welcome and found the Hutchinsons as pleasant as ever. Tom was a fine sensible fellow, uncommonly fond of his sisters. Mary was just as she had always been, slow-moving, tall, calm, handsome, with a rich carnation colour in her cheeks, a slight, rather engaging cast in her dark-brown eyes, and a faint meditative smile upon her full lips. She spoke very little, but looked as if she were pleased with her own thoughts. She was twenty-nine and a very steadfast creature, nothing put her about. She was a notable housekeeper, but never opened a book; however, she was by no means so stupid as a stranger might have supposed. The next sister, Sara, who had been unknown to Dorothy, proved to be a small light brown-haired creature, innocently frolicsome and shyly intelligent; she had read a great deal and was ready to argue with William, once she had got used to him. Little Joanna was away at school.

Somehow or other, the Wordsworths stayed there all summer; perhaps Mary had something to do with it. William seemed perfectly content to spend his time walking, reading, or playing at ball in the meadow, and seeing him so placid made his sister relax a little from the strain of their long German winter. It was a charming life at Sockburn, but not an idle one; however, the Wordsworths had it in their blood. They were quite ready to get up at dawn, breakfast on porridge and help with the work of the farm. William went out with Tom to the fields, with cheese and oatcake in his pocket, and stayed there all day long. Mary and Dorothy milked and churned butter, kneaded bread, set it to rise and baked it; they fed the hens, hunted eggs and plucked feathers for mattresses; they did the cooking for the whole of that large household.

At three they all dined together, with a rough north-country plenty which the Wordsworths had long missed in the south. All the farm-hands sat down with the master and mistress at the long table. They ate boiled beef and dumplings, broth, bacon and beans, rabbits smothered in onions, fat ducks and chickens stuffed with herbs and heaped with green peas, oat-cake and ewe's milk cheese. When they had killed a pig there were chitterlings and black puddings.

In the evening they all sat round the wood fire. The men mended harness, made snares, carved wooden spoons, bowls and platters while the women knitted and sewed. Mary sometimes span, though this was going out of fashion, but she liked the sound of the wheel. The shepherd's two dogs lay and panted on the stone flags, the cats blinked at the fire; in that cold country there was a wood fire every night, even in summer. Everybody went to bed at eight and rose at five; one day was exactly like the next, and the weeks slipped into months quite easily, with only the season's change of work to mark the time. Everybody turned out into the fields for haymaking. As soon as the dew was off the grass the long line of men would begin moving across the field with their scythes, while the women came in their print sunbonnets, to rake and turn the long scented swathes when ready. At night the wains came swaying home, loaded as deep as an East Indiaman, jingling and creaking.

In June the sheep were all driven down to the riverside to be dipped. They were herded through the fern by the shepherd and his two dogs, the long-haired yellow collie and the brindled lurcher with the wall-eye, both so clever that they could do all but speak. William helped the farm-hands to fling the terrified creatures into the stream and souse them; they struggled out and shook themselves and stared about stupidly for their bleating lambs, then hurried off into the fern. Dorothy, Mary and Sara picked currants and raspberries and made endless pots of jam. The kitchen was full of the hot sweet smell of it boiling for days together, and later in the summer there were bilberries and blackberries to be gathered for suet-puddings.

Some time early in July there was a great clipping-feast. The neighbours all came to help and sat astride the clipping-stools, there was a day-long noise of clicking shears and grating whetstones. The men caught the sheep in turn and delivered them to the shearers, all the women helped to carry the great soft yellow fleeces to the barn; after that each sheep was nicked in the ear, daubed on the flank with ruddle, and turned loose. The western sky was rosy with the afterglow before all was done. Afterwards they had a great feast in the barn, with singing and a fiddle going. Harvest was not so great a day, because Tom Hutchinson was a sheep-farmer and had little corn to get in; but they made it an excuse for a feast too. When the corn was reaped and carried into the barn ready for threshing they danced round the last sheaf and crowned it with flowers. There was beef and beer for every man and dancing on the floor of the barn. After that, quite suddenly, it was autumn, with gossamers on the stubbles, heavy morning dews and a smell of leaves burning in the garden. William had helped with everything most cheerfully. He was burnt as red as a labourer; he ate like a horse, slept like a pig and put on weight with the good country food, he seemed perfectly happy. He did not write a line all summer long.

7

All this time they had heard nothing from their friend Coleridge, though he was to have come back from Germany in June. Dorothy told herself that he had gone home to his wife, where he belonged, and she tried not to think about him more than she could help. The time slipped by so pleasantly that she and William made no plans, but towards October, when the bracken had all turned rusty, the fruit-trees were yellow and the nights were getting frosty, they began to ask each other where they should spend the winter. Then suddenly their friend appeared among them and everything was changed.

He was like Apollo in the sheepfold of Admetus and turned the household upside down with his bright wilful airs and ways. They had talked of him so often and with so much affection, that the young Hutchinsons felt as if they knew him already. Tom and his brother George listened with open-mouthed admiration to the talk of foreign countries, of Cambridge and London. They thought the stranger a wonderful fellow, he was quite unlike anything that these two young farmers had ever seen. Mary accepted him much more calmly. She gave him her sweet placid smile, just touched with faint amusement, and listened without comment to all that he said. He obviously laid himself out to impress her, but you could never tell what Mary thought. She was very busy just then with her preparations for the Michaelmas goose-feast, and her Christmas puddings. She simply laid another place for him at table and went on with her chopping and stoning, stuffing and mixing; it was never very easy to disturb Mary.

Her sister Sara took him far more seriously. She was twenty-four years old at that time, but romantic, inexperienced, and very young for her years. She had never guessed that there were beings in the world like this god-like stranger. She was a quiet girl in company; she would sit across the hearth from him in the long evenings and hang on his words, while he and William were talking. It gave Dorothy a jealous, pitying pang to see the girl's eyes fixed upon the visitor from her corner. They sparkled in the firelight with a hopeless eager delight which was only too familiar; it could not but remind the elder girl of her own emotions in the days when she knew him first. She had gone a long way since that time in knowledge of him and she did not choose to examine her own present thoughts of him, which were dark and bitter. She would not admit that it vexed her when Sara Hutchinson leant forward from the settle, until the firelight coloured her small pale face, and raised her softly timid voice to break in upon the talk. It vexed her still more when her friend turned his head, paused, smiled indulgently and interrupted his flowing stream of eloquence to answer Sara. After one or two evenings he was always ready to do this and presently Sara had drawn her stool forward out of the ingle-nook and was joining in the talk with a rapt eagerness, a sweet simplicity and innocent humour not easily resented. It was Dorothy now who drew back into the shadow by the baking-oven, and told herself obstinately that she would not interfere with little Sara's short-lived pleasure.

Presently those two were going walks together, short easy walks which suited her small strength and his idleness better than keeping up with the long-striding Wordsworths. Sara Hutchinson would lead her new friend gently along the river bank, to look at the hoar-stone in the field where a dragon was buried, or up to the church to gaze at the stone knight in armour and tell legends of chivalry. William very soon grew bored with all this loafing and pottering. He considered that his friend had come north to see him and after a very few days he proposed to drag his captive off for a walking-tour. They were to go over the fells by Haweswater to Bowness and at Temple Sowerby they were to pick up his brother John, the merchant sailor, who was just home from a voyage to the East Indies. They would all three go and walk in the Lake country. Nobody had ever been able to turn William, when he had set his heart on a plan, from the time that he was quite a little boy, so that was exactly what they did. Dorothy was glad that they did not ask her, this time, to go with them. She wanted to be left to her own thoughts. Sara Hutchinson moped a little after the men were gone, but Dorothy and Mary kept busy, stirring and mixing the Christmas puddings till their arms ached, in the warm sweet-smelling kitchen; and presently they got cheerful letters from the wanderers.

Apparently the tour had been a great success. They had met John and gone over by Windermere and up green Esthwaite to Hawkshead, where the Wordsworth boys had all been at school. They had seen the schoolhouse and the desk which still bore William's initials carved upon it. The cottage next the churchyard where William had lodged with that kind old dame, Ann Tyson, still had its ash-tree outside the window. William used to lie awake on summer nights and see the moon couched in splendour among the leaves of that ash-tree. He was going to put it into his great poem, *The Prelude*, and all that he could remember of his schooldays at Hawkshead, how he and the farmers' sons, his schoolfellows, used to ramble and play together, fly kites, go nutting and fishing in the brooks, set springes for woodcocks, play cards on winter nights, or go skating by moonlight. That was why he had been so set on going back to see Hawkshead again and he found that his brother John remembered those days just as clearly as he did.

After Hawkshead they had all wandered on to Grasmere and seen the twin lakes sleeping in the rich yellow evening light; Coleridge had been enchanted with their beauty. He had been obliged to go straight back to London, because he had the offer of some work on the *Morning Post*, but he had promised to come back again in the following summer and bring his wife and child. Meanwhile William and his brother John were staying at Robert Newton's inn, at Grasmere, and walking every day among the soft autumnal hills. William had been very clever, he had found out a place for himself and Dorothy to live in. He had thought at first that he would buy a plot of ground beside the lake and build a house upon it. John, that open-handed sailor, had offered to lend him the money for the building, if he might make his home with them whenever he came home from sea; but afterwards they had found a dwelling which was better in every way, and William had quite decided to take it. It stood in a group of three cottages, called Town End, on the old road from Rydal, a mile from the church and close to the lake; it was to let for eight pounds a year. It had formerly been an inn, called the Dove and Olive Branch, but they would call it Dove Cottage.

V

I

THE BROTHER and sister set out from Sockburn in a bitter December dawn, with the moon still bright in the sky. She rode pillion behind George Hutchinson, leaning against his broad back and holding to his belt, while William jogged beside them on another of the farm horses, with a lantern at his saddle-bow to use when the moon went down. It was so cold that Dorothy could not feel her fingers after the first mile, the horses' hoofs rang like iron on the frosty road. By and by they saw the sun rise behind them, round and red as a new penny, through the morning mist. It was high in the sky before they came to Richmond and saw the castle towers taking the morning light in the gap of Swaledale. They thawed themselves out at the inn with mugs of hot ale and then jogged on eight miles farther, through sleety showers and flying sunshine, by Hart-Leap Well to Wensley, where they ate their dinner. Here, at the mouth of the dale, George and the horses left them. The river was in full flood after the autumn rains and roaring in its screen of leafless trees as they tramped up the dale. They turned aside at Aysgarth to see the water pouring down in sheets of yellow peaty foam among the black rocks of the falls, and smelt the keen scent of wet woods, bracken and falling water. At dusk they reached Askrigg and were glad to see the glowing red curtains and fretted gables of the ancient inn.

They slept a cold stormy night there and next day tramped on over the brown winter moors, where the sheep huddled against the stone walls and the grass shivered in the wind. It was twenty-one miles to Sedbergh, but they were young, strong and happy and had a full easterly gale behind them. They did the ten miles from Hardraw over the saddle into Garsdale in two hours and a quarter by William's old silver turnip watch, which had been his father's, and the next seven miles of the downhill stretch into Sedbergh in an hour and thirty-five minutes; William wrote afterwards and boasted of this marvellous feat to Coleridge. Next day they went on more easily, over Hutton Moor to Kendal, with the outlines of their native mountains shaping before them all the way, blue and clear against the icy sky. They spent a charming afternoon in Kendal, laying out a timely legacy of a hundred pounds on furniture for the cottage; if Uncle Crackenthorpe, never a favourite of theirs, had to die, he could not have done it at a better time for his niece and nephew. They bought wash-stands and chairs, beds and tables as cheaply as they could. Next day they hired a postchaise and drove by Staveley and the shores of Windermere. The sun was declining in a rich yellow light, and the islands were all reflected in the water, as they went through Ambleside and past Rydal Water and climbed over the hill into Grasmere Vale.

She held William's hand in hers as they came down the winding road from White Moss; it was like driving backwards into their childhood. He squeezed her hand with his own bony fingers, lolled back in his corner and said nothing; but she knew that he was as absurdly excited as she was, for his weather-beaten cheeks were very red and his eyes shining. He gave her his convulsive grin as the postboy blew his horn, cracked his whip and rattled the two horses down the last of the hill. Her heart was beating as fast as the trotting hoofs. She put her head out of the window and exclaimed, "Oh! there is the lake; are we nearly arrived? Which is the house?" William would not say anything; he grinned and nodded with his lips shut tight, like a child taking you to see a hidden treasure. The postboy drew up his reeking foam-spattered horses suddenly, the chaise stopped with a jerk and they had arrived at Dove Cottage.

She fell in love with the place at first sight, and knew that she and William were going to be happy there. The house was charming, low and humble with diamond-paned windows and a slated roof. It looked small enough to put in your pocket; it had a tiny steep garden and a little orchard behind and it huddled close under the fell, but the meadow before it in those days ran down clear to the lake. The rooms inside were larger than she had expected and very dark at that hour, for it was five o'clock on the shortest day of the year. There had been little preparation made for her arrival, except a dying spark in the grate of the parlour and a couple of beds, without curtains, set up in the rooms upstairs, but she was not to be discouraged by such drawbacks. She stood in the parlour, in her striped gown and little straw bonnet, warming her foot on the hearth and gazing eagerly about her. The old woman, Molly Fisher, who had come in from the village to welcome them, thought that she had never seen a young lady with such bright wild eyes. The brother and sister were like a newly wedded pair, running about together over the house, upstairs and down, planning how they would live, candle in hand; it warmed her old heart to hear them at it.

The rooms downstairs had been the public-rooms of the inn and were wainscoted with dark oak panelling, all the grates had black iron hobs with pretty leafy patterns upon them. Dorothy planned to make the first room as you came in their common parlour, with a grandfather clock and a round table, brass rushlight-stands, some rush-bottomed chairs and a rocking-chair for William. It would look very well, and the dark, rather gloomy room next it would do well enough for her own bedroom. Behind these two front rooms was a slate-flagged kitchen, running back into the hillside, with a window half-underground, darkened in summer by green ferns. There was also a dairy and a cupboard under the stairs for wood and so forth. Upstairs she gave William the two best rooms in the house; a parlour where he could put his few books and do his writing, and a bedroom next to it, above her own, so that she could hear him in the night and go to him if he walked the floor and was wakeful as he so often was. Both these rooms of his looked across the lake to Silverhow, rising purple and shaggy brown against the western sky. Behind them was another bedroom, looking straight into the hillside, but good enough to put a visitor in for a night or two and a little closet opening out of that, which she planned to paper with newspapers when she had time. She meant to light the kitchen fire only for an hour or two, at midday, just to dress the dinner. She would boil kettles and cook supper and breakfast on the parlour fire, or in William's writing-room above stairs, where they would spend most of their time. They would live very simply and lay out their little store of money to the best advantage. William should walk or write all day long, she would live only for him and would not let herself think of their friend. She and William would be children again, they would be perfectly happy. So she planned, lying awake in her cold uncurtained bed, in the strange room, hearing the wind blowing through the trees outside, dreaming of the future.

2

There was a great deal to do before they could be comfortable in the cottage. William, manlike, had taken it as it stood and had done nothing to it. They both caught colds in the almost empty dwelling. One of the chimneys smoked like a furnace, everything was in confusion, doors had to be mended, rooms to be painted; Dorothy had so much work to do with her needle among the bed-curtains that she was absolutely buried in it. She scarcely went out for the first few days. When William did tempt her forth one evening to see the planet Jupiter shining on top of the highest of the Rydal mountains she had reason to repent it, for she came back with a raging toothache; but quite soon they settled down and felt as if they had lived in Dove Cottage all their lives. The valley was like a nest, deep, round and warmly sheltered, with thickets of ash and oak, birch and sycamore, climbing everywhere among the steep broken crags. Stone walls ran up hill and down dale, and waterfalls glistened like snail-tracks on the fells; it was a rich pastoral landscape, pleased and cheerful, yet with something wild in its nature. The village was not half a mile away, clustered about the church at the head of the lake, on which there floated a little ark-like island which pleased Dorothy greatly. Other cottages were star-scattered everywhere about the vale.

Quite early in their time they found out a perfect short walk, into the flat quiet valley of Easedale, which they called the Black Quarter before they knew its real name. It was a valley shut in by the fells, like an enclosed room, cheerful and silent, with a clear brook racing through it. There was a green terrace, on the Easedale side of Helm Crag, which was to become William's favourite place for walking up and down and making verses. They promised themselves fine tramps on the fells as soon as the winter should be over and gone; meanwhile they were happy enough in spite of much bad weather, settling into their new cottage and getting to know their neighbours.

The dalesmen were all very friendly to them. William was always stiff with strangers, until he had known them a long time, and he would never have made friends if he had been left to himself, but Dorothy had learnt the trick of it and for all her shyness she was quickly made welcome in every cottage. Old Molly Fisher, the witch-woman with the perpetually nodding head and trembling withered lips, who had lit the fire to greet them when they arrived, became their daily servant. She came toddling in for two hours a day, lit the kitchen fire, cooked and washed up after their three o'clock dinner, which was their main meal. She turned out very dirty, ignorant, foolish and difficult to teach, and at first Dorothy despaired of her; but she attached herself to her young mistress like a faithful muddy dog, and they had not the heart to dismiss her. At least she was honest and loving and she amused them with her north-country sayings, brought out with much nodding and trembling of her old head, in a broad Cumberland speech. It would have been almost unintelligible to any one from the south, but William and Dorothy had been bred up to understand it. Old Molly was enormously proud of serving them; boasting, "Aye, mistress, them 'at's low laid would have been proud creatures could they but have seen where I is now, fra what they thought mud be my doom."

She lived next door with her brother, John Fisher, and his wife. On the other side were a poor family named Ashburner; further off lived Farmer Lewthwaite and Fletcher the carrier. They were all very friendly, ran Dorothy's errands, baked her gingerbread and fetched her letters if she were not going into Ambleside herself. Jenny Dockeray promised roots of yellow lilies to set in her garden and blind Robert Newton London Pride to put in the chinks of the wall. She planned to make the neglected garden neat again and to enclose the ground between the cottage and the road; when the summer came she meant to make an arbour at the top of the garden, for William to sit and work in.

Once a week the great wagon came by with a rumbling of slow wheels and a jingling of harness, the great tilt swayed like a ship and everything inside banged and rattled. Old Benjamin the wagoner would halt his eight horses at her door, knock, knuckle his forehead, wipe his brow with his old red handkerchief and count out the change for some small purchase of hers; then go back to his horses' heads and start them up for the long pull over Dunmail Raise to Keswick. There was a letter-carrier, too, who came on foot once a week with letters in a box over his shoulders, a patient, bowbent man. A woman-pedlar from Cockermouth came regularly with a packful of trifles, needles and thread and so forth, she had travelled those mountains for thirty years. There were besides many beggars and vagrants, gypsies and tinkers, soldiers and sailors broken in the French wars. Every day somebody went past the cottage door, stopped and spoke.

On Christmas Day, which was her twenty-eighth birthday, as she and William sat by the fire roasting chestnuts, they heard the sweet wandering notes of a fiddle at the door. It was the village fiddler, going his rounds, as he always did there on Christmas Day and wanting to play for them. They called him in and he stamped the snow from his feet on the flags by the door. Then he stood by the fire, tucked his fiddle under his chin, and played three or four country tunes, "The Hunt is Up" and "Here's a Health Unto His Majesty" and a lovely tune which she did not know, called "The Days When We Were Young." It brought the tears into her eyes for pleasure when William said, "I shall tell him to come and play to you every year on your birthday," it seemed to assure her of many happy years to come. And all through that winter, for two unbroken months of bad weather, a pair of swans floated on the small open space of blue unfrozen water at the centre of the lake. They were strange birds, unknown in that valley, a solitary pair, who had chosen the island for a refuge. She could not but think that they were like herself and William.

3

At the end of January their brother John came to stay with them. He was not to make the China voyage again until the autumn and the cottage was to be his home whenever he came back from sea. She had hardly seen him for seven years and had only had glimpses of him between voyages to the East and West Indies and to the China Seas; the East India Company's was a hard service. She thought of him still as the quiet, friendly, rather stupid schoolboy, honest and clumsy, sweet-tempered and obedient, whom clever Christopher and stubborn William used to lead about by the nose. Now she found herself with a young man on her hands, who was at first almost a stranger, a handsome, slow-moving, sensible creature, modest and silent, even-tempered and loving, who surprised her continually by his affectionate consideration for herself. William, she knew, loved her very dearly, but she had spoilt him; he let her wait upon him hand and foot, used her with no ceremony, expected her to be at his beck and call continually, and released his irritable temper upon her whenever he needed an outlet for his nervous moods. It was a novelty to have John follow her about, lift her burdens, take her place, defend her in argument, and stare at William with his bright-blue far-gazing eyes, in blank astonishment, when the elder brother was in one of his bad humours. John was charming; she had leisure now to find out all his good qualities and she sometimes fancied that he would be of more value in the world than either of his brothers. He was balanced, calm and resolute; his seafaring life had made him so. She had never met a man more honest and gentle. He was sometimes a little hasty, when anything was done in a clumsy or bungling manner, to vex his practical soul; but she never heard an oath from him, or any loose sailor's talk. He was as modest as a woman, a rare thing in that free-spoken and violent age. He was meek, self-denying and simple in his nobility; he only thought and lived for others. Certainly he was the flower of the flock, although she had never known it. William would always be the nearest and dearest of her brothers, because he depended so much upon her; but she understood that in some respects he was inferior to John.

At first she did not know what to do with her new ally, she was not used to being helped. John, however, calmly took his own place in the life of the cottage and presently she wondered how she had ever got on without him. He went his own way with perfect placidity. She had feared that he might find the place dull, after all his sea-roving; but he seemed quite content to share their common employments. He was an excellent carpenter; he helped to furnish the cottage, he made chairs and cupboards and put up shelves for William's books. When the spring came in he dug up the whole garden for her, helped her with her planting and got in all the potatoes. There was a grove up the hill where he liked to go and walk up and down, enjoying the sea-sound of the wind in the dry branches of the fir-trees over his head. In the winter evenings, as they sat by the fire, he used to make nets, or splice fishing-lines and spin yarns for her amusement. If she questioned him skilfully, he could be made to talk by the hour of his life at sea.

He had a streak of his elder brother's poetry in him. She and William would sit enchanted while John talked of the broad-bowed, lumbering ships of the East India Fleet, all rocking together like a flock of white swans, great towers of canvas, loitering home in convoy round the Cape and up past the Atlantic islands. John could make her see the flying-fish skipping through the warm tropic waves, the palm-trees nodding to their own reflections along the green shore of Africa and the Peak of Teneriffe hanging between sea and sky, like the battlements of Heaven. He could make her smell the off-shore wind at night, heavy with jasmine-scent and spices, in a tropic harbour paved with glittering stars; he could show her the white domes and pagodas of an Eastern city mirrored in the sliding current of some enormous river.

John had seen fighting, too, for all his youth and air of innocence. In the Eastern seas merchant vessels had to look out for themselves against French privateers and Chinese and Malay pirates; they did not get much help from His Majesty's Navy. He boasted cheerfully, "Our ships are as well-found, well-manned and armed, as any; it hardly ever comes to a hand-to-hand fight with us. The Frogs mostly sheer off after a broadside or two. An East Indiaman has often been mistaken for a ship of the Line. We don't carry any of your native crews, our fellows are all regular old tarrytails out of English ports. The press-gangs have been warned off stealing our men from us and we keep good naval discipline aboard." He wandered off into a yarn of how, off Java, in the previous year, five East Indiamen, homeward-bound with Captain Lennox in command, had beaten off six French frigates and how their admiral had danced with rage on the poop when he found that he had been bluffed by a merchant-convoy. He had a string of wild stories about fires and wrecks, mutinies and floggings, mostly picked up from his brother officers, for he said that he had steered clear of such troubles himself, so far, touching wood; he hoped never to lose his ship. He blushed when Dorothy asked him where he got the scar on his forearm and said that had been a bit of trouble in port, with a Malay who was running amok; but he opened his blue eyes wide and shrugged his shoulders when William asked him curiously whether he had ever killed a man. He said, "Of course," and the two stay-at-homes looked at their brother for a moment as if he had turned into a stranger. John looked uncomfortable and said, "Well, what do you expect. You can't go to sea in kid gloves nowadays." He had gone when he was sixteen and been at war with the French ever since he was twenty.

4

As soon as they were settled they wanted to show the cottage to all their friends. Mary Hutchinson was their first visitor; she came for six weeks early in the year and was very helpful, made curtains, scrubbed and polished and taught old Molly Fisher some of her best dishes. She was a better cook even than Dorothy, they were all very comfortable while she was with them. She and John had always been good friends, it was charming to have her come while he was there. They took her all about the vale and named a pool in the woods for her. The family had a childish habit of giving their own named to places they liked. Presently there was *William's Rock*, *Joanna's Rock* (named for Mary's little merry laughing sister, the youngest of the brood, who had waked its echoes), *Mary's Rock*, upon which William had carved her name in sport, and *Point Rash-Judgment*, which had a moral tale attached about a sick man seen there fishing. They had a favourite place, too, for a long day's picnic in fine weather, on the shores of Thirlmere under Helvellyn, beside a rock which they called the *Rock of the Names*. Every one they took there had to carve his or her initials on its face. Before the summer was out they had collected William, Dorothy and John Wordsworth, Mary and Sara Hutchinson and the magic initials S.T.C. Their friend came to them for a month, when the vale was sweet with Easter, and was enchanted with everything. They took him to all their loveliest places and when he went away he vowed that nothing would content him save to come and live near them in the north. William said that he would find him a house at Keswick. They would go to and fro over the Raise and bring each other everything they wrote. It was a pleasant plan, if Mrs. Coleridge would agree to it.

On the fourteenth of May, 1800, William and John started for Yorkshire to visit the Hutchinsons, who had lately moved to a new house, Gallow Hill farm, near Scarborough, and wanted to show it to their cousins. They set out after an early dinner, at half-past two o'clock, with cold pork in their pockets. Dorothy went with them down past Rydal and through Ambleside and left them at the turning of the Lowood Bay, under the trees. Her heart was so full that she could hardly speak to William when she gave him a farewell kiss under the trees. She sat a long time upon a stone at the margin of the lake, and after a flood of tears her heart was easier. The lake looked to her, she knew not why, dull and melancholy and its weltering on the shores seemed a heavy sound. She walked as long as she could among the stones of the shore. There was a little wood there, at that season rich in flowers; she found a pale yellow flower, round and double, which smelt very sweet, and supposed it to be a ranunculus. She picked crowfoot and wild strawberries to nibble, wild geranium and anemones, white violets without scent, two kinds of orchids and a few late primroses; there were many tall shiny foxgloves already with their heads budding. The wild crab apple-trees were in blossom as she wandered beneath them. She came home by Clappergate and up the narrow Rydal valley, resting often, though the wind was cold, for she was tired with her long walk and her sad thoughts. She resolved to take a new notebook and to keep a faithful journal of her time until John and William came home again; she knew that this would please William.

When she got home she set some slips of privet in the garden and afterwards sat by the fire all evening till her face was flame-coloured with the wind and the fire. Then she wrote her journal for William and put all those flowers which she had gathered into it; that is how her Grasmere Journal begins. The house seemed very lonely, cold and quiet without her brothers and she went early to bed, wishing absurdly that she could have had a letter from William to console her.

The boys were away for nearly four weeks. It was the first time that she had ever been so long alone in her life and the first time for many, many months now that she had been parted from William. She missed him dreadfully, she had not known that days could be so long. Almost every day she wrote down something for him in her journal, counting the days with flowers and birds' nests. She had promised him to go on reading the plays of Shakespeare just as if he were at home and she persevered at this, though it was a sad *miss* not to hear them read aloud in his harsh chanting voice. She went all through *Midsummer Night's Dream*, *Macbeth*, *King John* and *Timon of Athens*, which suited her melancholy mood. She bound carpets, mended and made clothes, washed and dried linen, papered the little spare room with newspapers and worked a great deal in the garden. She planted her blind neighbour's London Pride on top of the wall and set yellow lilies and periwinkle, wild columbine and wild thyme in the borders. A neighbour gave her some lemon thyme one evening and she brought it home and set it by moonlight. She wanted to make the garden look gay for William when he came home again.

It was good growing weather; everything seemed green and overflowing with life. The streams made a perpetual noise, it rained mildly and sweetly in the early mornings and afterwards the sun came out. The little birds were very busy, making love, fluttering about and about and pecking the blossoms and bits of moss off the fruit-trees in the orchard. She wished that William could have seen the blackbird that she found, sitting quietly in its nest, rocked by the wind and beaten by the rain. She wanted him back dreadfully. She walked into Ambleside almost every day, hoping for a letter from him. One unlucky Friday morning she actually set out before breakfast, forgetting that the post did not come in till the evening, and had to come back empty-handed. William did not write to her nearly as often as she would have liked. She wanted to know everything that they were doing in Yorkshire, but his letters were very dull and brief. Even a letter from their friend Coleridge did not do much to console her. She tried very hard to be patient but she was only half-alive when William was away.

She took long daily walks, as she had promised William, who did not think that you could keep in health without them. The neighbours were very friendly and were always inviting her into their cottages, but she preferred to walk alone and think her own thoughts. She went up often into the little green chamber of Easedale, the Black Quarter, where she could be alone with a few sheep and rocks; or she climbed to the top of White Moss, where she could look down on the valley; but most often she did her round of the two lakes. She liked to walk by the shore and hear the regularly irregular sound of the dashing water. On a windy day the waves running round the island seemed to her like a dance of spirits about its small circumference. On a still day Rydal was very beautiful, with spear-shaped streaks of polished steel in the water. Grasmere was very solemn in the last glimpse of twilight, it called home her heart to quietness. Walking alone, she had many of her saddest thoughts, confusedly filled with her friend and with William. She could not always keep back her tears, but once when she was walking and brooding she was recalled from her reverie by a noise as of a child paddling without shoes. She looked up and saw a lamb close to her. It approached nearer and nearer as if to examine her and stood a long time. She did not move and at last it went past her and went bleating along the pathway, seeming to be seeking its mother. On that day she went smiling home.

So the time of her solitude went by and as June came in she grew increasingly restless. She would not go far from the cottage for fear lest her brothers should come while she was away; yet she slackened her pace always as she returned, dreading the silence of the empty cottage if William were not yet there. She sat up late at night sewing, wanting him to find a light in the window if he came after dark. She lay awake listening to every barking dog and village noise. At last, one night, after eleven o'clock, she heard a foot at the front of the house, it halted and there came the sound of the opening gate. It was William and everything was well. She was alive again.

5

He seemed very well and happy to be back and so did John. They both talked gaily and freely of their visit to the Hutchinsons. Of the two, it was perhaps John, that open simple sailor, who talked most fondly and continually of Mary, the dearest to him of the three sisters. Once or twice she fancied a slightly conscious warmth, a kind of surprised regret in his manner, as if he had liked Mary better than he realised. She said to herself, with her heart beating faster, "Oh, dear! if John were to fall in love with Mary, that would never do," but she did not admit what her reasons were against it. John, however, seemed cheerful enough and perhaps it was all her fancy. He made himself very busy that summer; she did not know how she would do without him when he went to sea in the autumn. Any little business of the house interested John. He made two more cupboards and put up a set of shelves, which were badly needed; for William could not knock in a nail straight and was so dreadfully untidy that he would just as soon dump his clothes and books on the floor for some one else to pick up again. John could turn his hand to anything, he helped her plant and stick peas in the garden and dug vegetables for her. He was a great fisherman, too; he was always dragging William out on to the lake, to set pike-floats above the reflections of the flowering hawthorns, or go trolling when there was a breeze to ruffle the water. Often they went up Langdale to fish the beck, and came back with a basket full of crimson-spotted trout to spread out on the larder flags.

Sometimes they went all the way up to Stickle Tarn, to Red Tarn, which lies under the black slate precipices of Helvellyn, or to Wythburn beck. William was not such a keen fisherman as his brother, he tired quickly of the sport. He would sit down on the hot stones and pull a book out of his pocket, or begin to walk up and down and string rhymes. However, he did catch a pike up at Wythburn of four and three-quarter pounds, a family record. They used to take old Mr. Sympson with them on these expeditions, a stout old parson, upwards of eighty, who stumped about the village in his broad hat, square-toed buckled shoes and voluminous unstarched white neckcloth. He always had a trail of children running after him, and he was welcome at every fireside in Grasmere, where the Rector was an old mad clergyman who did not go about in the parish. Any cottage woman was glad to sweep up the hearth and brew a dish of tea for Mr. Sympson; but the vigorous old man liked best to take his fishing-rod and climb to the tarns on the hilltops with John and William. He showed them very good sport. He had a charming gentle old wife, a simple soul who had lived in the vale for forty years, and a pleasant silent son and daughter, they were all good friends to Dorothy. Miss Sympson, who was a great gardener, like so many English spinsters, gave her roots for her garden and showed her where the rare Osmunda fern grew. Dorothy liked her because she often took roots of garden flowers and planted them in wild places, or beside the road, to pleasure wandering folk and such as had no gardens. They planned together that in the autumn they would take slips of Laburnum and plant it in the woods.

It was a very fine hot summer. They went on the lake every day, the men swam and they picnicked on the island. John was boatman and would row them about by the hour. His sister liked to see him in his white shirt and trousers, with his bare head and sunburnt neck, handling the oars with his tattooed arms. He used to say in the morning in his weather-wise way, "The sun looks very small, we shall have rain this evening"; or at night, "The moon looks greasy and the stars want snuffing; we shall have wind before morning," and sure enough, it always came out as he said. Once they were floating idly on the lake and they saw a raven, very high above them. It croaked again and again as it flew, like a dog barking up above them, the sky and the mountains echoed the sound. They heard the call of the bird and the echo from it long after it had disappeared. John rested on his oars and turned his face up to the quarter from which the sound came. She thought that she had never seen anything more beautiful than the simplicity and honesty of his face at that moment; it wore an expression which she could never forget. Then John roused himself, smiled at her, dipped the oars again and drove the boat smoothly through the crystal water towards the island.

6

There was some very hot and thundery weather towards the end of June in that year, 1800, and all through July it continued warm and beautiful. The shores of the lake were all dim with the scorching sun, the water was a dark mirror, day after day, still as glass, the house a hot oven. Coleridge, his wife and the little Hartley came to stay for three weeks and John had to have a bed over the way at the Ashburners. The Coleridges were on their way to a new house, called Greta Hall, which William had found for them at Keswick. That was thirteen miles away over Dunmail Raise, but perhaps it was as well that they would be no nearer; the distance might not keep their friend away, but it would spare Dorothy many visits to Mrs. Coleridge. The little woman was just the same as ever, talkative, silly, sweetly fretful. Dorothy saw with an immediate pang of bitter jealousy that she was within a few weeks of bearing another child. She cried a good deal to Dorothy, at their first meeting, about the death of her little second son Berkeley and complained, "His father has forgotten all about him, but I cannot. You do not know what it is for a mother to lose a child. His father hardly knew the boy, only saw him for a few weeks before he went off to that horrid Germany; but I had carried him in my arms, and fed him and watched over him for nine months. He was such a dear pretty little baby." It was impossible not to pity and console her, however much you might suppose you hated her; she was like a child that cannot understand why it must suffer.

Dorothy tried to be patient, but found her a very difficult guest to entertain. She evidently thought Grasmere a sad dull place and expected Keswick to be much the same. She could not, of course, walk far, and indeed had never liked walking. Dorothy took her to tea with the Sympsons and so forth, but it was a hard task to keep her cheerful. She was very watchful and suspicious and did not like her husband to talk much to Dorothy, who for that and other reasons kept away from him as much as she could, and left him to spend his time with William. She thought him tired, changed and much subdued by his long months of work in London. He said that he had slaved hard for the *Morning Post* and sadly needed a holiday.

He seemed very much taken with her brother John and talked to him whenever he could; he declared that nothing would please him better than to go a voyage with John to the East Indies, a notion which made his wife scream. John, however, smiled and kept himself aloof. His sister could not forgo the indulgence of asking eagerly, "What do you think of him? He says he loves to hear you talk of your voyages. He thinks you are as much of a poet as William, in your own way"; but John smiled and shrugged his broad shoulders, demurring, "That's his pleasant fun. Bless you! I don't open my mouth much when he's about. I couldn't hope to say anything that would interest a man like that; I leave him to you and William."

She murmured, "He is a wonderful man," and John said heartily, "I never knew any one like him. He fairly takes your breath away, with his fine talk and his grand air. It's my belief," concluded John innocently, "that a king would look like him, if you could see one." She could press the simple phrase into her sore heart, like the thorn that the nightingale leans upon, and find an aching pleasure in it; but she was taken aback when John shook his head and mournfully concluded, "I don't know why it is, but I feel it in my bones that he'll come to some bad end." She asked him why, uneasily, but he could not or would not tell her; he only muttered something about, "Too good to be true. Red sky at morning; shepherd's warning," and did not explain his foreboding. He did say however, "Pity the man's got such a fool of a wife. He deserved a fine clever woman, a girl like you." She coloured up and turned away for she did not want to meet John's eye, or talk to him about Mrs. Coleridge. She had begun to feel that she could not endure the little woman's company much longer.

Mrs. Coleridge herself apparently thought John the best of his family and certainly the sailor had been very kind about rowing her on the lake and talking to her. Once they all went on a picnic to the island and made a driftwood fire on the shore. Hartley danced beside it like a spirit on an aspen leaf. He was a fairy child, an enchanted being, singing, dancing to himself; the tears came into his father's eyes as he watched him. That was the best of their days together.

Presently the Coleridges went away to Keswick and Dorothy was not sorry to see them go. She was glad to have their first meeting safe over and done with, hoped that now everything would be easier, and believed herself cured of her folly. She devoted herself assiduously to John and William. The summer was slipping by terribly quickly and soon John would have to go back to sea. She felt that she must not waste an hour of his company in vain regrets.

At the end of July, on St. Anne's Day, they went down in the evening to Ambleside, to see the Rush-bearing. The village people all went in procession up and down the streets singing and carried *burdens* from the Market Cross to the old chapel on the hill, fantastic trophies of rushes and green boughs, stuck with coloured paper rosettes and with all manner of flowers. A pipe and tabor went before them and an old man playing a tune on his fiddle, always the same air, "The Hunt is Up"; and every child got a piece of spicy gingerbread. It was a charming outing. A little later in the summer there were village sports at Grasmere in the field called Pavement End, because it was on top of the Roman road. The dalesmen wrestled together for a leather belt and the shepherds raced each other up the crags and down again. John and William sat on a bench and watched the sports with great enjoyment all day long. She and William could not avoid going over once to Keswick to spend a few days with the Coleridges and see the new house, but they did not enjoy it greatly. There was an uncomfortable feeling in the air all through the visit. Dorothy tried to put it down to the hot thundery weather and the trouble of visitors in a new house. The whole place was in a sad muddle and poor Mrs. Coleridge, very near her time, too spiritless to put anything in order. Dorothy itched to help her, but was snubbed when she interfered with any household task. The house itself was charming, tall, yellow and classical in its proportions, with elegant fanlights, doorways and woodwork, marble mantelpieces and iron hob-grates wrought into delicate patterns of urns and skulls, wreaths and cherubs. When it was finished it would have a centre block of three stories and a semi-circular bay at each end, but the workmen were still hammering away in the further half. It was called Greta Hall and it was being built by old William Jackson, the carrier, who had made a good deal of money out of the weekly wagon plying between Keswick and Whitehaven and wanted a fine house to live in when he retired. He was an intelligent and charming old fellow, quite self-taught, but a great reader and he liked the notion of letting half his house cheap to a poet, even if the rent was not very regularly paid.

He was going to live in the other half when it was done.

Meanwhile the Coleridges were much better lodged than at Nether Stowey. Dorothy thought the position of Greta Hall enchanting. It stood on a little hill, just outside the town, and the River Greta, the loud lamenter, made a loop about it. There was a bridge just below the house and a forge near by it, you could hear the water-hammers going all day long. You went through the front door, between Corinthian pillars, and found a pleasant yellow and white parlour on the right and a breakfast-room on the left, shelved up to the ceiling for books. The family had christened these two rooms Peter and Paul, nobody quite knew why. Upstairs there were a dozen rambling rooms. Coleridge had a study on the first floor, an antique ill-shaped room with a huge old-fashioned church organ in it, never played upon, which had somehow taken his wandering fancy, an old day-bed for a sofa, many books scattered all over the floor and an Æolian harp hanging by the casement. He was enormously pleased with his new abode and boasted that it commanded a prospect of six different landscapes. There was an army of tentlike mountains encamped about the town of Keswick, which he said reminded him of a leaguer of giants.

He wanted the Wordsworths to quit Dove Cottage immediately and come and live in the unoccupied part of the house to be near him, but Mrs. Coleridge would never have agreed to that and even William did not think it a good idea. He said gloomily, "I could not work under the same roof as that chattering woman." She had certainly grown more garrulous than ever. Her husband used to shut himself up in his study to get away from her. She did not dare to go in after him and she complained to Dorothy, in her flat plaintive silly voice, "Mr. Coleridge is so strange nowadays. He is always out of humour. He never tells me anything. Sometimes he will not speak to me for half a day together," and gave her a sharp sour look, as if to say, "That is your fault." Dorothy was not sorry when this first uncomfortable visit came to an end.

She and William walked back home over the Raise, on a

heavy fatiguing afternoon. There were coppery clouds brooding on the mountains and a curious yellow reflection in the water of the lake, Helvellyn looked very black up above them. There was thunder at night in the mountains, echoing from one peak to another, and it rained heavily; but next day the air had cleared. Everything seemed green and beautiful, she was glad to be back again with her two brothers in her own dear cottage and her spirits rose. She persuaded herself that presently, after the child was born, Mrs. Coleridge would settle down in the new house and they would all be happy and comfortable again as they had been at the beginning.

Their friend was with them again inside a fortnight. He appeared at eleven o'clock one night, after her brothers were in bed, when she was walking in the garden, in the still clear light of the harvest moon. He had walked over the top of Helvellyn and was in wild spirits; he had brought them a new poem, the second part of that rhyme of the Lady Christabel, which had come into his head under the withered oak in the winter woods of Alfoxden. Nothing would do but that he must read it to both of them at once. William was got up out of his bed and came down to the embers of the kitchen fire and the three of them sat there talking till half-past three; it was just like the old days, though the second part of the poem was not quite so good as the first had been. Next morning they bathed and walked in the wood by the lake. It was a fresh autumn morning and there was a great deal of corn cut in the vale; the prospect was as mellow and gentle as their thoughts. After dinner they discovered a rock seat in the orchard and their friend cut away the brambles about it, so that she and William might sit there. She sat and watched him while he did it and pleased herself with the brief fancy that he was also one of her brothers, a dear creature who had been brought up with her. She vowed that now everything should be well between them. She had not been so happy for a long time as she was on that September afternoon.

On the third day, which was very fine, warm and sunny,

the men all went off fishing and came back, bubbling over with an absurd plan of building a house on Helvellyn. It was a lovely moonlit night and there had been a fair that day in the village. She walked with William and their friend up the lane and by the church and they listened to the sound of dancing and merriment which came along the still air. Afterwards she lingered with her friend in the garden, when John and William had gone to bed and all the lights were out. The moonlight was like snow upon the mountains, they looked as if they belonged to the sky and there was a bright soft radiance upon the island and the lake. They did not talk much, but they were both perfectly happy as they walked up and down. She could have wished that such a night might never end, but at last the church clock struck and recalled them to themselves. He took her hand and said, "You must go in."

After that, when he had gone home again, it seemed all too short a time before the bracken on the mountains began to spread like yellow veins among the trees and the coppice wood turned brown. There was a sparkling misty freshness in the mornings and gossamer threads everywhere; the leaves of the pear tree in the orchard turned yellow before anything else, while the apple trees were still green. They spent a sweet and lovely afternoon under the trees. William read aloud to her Boswell's *Life of Johnson*, which he had just discovered and thought a fine book. In the middle of the month they heard that Mrs. Coleridge had another son, a fine and lovely boy. He was to be called Derwent, after the noble stream which ran out of the lake at Keswick and went down to Cockermouth, the bright blue river which had run behind the garden of the house where she and her brothers were born, whose voice had flowed along their dreams in childhood. She was glad to think that her friend's child should bear that name. And on the twenty-eighth of September, while they were still unready to lose him, they heard that John's ship was at Portsmouth, ready for sea. Next morning he must leave them.

7

She packed up his clothes for him all that afternoon, on her knees in his bedroom, with the door open so that she could call to him for anything she wanted. He was in the front room, William's writing-room, putting up the bookcase beside the hearth, for he was determined to finish it before he went to sea. She could hear him humming to himself, softly and tunefully, as he drilled and screwed, notched and fitted and hammered; he had a pleasant tuneful voice and a better ear for a melody than either William or herself. She had often thought that she would miss his voice about the house and garden when he went back to sea. He was fond of simple ditties, about ships and sweethearts mostly, "All in the Downs the fleet was moored" and "Come, cheer up, my lads, t'is to glory we steer" and ship's shanties like "Way-ho, up she rises" and "Leave her, Johnny" and "Spanish Ladies," all with rousing tunes; but this afternoon he had got another song into his head, a ballad that had been made fifteen years earlier, when the King of England's son wanted to marry Mrs. Fitzherbert. It had a pretty tune and pretty words; she could hear him singing through the open door, "Sweet lass of Richmond Hill, Sweet lass of Richmond Hill, I'd crowns resign to call thee mine . . ." before he stopped hammering and called to her, "Come here a minute, Dolly, and lend me your straight eye."

She got to her feet, went in and found him hard at work. He did not lift his absorbed brown head as she entered, but murmured, "I'm not certain of this corner. The truth is, the whole wall's cock-eyed; it's always the same in these old houses. I can get on twice as fast if you'll bear a hand for a minute or two. I'm almost done." She knelt beside him, boy and girl again together. At Cockermouth he had always liked to have her beside him. watching open-mouthed, too little to do more than hold a tool or a nail for him, while he knocked a rabbit-hutch together or made bows and arrows and such. He had always been the handy one; Chris and William were bookworms, and clumsy with their fingers, and Richard was idle and stupid. She liked to watch John's neat hands at work as he murmured, "Easy now," and "Handsomely" and "Keep that corner straight." She wondered where he had had such a fine red and green serpent tattooed round his sunburnt arm. Presently the last bracket was fixed, the screws were all driven home; he sat back on his heels, dusted the sawdust from his hands and grinned at his sister. He said, "That's done; all shipshape and Bristol fashion. It'll hold more books than William will be able to afford for a year or so yet. It's a good bit of carpentering, though I say it as shouldn't. It'll do to remind you and William of me while I'm at sea."

She said, "We shan't need to be reminded, John," and for the moment her wild eyes, stilled from their restless glancing, dwelt upon him with the deep and steady affection which she had for him. It was a calm and happy feeling, quite different from the emotion which she had for William. John had never tormented her, or exacted anything from her. He did not draw strength away, he gave it; she knew that she could rest in him. She felt a sudden need to assure him of her love and she told him. "We shall think of you and talk of you continually. When we hear the wind in the chimney at night we shall wonder if there is a storm blowing where your ship is. Whenever we go down to Ambleside for the letters we shall ask first whether there is one from our sailor brother. Whenever William takes his fishing rod up to the tarn on Helvellyn, or down to the lake, he will say, I wish John were here to go with me, he always catches more than I do. When we walk in the fir grove on summer evenings, and hear the wind in the branches making a sound like the sea, we shall say to one another, Perhaps John is walking up and down now on the deck of his ship and timing his steps with ours."

John coloured deeply, pressed her hand and smiled. He said, "Wherever I am I shall think of you two living happily here together." She tried to meet his look, but her lip trembled as she turned her head away lest he should see the tears in her eyes. A shade of trouble came upon his face. After a moment he urged her anxiously, "You are happy, Dolly?" and gave her a doubtful stare. She said eagerly, perhaps too eagerly, "Of course I am, very happy," but he shook his head and grumbled, "Sometimes, you know, I think you give in too much to William." She protested, but he would not be convinced; he rubbed the top of his head and said, "William's a queer fish, an uncommonly queer fish. He doesn't think much of any one but himself. I like the old fellow, but I'm damned if I understand him. There's something a bit frightening about William, a kind of fire in him, smouldering away down underneath." His ingenuous forehead puckered itself into a bewildered frown. He said, "William's not quite like the rest of us."

She replied gently, "No, dear; he isn't quite like the rest of us." John grumbled, "Of course he's a genius, I know that. He was always Mother's favourite, she said he'd go farther than any of us. She wanted him to have his chance, she told me always to look out for William. I promised I would and I shall do it. If ever I have any money it shall be for you and for William. A fellow like him ought not to have to worry about how he's to pay his bills. I shall be a rich man one of these days and then you two shall live in comfort. Once I'm a captain I can do a bit of trading on my own account. You know John Company lets us have cargo space for our own ventures and we can get the fares of twenty or thirty passengers, besides letting our own cabins if we choose; an old general going out or a nabob coming home, will pay a hundred or more for quarters in the master's cabin. Oh! I shall get pickings, never fear; we three shan't starve in our old age. The captain of an East Indiaman can make his six thousand a year, while he's at sea; there was a captain once made thirty thousand pounds in two years, out of the China voyage." His sister smiled at him and said, "I am sure you deserve to make your fortune." He gazed at her with a long troubled look, then burst out suddenly, "Don't let William suck you dry, Dolly;

don't spend your whole life running after him and waiting on him hand and foot as you do. He's too much wrapped up in himself, he'd never see it if you killed yourself for him." She was startled and protested, "Don't be foolish, John, I want nothing better than to look after him," but her brother shook his head. He sighed, "I want you to have some life of your own," and then concluded, "There's something great in you, too, I don't want to see it wasted."

This seemed very foolish and touching to her, she thought that he only said it because he loved her. She protested, "Why, there's nothing great about me, John, all I'm good for is looking after William." He said stubbornly, "That's all very well for a time. You've got him to yourself here and you two always did like to get off together, but it can't last." Her smile faded as he told her gravely, "Don't you see what's going to happen? Don't you feel it coming? Sooner or later William will marry and leave you. He's got over that business with the French girl, though it took him longer than any of us expected. He's getting to an age when he wants a wife and children. You can't keep him to yourself for ever. I tell you what I think, Dolly, though I haven't said a word of it to any one but you." She waited, with her lips parted and her wild eyes fixed on his. John said, with a gravely pitying look, "I think he'll end up by marrying Mary Hutchinson."

She shrank back from him and a long breath, a sigh of utter dismay, escaped from her parted lips. She faltered, "Oh, no; oh, no!" but John still gazed at her mournfully and shook his slow head. She found herself babbling, "William will never marry. He wants nobody but me, we shall live and die here together. I could not bear it if he left me." John continued to gaze at her as if he knew something that she did not, and she felt as if a great weight were settling down upon her, pressing her to death. She stammered, "D-did anything happen between them, when you were all at Gallow Hill?" because he seemed so certain, but John said, "No" and smiled gravely, admitting, "William will stand off and on for a long time yet, I dare say; but I felt it coming, like a change in the wind, or the tide turning. He'll swing her way in the end, she'll be his anchorage. It's what he needs. You won't keep him from it." And he added, with some dejection, "William always was a lucky fellow. He gets what he wants in the end. Other people have to stand aside for him."

She had been sitting beside him all this time, on the floor, in the sawdust and shavings of his carpenter's work, listening and curling a bit of wood-shaving round her fingers. Now she got uncertainly to her feet and walked away from him, stumbling a little as if she were giddy from long kneeling. She went over to William's writing table by the window, all strewn with the papers on which he had been at work, and looked down at them but she did not really see them. Behind her she heard John murmur, "If he would but spread a little more canvas, take her in tow and bring her into harbour! But I dare say he will hang in the wind for a year or two yet and never guess how the poor girl feels about him. I've no patience with William sometimes. If I had a girl like Mary Hutchinson waiting for me to speak, I'd not beat about as he does, I can tell you." His voice became rueful as he said, more to himself than to her, "But a girl like that would never come my way." She turned round and said to him, she did not know why, "You would make her a better husband than William," but he smiled unhappily and said, "She will never look at any one but him." Dorothy nodded slowly. It seemed to her now that she had always known it, but she said sternly, "William never thinks of her. I am sure of that. He tells me all his thoughts."

John said wretchedly, "It's hard on you, I see that; you'll be all adrift." He brooded on that, while he gathered his tools together and she stood watching him, kneeling on the floor. When he had everything collected he looked up at her and his face broadened into a doubtful, humble smile. "Tell, you what, Dolly"; he burst out like a schoolboy, "when William's spliced you shall come a voyage to the Indies with me. We'll run off together. I shall have my own ship by that time and you shall have the captain's cabin. How would you like that, my girl?" She summoned up a pale smile for him, hardly listening and he ran on, encouraged, "I'd show you all sorts of fine things. You've never been out of England except that one time into Germany. You've never seen mid-ocean in flying-fish weather, all blue and shining, or a clear night with the moon like snow on the sails and the water hissing alongside." She smiled and murmured, "Why, John, you're quite a poet!"

He was checked immediately; he stammered a little, reddened up to his ingenuous forehead and muttered, "Oh, I can't spout poetry like old William, but I enjoy a fine night at sea as well as any man." She said, "Indeed you have called me out in an evening many a time, to look at the moon or the stars. I believe you love them as well as either of us." At that he burst out into a great guffaw and said, "I may not love them as well as you do, or William, but I know more about them. You and he always call the biggest star Jupiter." This had long been a family joke about them. She had put it down against herself in her journal. She gave him a vague smile and encouraged by this John promised, "Well, you shall come with me to the Eastern seas whenever you say the word. We'll go to Canton together if we both live long enough; I'll buy you a Kashmir shawl, or a fine worked India muslin and bring it back for you to wear at William's wedding. I hear the French ladies all begin to wear Kashmir shawls, Madame Buonaparte has made them the fashion; and our William shall have a set of red and white ivory chessmen, or a chest of tea, or a ship in a bottle, or a parrot to recite poetry to him. So cheer up, Dolly! There's bad weather coming to you for a bit, maybe; but you're a brave girl and you'll ride it out." She set her lips into a rueful grin which made her look, for the moment, uncommonly like William; but did not speak, only squeezed John's hand in her brown fingers and then went off to finish his packing.

They sat up late that night talking, but only of cheerful everyday things; she did not realise that it would be two years before she could see John again. She still felt absurdly that he was only going off as far as Penrith, or maybe Carlisle; as if she would see him and hear his strong cheerful voice again quite soon. They set off with him next morning. He was going over Grisedale Hawes to Patterdale and so down Ullswater to Penrith, where he would get the coach. They went with him as far as Grisedale Tarn. At first it was a gay and sunny walk, with the water tumbling cheerfully down the rocks under the rowans in Tongue Ghyll. A shepherd boy whistled to his dog as they herded the sheep among the feathery bracken; but higher up the travellers got above the trees and the fern. The far peaks came up stealthily behind their backs and looked at them over the shoulders of the fells. There was little astir up there except sheep like stones moving, a glassy shimmer flowing over the hot ground, a carrion crow wheeling out from a cleft, or a buzzard tilting with the sunlight on his wings. At the top of the hill there was nothing but a golden afternoon cloud, building itself up in the nick of the pass, to be reflected in the tarn, and the wind talking to itself very quietly among the stones. Here they parted from John and sat a while to watch him go down the valley, jumping cheerfully across the brook from stone to stone. There was a great quantity of a small purple flower growing in the turf all about them as they sat. She plucked a little of it idly, rubbed it between her fingers and said to William that she would always think of John when she saw it growing; but she did not guess that he would never come back to the valley again.

VI

I

All that autumn brother and sister were hard at work, getting a second edition of *Lyrical Ballads* ready for the press. William was writing a new preface to explain just what people ought to think about his poems. They had fine golden weather for a long time, with a bite in the air and patches of snow on the mountains above the many-coloured woods. The oaks were dark-green, the sycamores crimson-tufted, the mountain-ash deep orange, the common ash lemon-coloured, but many of the ash trees remained of their own peculiar green all through October; those that were discoloured were chiefly near the water. She had never seen such a soft autumnal confusion of sweet hues as among these mountains. Later the rainy weather closed down upon them and turned to snow. There were new waterfalls like snail tracks everywhere upon the mountains and on moonlit nights the moon was bright as herrings in the water of the lake. They got long walks, however, in all weathers, sat by their fire and could write and read; William and she were very snug together.

He was working that winter on a long poem about a sheep-fold which they had often passed in their walks, a ruin built nearly in the form of a broken, or unequally divided heart. There was a sad story about the old shepherd, Michael, who had built it, and William could not rest till he had cast it into verse. For some reason he found it difficult and fatigued himself by altering it, again and again. His sister thought that he missed the talk and company of their friend, who could not come to them over Dunmail Raise in snows and rain. He could not stand the weather as they did. He was often rheumatic, feverish and wretched; his wife complained that he should never have come to live in Cumberland. He came over twice in

November when they had Sara Hutchinson staying with them. He still made a great fuss of this young creature and she followed after him like a little dog, hung on his words and sat at his feet. He changed her name to Asra, because to call her Sara reminded him of his wife. They were quite absorbed in each other and poor Dorothy was wildly jealous when she saw how long they talked together. Otherwise he did not come very often to Grasmere during that winter and William and she felt very low without him. William fidgetted and fussed a great deal over the notes and prefaces for the *Lyrical Ballads*, altering again and again; he became nervous and jaded and slept badly.

At that time the mail used to pass through Ambleside at one in the morning. William several times insisted on walking down to the post office to get back the packet of proofs and make yet another alteration of some phrase which had troubled him. Mrs. Nicholson, the old postmistress, or her husband would get up, let them in and give them their letter back out of the box. They would sit there in the parlour or the kitchen, discussing over it, reading and changing, till they made it quite to their minds. Then they would seal up the packet again, knock at the Nicholsons' bedroom door and say, "Please will you bolt the door after us. Here is our letter for the post. We'll not trouble you any more this night." Mrs. Nicholson used to tell the story to the day of her death; she never forgot how friendly the brother and sister were to her and how loving to one another. Their friend did not finish his *Christabel* in time and the *Lyrical Ballads* had to be made up without it, a great disappointment.

After all the sheets had gone off William was very much depressed and could not settle to anything. She walked out with him upon the White Moss, on a calm and lovely October morning, the morrow of a stormy night when the grass was bright with raindrops and the air was full of a pleasant noise of water falling. First they saw a hare running races on the moor for pure pleasure, splashing up a glittering mist of water with her feet from the wet turf; and then they saw an old man standing motionless as a cloud, beside a little pool, stirring it with his staff and gazing upon the muddy water. He was a queer creature, bent almost double, with a nightcap, and an apron on under his long coat, which hung loose about his stooping shoulders. He carried a bundle under his arm and with his long nose and dark eyes looked like a Jew. They went to him and asked him how he lived and what he did.

He told them in his slow speech that his trade was to gather leeches, but he had not the strength for it. They were getting very scarce, because they were much sought after, and did not breed fast and were of slow growth; he used to get half a crown a hundred for them, but nowadays they were worth thirty shillings. He lived by begging and was making his way to Carlisle, where he would buy a few goodly books to peddle. He then rambled off into a long story about how he had been hurt driving a cart, his leg broken, his body driven over, his skull fractured. He seemed very poor and decrepit, yet uncomplaining. Dorothy gave him some money to help him on his way. She was sorry for him; he had lost his wife and ten children and was alone in the world. William said afterwards that the old man had made him ashamed of his own melancholy. He said, "I shall think of him when I am ready to grumble," and he began a poem about the leech-gatherer. Two years later, when it was finished, he called it *Resolution and Independence*.

The second edition of the *Lyrical Ballads* was published in February, 1801, but it did badly. It was a weeping spring, the mountains were veiled in cloud for weeks together, the rain came through the roof of their cottage and all the chimneys smoked. They got no word from their friend and in April they walked over to see him.

They found him sitting in the parlour, looking dreadfully ill. He complained of aches all over him, swollen eyes and a pain in the back of the head; he was so weak that he changed colour when he tried to move. They were dreadfully anxious about him. The doctor had told him that he ought not to spend the winter in England and he was rambling about how the climate was killing him and wondering who would lend him the money to go to some warm island. He was very low and complained that nobody understood how ill he was. Their company did him good at first, but he was never well for more than an hour together during the whole time they were there. The weather was fine, but it did not set him up as they expected.

He talked of Lisbon, the South of France, or Nevis, in the West Indies. The Pinneys of Bristol had property in Nevis and they had described the gorgeous isle. His sick eyes sparkled again as he talked of the cloud-capped peak, rearing its volcanic cone three thousand feet out of the sea, fringed with palm trees and cane fields and ringed with coral surf. He said that the place was a health resort for all the white folk in the West Indies and that a winter there would cure him of all his ills. He pictured himself lolling pleasantly in the wide airy veranda of the Bath House, drinking sangaree and listening to the trade wind rustling the banana fronds in the for some one else to contrive.

His wife was unsympathetic; she said, "He will not take any care of himself. He goes out in the rain and will not change his clothes, he sits up half the night writing and lies in bed all day. I wash my hands of him; he is more trouble to me than either of the children. What with his grumbling and their crying I never have a moment's peace. He does not understand how busy I am. He is always teasing me to read this book and that book, as if I had nothing more important to do than to sit down and study. He must go to you, or to this Miss Sara Hutchinson, if he wants a woman to read books. I have no time for that." She hardly knew Sara Hutchinson, but she complained that her husband was always talking about her and saying what fine letters she wrote. This was news to Dorothy.

Mrs. Coleridge was certainly very fortunate in her two children. Hartley was now a splendid child, with steady roses five years old in his cheeks and Derwent a sweet lovely fat baby. His mother sat in the nursery all day long, suckling him and playing with him, she hardly troubled to dress herself before the two o'clock dinner. She had no method and wandered from one household task to another, never finishing anything. Dorothy said to William impatiently, "Mrs. Coleridge is a sad fiddle-faddler." She could not get servants to do the work of that great house cheaply and lamented, "If you tell a servant nowadays in the mildest manner that she has not done her work to please you, at once you are told to provide for yourself and if you speak again, they are gone. They are all so impertinent. It is because they can get such high wages in the factories. When they had five or six pounds a year, they could not afford to be out of a place, but now they get double. Not that they ever think of laying by for sickness; oh no! they squander it all on ribbons and bonnets and fairings. I have no patience with such people." As always, she made Dorothy feel unwelcome and glad to go home again.

The second summer in Grasmere was perhaps not quite so happy as the first one had been. John was not there to keep them cheerful and the first pleasure of discovery had worn off the valley. It was a wet summer, heavy and green and dripping. William was translating Chaucer and getting on slowly with his long poem, if Dorothy kept a journal it has been lost. In the autumn their friend suddenly took it into his head to go to London for the winter. He had an offer of work on the *Morning Post* and had persuaded himself that dry pavements were the next best thing to a winter in the south; besides it seemed that he was wild to get away from his nagging wife for a time. They could not but advise him to accept, though they knew that they would miss him sadly. On the tenth of November, 1801, they went over to Keswick to say good-bye to him and stayed a night. He walked back with them next day and parted with them, in a mild soft October afternoon, under the slopes of Helvellyn, near the rock on which they had all carved their names during that first happy summer, when they had thought that they had brought him to live near them always. It was a sad parting. He had a sweet day next day for his ride to London, but at the cottage every sight and every sound reminded her of him, of his many walks to them by day and night, of all dear things. She was melancholy and could not talk, but at last eased her heart by weeping. William was cross and said, "Nervous blubbering"; he was dreadfully unsympathetic. She dried her tears and said proudly, "I have done; I shall cry no more," but she could not but feel how many, many reasons she had to be anxious about her friend.

2

Mary Hutchinson came to stay with them for several weeks that winter. She arrived just after Coleridge left, and Dorothy found her a great comfort, though she had dreaded the visit, because it made her think of what John had said to her before he went away. She had struggled to put that warning out of her mind and had thought that she had succeeded, but when William said suddenly in August, "It is time Mary was asked here again," her fears and suspicions all woke up. She put off the invitation as long as she could. However, in the end Mary came and for a time seemed unlikely to threaten their peace. She was placid and pleasant as ever, and quite good company in her own silent fashion; she helped with the work of the house, washed and baked and ironed, took a hand at cards in the evenings when the neighbours came in and sat sewing by the fire while William read Chaucer or Spenser aloud to both of them. They made him a set of new waistcoats. It was a pleasant change to have another woman in the house again, and she had always liked Mary very much better than Sara. William left them very much to themselves at first; he was in one of his sulky moods and shut himself up with his books all day long. The two girls had to amuse each other. Mary, though she was not such a great walker as Dorothy, was country-bred and as sturdy as a pony. It was pleasant to have her company tramping round the lakes, going into Ambleside to do the shopping and fetch the letters, or up into the Black Quarter to get cream from the farm. Once the two girls rose by candlelight, put on their full broadcloth riding skirts and jogged over the Raise to Keswick. It was a cold ride, with the snow blowing away in a straight line off the top of Helvellyn, but they both enjoyed it and laughed a great deal together over the adventure. Dorothy was never very happy on a horse, but Mary was a famous jockey, all the family said so.

Mrs. Coleridge was stiff and cool and out of humour, but the little boys were sweet. It was amusing to sit with them in the nursery, look at Derwent fatly asleep in his cradle, and listen to Hartley's quaint chatter. Mary said to him teasingly, "Shall I take Derwent away with me?" Hartley said, "No," in the sweetest tone possible, "I cannot spare my little brother, and he cannot do without his mamma." Mary said, "Well, why can't I be his mamma? Can't he have more mammas than one?" but this did not please the child who said, "No" very stoutly and when she persisted, "Why not?" made round eyes and explained, "Because they do not love and mothers do." Dorothy and Mary exchanged a smile above his unconscious head and Mary asked him, "What was the difference between mothers and mammas?" This did puzzle him for a little, but not for long; he peeped up at them with his bright mischievous eyes, then found a thing to say and informed them gravely, "Mothers wear sleeves like this," pulling his own right down, "And mammas so"; and he pulled his sleeves up and made a bustle about his shoulders. Mary burst out laughing, picked him up and kissed him. She rolled him on the bed, and tickled him, while he screamed with delight. Dorothy stood by and endured a pang of envy because he could never be hers. Mrs. Coleridge did not press them to stay the night. She did not much like any of the Hutchinson sisters, though she was chiefly jealous of Sara, for she detested any woman who could talk about books and poetry to her husband. So the two girls rode home through the misty winter evening and found William translating Chaucer's *God of Love* and the fire out; he could never remember to mend it when he was working.

Two days later the girls went up the green lane to collect mosses and make the chimney gay for William; but Dorothy had stayed so late, finishing a letter to her friend, that it was too dark to see to gather them. She and Mary turned aside into Easedale and walked backwards and forwards in a large field. The river had been galloping past the church as fast as it could go and from the field they could see Churn Milk Force like a broad stream of snow at the little footbridge. The valley was full of streams with that great waterfall at the head, and lesser falls in different parts of the mountains. The whole place was loud with the noise of roaring water. They walked backwards and forwards until all distant objects except the white shape of the waterfall and the outlines of the mountains were gone. A few stars shone dimly in the grey cloudy night. They talked of the man who was dearer to them both than any other being. Mary said, "This is a sweet place and you have made it home to William. I think he loves you more than any one on earth. You must be very happy here together." Yet her voice was sad.

Dorothy listened to the falling water in the dark; after a little she said, unwillingly, "I do not know; I cannot tell you. Sometimes I think that William is wretched." She had not known that she felt this, yet when it was put into words she saw that it was true; she repeated, "Yes, William is wretched. He wants more than I can give him. He is too much shut up in himself. He works too hard, he drives himself, he cannot be at peace. I do not know what more I can do for him. Sometimes I think that he is sorry we ever came here. I cannot tell what he wants."

They walked a few more steps in silence. Then Mary stood still and asked abruptly, "Does he ever write to that girl in France?"

It was the last thing that Dorothy had expected; she could

only say stupidly "Annette?" and Mary retorted, quite shrewishly, "Yes, Annette, of course; there was never any other that I heard tell about." Dorothy said, "I did not know that you had been told." It astonished her to hear Mary say, quite calmly, "Dear me, yes; I've known about Annette for years. William told me himself." She walked on again and Dorothy had to hurry to catch her up in the darkness. A little breathlessly she stammered, "I d-don't b-believe William has heard from her since we came here." Mary said, quite tartly, "Well, he may think of her for all that, and make himself wretched about her. He has always been so miserably ashamed of the whole business. You do not know everything that goes on inside William's head." She sounded quite unlike herself, sharp, jealous, and impatient; Dorothy expostulated, "Why, Mary; what's come over you?" but Mary only said, in a hard voice, "Nothing new"; and then with an odd sound, half-sob, half-laugh, concluded, "You must know that I have always loved William."

Dorothy did not deny this; it seemed to her now that she had always known it. She said with concern, "Can you not stop thinking about William? He will only make you unhappy"; and took the other girl by the arm, but Mary withdrew herself and retorted, "Easier said than done. You should know that of all people."

Dorothy admitted, "Yes, I should know," but she was not thinking of her brother as she said it. The two girls walked on a little way in silence, turning towards home; then Mary burst out, in a voice which sounded as if she were crying, "He loved me first, I am sure of it. He taught me to love him, years ago, when we were all in Penrith together; but then he went away and that French girl stole him from me. I understood that; I thought he would forget her, I expected him to come back to me, but there is something holding him from me. When we were at Sockburn I felt him turning back to me, but now he is quite different; he will not talk to me, he will not be alone with me, he is full of moods, he is angry with me about nothing. Sometimes I think he is tired of me and sometimes I think he is beginning to love me again and will not give way to me. He fights against me, he holds me off; and I cannot bear it. He makes me too unhappy. I cannot endure it any longer." She was fairly crying now, wringing her hands and exclaiming, "I must go home, Tom wants me, I ought not to have come here. I cannot stay with you."

She was quite changed and possessed; Dorothy would not have recognised the gentle creature and her heart leapt with a pang of jealous relief. She thought, "Well, let her go. William does not want her, after all. She disturbs him with her brown eyes and her soft ways, but he would forget her as soon as we were alone together again. I could drive her out of his head as I have always done. What use is she to William? She can never love him as I do, she does not understand him. She would make him as dull and contented as herself. She knows nothing of the world that he and I live in, there is no fire in her, she cannot understand his thought. Why should she come between us, always making a third in the house? Why should I let her take him away from me? I have nothing left in the world but William." But when she had got so far in her thoughts she was ashamed of herself. She said, "You cannot go away from us yet, Mary. There is more snow coming; all the village people say that. You could not travel, the roads would be blocked and the valley shut in. You must stay with us a little longer, we could not have Christmas without you." Mary cried and clung to her and was persuaded. Poor girl! she was only too ready to stay where she could see and talk with William.

3

The country people had been right about the snow; it came, sure enough, five days later, a great fall, hiding and smoothing over grass and rocks alike. All the mountains looked like solid stone, smooth and white as marble. The birches on the crags were beautiful, red-brown and glittering, the ashes looked like bright spears, the brooms waved gently with the weight of snow upon their branches. The air was sweet and sparkling, as pure and sharp as fire. They all walked out to look at their favourite birch tree; it was yielding to the gusty wind with all its tender twigs. The sun shone upon it and it glanced in the wind like a flying sunshiny shower. It was a tree in shape, with stem and branches, but it was like a spirit of water. The other birch trees that were near it looked bright and cheerful, but it was a creature by its own self among them. William stood footbound and gazed at it, with his mysterious absorbed stare, and Mary stood by him, with her hand through his arm.

Dorothy left them and walked forward among the bushes. There was a small bird, with a salmon-coloured breast and a white cross upon it, piping and fluttering among the branches; it seemed to have no fear of her. She stood a long time and watched it. The snow upon the rock was as soft as a down cushion, round and white, the mossy rock behind looked soft as velvet, vivid green and tempting her to sit upon it. There was a young foxglove, like a star, in the middle of the snow. All else was thick snow without a footmark, not even the foot of a sheep; all smooth and innocent. She walked among the snowy bushes and nibbled the red hips and haws which her friend loved so absurdly; she ate twenty for him, when she was walking and thinking by herself, but still she got home to the cottage before the others. They came in cheerful, blooming and happy; she had not seen William look so for a long time and her heart smote her.

It was a hard winter, with sickness and poverty in the cottages. There were many tramping the snowy roads, with patched garments and sacks of meal on their shoulders. They often came to beg at her door. There were tales going about of rick-burnings and thefts, hangings and transportations, the war had sent up the price of bread. Dorothy could hardly sleep for cold in her icy, stone-floored bedroom and when she lay awake she could hear poor Peggy Ashburner, in the cottage next door, coughing her heart out; the woman was dying of consumption. They missed their friend sadly and he wrote them dreadful melancholy letters; scarcely a week passed but they had some affecting heart-rending complaint from him. They used to tramp down to Ambleside for the letters, by starlight or lantern-light, with straw in their shoes when the snow was deep on the ground. Sometimes they would meet the carrier trudging along half-way, with his little wooden box at his back, and he would lift the lid and give them the letters to save them walking further. Dorothy would break the seal to see whether their friend were sick or well and then carry the packet home in her bosom for safety. She could not bear to think of him, ill and unhappy and lonely in London. She was stopped in her writing and made ill by his letters. A sad one, coming late at night, would keep her from sleeping. When she slept she often dreamt of him, but mournfully and confusedly; and when she awoke in the morning she could not remember her dreams.

On the shortest day of the year Mary walked into Ambleside and brought back four letters. Two were very melancholy ones from their friend; the third was from her sister Sara, the fourth, as Dorothy saw immediately, was from France. She did not dare to look at Mary; William, with a very red face, put the letter in his pocket and went up to his own room to read it there. On Christmas Day they had another letter from Coleridge, the saddest that he had ever written. She took it into the warm kitchen and read it kneeling by the fire in the chimney corner, where William's muddy boots were drying, full of oats. Mary was cooking the Christmas dinner; there were two plum-puddings rumbling in the pot and a sirloin smoking before the fire. Mary had turned back the checked tablecloth half-way across the table and was rolling out her pastry for the mince-pies on the board. The firelight danced on her fine bare arms and was reflected in the copper pans and pewter plates on the dresser. Snow went whirling past the window, heaped itself grotesquely on the dead ferns which choked the pane and cast a queer white light up to the rafters. Mary stopped her work and leaned upon her rolling-pin for a minute or two, watching Dorothy; then she said, in her gentle voice, "I fear you have no good news from London."

Dorothy's lip trembled and she could not speak; she blinked and turned the page. Mary began to roll out her crust for the second time, with energetic, angry thumps. Presently she burst out, "I wish he would not write you such letters. He has no right to burden you with his troubles." Dorothy protested, "Who should he write to, if not to William and to me? We are his oldest friends," but Mary only pursed her lips and said, "You are always unhappy when you get a letter from him." She turned the dough this way and that and slapped it on the board; then said, "He writes to my sister Sara in the same way, whenever he is lonely or unhappy. If I see her crying I always know that she has had a letter from London."

That startled and silenced Dorothy; but she would not admit how nearly it had touched her. She had not understood that he was writing to Sara for consolation as well as to herself. The two girls stared at each other for a moment as if they were enemies; then Mary looked down and began rolling out the pastry thin and flat, for the last time. There was a warm crackling firelit silence in the kitchen. Mary began stamping out the crust into thin rounds and between two stamps of the cutter she demanded, "Why can't he write to his wife?"

Dorothy looked into the fire; she said, in a strangled tone, "He tells her nothing. She is no use to him. She is the lightest, weakest, silliest creature I have ever known, she cannot understand him. They should never have married each other." It sounded as if she were clinging to her only justification. Mary said grimly, "At least they have lived together for six years and he has given her those children." Dorothy shrank back at that and the other girl burst out, "Why do you make yourself unhappy over him? He has never brought you anything but trouble since he first met you and now it will be the same with Sara. She has persuaded herself already that she is the woman he ought to have married, she thinks she understands him better than his own wife. I have no patience with such ways; why cannot he leave you both alone?" She concluded, in a lower tone, "Some day, when it is too late, and he has spoilt your life for you, the time will come when you will wish that he had never known you." At that Dorothy raised her head and gave the other girl a strange wild look out of her grey eyes, saying, "Do you wish that you had never known William?" Mary started and stopped working; she leant forward with her hands on the table, stared and groaned, "Oh! my dear, is that how it is with you?" but Dorothy did not answer. She got to her feet and walked out of the kitchen. It was her birthday, Christmas Day in the year 1801, and she was thirty years old.

The fiddlers came that night, several of them, and played their Christmas tune, scraping their fiddles in the cold outside the cottage. Dorothy flung the door wide and welcomed them in and they played "The Days When We Were Young," standing in a ring by the door. William sat by the hearth while they played and covered his eyes with his fingers, but presently his hand dropped, and Dorothy saw him raise his head. He thought himself unseen and he sat and stared at Mary with a yearning hungry look. He never stirred while the music played, only a bright spot of red fixed and deepened itself on either cheek-bone. He looked like a starving man in sight of food. Mary did not look up, she was watching the fire in a soft and tender reverie, with the rich carnation colour burning in her cheeks. He could gaze unobserved for as long as the music lasted with that craving bewildered look, while his sister hid herself in her corner and felt as if the tune would break her heart.

VII

I

Directly after Christmas Mary insisted on going home. William seemed astonished and disappointed that she would not stay longer, though he had spent so little of his time in her company while she was there, but Mary was firm. So then he said that he and Dorothy would go part of the way with her and see their good friends, the Clarksons, at the foot of Ullswater; they had a standing invitation to visit them and so it was arranged. On the twenty-eighth of December the three of them set out through the inverted arch of Dunmail Gap. It was fine weather, but very cold, and there was snow upon the mountains. They carried cold mutton in their pockets and stayed to dine at John Stanley's inn, the Nag's Head at Wythburn, where they roasted apples at the fire; this was their usual half-way house on the way to Keswick. William had a fit of verse-making upon him and was uncommonly absent-minded. He left his gloves behind at the inn and his pocket volume of Spenser on a snowy bank where they had rested, but Mary turned back and found it for him. They spent the night at Greta Hall, a sad and deserted house when its master was away. Next day they made their difficult way down the Vale of St. John, past Threlkeld, though the road was often very slippery and the wind so high that the girls could hardly keep their feet. Dorothy was often obliged to crawl on all fours and Mary fell many a time; they missed their way and it was nearly dark before a stray traveller set them on the right road. They got to the Clarksons' new house, Eusemere, at tea-time and were made very welcome.

These Clarksons had been their friends for more than a year. Tom Poole had written from Somerset to ask them to visit his dear Wordsworths, and they all suited each other very well. Mr. Clarkson was a big florid tedious man, with a fleshy square face and a reserved serious manner. His wife was a pretty witty creature thirteen years younger than he, who teased and petted him. She had charming eager manners and was a very pleasant hostess to his friends. The Clarksons were devoted to each other and they had a lively five-year-old boy, called Thomas after his father. Mr. Clarkson had devoted his youth to intense exertions in the anti-slavery campaign; that was how he had come to know Tom Poole. While he was still at college Thomas Clarkson had felt the call; riding alone on a journey he had climbed off his horse, knelt and prayed and vowed himself to the cause. For the next nine years he had been, as he said himself, the "slave of the slave." He had worn himself out going about the country from one seaport town to another, from Bristol to Liverpool, from Portsmouth to Bridgewater, getting evidence of barbarous cruelty, of torture, overcrowding, disease and death; collecting signatures to petitions, persuading timid witnesses to give their testimony, writing letters and pamphlets, making speeches, going all the time in fear of his own life from the enemies he made. Finally the outbreak of war with France had brought all his hopes to a standstill for the time, nobody had any more leisure to think of the slaves. He had broken down then in health and mind, he could work no longer.

He came to Cumberland to visit a Quaker friend, Thomas Wilkinson of Penrith, a man who had known the Wordsworths since they were children. This friend found him a piece of ground near the foot of Ullswater, in the pleasant green pastoral country near Dailmain. Here the abolitionist built himself a long low white house overlooking the lake, married a wife and settled down to farm his land. He was still more than a little insane on the question of the slave trade and could talk of little else. When some other subject was introduced he would often listen for a moment or two and then burst out impatiently, "I cannot think of anything but the poor wretches in Barbadoes." He insisted on exhibiting to Dorothy the whips and fetters which he had collected from the slave-ships and the plan which he had drawn between decks, with the packed negroes like herrings in a barrel. This plan he carried about with him everywhere. He allowed no West India sugar or rum on his table and he always carried and displayed a snuff-box made at the Wedgwood works, with a black-and-white cameo in the lid, a chained negro kneeling and praying, with the motto, "Am I not a man and a brother?" The sufferings of the negroes had become an obsession with him and he declared that he should begin to work for abolition again as soon as the war should be over. Meanwhile, he had grown very much interested in the Quakers, who had done so much for the cause, was writing a weighty history of that movement, copied their ways and turns of speech, attended their worship, and fancied that he might end by becoming a Convinced Friend and being admitted to Meeting.

He and William were alike in many ways, though Thomas Clarkson had not a spark of poetry in him. He was a person of great fervour and no sense of humour, very earnest, impatient, persevering and narrow-minded. Coleridge laughed at him and called him "the moral steam-engine," but he suited William very well. They used to talk about religion by the hour together. Dorothy found herself preferring Catherine Clarkson, who was about her own age. Catherine had a charming impulsive nature, and the most elegant airs and graces, only slightly checked by her attempts to behave in a Quakerish fashion, to please her husband. She adored the good tedious fellow, listened with a pretty blend of indulgence and admiration to his solemn discourses, sighed over his obstinacy in fatiguing himself for his blacks, and did whatever he told her. She was a delicate creature and complained that the damp Lakeland climate made her ache in all her bones, but she was very active in her house and garden, which she managed with exquisite taste and skill and ran about with her little boy like the girl that she still was. She found time to read a great many books and was fascinated by William's poetry, but declared herself a little afraid of him. She thought it wonderful to find herself in literary society, quoted William all day long, and so won Dorothy's heart. She was in fact a little inclined to gush over William; but did it so prettily and innocently that she disarmed him and struck up a great friendship with Dorothy, which was destined to endure for many years. She said that she had been dreadfully homesick in the north-country. Her own home was at Bury St. Edmunds.

The Wordsworths stayed at Eusemere for the whole of January. Mary had left them on New Year's Eve, but only to go as far as her relatives at Penrith; she came back twice to see them. Mrs. Clarkson seemed to have taken a fancy to her and Mr. Clarkson liked her quiet ways; he once declared that she never said anything but "God bless you." They walked every day in the frosty weather; several times they went over to visit Thomas Wilkinson. He had a house called the Grotto, at Yanwath, on the banks of Eamont, where he had amused himself by twining pathways along the stream and making little cells and bowers with inscriptions of his own writing, all very pretty, though not spreading far. Like many old bachelors he was a great gardener. He was a stiff opinionated Quaker of the old sort, with long hair falling to his shoulders, drab clothes, knee-breeches and heavy buckled shoes. He held very strong views against war and slavery and was a great crony of Thomas Clarkson's. William admired this queer fellow very much and later wrote a poem to him, all about his garden. "*Spade, with which Wilkinson hath tilled his land,*" it began; Dorothy had not much sense of humour, but she felt dimly that it was not one of William's happier efforts. However, Thomas Wilkinson was a very good fellow, for all his narrow views and interfering ways. She admired the simple life which he led with his devoted sister at the Grotto and would have liked to be sure that she and William might long live so together, but her heart was full of fears, for it seemed to her that William had changed since Mary went away. He was always speaking of her and looking for her, he seemed almost ready to love her, against his will.

On Saturday, January 23rd, they left Eusemere at ten o'clock in the morning and rode on horseback as far as Grisedale, where they parted from Mr. Clarkson. It was a threatening day, the wind was cold, the mountains looked large and dark and were thinly streaked with snow. There was a strong wind and it rained all the way home. They struggled with the gale and often rested as they went along. A hail-shower met them before they reached Grisedale Tarn, and the way was often difficult over the snow, but at the tarn the view closed in. They saw nothing but mist and snow; and at first the ice on the tarn below them, cracked and split, yet without water, a dull grey white. Then they lost the path and could see the tarn no longer. They found themselves struggling and slipping among black shining screes. They were afraid of being bewildered in the mist; there was no footmark upon the snow, either of man or beast, only once they saw four sheep in a hollow. People were often lost and benighted upon those hills in winter; only the year before an old man had been lost in Boardale and sheltered all night in the angle between two walls of a ruined chapel, where he was found stupefied and well-nigh frozen to death by the dalesmen who went in search of him. She had that tale in her mind as she struggled with William through the driving snow-wreaths. Drowsy and stunned by the cold, she clung to his arm and found it in her heart to wish that they two might lie down like lost children and sleep for ever in the drifted whiteness about them. But William had been bred to those hills. He kept his glistening red face obstinately upturned to the driving storm and at last he guided her to the right track, by a heap of stones which they both remembered. Presently the mists parted and looking down through gulfs of air she saw the vale of Grasmere, soft and yellow beneath her. They reached the cottage in the dark. It was sweet and comfortable after all to get off her wet clothes and sit by her own fire with

William and not think of the morrow. He was hers for a little longer; she would be happy with him and shut her eyes to the future.

2

So they fell into their old life again for a time and yet it was not altogether their old life, for William was restless day and night and she knew from what he let fall that he was thinking continually of Mary. He tired himself with his long poem. He was composing that part of it which he called *The Pedlar*, and afterwards used in *The Excursion*; a character based partly upon the old Scotsman who had brought Sara Hutchinson up, and partly upon a packman who had lived at Hawkshead in William's schooldays. He wrought upon this and changed it so laboriously that he made himself quite ill. He wrote an epitaph and altered another that he had written when he was a boy; he was in miserable spirits and so was Dorothy. He had sent off a letter to Annette in France, within three days of coming home, an answer to the one which he had received before Christmas, but he did not tell her what he had put in it and she would not ask. She knew that he was sleeping badly, for when she lay awake in her own icy bedroom, with clothes heaped upon her, staring into the dark with hot eyes, she often heard him moving overhead. Once at a quarter-past three he called out to know what the hour was. She felt dull and stupefied with misery. Next day he was very unwell, worn out with his bad night's rest. She read aloud to him, to endeavour to make him sleep. One day he went with her down to the shore to a place where he had carved Mary's name upon the rock, and cut at it with his knife to make it plainer; a lover-like thing to do, if it had been any other man, but you could never tell with William. He was wearing himself out with labour and to little purpose. One day he kept the dinner waiting till four o'clock and was much tired, but yet dissatisfied with what he had done. When they went out walking together he must still be trying to polish his verses, he could not stop working even if he wished. So it went on for a fortnight or more. William wore himself out, and her too, with labour, altering and refitting. She copied his rough drafts for him again and again, they were both tired to death. It could not continue. She saw that she would have to deliver him from his prison of silence and at last she found words.

It was at the closing in of a hard bright day of frost, in the middle of February. She heard a cart pass the door and at the same time the dismal sound of a crying infant. She went to the window, and had light enough to see that a man was driving a cart, which seemed not to be very full. A woman with an infant in her arms was following behind and a dog close to her. It was a wild and melancholy sight. She stood a long while at the window looking after them down the snowy road and pitying their poverty, until William called her back with his harsh voice, saying that he wanted to go on with his poem. So they lit the candles and sat a long time with the windows unclosed on the wild moonlit night. They almost finished writing *The Pedlar*; but William came to some ugly place, found it uninteresting and must have it altered. He could not be satisfied; he walked up and down like a beast in a cage on the stone floor, muttering his sing-song lines to himself, saying, "Try this," and "Try that" and "No use," until she was distracted. At last she dropped her pen and said, "I cannot go on any longer."

He stopped in his tracks and stared at her, as if he could not understand what she said. Then he passed the back of his hand across his forehead and looked at it as if he feared to see some stain there and muttered, "What was I saying? How did that last line go? It has got to be finished, I cannot leave it. Read me what you have there." She pushed her papers from her and rose, with her hands on the small folding mahogany desk. She insisted, "I cannot go on any longer, nor can you. It is no use. You are killing yourself and me too, all to no purpose. You are spoiling the poem with working it over. You must let it lie for a time." He stood in the middle of the floor, gaping at her stupidly and said, "I can't stop . . . I can't stop . . ." over and over again, as if he were going out of his mind.

She went to him then, took him by the arm and led him to his own old wooden chair by the fireside. She made him sit down, knelt beside him and fixed her wild light eyes upon him steadily, trying to read his soul. He could not sustain that passionately loving gaze. His eyes fell and glanced sideways, then he turned his head away as a captive animal does when it is stared at. She said, "You have been working night and day since we came back from Eusemere, you cannot rest or sleep, you are almost out of your mind. It is because you will not let yourself look into your own heart. It is because you dare not admit that you are thinking all the time of Mary."

He sat huddled in his chair, looking at the ground, for so long that she thought he had not understood what she said; then he groaned, "Mary," in a voice so harsh and tormented that she would not have known it. She urged him softly and eagerly, "You love her, William," and felt as if she were driving a knife into her own heart, but he only twisted his hands together and muttered, "I have had too much of that. I could not endure such misery a second time. When I left Annette I swore that I would never love again." He leant his head on his hand, so that she could not see his face; from behind that screen she heard him say, "Once in a lifetime is enough for me to break my heart."

She was very much troubled; she protested, "But Mary is not like Annette." He uttered a dreary laugh and said, "All women are alike, except yourself. I want nobody but you about me. I cannot do with any other. You do not mean to marry and leave me, do you?" And he dropped his hand and stared at her with a strange devouring look, which frightened her, but she answered him steadily, "I shall not marry." He nodded once or twice, mournfully, and sighed, "You and I are not very cunning in love, are we? I think we were not meant to be happy." His tone was so wretched that it brought the tears to her eyes; but she persisted, "You would not be unhappy with Mary. She loves you dearly, she has loved you all her life, I believe." He said, "I am afraid that is true," and afterwards dropped out, "Poor fool," in a hollow brooding tone which chilled her. It was strange to find herself urging upon William the very thing that she had fancied she dreaded most; yet she persisted, "Sometimes I think that Mary is wiser than either of us," and added, to herself rather than to William, "She knows how to endure life, and we do not."

He said, after a pause, "I have thought that too. I have fancied that I should be glad to see her in this house, moving quietly about, making her home with us, lending me her strength and her peace, bearing and bringing up my children." He confessed, "I wrote to Annette lately; I asked her whether she still thought me bound to her. I said I must know whether she wished to see me, if peace should come this year, as they say it will. I told her I had long ceased to love her." He put his hand to his brow and said confusedly, "I am half out of my mind with trouble. Sometimes I think that only Mary can save me, but then I remember you and I cannot go on." She turned very pale, but she did not flinch, only stammered a very little as she said, "You m-must not think of me." He took her hand in his strong bony fingers. They trembled very much as he said, with his face close to hers, "I shall never love any woman as I love you." Her heart was beating so hard and fast that she could scarcely breathe, but she put her arms about him, fumblingly, and drew his head to her shoulder. He clung to her and murmured, "You'll never leave me." And she sighed, "No, never, never"; and found his lips with hers, but afterwards she drew back and, took his face between her hands and said to him, quite steadily, "Mary would not part us. Indeed you must marry Mary. I love you and I tell you to do it. Some day you will thank me." He gazed at her forlornly, like a child, then bowed his head on her breast. She put her arms about him and comforted him.

3

Next day the snow began to melt and run, though a little fell in the early morning. The February sun shone, the frozen snowdrops and hepaticas in the orchard lifted their heads again; and though there was a hard frost in the night the third day was fine and sunny. It was Sunday and William went walking in the orchard after breakfast, while she copied some alterations into the *Pedlar* poems. After half an hour he came in, looking quite wild and strange, and said that he would ride over to Penrith to see Mary. She was afraid to say anything that might turn him from this purpose. She sent old Molly off to hire a horse for him and worked hard to get the writing finished. She wrote a note for him to take to Mrs. Clarkson, for he must spend the night at Eusemere, and put up some letters for Mary; and off William went in his blue spencer and a pair of new pantaloons fresh from London. He turned the cottage upside down before they got him off. She could have cried over the fuss he made, he was like a child going to a party. Old Molly knew well enough that he was going courting, she laughed and nodded her kindly witch's head and said that was right enough for St. Valentine's Day.

After he was gone Dorothy set the house in order and read to quiet her mind. Before sunset she put on her shawl and walked out. The snow-covered mountains were bright in the rich sunlight; she walked as far as the gate which they called the Wishing Gate, and when she came in view of Rydal she cast a long look upon the mountains beyond. They were very white, but she concluded that her brother would have a safe passage over Kirkstone and she was quite easy about him.

After dinner, a little before sunset, she walked by the lake and met a train of carts, some tinkers travelling the roads. She stood to watch them up the hill. The carter was cheering his horses and talking to a little lass, about ten years of age, who seemed to make him her companion. She ran to the wall and took up a large stone to scotch the wheel of the cart and ran on before with it in her arms to be ready for him. This light and gay little creature seemed all pleasure in her own activity and the man looked at her as if he too were pleased, and spoke to her in the same tone in which he spoke to his horses. Her mother followed the last cart with a lovely child, perhaps a year old, at her back and a good-looking girl about fifteen years old walked beside her. They were all wild creatures of the road, travellers from birth, wanting neither food nor clothes, but pleased to wander; Dorothy could have found it in her sore heart to envy them their careless freedom. She went home alone to her empty cottage, read German till nine o'clock, wrote a letter to her friend, and went to bed; but she slept badly, for her thoughts were full of William.

Next day it snowed again and was terribly cold; when she went out she was obliged to run all the way to the foot of White Moss, to get the least bit of warmth into her.

When she came back she found a letter from her friend, and one from Annette, round which she prowled like a hungry cat, longing, yet not daring to open it. She wrote part of a letter to Coleridge. William had confessed that he had begged their friend to advise him and she too felt that nothing could help her so much as that dear company. She went to bed but slept badly; she was always thinking what could be doing at Penrith between Mary and William. She spent the next day ironing linen, having persuaded herself not to expect William for fear of being disappointed; but he came in at tea-time, just as she had closed the shutters, brightened the fire and put the kettle on and she could tell at once, from his closed and wretched look, that he had no good news for her. It came out after a time that he had only seen Mary for a couple of hours, between Eamont Bridge, he said, and Hartshorn Tree. He told her, "We walked up and down," and said, "Mary looked well and sent you her dear love"; but when she burst out, "Did you not speak to her?" he turned his face away and muttered, "I could not bring myself to it." So all was to do over again.

They passed a second uncertain week, William was tormented by indecision. He read her the letter from Annette. It was one of her long rambling scrawls and spoke tenderly of the past, but the Frenchwoman told him clearly that she did not hold him bound to her. She had made a life of her own and it was plain that William had no place in it. There was a scribble at the end from the little girl, Caroline, which affected Dorothy very much. William answered the letter within two days and sent it off by Fletcher the carrier. He did not show it to Dorothy, but he told her that he had promised, if peace should be declared, to go over to France and see Annette and her child once more, whatever else happened to him. It was wet spring weather and the nights were wild with wind and rain, there was still snow unmelted on the tops of the black mountains and the vale was loud with streams. William could settle to nothing. Dorothy was so unlucky as to propose, on the first fine day of March, that she should re-copy *The Pedlar*. William got to work and was worn to death; they did not walk out and she wrote all afternoon. She was thankful when he decided to ride over next day and visit the Calverts at Windy Brow.

These were old friends; she and William had stayed at the farm, with its lovely view over Keswick, when he first came back from France. It was the earliest place in which they two had lived together; and it was the younger brother, Railsey Calvert, William's college friend, the consumptive boy, who had left William that small legacy on which they now made ends meet. William was always glad to spend a few days at Windy Brow and she was glad to have him go, hoping that the change might distract his restless thoughts.

4

He rode away at half-past eleven on a bright morning, the fourth of March, 1802. She spent the morning putting the drawers into order, laying by his clothes, which he had, as always, thrown here, there and everywhere; then filed two months' newspapers and dined, as women do when the man of the house is away, on two boiled eggs and two apple tarts which were left in the larder. When she found one of William's bitten apples she had not the heart to throw it away; she stood with it in her hand, sighing and smiling, it seemed to bring him back to her. She set old Molly to dust and sweep and afterwards to clean the garden a little. She herself transplanted some snowdrops. The bees were busy and the sun was shining. She was determined that she would be busy, so as to look well, and be well, when he came back to her. After tea she walked round the two lakes, crossing the stepping-stones by Rydal foot and sat down where they two always sat; her thoughts were full of William. When she saw the new moon over Silver How, like a gold ring snapped in two and shaven off at the ends, with the old moon within it, she wished for a blessing upon her brother.

She was alone four days and did her best to be cheerful. William came back on the Sunday, earlier than she had expected and immediately she saw a happy change in him. It was evident that the ride and change of scene, or some turn of the tides within him had cast him into a fit of versing. He sat down in the sweet glittering weather which had followed the rain and snow and finished his last alterations to *The Pedlar*; and when that wretched millstone was at last off his neck he fell upon a lyric which he first called *The Singing Bird*, but afterwards the *Sailor's Mother*. He had found the subject for himself, in an old woman, as tall and straight as a Roman matron, who had begged from him on the road that winter. She had sheltered under her cloak a caged linnet; it had been the pet of her sailor son and he had been drowned at sea. William finished the poem in two days and made his sister cry for the sad mother and the bird.

After that he cast into verse a little story told her by a kind neighbour and noted down for William in her journal. This neighbour had been riding in a post-chaise on a wet and windy night and heard a strange crying which he could not understand. He stopped the chaise and found a little girl sitting behind, crying as if her heart would break. Her cloak had been caught by the wheel and torn to rags and she had no other. It was the greatest sorrow that could befall her. He took her into the chaise and comforted her; her name was Alice Fell, she had no parents and belonged to the next town. It was a simple story, which ended like a fairy-tale in the nicest way possible with a new cloak of duffel grey for the orphan, as warm a cloak as man could sell. William was so delighted with this that his sister ventured to bring out for him another story which she had set down for him two years earlier, when he and John were at Gallow Hill, of a tall brown beggar woman, "tall beyond the measure of tall women" and her naughty ragged boys. Dorothy had seen the pair of them chasing a butterfly. One had a wreath of yellow flowers in his hat, the other, whose hat was but a rimless crown, had stuck it round with laurel leaves. They had whined and begged from her with a delightful impudence which she had never forgotten. She fetched down her old journal to read her account of them to William and at first it seemed an unlucky thing that she did so, for he could not escape from those very words, and so he could not write the poem. He left it unfinished and went tired to bed, though in their walk from Rydal he had got warmed with the subject and had half cast the poem.

Next morning, however, he was fresh and happy again. It was a fine Sunday and he shouted out to her from his bedroom upstairs, before he had done dressing, that he had finished the beggar boys. While they were at breakfast he wrote the poem *To a Butterfly*. He ate not a morsel, but sat with his shirt neck unbuttoned and his waistcoat open while he did it. The thought first came upon him as they were talking about the pleasure they both always felt at the sight of a butterfly. She told him that she used to chase them a little, but that she was afraid of brushing the dust off their wings, and did not catch them. He told her how he used to kill all the white ones when he went to school, because they were Frenchmen. She wrote it down and the other poems and read them over to him and they talked of summer days when they were young, "Sweet childish days," said William, "that were as long as twenty days are now." She had not seen him so happy or so much at peace, all that year. She told him that, but he only laughed quietly and said that he had seen the new moon, too, at Keswick. He had turned his money and wished and that must have brought him luck. She felt that before that moon had waned his life might have turned into its new channel, and she was able to endure the thought.

All that week they were waiting for their friend Coleridge, who was travelling to them from London. He had promised to visit them on his way to his own home, because he knew the trouble and uncertainty in which they had been; she could not but feel that when he came everything would go right. They had not seen him for months and she could have no peace until he came. William seemed happy but weary; after his furious fit of verse-making it was natural for him to be a little idle and she let him alone. It was sweet fine weather, he could walk in the orchard every morning and repeat verses to himself. When she had done the work of the house she went out to him and they walked backwards and forwards in the orchard till dinner-time. In the afternoon they sat under the trees and she would read to him until he fell asleep in that budding grove. She could walk by herself along the shore of the lake with quiet thoughts, in that twilit hour when the lake and the hills were still, the owls had not begun to hoot, and the little birds had given over singing. One night she saw the moon, far distant in the sky, the moon of her wish; with two stars beside it, that twinkled in and out and seemed like butterflies for motion and lightness, they looked to be far nearer than the moon. On the next night she saw a red light upon Silver How, a light of most strange birth, as if the hill burnt with a fire of its own. She was going on when she saw the shape of her beloved in the road at a little distance. They turned back to see the light, but it was fading and almost gone. The owls hooted when they sat on the wall at the foot of White Moss; the sky broke more and more and they saw the moon now and then, the vale looked fair and quiet in the moonshine. There were huge slow-travelling clouds in the sky, which threw large masses of shade upon the mountains. They walked backwards and forwards in the road till she was tired. William kindled and began to write his poem. They carried cloaks into the orchard and sat a while there. She left him and he nearly finished the poem. She was tired to death and went to bed before him. He came down to her and read the poem to her in bed. It was called the *Emigrant Mother*.

So passed that week of spring weather, but their friend did not come to share it with them. They knew that he was on his way to them from London and might walk in at any moment, but on the Friday it rained so dreadfully that they did not expect him or wish for him. She went up the lane to collect a few green mosses to make the chimney gay and came back dripping wet, saying to William, "He will never come to-day. If he is at the inn at Ambleside he will stay there until the rain is over." William agreed; but as they were sitting by the fire together in the dusk there came a knock upon the door and suddenly he was with them, looking like a drowned man come from the sea. He was wrapped in a sodden cloak and his black hair was streaked on his forehead. His eyes were swollen with the wind and he stared at them as if he were half-stupefied. She was quite terrified by the sight of him.

She sprang to her feet and cried out his name; then she ran to pull off his steaming cloak and thrust him to the fire. She knelt at his feet and tugged off his wet riding-boots as she often did for William; then felt him all over with her eager hands and sighed, "Oh! you are ill; you are shaking from head to foot." He groaned, "Yes, I am ill; I am very ill," in a hollow tone which struck her to the heart. Then he leaned his head on his hand and seemed not to understand where he was. She glanced, terrified, from him to William, but her brother only looked strange and troubled, he did not give her any help. She had to think of what to do for herself. She packed William off up the road for brandy from the inn, for they kept none in the house; she filled the kettle, put it on the fire and made William get out dry clothes and blankets. Presently they had their friend sitting in a daze by the fire, sipping hot grog made sailor-fashion, turning the glass about in his hands and staring round the room with eyes which scarcely knew them. It made her heart ache to look at him. He drank and sighed and drank again; then gave the two of them a dreadful bewildered stare, like a sick animal, put his hand to his head and asked them, "How did I come here?"

She knelt before him and urged in her soft stammering voice, "Do you not remember? You came down by the coach from London, you are going home to Keswick; this is Grasmere and you shall stay with us till you are fit to travel again. We will take care of you." He seemed unable to take in more than a sentence or two. He repeated, "Home," and "London," in a slow wandering voice as if the words meant nothing to him and then he said, in a voice which pierced her heart, "I should never have gone to London. I am not the man I was when I went away." He sank his head on his breast and a stupor overcame him. She rescued the glass from his nerveless hand and gazed up imploringly at William. Her brother said glumly, "We had best put him to bed, he should not sit here, but I do not know how we shall get him up the stairs." She said that they would put him in her bed, because her room opened out of the parlour where they were sitting. So they got him there, wrapped him up in blankets and carried in shovels of hot coals from the parlour to make a fire in the basket-grate.

They left the door between open, so as to let the warmth of the parlour flow into the bedroom and they themselves sat up till four o'clock, talking quietly together and listening for a call from him, but there was never a sound. He slept as heavily as a drunken man, snoring in his blanket. William said, "It is not that he has been drinking. It is this cursed Kendal Black Drop again, he is stupefied with it"; and when his sister stared, affrighted, looked down and said heavily, "Did you not know he was an opium-eater? I have known it for a long time. John spoke of it to me when he was at home, he has seen it in the Eastern ports. He said that he could tell what was afoot as soon as he touched the poor fellow's hand and looked at his eyes. He said black men could eat opium all their lives long and get little harm from it, but white men could not take it safely. We talked of whether he could be cured or not; John thought it was too late. He has been taking the cursed stuff ever since those wet winters he had at Nether Stowey. He got into the way of dosing himself with it because it helped the pains of his rheumatism. Do you not remember how he came to us one night from Porlock, and read us his poem of *Khubla Khan*? Why, he had it on him then. Did you not see it?" She said, "No, I did not see it; I never knew. I have heard him speak of the Black Drop, but I fancied it was just some doctor's stuff that he used when he needed it. You know he is always dosing himself for any of his aches and pains." William stared gloomily at the fire and said, "It is more than that now. I greatly fear he will never escape from it. This is why his wife did not wish him to go to London; she knew he would take to it again once he was out of her way. Poor woman, she is much to be pitied. She has done her best to cure him, but she is so light and weak, that he does not listen to her. She will see a sad change in him when she gets him home again." Dorothy was very much agitated; she cried out, "Oh, God! what can we do to save him?" but her brother had little comfort to give. His face was set in its heaviest and most forbidding lines as he said, "I think he is past any help from us."

5

Next morning, when they awoke, the whole vale was covered with snow and it was wretchedly cold. Their friend spent two days with them, shivering and sitting by the fire, or lying late abed. He talked of little but his own bodily miseries, his pains and headaches. He was very low in his spirits and this saddened them both. He would not give them any advice, for he said, "A poet makes a good lover, but a bad husband; we do better single, I believe. The fire in us will not warm a hearth. I did not marry my first love, though I ran away from college for her sake, and went for a soldier and fancied my heart was broken; but I dare say she would have wearied me in the end, as my poor Sara has done. A man who marries for love is like a frog that jumps into a well; he has plenty of water there, but then he cannot get out, and so your brother will find." He put out all this with a most melancholy smile, less cynical than utterly miserable. He wrung William's hand at parting and said, "I wish you luck with your Mary; she is a good creature"; then rode away up the valley towards Keswick and his wretched home.

After he had gone William was very sad and she had to put aside her own feelings in order to cheer him. They talked over their plans, reread Annette's letters and made many desperate calculations. While Lord Lonsdale's debts to their father remained unpaid William did not know how he could support a wife. He said that they might go and live at Gallow Hill, but to that his sister would not agree. She reminded him that Mary had a little money of her own; she said hopefully, "Lord Lonsdale cannot live for ever." They wrote many letters; to brother Richard, who mismanaged the family affairs, to Mary, to Sara and to Coleridge; they resolved to see Annette, and that William should go to Mary. Once he had taken this decision William seemed easier in his mind. He sat all one mild morning working at a poem about a cuckoo. He had just heard that blithe new-comer's wandering voice in the orchard, for the first time that year, and its double call had chimed in with his singing mood. The fire of spring and poetry was still burning brightly in him. His sister sewed beside him as he worked, or studied her German book; at the closing-in of the day they walked backwards and forwards in the orchard and he repeated the finished poem. In the evening they sat together with their books by the hearth; the fire flickered and the clock ticked, she heard nothing save the breathing of her beloved as he now and then pushed his book forward and turned over a leaf.

6

On the Sunday they started for Keswick in the rain and arrived wet to the skin. Mrs. Coleridge flung up her hands at the sight of them. She had got her husband in a chair by the fire, very sorry for himself because of a neuralgic headache, and she was clucking over him in her most possessive fashion, saying that he had taken no care of himself in London. He let her bustle him about as she chose and seemed quite under her thumb. Dorothy hated to see him in such close captivity.

They stayed three days in Keswick. Dorothy did a thing that she had always wanted to do and went to a Quaker meeting. Her friend had told her how, for many years, there being no congregation of Friends in Keswick, a single old Quaker woman used to go regularly every Lord's Day to perform her worship alone in the tiny meeting-house among the fir-trees in the spacious vale, under the great mountain of Skiddaw. This enchanted Dorothy, but Mrs. Coleridge laughed at the story when her husband related it. She said, "Yes, they went and sat there and nobody ever said anything; until at last they all died and so they gave it up." She laughed her high shrill nervous laugh and ran on, "The Quakers are very dreary people. I cannot think what you will do at the Clarksons' while your brother is gone into Yorkshire. I am sure you will be very dull there. Nobody is so stupid as Mr. Clarkson, he can talk of nothing but the blacks in Barbadoes, and I cannot see that Mrs. Clarkson is so pretty as they say. For my part I think her a very silly forward woman. I do not know why your brother does not take you with him." She did not like Catherine Clarkson, because her husband admired the little woman and had once incautiously declared that he wished she had been his sister; and she was wild to know what errand William had in Yorkshire that could not be talked about, but William would not have her told of it.

Dorothy, for her part, was glad enough to be with the kind Clarksons at such a time. William left her at Eusemere, and on his thirty-second birthday, April the seventh, 1802, he set out for Middleham, where his Mary was staying. His sister walked six miles of the road with him and they parted with a long kiss. The Clarksons knew well enough what his errand was and approved it. Catherine Clarkson hung about Dorothy in a loving flutter, eager but afraid to speak of the matter. Mr. Clarkson said in his solemn fashion, "The Lord will show your brother what he should do." She knew that they meant well by her, but even their affection teased her. She hardly knew how she could endure her days and nights, while she waited for news from William.

When she had been there five days she could sit still no longer. She started out late one afternoon for Yanwath, went to Thomas Wilkinson's house and begged him urgently to send into Penrith for any letter there might be. She made up some lame excuse for her impatience, saying that it was a matter of family business. The kind Quaker fellow sent off a messenger immediately and he and his sister gave her tea and sat with her by the fire. They were obviously very curious to find out why she was so agitated, but she could not bear to tell them. She did not know how she got through the time, until the messenger came back. There was a letter for her. It had come that very afternoon by coach and she opened it with her trembling hands. Her heart was beating so fast that it choked her, she could hardly see for a moment; then her eyes cleared and she was able to make out part of what it said. Mary and William had written it together and that told everything. They had made up the match; the wedding was to be in the autumn, she was to live with them always and be their dear sister.

She must have turned as pale as a sheet, for Thomas Wilkinson took her by the arm and made her sit down. His sister was for taking the letter from her failing hand, but she snatched it back and put it in her bosom. She stammered something, she knew not what, and got to her feet; she said she must go back to Eusemere. They looked at each other and tried to restrain her. Miss Wilkinson urged that she was not fit for the walk and when she persisted her brother said that at least he would go with her as far as Barton. There was snow upon the ground, a late April fall, and it was a sharp windy night. He questioned her like a catechiser all the way and every question was like the snapping of a little thread about her heart, but she was so full of thoughts, of her half-read letter and the future that she scarcely heard what he said. She was thankful when he turned back and left her. Then she had time to look at the moon and think her own thoughts of William. The moon travelled through the clouds, tinging them yellow as she passed along, with two stars near her, one larger than the other. These stars grew and diminished as they passed from, or went into, the clouds. She thought that they were like herself and Mary.

William came back next day, before she had dared to look for him. She had been walking all by herself, as lonely as a cloud, along the shore of the quiet slate-coloured lake, among the dark hills, thinking only of him. When she approached the house one of the servants met her to tell her he was come. She screamed and ran forward; then recollected herself and told the maid to go on before and tell him that she was coming. In her heart she hoped that he would set out to meet her; but the girl was stupid and did not deliver the message, so she had to go on and meet him in the parlour, under the eyes of the Clarksons. She flew to him, in spite of them, flung her arms about him and hid her face on his breast. Then she held him off and gazed at him, as if she feared some change in him, but he looked just as he always did, only fatigued with his long ride, and his face caught and reddened by the wind. He said in her ear, "My dear, dear sister" . . . but no more. Mrs. Clarkson came up and kissed them both and cried a little, in her pretty loving way; Mr. Clarkson said, solemnly, that this was blessed news. They two were so happily married that they wished all their friends to follow their example.

They would not let William go until he had taken time to recover from his ride, so that Dorothy did not get him away until the second day after his return. They set out after their midday dinner and Mrs. Clarkson went a short way with them, but the fragile creature could not stand against the wild April gale which was blowing, she had to turn back at the foot of Dunmallet. The wind was so furious that it took their breath away. They could hardly battle against it themselves and they rested wherever they found a shelter. There were high waves running on the lake, and it was roaring like the sea.

When they were in the woods beyond Gowbarrow Park they saw a few daffodils close to the waterside. They fancied that the lake had floated the seeds ashore and that the little colony had so grown up. But as they went along there were more and yet more; and at last, under the boughs of the trees, they saw that there was a long belt of them along the shore, about the breadth of a country road. She had never seen daffodils so beautiful. They grew among the mossy stones about and above them; some rested their heads upon these stones, as on a pillow, for weariness; and the rest tossed and reeled and danced and seemed as if they verily laughed with the wind that blew upon them over the lake; they looked so gay, ever dancing, ever changing. The wind blew directly over the lake to them. There was here and there a little knot, and a few stragglers higher up; but they were so few as not to disturb the simplicity, unity and life, of that one busy highway. She stood with her hand on William's arm and looked at the daffodils for a long time; she knew that all her life her heart would fill with pleasure when she thought of them dancing beside the stormy water.

They reached Patterdale in the twilight, in heavy rain; they were both wet through and she feared that she had ruined the new cashmere shawl which Joanna Hutchinson had lent her. The landlady at the inn looked sour at such bedraggled travellers, but a young woman staying in the house lent Dorothy dry clothes while her own were being dried in the kitchen. She came down to William and said gaily, "That stranger has made a smart lady of me; it is more than Mrs. Coleridge would do for her own sister," a flash of an old resentment which made William grin. They spent the evening sitting by a bright fire, had a good supper, talked lovingly of Mary and went to bed. In the morning when she opened her curtains the sun shone, the wind had passed away, the hills looked cheerful and the river was very bright as it flowed into the lake.

It was Good Friday morning and they set forward up the vale to Brothers Water about half-past ten. She had never travelled that way before and everything pleased her. It was a happy day; they sauntered and rested, lounged and were lazy and loved all that they saw. William sat on the bridge at the foot of Brothers Water, while she walked forward along the shore of the lake. When she came back he had begun to make up a little jingling rhyme for her sake out of the sweet sights and sounds about him in the bright March weather, the gentle flowing of the stream, the glittering lively lake under the young sun, a dog barking, cocks crowing, birds twittering, and the grazing cattle, forty feeding like one, in the flat pasture behind him. He was very happy that day, it was young man's weather and he was in a singing mood. She could not but rejoice with him.

They dined at the foot of Kirkstone on some pies which the Clarksons' cook had baked for them and then climbed up over the great pass, where the streams among the rocks were all alive and running, and the dried yellow winter grass was blowing in the wind on the enormous shoulders of the hills. They rested at the top and sat looking over the wide prospect to the south, then went down into Ambleside. The vale looked green and very beautiful in its own evening brightness. It was half-moonlight, half-twilight, before they reached their own door; no fireside, they said, was like their own and soon Mary would come to share it with them.

Next morning she was wearied out, utterly drained of feeling, but at peace. It was a mild warm rainy day to suit her mood. They sat in the garden all the morning, William dug a little and she transplanted a honeysuckle. It was so still that the sheep on the island were reflected in the water. They were idly pleased by the sight of a robin chasing a scarlet butterfly. William said that he would put it into a little poem for his sister and then he told her, in his shy harsh fashion, that he had written another for her while he was away, a poem about a glow-worm. He repeated it to her, calling her his love. She was very much moved and said with tears in her eyes, "But that was the glow-worm you brought to me at Racedown. I did not know that you remembered it still."

He smiled very sweetly, assuring her, "I have never forgotten it. Whenever I chance to see a glow-worm I remember your pleasure in that one. You were like a child over it, you had never seen one before. I was riding between Middleham and Barnard Castle, by myself on Monday night, after I had parted from Mary, thinking of you and then I remembered the glow-worm and cast it into verse." She said, "And I was walking between Barton and Eusemere, looking at the moon with two stars near her, and thinking of you." It gave her a strong thrill of mingled pride and anguish to find that she had been remembered at that hour, when all her brother's thoughts must have been full of his own happy future. She found that she could not utter her troubled mind, but she looked down and murmured, "It is a lovely poem." William said with his usual simple interest in what concerned himself, "I began it coming to a well, or trough, which there is in Lord Darlington's park; I was interrupted in going through the town of Staindrop and finished it about two and a half miles beyond. I did not feel the jogging of my horse while I was writing; but when I had done my hands were so cold that I could not feel them in my gloves and I let my horse down. Still, there was no harm done and that is how I came to write the poem. You can put down the time and place in that journal of yours, Monday, the twelfth of April, 1802"; and so recorded it stands.

7

The next day was Easter Sunday, a mild grey morning with rising vapours. They sat in the orchard and William wrote out his poem on *The Robin and the Butterfly*. On the Wednesday after their friend came to the door, to know how William had sped. She sprang up and startled him with her cry of welcome. He was sad and quiet, she and William knew that he could not but feel the contrast between William's rising hopes and his own declining fire. He brought them some most melancholy verses which he had written to Sara Hutchinson. They three sat out in the orchard, on the morning after his appearance, under the flowering branches, but there was a sad weight on all their spirits. They talked of other springs, when their hearts had been light as the skies above them. Dorothy said, "I do not think the spring here is as gay as it was in the south, at Alfoxden or at Racedown," and her friend sighed, "I believe the spring is nowhere so lovely now as it used to be when I was young. I am certain that the primroses in the woods, at Ottery St. Mary, when I was a boy, were larger and sweeter than any I see here"; and then he said, smiling mournfully, "Perhaps it is because I am beginning to grow old."

William lay at their feet, sprawling on the ground, and crushing the daffodils, in the sunshiny shade, frowning up through the clotted pink and white apple-blossom. He said heavily, "The spring is lovely still, but I cannot rejoice in it as I did once. There was a glory and a dream, but it is gone and I cannot find it again. There was a time . . ." He broke off and they waited for him to speak again, but he seemed unable to find the words he needed; and their friend assented with a dreary passion, "Yes, the change is in ourselves. I feel it continually, a dreadful dejection, a dull grief that stifles me. There is a weight *here* which nothing can relieve." He put his hand to his breast, as if some physical oppression choked him and complained, "Oh! I am sick, sick to the heart, my life is withering away. I had a fire in my heart once, but it has burnt down and choked itself with ashes. Nothing pleases me now. Last night, at sunset, I went out and stared at the sky; there was a green light that lingered in the west and the crescent moon was sailing above it. I gazed upon it and saw that it was beautiful, but I felt nothing; not even a regret for the days when it would have delighted me. It moved me no more than if I had been a dead man." She could not bear to listen to his sad voice and meet his changed and melancholy glance; she was in miserable spirits. The sunshine, the green fields and the fair sky made her sadder; even the little happy sporting lambs, running races by twos and threes, seemed but sorrowful to her, while her friend was so ill and so wretched.

They did what they could to cheer him; they walked daily together about the flowering vale, in the mild weather after the rain. William at least was in good spirits, she had not seen him so gay since John left them. He dragged them up into Easedale, to fling stones into the roaring river and hear the *stunning* of the swollen falls; this was a country word which always greatly pleased him. On another day they must climb up to the rocky seat under the brier-bush on the face of the precipice called Nab Scar and sit there while he read out the poems which he lately had made, about the broom and the eglantine. They sat in the sun and were lazy, looking down upon Rydal, alive and glittering, and their own dear little round lake of Grasmere with the river flowing out of it, full of delicate purple and yellow reflections, like Derbyshire spar.

They were so high up that they could look across to the Coniston Fells, with the shadow of the clouds moving upon them; she thought that they were not like man's hills, but belonged to themselves, to the sky and the clouds and a few wild creatures. Their friend went to search for something new. They saw him climbing up towards a rock. He called them and they found him in a bower, the sweetest that ever was seen, under a high rock, with ivy hanging loosely about it in bunches of brown berries. There were ash trees, hollies and yews about this bower and a carpet of moss underfoot; and a little higher yet was a parlour among the rocks, so small that only one person could sit in it. They resolved to take roots of flowers and plant them in both these places. It was a happy blessed day, such as these three friends could still make for themselves when they were alone together. But next day the valley was blotted out with rain. They could only walk a little way towards Rydal in the evening, childishly stopping to dam up the little tunnel by the roadside and make a lake; and on the following morning their friend drove away from them to his own home. She and William spent the morning in the orchard, reading the *Epithalamium* of Spenser, walking backwards and forwards. She kept her hand in her brother's arm and thought that next year Mary and he would be walking under these trees together, a happy man and wife.

The valley had never been so beautiful as it was that spring. All through May and June the days dropped away, one by one, exquisitely lovely, like petals falling from the pink and white appleblossom. Each day was marked for her in her journal by its own symbol of bird or flower. William and she were always together, because their time was so short; he did not want any company but hers and had never been so tender or so loving. One day they went to John's Grove, and sat a while under the fir trees; then William lay, and she lay, in the trench under the fence, he with his eyes shut and listening to the waterfalls and the birds. There was no one waterfall above another, it was a sound of waters in the air, the voice of the air. William heard her breathing and rustling now and then, but they both lay still and unseen by one another. He said dreamily that it would be sweet thus to lie in the grave, to hear the peaceful sounds of the earth, and just to know that one's dear friends were near.

They used to sit in the orchard every day, in the long hot May mornings, listening to the cuckoo calling, the lambs bleating, the small birds singing, rooks cawing, hens cackling, Thomas Ashburner's axe going quietly, and old women talking at their cottage doors. Often in the afternoon they would carry a fur cloak and spread it out upon the ground, in the rocky pasture called the Hollins, where William could sleep undisturbed beneath a holly tree, while she watched beside him. Often they stayed there until the light of day was going and the landscape fading, the little birds had begun to settle their singing and the sheep and lambs were quiet among the rocks; but there was always one thrush, not far off, which seemed to sing louder and clearer at that hour than the other thrushes had sung when it was day.

Once they spent a cloudless May day by Wythburn water, in a place which now lies drowned in the bed of Thirlmere. Their friend Coleridge had walked over from Keswick to meet them and crossed the beck when he saw them coming. They went up to the waterfall, in its own glorious wild solitude under its lofty purple crag. There was a bird flying round and round above it, transparent and fluttering, like a moth in the sunshine. She and William climbed up out of the bed of the stream above the fall, but looked in vain for any other shade; there was none in all that wide valley and the hills slept in the burning sun. So they came down again into the ghyll and rested upon a moss-covered rock rising out of the bed of the river. There they lay, ate their dinner and drank the cold peaty water, laced with brandy; the two men repeated and read verses all through the long happy silent afternoon. It was as quiet as if they were in heaven. They drank tea at a farmhouse and parted beside the *Rock of the Names*, where they had all carved their initials in that first happy summer. William took his friend's penknife and cut at one or two of the lichened marks to make them plainer. They sat on the wall for a little time afterwards, seeing the sun go down and the reflections in the still water; then their friend parted from them cheerfully and went over the brook, hopping upon the side stones. The brother and sister went home lazily, resting often, always upon the bridges, looking at the crescent moon with the old moon in her arm. She could have wished that such a day might last for ever. They got home at ten o'clock and William went to bed soon, tired out and drugged with fresh spring airs. She repeated poetry to him when he was in bed, *This is the spot*, and *The Lover's Complaint*, and such simple verses, to help him to sleep; he was soothed and presently she left him.

He had many white nights about that time, because he was working very hard at his spring poems, the *Celandine* and the *Tinker*, the *Rainbow* and *Children gathering Flowers*, besides the first part of his great ode on Immortality, which he had begun after the morning when they sat with their friend in the orchard. He wearied himself to death sometimes over these and other poems, hammering away at a passage, altering and recopying it till his sister grew sick at heart. He tired himself and her. She tried to distract him from his writing with simple cunning, persuading him to dig in the garden, clean out the well, sow flowers and scarlet beans and make a bower in the orchard, so that everything might look beautiful for Mary when she came. All these plans kept him out of doors and away from his work while the sun shone; but when evening came he could not keep from working and when he went to bed thinking about a poem he could not sleep. She heard him continually pacing up and down overhead, hour after hour; it robbed her of her own sleep and she lay awake, thinking of the past and the future. One night his walking went on till past three. She could bear it no longer; she groped for the tinderbox, struck a light, and carried her glimmering candle up the stairs to his room. He opened to her knock and stood before her, not yet undressed, with his waistcoat unbuttoned and his shirt open at the neck, looking haggard and wild; the candle light glittered in his eyes.

She said, "My darling, it is almost four o'clock. What is the matter? What keeps you walking the floor all night long?" She went in, shut the door and set her candle on a chair. He turned from her and sat down on the edge of the bed. He put his hands to his head as if it ached intolerably and complained, "I cannot sleep, I tell you I cannot sleep. For three nights now I have been walking the floor. I shall go out of my senses."

She sat down beside him, drew his head to her shoulder and made a pillow for it. After a moment or two he turned and buried his face in her breast. She heard him groan as if his heart would break. She soothed him with her hands and murmured, "You are working too hard. You will wear yourself out. I cannot bear to see it."

He raised his head and began to babble despairingly, "I cannot stop thinking. The words go round and round in my head like a mill wheel. I've counted sheep going through a gate till I was tired. I've thought of the sound of rain and bees murmuring and water falling; I've thought of smooth fields, white sheets of water and pure sky, by turns; but it was all useless. Soon the birds will begin singing in the orchard and I shall hear the cuckoo calling. That bird will drive me out of my mind." He rubbed his aching forehead distractedly. He sounded as cross and peevish as a tired child, and she scolded him like a young mother. "You cannot go on so. You must lie down and cover yourself up; shut your eyes and let me read you to sleep." She had often done so before and she knew just the tone which habit might force him to obey. He sat still beside her for a moment, fighting her will; then he yielded, shivered all over and said meekly, "Very well, if you still stay with me."

She wasted no time, but laid him on the bed as he was and drew his harsh brown blankets over him; then sat down beside him and moved her candle out of his sight to the mantelshelf at the bed's head, beside the curtains. She thought as she did so that she would never do it again after this spring. When they came home again Mary would be with him in this room, if he lay awake in the night her face would bend over him, her voice and hands comfort him. William turned away and buried his face in the pillow; she heard his stifled murmur, "Yes, read to me, Dolly; your voice will send me to sleep." Her brothers had all called her by that name when they were children together, but only John used it still. William had given it up for years, except when he was very tired or in great trouble.

She glanced about her for the book which he had been reading, and found it open upon the table; it was *Paradise Lost.* He had been reading in the second book and had flung it down impatiently, for he was always careless with his books. She took it up, smoothed the page and turned a leaf; she read from where he had left off, beginning:

"Far off from these a slow and silent stream,
Lethe, the river of oblivion, rolls
Her watery labyrinth, whereof who drinks,
Forthwith his former state and being forgets,
Forgets both joy and pleasure, grief and pain. . . ."

She purposely made her voice monotonous and without expression. She fancied that the long slow roll of the Miltonic blank verse might compose his thoughts; their sound was like the sea. She read on and presently found from his breathing that he had fallen asleep. The candle began to flicker and the shadow of the chair grew great and small by turns on the ceiling. She extinguished the flame but she would not move, for fear of disturbing the sleeper. She sat on alone in the dark, until the window turned grey with the coming dawn; a cock crew in the village, and the birds began to twitter in the orchard trees.

8

They spent all the time that they could out of doors, during those last weeks together. When it was too cold to lie in the open they would take shelter in John's Grove, where there was always cover from the wind. She could sit upon the mossy stone which had been her seat in summer, with William's place unoccupied beside her and the space between where her friend had so often lain, while William walked to and fro among the trees and wearied himself with seeking an epithet for the cuckoo. At such times she thought long of their friend, but indeed he was always in her heart.

One evening in May they had a sad letter from him. He said that he had had a great quarrel with his wife, about a letter from Sara Hutchinson; he declared that he could not endure his troubles, he was quite distracted, he should go out of his mind from misery. She started up and cried out that they must go to him. William told her that it would be foolish and useless, she would get no thanks for her interference. He was in one of his jealous fits, when he could not bear her to occupy herself with any one but him. He made himself so difficult that next day she changed her mind and agreed to stay at home. He kept her at work all morning, copying the *Leech-gatherer*, which he had lately completed, and other poems; but on the blotting-paper in her journal, opposite that date, she traced an unconscious and symbolic pattern, which betrayed the confusion in her mind. It had her friend's name at the head, followed by her own and her brother's, then came the names of Mary and Sara Hutchinson, in one grouping after another, as if she had sought to clear up all the changing relations between them. It stands there to this day. When it was done she stared and stared at it as if she could not tell what it meant; then she raised her head and said to William, "I am going to Keswick to-morrow."

William retorted, "You will be a fool if you do," but afterwards he yielded and let her go, though he would not go with her. He had been right, however, and so she found when the got to Keswick. Mrs. Coleridge flew out at her, said that nobody should interfere any more between herself and her husband and burst into a hysterical fit of crying. Her husband said, "You cannot help us." Dorothy went home again quite dejected. Next day they got a letter saying that Coleridge wished them not to come to Keswick at present. He would visit them when he could, but he did not want his wife to be disturbed in her present state. It seemed that she had a reason for her jealous temper and misery; there had been some brief reconciliation between them on his return from London in March, and now she was to have yet another child. When she heard that Dorothy burst into a dreadful fit of sobbing. William said, "Well, I told you how it would be. He has made his bed and he must lie on it"; but afterwards he was kind to his sister and comforted her as best he could.

After that the time went quicker and quicker, she could not bear to think how little she had left. She marked the coming and fading of the primroses, the blue hyacinths, the stitchwort and speedwell and wild columbine, the violets and the celandine which William, one hot morning, put into a poem. Presently the oak trees put forth yellow knots of leaves; the plums and pear trees flowered and the wild sloe and the hawthorn came out on the mountain sides, like orchards in blossom. There were a thousand buds on the honeysuckle which she had transplanted for Mary. The cuckoo sang all day long, and the thrush too; the young bullfinches, in their parti-coloured raiment, bustled about among the blossoms and poised themselves like wire-dancers or tumblers, shaking the twigs and dashing off the blossoms. William loved to sit and watch them.

He was writing the springtime Ode, which he had begun after their friend left them, but he did not get on with it very quickly, because of watching the birds. Once a young fledgling perched upon his knee, a little creature that had just left its nest, equally unacquainted with man and unaccustomed to struggle against the winds and storms. He thoughtlessly stirred himself to look further at it and it flew on to the apple tree above him; there the wind blew about the stiff boughs and the bird seemed bemazed and unable to strive with the rough weather. The sparrows in the orchard were full-fledged, the nest was so full that they lay upon one another, resting quietly with closed mouths. And the house-martens, which she and the country folk called swallows, came to the parlour window as if wishing to build. She was afraid that they would not have courage for that, but she believed that they might build in her bedroom window. They twittered and made a bustle and a little cheerful song, hanging against the panes with their soft white bellies close to the glass and their forked fishlike tails. They swam round and round like a fish and presently became very busy. As soon as the nest was broad enough to make a ledge for them they sat there morning and evening and she watched them. Every now and then there was a motion in their wings, a sort of tremulousness, and they sang a low song to one another.

She used to go out into the garden and see them there, looking down upon her with their small sweet faces. Once, at the end of June, she went out to look up at the nest and it was gone, it had fallen down. The poor birds themselves could not be more distressed than she was. She went upstairs to look at the ruins which lay upon the window ledge in a large heap; the swallows had been ten days employed upon the nest and it had seemed to be almost finished. It was like an evil omen. However, the birds set to work again next morning undaunted; so the omen was for good, after all. Brother Richard sent them wonderful news; the Lonsdale debts were all to be paid by the new heir, William and Mary would have enough to marry upon and even Dorothy was to have a little money of her own, which she had never yet had all her life.

Everything seemed to be coming right; when she and William went out walking they could talk sweetly together about the disposal of what they called their riches. The spring flowers were all done; but the guelder rose and the wild rose had flowered, there were foxgloves everywhere in the June woods.

The time went by faster and faster, but now she no longer wished to hold it back. She wanted to have all done and be at peace. William had finished his poems and she all her preparations and the swallows, too, had completed their nest. She went to look at them on the last evening of all, the eighth of June, just before she and William went away. They stole in and out of their nest and sat there quite still, or sung low, for two minutes or more at a time, just like a muffled robin. William called her out to look at the moon before it set and they walked together arm in arm on the top of White Moss for the last time. They heard the owls hoot and the nightjar cry and saw glowworms in the grass; there was a skylike white brightness on the lake. They came in and William went up to sleep before his wedding journey, but she could not sleep. She took out her journal and tried to put down her thoughts, but they were too confused for utterance. She wrote, "O beautiful place! Dear Mary, William. The hour is come." And then, "I must prepare to go. The swallows, I must leave them, the wall, the garden, the roses, all. Dear creatures! they sang last night after I was in bed; seemed to be singing to one another, just before they settled to rest for the night." She looked at the page and her heart swelled until it almost choked her; she wanted to record all that William had been to her, but she could not find any more words. She wrote, "Well, I must go. Farewell," laid down her pen and hid her face in her hands.

VIII

I

THEY SET out from Grasmere on the ninth of July, 1802, a Friday, which the country people said was an unlucky day to start on a journey, but Willian had arranged it so. They tramped over the Raise to Keswick, and spent the Saturday and Sunday at Greta Hall. Mrs. Coleridge had settled down into the placidity of an advancing pregnancy, and was amiable enough to them; she even displayed a mild plaintive curiosity about the wedding, congratulated William, who took it awkwardly, and asked some inconvenient questions about why they were going to France first. These had to be parried, since she had never been in the secret about Annette. She complained, "It seems such a strange time to take a holiday; why do they not go to France for their honeymoon and take you with them? You will be bridesmaid, I suppose. Well, I am very glad your brother is to be married, though I am sure I never thought he would do it. I suppose you put it into his head. I am certain he would never have thought of it for himself." This was all so uncomfortably near the truth that Dorothy found it difficult to answer.

She stammered something lame about William having been very fond of Mary for a long time, but not having the means to marry earlier. Mrs. Coleridge said, "Yes, I hear Lord Lonsdale has paid all his father's debts to your family and you are to be quite comfortable in the future. I envy you, I am sure; now that we have two children to provide for and another coming, I do not know how we are to make ends meet. Your brother will find it just the same when he has a family, but I hear Miss Hutchinson has a little money of her own. I dare say that is why your brother chose her." She seemed to say everything that she could find most likely to tease the girl's sore heart. Dorothy bit her lip and tried not to show how angry she felt; and Mrs. Coleridge, with a sharp spiteful look, ran on, "Well, I wish it were you, my dear. It will be very uncomfortable for you, will it not? having another woman about the house, when you have had your brother to yourself all these years. I wish you and she may not quarrel," Dorothy said, with a voice which anger made unsteady, that she and Mary had never quarrelled, but Mrs. Coleridge persisted, "Oh! my dear, it will all be quite different now. I am sure you will not like having her over you. Why, my own sister Edith talks of coming to live here next year with her husband, and I am not at all sure how it will answer, though she and I have always been very fond of each other. Edith is the sweetest creature, but you know they say two women in a house are like two cats with one mouse. It will not be at all easy for you." The thought seemed to gratify her. She laughed her silly tinkling laugh, which had lately grown rather shrill and said, "I cannot picture your brother as a married man. He does not seem particularly happy about the prospect."

It was true that William was hardly the picture of an eager bridegroom. Now that all was settled and he was actually on his way to his wedding, the singular fellow seemed quite nervous and dejected, but perhaps it was the thought of Annette and Calais which was hanging over him. He was in a sad nervous state and Coleridge did not do much to cheer him. He made sour jokes about the matter, snubbed his wife's timid attempts at polite congratulation, teased William uncomfortably and seemed determined to parade the unhappiness of his own affairs. Dorothy was sometimes quite sorry for Mrs. Coleridge, whose large blue eyes filled with foolish tears when her husband scoffed at love-matches and said that the only happy marriage which he could picture or imagine would be a union between a deaf man and a blind woman. He seemed quite unlike himself. Dorothy could have found it in her heart to be vexed with him for spoiling their visit, if she had not seen how unhappy he was. He said to her, "A poet should not marry. William will do no more good work after this." He walked along the valley with them, when they went away, for six or seven miles. He was not well and they had a melancholy parting after having sat together in silence by the roadside. He stared at the ground and looked utterly wretched; then he jumped up, wrung William by the hand, gave her a last glance filled with reproach and misery and tramped off without once turning his head to look back.

Not for the first time they found themselves happier without his company. They lingered and loitered and sat down in pleasant places together to be alone. It was evening, and the swallows were flying about and under the bridge, where the river ran out of the lake, before they got to Eusemere. They spent two days in that good Quaker house, where it was not so hard to believe in married happiness as it was at Greta Hall. William seemed quieter and more at peace and talked a great deal of Mary. Mr. Clarkson wished him well at parting and said, "I am sure thou wilt have great comfort in thy marriage, friend." Catherine Clarkson kissed Dorothy and said in her ear, "The Lord strengthen thee." The brother and sister set out again on their travels in good spirits. They walked to Eamont Bridge and mounted the coach between Bird's Nest and Hartshorn Tree. They had a cheerful ride over the moors till they got to Stainmoor, then a heavy shower came on, but they buttoned themselves up together in one coat and liked the hills and the rain the better for bringing them so close to one another. They never rode more snugly.

At Greta Bridge the sun shone out again cheerfully and they had a glorious ride over Gaterly Moor. Every building was bathed in golden light; the trees were brighter than earthly trees and they saw round them miles beyond miles. They reached Leeming Lane at about nine o'clock, stiff, tired and cold, but happy in each other's company and spent the evening talking by the fire. Next morning they set out before seven, while the dew was still on the grass, and drove post to

Thirsk to breakfast. They were well-treated, but the landlady threw out some saucy words in their hearing when she heard that they were going to save the few guineas in William's slender purse by sending the luggage forward and walking over the Hambledon Hills. Poor folk must endure such scorns.

It was hot walking among the July heather under the misty scorching sun. Dorothy was tired and thirsty and had a blistered heel long before they came down through the wooded glen to the ruins of Rievaulx Abbey. She would gladly have stayed in that solemn quiet spot until evening, but William would not linger among the broken arches and cloisters for more than a quarter of an hour, after that he hurried her away. His impatience seemed to grow with every mile. They pushed on to Helmsley, where they slept in the clean and pleasant inn, with its yellow walls wreathed in jasmine, its low double gable-ended front and its floors smooth as ice; and next day they went on over the wolds by Kirby and Pickering to Gallow Hill.

Mary and Sara Hutchinson had come seven miles along the road to meet them; at a turn in the way the two comely young women appeared, walking together, swinging their straw bonnets in their hands. William stood stock still when he saw them, but Mary ran to him, flung her arms around his neck and lifted her face to his. He returned the embrace with awkward violence. Afterwards the girls, who were to be sisters, kissed each other silently and fervently. It was the first time they had met since the betrothal. Little Sara stood by, pulling wild roses from the hedge. William was ill at ease; he stared at Mary as if he hardly recognised or remembered her and was dreadfully shy of her. That was his way. He got Dorothy between them as soon as he could and talked across her, sticking closely to the incidents of the journey and avoiding any allusion to his journey to Calais. In this order they returned to the farm, Sara following behind, for most of the way, pulling flowers out of the hedge and adding them to her posy as she walked.

2

There were only two days for the lovers to spend together before the Wordsworths went off to France. William mooned about after Mary in his usual absent fashion or sat staring at her with that smouldering look of his, which his sister knew of old. Mary for her part took his oddities very quietly, as she always did, and went about her work in house and dairy as composedly as ever, though with a lovely heightened colour and shortened breath when she found him close at hand. They did not get much time to themselves, for the household was a large and busy one, but Mary seemed absolutely sure of him. They behaved to each other, thought Dorothy, watching hungrily, as if they had been married a long time. She herself rested from the fatigues of the journey, kept away from Mary and William as much as she could and talked a good deal to little Sara. The shy girl, who always had a timid admiration for Dorothy, was shocked on this occasion by the simplicity of her outfit and insisted on lending her a couple of light gowns to take with her to Calais, saying, with a doubtful smile, "You must do William credit among the French ladies." That was as near as anybody got in public to mentioning Annette. The gowns were tried on and fitted very well. Sara and Dorothy were both small-boned, delicate, virginal creatures, light and restless; the ripe slow-moving Mary was cast in a different mould. So a pink and a lavender print were packed in Dorothy's basket and in the third week in July they set out on the long drive to London.

They went by Beverley and Hull, Lincoln and Peterborough, a pleasant summer journey, rattling south down between the dusty hedges. The July sun had sucked all the colour from the brown and yellow midsummer fields; the elm trees were heavy in leaf, the hay all carried, the corn not yet cut. The fen country simmered in the heat and the cattle stood flicking their tails, knee-deep in the slow midland streams. There was a great deal of traffic on the roads, because of the fine weather.

At night the inns were very busy with travellers coming and going, pretty maids in mob-caps whisking up and down the stairs or leaning over the galleries of the crowded courtyards, old waiters hobbling to and fro with covered dishes to the coffee-room.

Dorothy was wakened every morning, before it was quite light, from her broken sleep in the curtained four-poster of each unfamiliar bedroom, by the rumble of wheels in the courtyard, horses stamping, postboys shouting, ostlers whistling, coach-horns blowing and the pump handle going under the window. All the way the traffic grew thicker and thicker; coaches and carriages, wagons and gigs, flocks of sheep and droves of cattle coughing in their own dust, on the way to the slaughter-houses, flocks of geese from Norfolk with their feet tarred and sanded, all coming down to London in a cloud of golden dust. She heard the roar of the town, and saw the smoke of it in the sky, long before she came to it; she was wearied out before they rattled down Islington Hill full gallop on the last stage with the horn playing.

It was a fine July evening and very warm. She had never seen so many people gathered together as were out that night in the streets, walking to and fro to enjoy the air, under a rosy dusty sunset sky, with the lights being lit in the windows. The yard of the Sun Inn was a bewildering confusion of people kissing and greeting, ostlers running this way and that, blown and sweating horses being led away, luggage being unloaded; she clung to William's arm and felt very rustic. It was a relief to see Richard's prim attorney's face come peering through the crowd. He was her least beloved brother, but she had never been so glad to see him.

He was now in chambers at number eleven Staple Inn, two rooms with low roofs and tilted floors, in a crooked house hidden away from the roaring traffic of Holborn. You reached it through a cobbled courtyard, where there was a little hall with a leaded cupola upon it and great windows to be lighted up at night when the students were dining inside. She went there with William several times and sat in the window seat while her brothers talked business together. Richard was just the same as ever, slow, peevish, fidgetty, quibbling at everything that William suggested and making endless difficulties about money. There was a great deal to be settled about Lord Lowther's debts and Dorothy's portion, about William's and Mary's settlements and what provision could possibly be made for Caroline and Annette. Richard looked down his long Wordsworth nose and primmed up his mouth whenever it was suggested that something should be done for them; he hated the thought of letting good money go out of the family. Dorothy supposed that lawyers were always like that. It was very difficult to get figures out of Richard, but he did explain to her that she could now count upon fifty to sixty pounds a year of her own, when the Lowther debts were settled. It was more than she had ever expected. Richard said gloomily, "It will keep you well enough, for I know you are a thrifty creature and I suppose at your age you do not expect to marry." Dorothy said cheerfully, "Well, I am thirty years old," but she thought to herself that she still felt like a young girl, sitting there in Richard's window, looking into the branches of the dusty London trees.

They left London at the end of July, very early in the morning, by the Dover coach from Charing Cross. Crossing Westminster Bridge it was lovely; the city wore the beauty of the morning like a garment, the river went gliding at its own sweet will beneath the bridge, the very houses seemed asleep, spread out endlessly under the rising sun, all bright and glittering in the smokeless air. William smiled and stared and fell into a musing trance, with his lips moving. His sister sat beside him, wrapped in her old grey cloak, gazing about her with her wild shining eyes, as the coach rattled over the cobblestones. They got down to walk as the horses toiled up Shooter's Hill and looked back to see the city spread below them with ships sailing on the river in the morning sun. They were happy to be travelling together and like children they picked out a house for themselves to live in, and another for their friend Coleridge, as the mail coach went swinging over the North Downs and through the Kentish hop-gardens by Canterbury to Dover. It was almost dark when they clattered into the little crooked town, smelt fish and seaweed and saw the masts in the harbour under the white cliffs. There was a packet sailing with the tide and they went aboard. It was almost four years since they had set out for Germany with their friend. Dorothy could not but think of that voyage and all the changes that had happened since, but she would not speak of it to her brother. She stood on the crowded deck with him, arm-in-arm, and watched the land slide away; when the first star came out in the evening sky she looked at it and wished a wish for William.

3

She was sea-sick on the crossing, as she had been before when they went to Germany. William stayed on deck and walked up and down all night, wrapped in his grey Cumberland shawl, snuffing the salt airs, but his sister was down below in the smells and noises of the crowded cabin with a crowd of sick scolding women and crying children. She did not struggle up again until the packet was at anchor in Calais roads, at four o'clock in the morning on the last Sunday of July. It was a bright windy morning and the blue water was sprinkled far and nigh with ships like stars in heaven. She found William standing by the rail, with his arms folded, watching a French frigate coming out of harbour with the sunrise on her sails. She put her hand through his arm and stood with him while that tall stately beauty went gliding by them. The frigate passed so close that they could see the two rows of brass guns in her ports and the faces of the men on her decks. William pursued her with a lover's look and muttered, "Where is she going?" John had taught them both to like to look at a fine ship.

Later they went ashore in one of the many little boats which gathered about the packet. There was a great deal of bawling and shouting and confusion. Dorothy had fancied that she knew a little French, but she could not understand anything that was said. She sat on her box, with her feet gathered up under her out of the water in the bottom of the crowded boat. William sat beside her, with his most forbidding and impenetrable look. He did not say anything to her. She glanced sideways at his drooping eyelids and compressed lips and realised that he had forgotten her presence. They were already gliding close to the black timbers of a jetty, rough with barnacles and fringed with trailing green weed. A row of people stood above them peering down upon them, chattering and grinning. Most of them were dock loafers, in blue blouses, wooden shoes and red cotton nightcaps, or fishwives in crimped caps and striped kilted petticoats, but there was one buxom woman standing a little apart from the others, anxiously scanning the faces of the passengers in the crowded boat. She wore the deep mourning in which a respectable Frenchwoman spends so much of her time and held a leggy child by the hand.

William sat staring up at this motionless creature with all his eyes and his sister felt him draw a long troubled breath. She murmured in her soft stammer, "C-can that be Annette?" and he answered, "I suppose so," in a whisper so harsh and restrained that it barely parted his lips. Dorothy could not speak; she sat motionless while the green oily water narrowed between the boat and the jetty. Presently the woman up there caught sight of the brother and sister and began to gesticulate and call out to them. They saw her mouth open but they could not hear what she said. Dorothy's head was swimming still with the sickness of the night. The sun beat down upon her and the smell of harbour mud, drains, dead fish and seaweed rising up from the water made her feel as if she were going to faint, but she lifted her hand and waved to the staring child and William did the same, with a jerky stiff movement, like a wooden marionette. His face turned very red as he stared at his mistress and his child, but he did not speak. The boat bumped quietly against a flight of wet stone steps. There was a rush to get on shore first and it lurched this way and that, while the boatmen swore and shouted. William put his hand on Dorothy's knee to keep her where she was. They were the last to land. Dorothy nearly fell as she was lifted to the steps by one of the boatmen; the world swayed round her and a wave lapped over her shoes. William took her by the arm and made her climb to the top of the jetty, but she could not have told how she got there.

Then the world swayed steady again and she saw the woman in black hurrying towards them, pushing and scolding her way through the crowd, dragging her little girl by the hand. She advanced upon them like a rushing black wind, swirling her crape veils and draperies behind her. William braced himself for the onslaught and disappeared in her embrace. She flung her plump bare arms round him, kissed him hysterically on both cheeks, held him off at arm's length and embraced him again. He emerged from this bath of welcome very red in the face, grinning his convulsive sheepish grin. Then the child Caroline was dragged forward with an excited incomprehensible babble of French ejaculations. She was a lean plain sallow little creature, with arms and legs like sticks and a thin neck under a round dark head, cropped short like a boy's. She wore a long high-waisted white frock which came down to her red shoes, a red sash under the arms and a string of coral beads round her thin brown throat; she had a quaint little short cloak of coral-coloured silk and she carried in her thin hand a wide straw hat, slung by a red ribbon. She hung back and stared at the grown-up strangers and they stared at her.

Dorothy saw at once that she was William's daughter. She had his long Wordsworth nose and just the same fashion of compressing her full wide mouth, but her eyes were as dark as her mother's. Annette urged her forward, whisking off the red cloak, twitching the white frock, babbling, "*Viens, chérie; viens, petite. Regarde comme elle te ressemble, mon cher:*

elle est tout-a-fait la fille de son père." It was an embarrassing moment. William looked as red as if he would choke, but he stooped and kissed the child awkwardly upon the cheek and Caroline piped "*Bonjour*, *papa*," as obediently as a talking bird. Dorothy embraced her niece in her turn and felt the small body stiffen and tremble in her arms; when she was released Caroline shrank back against her mother. Annette continued to chatter with loud hysterical animation, turning from brother to sister. Dorothy's swimming head could not take in more than a phrase here and there. All her French seemed to have deserted her in a moment, she could not pronounce a single word. She gazed at the stout dark common animated Frenchwoman, with the full bust and the moustache on her lip, bursting out of her low-cut, high-waisted, skimpy black gown, nodding her gold earrings, flashed her white teeth, sweeping her crape scarves about her with an ample theatrical gesture as she drew her child to her side. Was this William's Annette, long loved, long lost, the girl whose forsaken face had tormented his dreams and driven him half-mad with remorse and longing? It did not seem possible to Dorothy.

Presently William gave up the struggle to answer Annette's hail of questions and said to Dorothy in English, "For God's sake let's get away from here." He caught hold of a surly porter in a blue blouse, who shouldered their few boxes and bundles and started ahead with him, striding along in his own ungainly fashion, never turning his head to see that he was followed. Dorothy wandered obediently after him, her head still swimming and her feet uncertain from the voyage and Annette trotted beside her, with the child hanging back from her hand.

Presently they were all stumbling together over the cobbles of the quay in the hot morning sun. Tall crazy houses, painted grey and white and brown, crowded round the harbour basin with their shutters closed against the hard glittering light which danced upon the water. Ragged laundry flapped from iron balconies, or looped itself across the mouths of alleys, which gave forth a mingled smell of burning wood and roasting coffee, a stench of rotten fish, soapsuds and drains. They picked their way between lobster pots and rusty chains, drying nets and blackened seaweed. William complained in English that the street was ill-mended and dirty and had to translate for Annete, who flung up her hands and complained, "How you have forgotten the French that I taught you!" He gave her an unamiable look and said sulkily, "I have spoken no French for ten years." Her face changed then and looked suddenly older, she admitted, in a checked and mournful tone, "*En effet, c'est dix ans.*" Dorothy pitied her.

They plunged down a winding alley between small shops, exposing sacks of charcoal and fly-blown meat, copper pans and brown pots, coloured heaps of vegetables and shiny strings of onions. Old women sat knitting or making lace on the doorsteps, soapy water ran in the foul gutter between the cobbles and Dorothy's head swam again in the breathless heat and enclosed stench between the dirty houses. William had his sick white look, which he had not worn for a long time; he too glanced about him as if he felt that the walls might totter and fall upon him. Annette scrambled along beside her, panting, "You English walk so fast; I cannot keep up with you." She tried to make polite conversation, stringing her schoolgirl French together to say, in her soft stammer, "I am sorry that you are in mourning, Annette." She had resolved to use the name, but it did not come easily, she could not feel that the stout woman was anything but a stranger. The Frenchwoman glanced down indifferently at her black gown and shrugged, "Oh! this is nothing recent. I call myself *la veuve Williams*, naturally; it is more convenient so. People imagine that my husband is dead, I have my child with me, nothing is said."

Dorothy was bewildered. She echoed, "Williams" in a tone which seemed quite stupid even to herself; and Annette, opening her black eyes, said, "But naturally; that is the name he always used when he was with us, did you not know?" She uttered a shrill harsh laugh; she said, "A young man does not always wish to give his true name. Besides, Wordsworth; what is that for a name? None of us could have pronounced it." She called it Vordsvorce, explosively, and Dorothy's head felt as if it were being split open by the sound of her harsh voice. The two women hurried on in silence, trying to keep up with William.

Presently they emerged into a dusty square, planted with clipped lime trees which rustled in the wind from the sea. Women were washing clothes in the chequered green shade, laughing and chattering shrilly together. From this leafy square a shuttered silent street led the party to the house of Madame Avril, in the *Rue de la Tête d'Or*, where they were to have their lodging. Dorothy found herself with thankfulness alone in a tall grey bedroom, as cool and dark as a well. William had carried up her box and Annette had embraced her again, expansively, and bidden her rest till the midday meal. The morning sun pushed long gold fingers through the cracks of the closed grey shutters, revealing dimly a room in which everything seemed unfamiliar. She wondered at the red waxed tiles on the floor, the heavy battered mahogany chairs with threadbare yellow cotton upholstery, the bed piled high with a billowing feather cover and curtained with *toile-de-Jouy*, an innocent design of shepherds and shepherdesses, eternally dallying in a red and white grove. She lay on this bed for a time, with her head aching and her heart oppressed; perhaps she slept a little, for the sunlight had moved some way across the floor and up the wall before she sat up and pushed her hair away from her damp forehead.

She opened the shutters, struggling with their unfamiliar fastening, and looked down into a secret, sour-smelling alley, only tenanted by a slinking cat. In the distance she heard a shout and a clatter of sabots, and then the midday bugles from the barracks, clear and far away, to remind her that she was in a foreign country still at war with its enemies. She drew back, washed face and hands in cold water in a doll's copper jug and basin, smoothed her hair and stared in a blotched dim mirror, but not for love of anything that she saw there. Then she opened the door and felt her way down the dark stairs. There was a savoury smell of cooking and a door stood open below. She found Annette and her brother sitting side by side on a couch, like married folk, not speaking to one another, behind a table spread with a checked cotton cloth, yellow plates, a yard of crusty bread and a carafe of red wine. They looked straight before them and seemed as if they had nothing to say to one another. The child was on the floor at their feet, absorbed in some play of her own. Dorothy stopped on the threshold at sight of them. William gave her a gloomy look, but Annette sprang up, with exaggerated gestures and a shrill incomprehensible flood of welcome. A bare-armed maid came in with a smoking dish and they sat down to dinner, a meal all silence and polite oppression, a funeral feast for a dead love.

4

It was a strange uncomfortable holiday; when Dorothy looked back upon it afterwards she wondered why William had insisted so firmly upon it. Once they were in Calais, he was no help at all; he seemed to think that he had performed a sufficient penance by making the journey and need not trouble to make himself agreeable. Annette was constantly angling for his notice, poor woman! but he took strangely little notice of her or of his daughter. He knew Calais quite well; he had been there twice before, once with a friend on a walking tour, when he was a raw undergraduate from Cambridge and again after he had taken his degree, in the year when he first met Annette. He was always wandering off by himself into the town, to sit outside a cafe and follow the war news in the French papers with a long forefinger, or sip coffee and watch the troops go marching by, with drums beating and bugles blowing and the children running after.

There were soldiers everywhere in the bright clean windy

town, and men drilling in the squares. People stood in their doorways to watch, or whispered together in corners; there was an electric uneasy feeling in the air. It was very hot, almost too hot to go out in the middle of the day, and Annette herself would not do it. She took her basket to market early, but all day long she sat indoors sewing. She would not even go out with William and Dorothy for their evening walk upon the sands. Dorothy did her best to leave them alone together, sitting by herself in her own room, or going out for solitary walks in the strange town, but when she came back they were usually silent, as they had been on that first evening. Sometimes, it is true, they appeared to be quarrelling, but that might only have been the effect of Annette's shrill Latin voice, and William's doggedly brief and sullen replies, indistinctly heard through a half-open door or thin uneven flooring. Several times, when Dorothy returned unexpectedly, they appeared to be discussing money, as of course they must needs do; and once at least, when she came upon them in an engrossed moment, they were merely talking politics, with considerable violence. William had a red spot on either cheekbone and he was drumming on his knee with his bony fingers, while Annette's black eyes were sparkling with impatience; but when Dorothy asked them what was the matter, Annette only shrugged and sat breathing rapidly, with her lips compressed. William said heavily, "We were talking of how the place had changed since I was last here."

Dorothy came in and sat down, looking doubtfully from one to the other. William continued in his sombre fashion, gazing at the floor. "When I was first in Calais, twelve years ago, it was like the Golden Age. Every one seemed happy. The people had all dressed up their houses with tricolour flags and laurel wreaths and flowering garlands and they were dancing round the Tree of Liberty, singing and kissing each other because the Republic had just been proclaimed. I thought then that it was heaven to be young and alive in such a brave new world." He spoke in English, as he usually did to his sister and Annette glanced from one to the other jealously. "I walked through the streets to-day," said William drearily, "it was a public holiday. The crowd had been told to rejoice, because it is Buonaparte's birthday and he has just been proclaimed consul for life. Presently I suppose they will call him king, or maybe emperor. Well, other cities may be gay, but Calais is not. There was not a smiling face to be seen, it was like a working day. You cannot make slaves rejoice to order. These people here are terrified. They look over their shoulders even while they are at work, they dare not be seen speaking to a stranger, they cannot call their souls their own. This dictator has put them back where they were before the Revolution."

Annette had been glancing from one to the other, knitting her dark heavy brows. She had forgotten most of her English and only partly understood what her old lover was saying; but when Dorothy turned to her and tried to explain William's regrets she burst out into a torrent of vexation. Dorothy only collected part of it. "But it is absurd what he says there, this brother of yours. He still believes in that nonsense of a dozen years back, he thinks there really was freedom, equality, brotherhood. He was not here during the Terror, he does not know what we suffered. You English, you are all the same . . . you make theories . . . you are not practical . . . you imagine that you can settle the affairs of the world, but you know nothing, nothing, nothing. . . ." Her shrill voice cracked on the last, "*Rien*" and Dorothy winced. Annette seemed much older than the brother and sister as she sat there enthroned in her upright chair, stout, common and contemptuous, turning her brilliant black eyes from one to the other. Suddenly she burst into a farrago of all that had happened to herself during the troubles of the last ten years, a long confused story of midnight meetings, rope ladders, house-to-house searches, bribes, codes, arrests, spies and goalers. Her brother Paul had been obliged to hide for months during the Revolution, her sister and she had helped numberless aristocrats to escape, their house in Blois was still a centre of Royalist plotting and intrigue. Dorothy could not understand half that she said.

She rocked herself about, laughed, wept hysterically and wrung her hands, lamenting, "You do not understand . . . you cannot understand. You talk philosophy while we are fighting for our lives." Dorothy took the Frenchwoman's brown hand and stroked and caressed it, with a bewildered stammering attempt at consolation. William only looked awkward and disgusted; he always hated uncontrolled female emotion. His sister heard him say under his breath, in English, "You are trying to bring back the bad old times again, the whole lot of you." Annette seemed not to hear him, but she melted into a flood of tears, sobbing, "Ah, you do not know what I have suffered . . . myself deserted . . . my child torn from me . . . my country in misery. . . ." William gave a loud snort of disgust, pushed back his wooden chair with a grating screech across the tiled floor, got to his feet and strode out while Dorothy was left to console the weeping woman.

Annette recovered with a striking and comical rapidity after he had made his escape, it seemed that she would not waste her grief on another woman. She dried swollen eyes, wiped the tears from the front of her heaving, well-filled bodice, and sighed, "What must you think of me?" in a somewhat perfunctory fashion. She got up, looked at herself in the glass on the wall, exclaimed, "How I have suffered," but with less conviction; then settled her kerchief, straightened her black glossy curls, put a hand on each of her gold earrings and returned to her chair. She laid her hand on the English girl's knee and murmured, "How good you are to me!" then inquired with a hopeful sidelong coquetry, "Tell me, does William find me much changed?"

Dorothy did not know how to answer this; she stammered something about William never liking to talk of the old days and saw the sparkle fade from the black eyes. Annette sighed, "In effect, they are better forgotten," and then lamented, "But I find him changed, greatly changed. He is not what he was," and with a deep sigh, "*Ah! ce pauvre garçon, il était si gentil autre fois. Je l'aimais tant.*" Dorothy had a glimpse of regret and profound disappointment behind the false airs and graces which had displeased her daily; she pressed the hand of William's mistress and struggled to express her pity, "It must be so difficult to see him again. There must be so many memories . . . you must be so unhappy. We ought not to have come . . . I am so sorry. . . ." She went on stammering, in her schoolgirl French, "*Je regrette . . . je regrette tant . . . ce mariage . . .*" She wanted to say that William's bridals must be a great distress to the woman whom he had loved in his ardent youth; but either she did not get the right words or Annette did not choose to confess her wound, for she only shrugged her plump shoulders and said, with a hard composure, "*Mais naturellement, il veut se ranger. On attendait ça.*"

There was a sparkle of interest, however, in her beady black eyes as she edged her chair closer to Dorothy's and inquired, "You are content with this marriage for your brother; he has chosen well?" Dorothy said steadily that William and Mary were devoted to each other, and for the moment Annette looked stricken; she said, "*Je me figurais que ce n'était qu'un mariage de convenance.*" She clearly was most unwilling to think it a love match and said, "I thought you had made the match for him." Dorothy clasped her hands in her lap to still their trembling and steadied her voice to affirm, "I think that he loves Mary as well as she loves him. I believe that they will be very happy together." Annette looked quite sour and old when she heard that. She drew up her neat dark head, gave her sharp laugh and scoffed, "*Ah, bah! l'amour d'un poète, ça ne dure pas longtemps.*" Dorothy was cut to the heart; she murmured in her own tongue, "You should know," Annette made an affronted movement. Evidently she had understood the meaning of the speech, for she said bitterly, "*Ah! on doit se méfier des poètes.*" Dorothy thought of the two men whom she loved and the pain which they had both given her; she looked on the ground. Annette gave her a glance as sharp as a sparrow's; then she laughed again and said, "Why do we talk of love? This is a question of marriage. Who is she, this Marie, this Hutchinson?" She made a hopeless shot at the name and flung up her hands, complaining, "Otchinson . . . Vordsvorce . . . I cannot pronounce such names. Tell me, *Dorothée*, what is her father, what money is there? has he many children? *est-ce une famille honorable?*"

Dorothy explained that Mary was William's cousin, and an orphan, that her father had left her a little money, made in the snuff and tobacco trade, that she had three brothers and three sisters still living, that the eldest two boys were farmers and the third a sailor. Annette picked over all this information as minutely as a scavenger; she said finally and with grudging approval, "*En effet, c'est un mariage convenable.*" Dorothy supposed that, yes, it was suitable and waited for some inquiry about Mary herself, but only got one, a doubtful, "*Elle est Protestante?*" to which she returned firmly, "Yes." She was oppressed by the Frenchwoman's commercial outlook. Annette seemed chiefly interested in the amount of Mary's dowry and grumbled that William might have done better for himself. Dorothy attempted a protest, perhaps rather more fervent than it need have been, because of the little lurking doubt in her own heart; "But William is going to marry her because he loves her." Annette said, with a jealous flash, "But he is avaricious, your brother, he counts his money carefully. He will not give a sou in charity, he will hardly pay his just debts. I think he knows very well what he is doing, when he makes this marriage. Come, the *dot* is larger than you tell me."

Dorothy flashed out in hot indignation, "You do not understand English people," and the two women stared at each other over a gulf of mistrust and hostility. "No," cried Annette, "I shall never understand the English. You are so foolish, so romantic; you must always have sentiment, you will not realise that a love affair is for two people only, but a marriage concerns two families. You are absurd, you make no arrangements, you leave everything to chance." And with a gesture of despair she concluded, "*Enfin, vous n'avez pas le sentiment de la famille.*"

Dorothy, who did not appreciate the force of this criticism, remained silent, biting her lip. The Frenchwoman, staring at her, shook her dark head as if utterly bewildered, while she murmured, "*Et apropos, ma chère,* what will become of you? Am I to congratulate you, too, on your marriage, perhaps?" The English girl started, trembled and involuntarily folded both her hands over her heart as if to protect herself, while she stammered, "No, no; I am not to be married. You make a mistake." Annette said spitefully, "But, *ma chère,* it is time. They should arrange a marriage for you before it is too late. Such things should not be left to chance. If one has no *dot,* it is more difficult, but not perhaps impossible, *surtout en Angleterre. Tu dois te dépêcher, si tu ne veux pas etre vielle fille. Tu as plus que trente ans.*"

She looked Dorothy up and down and gave her short mirthless laugh. The girl sat still with her hands over her heart, as if the fire within were consuming her. She said with her stiff lips, "I shall never marry." Annette was shocked and evidently bewildered by the intensity of her tone, she exclaimed, "But what will become of you?" Dorothy looked for the moment as if she scarcely knew, then she murmured, "I shall live with Mary and William. They have promised me that. It is all that I wish." The Frenchwoman retorted, "But that is not enough. You do not want to spend your life with them, you want your own home . . . your own children." The English girl said stubbornly, "There will be William's children," and Annette laughed again harshly, she said, "Do you wish to be nothing for the rest of your life but *Tante Dorothée . . . Tante Dorothée . . .*" She made the words sound like an insult.

Dorothy flushed up hotly under her Egyptian-brown tan. She turned her head aside and her wild eyes slid this way and that. She looked like a captive creature seeking escape. The Frenchwoman thrust her head forward and stared greedily, then exclaimed in triumph, "Ah! I see what it is. You talk of William . . . William always because you have lost a lover." Dorothy cried out passionately, "No, no," but Annette would not listen; she nodded her head once or twice as if satisfied and repeated, "Yes, you have lost a lover. *Ah! j'ai passé par là, moi-même*; but it did not spoil my life. You must not let it spoil yours. You must find another man to put in his place, that is the only cure." Dorothy shrank back, as if a rough hand had uncovered her wounds; she persisted in her bad French, "No, no; I love nobody but William. I shall never love any one but William." The Frenchwoman stared, sucked her lip, shook her head and murmured stupefied, "But it is not natural that, I cannot comprehend it," and then she leant forward and repeated urgently, "You must not sacrifice all your life to this brother of yours. He takes everything, he gives nothing; you may cut yourself in pieces for him and he will never notice it. I tell you he is selfish, he thinks of no one but himself. He deserted me, he left me to bring up his child alone, even now he will not give me what I need to bring her up; he will not listen when I beg for help." Dorothy interrupted her with stammering violence, "You shall not speak so of William. He is doing all that he can for you both, he is a poor man, he cannot give what you ask. You are greedy . . . you want to rob him." Annette screamed against her, "The English are all rich. He is selfish, selfish. If you waste your life on him you will live to regret it, as I have done." Dorothy's head swam with the effort of the long discussion in the foreign tongue, as from a great distance she heard Annette repeating, "He is not worth it, he is not worth it." She clasped her hands before her lips and vowed, in her own tongue, "He is worth it to me. There is nobody like William."

5

She asked William whether they might not go home sooner than had been arranged, but William would not alter his plans. Apparently he was determined to perform his penance to the full, or perhaps the singular fellow found nothing irksome in the situation and merely wished to enjoy his foreign holiday. It was very hot weather and every evening he walked with Dorothy upon the sands. Annette still refused to come with them, for her tripping step could not keep up with the long-striding brother and sister, but once or twice during their last week she allowed Caroline to go, saying with her sharp jealous laugh, "Since she is your daughter, William, she should like walking." So Caroline came with them and ran in front of them like a little dog, picking up green seaweed and cockle-shells from the pools. The tide was low in the evenings that week; they could walk far out on the firm sand from which it had receded, crossing fans of trickling water and sweeps of scattered pebbles and shells. The last evening was the loveliest of all. It had been a singularly clear and windy day; but in the evening the wind fell and there was a great wide sunset burning over half the sky. It coloured their faces with its own fires as they walked towards it. Sea and sky were brimming with liquid light; the reflection in the water were more beautiful than the sky itself, purple waves brighter than precious stones, for ever melting away upon the sands. They could see far off in the west the coast of England, like a cloud.

Dorothy called Caroline and showed her Dover Castle, like the summit of the cloud, with the evening star above it, saying, "That is England," but the child only laughed in their faces and ran on; at a distance they saw her dancing over the melted reflections of the sunset in the wet sand. Dorothy was disappointed that the child would not stay with them; she said, "Annette has never taught her to love beauty. She does not see the sky that we see; she is her mother's child, not yours." It vexed her to think that they were leaving William's child behind, to grow up unknown to them in a foreign country, inheriting none of her father's thoughts; but William only pressed her arm and stood still and said "Listen." She fell silent then and heard the distant and eternal thunder of the waves breaking a great way out on the shore. William stood gazing at his daughter, running alone on the shining sands. Then he turned his gaunt face to his sister with the rare smile which so strangely transformed him. He said, "She does not need our teaching. Such a child lies in Abraham's bosom, all the year. God is with her, though we may not know it." And he continued to gaze at the sunset, wrapped in his own mysterious contemplation. Presently the child came running back to them with her treasure of leathery brown wrack and coloured shells, cramming it all into their hands.

William accepted a blue mussel-shell gravely. His sister passed her handkerchief over Caroline's hot face and neck and they turned from the fading sky to walk eastward towards the town. The sky was rosy in that quarter with the reflection of the sunset. The fort at the entrance to the harbour stood up black against the eastern strait, as if it were reared upon pillars of ebony and the coloured water shone between them. As the evening star sank down and the colours of the west faded away, the coastwise lights began to come and go, and the heat lightning to flicker round the horizon, as if a storm were breaking somewhere far over Europe. The waves of the returning tide, as they roared and broke softly against the pier, were interfused with a green fiery light. The fishing-boats began to steal out of harbour, with their lights reflected in the water. They came on wings of fire, cutting a phosphorescent track which closed up after them with a hundred thousand sparkles, balls, shooting-stars and streams of glow-worm light. Caroline was delighted with the pretty spectacle; she danced beside the brother and sister, tugging at their hands with her hot hands and twittering and chattering incomprehensibly to them. They smiled at each other over her cropped head. Dorothy thought, "When she is grown-up perhaps she will remember this evening and think of us."

Annette was at the door when they returned, they saw her mob-cap turning this way and that as she glanced anxiously up and down the street. When she saw them coming she came a few steps to meet them, looking vexed. William had been carrying his daughter in his arms, but he set her down at her cry of welcome and she ran to her mother, holding out a long tress of salt weed. She got a slap and a shake which made her burst out into shrill crying. Annette hustled her indoors, scolding volubly, "Where have you been so long? I thought you had fallen into the sea, or been set upon by thieves, or arrested for loitering near the fort. Do you not know that all foreigners in Calais are suspected of being spies? Why did you take her so far? She is tired out and her new shoes are soaked with salt water; she has torn her clean white dress and stained it with green seaweed. These are your English ideas, I suppose. You are not fit to look after a child, either of you. I should have kept her at home with me. *Viens donc, chérie, viens avec ta mère.*" She carried Caroline upstairs, still crying. William grinned and looked foolish, but Dorothy was angry that the lovely memory of the evening should have been spoiled. She had wanted it to remain with Caroline all her life.

The last morning was a bright windy day of flying cloud and sunshine, the air tasted of sand and salt and the clear hard light danced upon the water. They walked in the cobbled streets of the town and passed an old woman who sat hunched on her doorstep, making pillow lace. The coloured glass bobbins flew this way and that under her lean fingers and her absorbed head, in its neat white cap, was bent down over her work; but when Dorothy lingered a moment, hanging on her brother's arm, the old creature glanced up as quickly as a robin, and her wrinkled brown face split in a toothless grin.

She stopped work to wave her hands and gabble. Then she called back into the house and a younger woman, stout and comely, came out with an armful of veils and laces and began to offer them for sale. William would have stalked on, but his sister pulled at his sleeve; the work was really charming and she was taken by the women's friendly smiles and chatter. She began to finger the lace and try to reckon the prices in English money, while her brother stood fidgetting beside her; finally she drew him in, appealing to him to interpret, for his French was readier than hers. He admitted grudgingly that the lace was cheap. "But you'll have to smuggle it home in your petticoats if you buy any," said he grinning. It did not occur to him to offer her any, he was too fond of his money ever to give small presents. Dorothy had long accepted this carefulness of his as the fruit of years of poverty, but she whispered in his ear, "Would you not buy a wedding-veil for Mary?"

He started at once and looked shy. His lean red weather-beaten face took on a deeper hue, but she saw his big hands linger doubtfully on a fine veil of the true Calais *blonde*, sprigged all over with a frostwork of tiny leaves and blossoms. The women saw it too and began to press him shrilly, holding up fingers and shaking them in his face to give him the price.

At that moment Annette came up behind them, leading Caroline by the hand. She took in the situation with one shrewd French glance and said briskly, "But you must not let them cheat you," then engaged in a wordy warfare with the lace-women, while Dorothy fingered her corner of the pretty veil and William stood back, looking very English and sulky. Annette pounced on Dorothy. "That is the one you prefer. Then make him give it you, *ma chère*. It is not too dear. Buy it for her, William, it will make her a souvenir of Calais." William reddened still further and fidgetted from one big foot to the other; Dorothy said in her soft stammer, "It is not for me, Annette." The Frenchwoman's glance went from brother to sister, as sharp as the prick of a needle; she said, "*Ah*!

pour la fiancée. Then we must find you something better and you must pay a little more for it. These are not good enough for a bride."

The younger woman caught at the word, ran into the house and came out again with a wide cream-coloured web of lace, most exquisitely patterned with a border of leaves and flowers of orange-blossom. She spread it out before them and praised it volubly, while Annette exclaimed, "*Voilà ce qu'il te faut.*" William tugged helplessly at the steel rings of his knitted silk purse and whispered to Dorothy, "Would Mary really like it?" His sister whispered back, "Yes, do buy it for a wedding present. She would wear it over her white silk bonnet, she would look lovely in it." Annette stood smiling maliciously upon them and William, with a sulky defiant stare at her, turned his back and began counting out the unfamiliar French coins into the old woman's brown and wrinkled hand. Annette bit her lip and said, with a spiteful disappointed laugh, "Well done, my friend; a bridegroom must not be stingy." He did not answer, but took the parcel and crammed it clumsily into the wide side pocket of his blue coat. He did not offer to buy anything for either of the two women who were with him, probably the notion did not even occur to him. Dorothy eased the situation by purchasing a handkerchief with a tiny lace edging and a flower in the corner, and giving it to the woman whom William had not married; then she saw the child's black eyes, watching greedily, and stumblingly asked for "*quelquechose . . . un cadeau . . . pour la petite.*" They brought out some trifles and she chose a needlebook with flannel leaves inside and sea shells stuck on the wooden cover. She presented this treasure to her niece and Caroline was delighted.

That night they went back to England. Annette and William parted dry-eyed under the swinging lamp at the head of the cabin steps. The Frenchwoman even laughed as she waved her hand and said, "Perhaps some day you will bring your wife to visit me." William reddened and looked awkward and ashamed. The child gave them an obedient uninterested kiss and then buried her face on her mother's shoulder; it was nearly midnight and she was tired and sleepy. Dorothy and William watched the boat which took them back to the shore disappear in the darkness. Presently the packet put out to sea. It was a night of faint wandering airs and dewy stillness, the shore lights were visible in either country all the way over. William walked up and down much of the time, or talked to a negress who sat by the rail, a languid white-robed creature, meek and destitute, who told an uncomplaining tale of how all women of her colour were now to be banished from France. Mr. Clarkson had taught him to pity that afflicted race. Dorothy lay on deck, long after the packet was in harbour, watching the stars tangled overhead in the ropes of the rigging, thinking of many things, until the sky faded into the blue of morning. Cocks began to crow and bells to ring in Dover town, smoke curled up from the crooked red chimneys; then the sun came up to turn the white cliffs rosy and polish the sea like the inside of a coloured shell.

Later in the morning they went on shore and William with his dear companion sat in a hollow ground of the cliffs. They heard boys shouting at cricket down below them, running between the wickets and the noise of the waves breaking on the chalky shore. The sea was brushed by light airs and veined with silver currents like a peacock's tail; it looked like a bright river running between the two opposing shores. The coast of France hung between calm sea and clear sky, like the ghost of a dead country. She gazed upon it with many a tender and melancholy thought and fancied that William did so too; but when she said to him with a light sigh, "How near it looks." He shuddered and said, "Frightfully near." He glanced about him with satisfaction at the smooth green shapes of the downs, snuffed the thyme-scented, salt-bitten air, stretched himself in the familiar sunshine and sighed, "It's good to be home again. France is a wretched country now. I was glad to shake the dust of it off my feet." And he gave her a strange wild look, as if he hardly yet felt himself free of his own past, from which he had so lately escaped. She pitied him more than his lost Annette, for she thought that he had suffered longer than the woman whom he had deserted. She blamed herself for thinking so, but she put her hand on his arm and said, "Very soon now we can go to Mary."

6

At midday they took two outside seats on the mail-coach and travelled through the Kentish hop gardens, smelling the sleepy September smell of the hops drying in the oast-houses. The road was one string of coaches, gigs and chaises, all loaded up with jolly noisy folk who had been pleasuring and were going back to London. Riding down Shooter's Hill in the evening they saw the city below them, shimmering in a dun-coloured haze, and when they reached it the walls breathed out the heat of the September day, a dry comfortable dusty warmth like the breath of a baker's oven. Every window was open, every shop lit up, there were people on all the doorsteps, or walking in the streets, the river was covered with row-boats, and every inn-yard was full of noisy folk shouting and drinking; London seemed a huge cheerful crowded careless place after the provincial military bustle of Calais.

The Wordsworths stayed with their old friend, Basil Montagu, the barrister, and saw little Basil again, now grown into a fine noisy schoolboy and full of chatter about his own doings. They went down to Windsor to see their uncle, Canon Cookson, and passed two days with him very pleasantly. The Canon had strongly disapproved of his nephew's behaviour in the past, but now that William had enough to live upon and was to be respectably married to an English cousin, his uncle was prepared to recognise him again, though it was still felt that he ought to be using his energies in some more profitable fashion than in writing poetry. The Wordsworth brothers and sister were all together again that September, for the first time in fifteen years. Richard was in Staple Inn; Christopher, the youngest and cleverest of them all, came down from Cambridge, where he was now a Fellow of Trinity; and dear John was home from sea. Dorothy was delighted to see Kit again, and hear him boast of prize-essays and college dinners. She congratulated him on his engagement to Priscilla Lloyd, the pretty Quaker sister of that same Charles Lloyd, so queer and quarrelsome, who used to stay with the Coleridges at Nether Stowey and had lately become the Wordsworths' neighbour at Brathay. Neither William nor Dorothy liked Charles Lloyd much, but they thought Priscilla charming and so Dorothy told Kit. She was pleased with her youngest brother, who had grown into a serious, rather dandified young scholar in black clerical clothes and a fine white neckcloth; but it was John's return which made her cry and laugh together and kiss him as if she would never leave off. He had been down to the East India House to wait upon the board and he came in very fine indeed in his full-dress uniform, which she had never yet seen, a blue coat with the cuffs and collar set off by gold embroidery, with the crest of John Company on the buttons, buff waistcoat and breeches, a cocked hat and a black stock. He was now the captain of his ship. It was two years almost to the day since he had parted from his brother and sister at the top of Grisedale. He had put on weight in those two years and grown into a solid broad-shouldered heavy fellow. His face was as brown as an Arab's and his hair and eyebrows looked bleached against it, but his eyes were as bright and blue as ever. His sister thought him exceedingly handsome. She hung about him and could not have enough of looking at him. She got him to herself, for William was gone to Staple Inn to talk business with Richard and almost the first thing that John said to her was, "So William is to have Mary Hutchinson after all."

Dorothy said, "Yes, you told me that would happen, before you went away. It was clever of you, John." He wagged his head and boasted, "I guessed it before any one, didn't I? You wouldn't believe me, but it was true." Then he turned rueful, twisted up his handsome sunburnt face and grumbled, "I only hope William knows what a good girl he's getting." She said gently, "I think you can be sure of that" and he agreed, with something of an elder-brotherly air, "Yes, William always did know how to look after himself. Mary is the best girl in the world." He looked on the ground and said, rather mournfully, "I've thought a good deal about Mary and William while I've been away, fancying her sitting on one side of the fire at the cottage and him on the other; well, that's how it will be. She wrote to me, you know, to welcome me back, and asked me to come to the wedding. I read it over and over, till the tears came into my eyes, like a fool; I don't know how to answer it, best leave it. You shall write to her, Dolly, and tell her that I can't manage to be there, but I wish her well and William too and I shall drink their health wherever I am." His sister urged him, "I wish you would come too. William would like it of all things and so would she. They will have nobody there, but me, you know, out of our family; neither Richard nor Kit can get to Yorkshire."

John shook his head and told her hurriedly, "It can't be done, my dear; I haven't the money or the time for that long journey north. Time and tide wait for no man; besides, to tell you the truth, I've no fancy to stand there and see them give her to William, though you needn't tell him I said so." He reddened under his brown skin and looked for the moment uncommonly clumsy and awkward, as William did himself when he was ashamed of a generous impulse; then said, "I've a bit of a present for her, Dolly, I wish you'd take it along with you and give it to her for me, some time when William isn't by. A length of China silk it is, that I bought in the bazaar, with her in my mind, one of their thick rough wrinkled silks, like Devonshire cream, with apple-blossoms embroidered upon it. She can use it for a gown, or a shawl, or something, I suppose." He looked anxiously at his sister, who said, "I know the silk you mean. Miss Lamb has some like it, and our

Mary would like nothing better; but I wish you would come and give it to her yourself." He shook his head and said, between jest and earnest, "I'd rather not see her till she's been married to William a year or two and they're both happily settled down; it will be easier to look at her then." He added with his rueful grin, "I suppose by the time we next take soundings in the Channel I shall just about be in time to stand godfather to a niece or a nephew. Better bring home a coral in case of that, I reckon." His sister laughed at his disgusted face as he said, "Lord, fancy a boy with a nose like William's."

John laughed too, but not so loudly as usual; he said, "Well, I hear you made the match in the end, so I suppose you're pleased." She said steadily, "I have hardly anything left to wish for, except that the wedding were over and we were all back home again in Grasmere." He gave her a long gentle pitying look, but said nothing; only shifted his shoulders as if to relieve some burden upon them, while his broad weather-beaten face took on its accustomed patient look, as of one trained to ride out bad weather. She said, "I am just writing to Mary to tell her that we shall wait another week in London, to see you and Kit. She will understand the delay, because it is so many years since we were all together and she loves her own brothers so dearly. I will send her a message from you." He said slowly, "She is a kind and dear creature. Whatever fate befalls me I shall love her to the last and bear her memory with me to the grave. You may tell her that, if you choose; but I can't go and dance at her wedding. No, that's too much to ask, Dolly." She smiled and said proudly, "Well, I shall do it, whatever it costs me. Mary is my dear sister."

7

One other thing she and William did while they were in London that September, was to dine with Charles Lamb and his sister in the Temple and go with them to Bartholomew Fair. The Lambs were then living in a set of low-browed attics at the top of a tall red brick house in Mitre Court Buildings. Their dormer windows looked out over a parapet haunted by pigeons, down through the tasselled plane-trees to the river; Charles boasted that by perking up on his haunches and supporting his carcase with his elbows he could, without much wrying his neck, see the white sails glide by the bottom of the King's Bench Walk, as he lay in his bed. He was enchanted with his quarters, which he had now occupied for rather over a year, and limped round with his visitors, showing off his tattered innumerable books, his Hogarth prints and all his modest comforts and contrivances, stammering more than ever in his excitement, with his face screwed up into a comical grimace of delight and his eyes fairly starting from his head.

His sister Mary sat by, calm and cheerful, in her plain old-fashioned dove-coloured gown, with a muslin 'kerchief crossed upon her bosom, listening to the talk and turning her sweet square pale face from one to the other. She seemed to Dorothy, who had never seen her before, the most reasonable and placid creature imaginable. It was extraordinary to sit there beside her, watching her small white delicately-formed hand, hovering about her snuff-box and remember that this same hand had once snatched up a knife and plunged it into the heart of a crippled mother, in a fit of raving madness. Mary sat there smiling quietly at her guests and indulgently at her brother as he displayed his bookshelves to William, saying, "Charles and I are very glad to be back in the Temple. We were born here, just round the corner, in Crown Office Row. My father was clerk to Mr. Samuel Salt, one of the Masters of the Bench of the Inner Temple and my mother kept house for him. Charles and I used to walk in the gardens and feed the pigeons when he was quite a little boy. I taught him his letters off the tombstones in the Round Church. He was always such a very good little boy. I am ten years older than he is, and he was my special charge because he was the youngest and was sickly. I suppose that is why I love him so dearly."

She smiled at Dorothy and said, "You can guess how much we love each other. You have a brother who is everything to you." The two women would always have that in common and it had made them friends before they ever met. Mary gave her brother a long look and said, "He has been so good and patient with me, he does everything in his power to comfort and help me. I am a sad trouble to him, I know, but I believe I am mending. I have not been from home now for over two years." She spoke with calm simplicity of her madness and said, "I always know when it is coming back upon me, but I have been quite comfortable of late, only sometimes I am in very low spirits. I strive against my melancholy all I can, but I fear my dismal faces are a sad affliction to Charles." Her brother heard his own name and turned from his books to come and see whether his sister needed him. She gave him a sweet upward look as he paused behind her chair and seemed to assure him that all was well with her; he clapped her on the shoulder and stammered that it was time to eat their dinner.

It was a pleasant simple meal and over it they all talked of the north country, for the Lambs had just been to Cumberland for three weeks. It had been a great expedition, long talked of and saved for. They had stayed at Greta Hall with the Coleridges, climbed Skiddaw and waded up the bed of Lodore. The Clarksons had taken them to see Dove Cottage and old Molly had made them welcome, but it had been a great disappointment not to find William and Dorothy at home. Charles said in his stammering whimsical fashion, "We should never have gone there if we had thought that you were from home. Separate from your company I don't care if I never see a mountain in my life. I have no passion to groves or valleys." William looked much shocked at this, for he never knew when he was being rallied. Miss Lamb said in her quiet way, "Charles and I, you know, are sad Cockneys. We like to go on a Sunday to the Lea Valley, to Enfield or Potter's Bar or Waltham. We take our savoury cold mutton in a basket and drink our glass of ale in a fishing inn, but we cannot be happy long away from houses and pavements." Her brother stammered, "Skiddaw, to be sure, is a fine creature. Mary was excessively tired when she got about half-way up, but we came to a cold rill running over cold stones and after a draught of the water she surmounted the hill most manfully. Oh! its fine black head, and the bleak air atop of it, with the prospect of mountains all about and about making you giddy; and then Scotland afar off and the border country! It was a day that will stand out like a mountain, I am sure, in my life. When we first came home again I felt very little, I did not like to come back to work, I had been fancying myself a great man."

He shook his fine head and looked mournful, but presently cheered up, glanced round upon them with his teasing quaint smile and said, "But that is wearing off. I shall conform again in time to that state of life into which it has pleased God to call me. After all, Fleet Street and the Strand are better places to live in for good and all than the mountains. I could not live in Skiddaw." Dorothy laughed and said that he might do worse, but he screwed up his face, shook his big head and maintained, "No; I could spend a year or two among the mountains, but I must have a prospect of seeing Fleet Street at the end of it." Then he turned the conversation to William's marriage and teased him very pleasantly about his future captivity. William took it better than he usually did, for it was impossible to resent such quaint and kindly mockery. Miss Lamb wished that she could have been at the wedding, for she said, "Next to the pleasure of being married oneself is the pleasure of making or helping marriages forward." She wanted to hear all about William's bride and their future. Afterwards in the little panelled bedroom, while Dorothy was putting on her cloak to go to the fair, she pressed her hand and said. "This will make a great change in your life, but it is better so. I am sure your brother has found a good wife and I wish she may be a good friend to you; but I know what you must lose." They kissed each other and Dorothy said, "I only want William to be happy." Mary said, "I wish Charles could have married, but I think he is afraid to do it, because of me and my affliction. He and I are everything to each other, but he has given up his own life to me and I can never repay him."

They went back into the parlour and found the two men sitting together by the table still, Charles was flushed, talking very fast, but William looked a little stiff; he got up when he saw his sister and said, "It is time we were going." Mary Lamb came and stood beside her brother's chair. She moved his glass away from his hand, looked down at him with an anxious loving resignation and said, "You will be late for the Fair." He worked his face about into a strange tormented grimace and stammered very much, as he did when he was moved; he managed to say, "She is the best sister in the world. She lives only for me; she would share life and death, heaven and hell with me and I waste and tease her life incessantly with my cursed drinking and ways of going on." Mary smiled, pressed his shoulder with her hand and said, "You must not listen to what he says," and the little man struggled to his feet and hobbled down the stairs with them.

They walked through the echoing cloisters and courtyards of the Temple; then out by the bookstalls and booths of the Fleet Market, up Newgate Street and past the blue-coat school, Christ's Hospital, where Charles and their friend Coleridge had been boys together. For his sake they stopped and looked through the wrought-iron gates. The autumn term had just begun and the boys were all running about together in their blue gowns and canary stockings, under the flickering shade of the yellowing plane-trees, as lively and chattering as the immense congregation of starlings which bowed down the branches overhead. It pleased Dorothy to stand there and fancy the two of them sitting under the trees, the tall scholar and the little limping comical child; she lingered and listened with delight to the stammering voice at her ear recalling childish miseries.

"Ah! poor Col, he and I spent many most unhappy hours here, but that's all over. He was three years senior to me and a Grecian. I remember how I looked up to him and admired him, but so we all did. We thought him the most wonderful fellow. Even old Boyer admired him, the terrible old flogging tyrant, with his dirty wig and his great birch-rod. Oh! you don't know how ill we were treated; how hard we had to work and how badly they fed us, on raw beef and stinking mutton and pea-soup and porridge. We were half-starved and could not sleep at night for hunger. I did better than the rest, because my own home was nearby. Many a time has my old Aunt Hetty come toddling up from the Temple, sat herself down on the coal-hole steps, as you go into the old grammar school, opened her apron and brought out her bason, with some nice thing that she had caused to be saved for me. The other boys envied me sadly, I fear."

They turned and went on to Bartholomew Fair in Smithfield. It was a rowdy business, with the lights of the booths all lit and flaring under a dusty sunset, drums beating, men shouting, people pushing and staring, and a smell of roasting pork, frying cakes, old clothes, sweating bodies and choking dust. They ate cake and sweets, watched tumblers, dancing bears and rope-walkers in spangles, bought toys and apples, saw fire-eaters and sword-swallowers, the fat woman, the living skeleton and the mermaid. William kept tight hold of his purse all the time, like a true north-countryman, for the Fair was a famous place for pickpockets and cut-purses. It was a very noisy tiring evening, a fit end to a London visit.

A few days later Dorothy and William set out for Yorkshire. The corn was all cut along the road and the sheaves looked like couples setting to partners in a country dance in the stubble. When they got back to Gallow Hill, on the twenty-fourth of September, Mary and her sisters met them in the avenue, while Tom was forking corn, standing upon the cart. The year had come to fruition and William's slow courtship with it, Mary and he had nothing now to wait for. On Monday, the fourth of October, 1802, they two were married at Brampton village church. Dorothy had slept a good deal of the night, but she could not bring herself to go to church with William. He came and parted from her upstairs, with a long kiss and a silent look. She watched him go down the avenue in a cold silvery autumn morning, with John Hutchinson; Tom followed with Mary. When they had all disappeared it was very quiet in the house and in the autumn fields, only once or twice she heard Sara Hutchinson moving about downstairs, preparing the breakfast. She did not feel anything at all, it was like a pause between one life and another. She stayed at her window, hardly breathing; but when she saw the two Hutchinson brothers running up the walk to tell them that it was all over, she could stand it no longer, and threw herself on the bed. There she lay in stillness, neither hearing nor seeing anything, until Sara came upstairs to her and said, "They are coming." This forced her from the bed where she lay and she moved, she knew not how, straight forward, faster than her strength could carry her, till she met William in the avenue and fell upon his breast.

IX

I

As soon as they had breakfasted the three set out together in the rain. Mary cried a good deal at parting from her brothers and sisters, but afterwards she dried her tears and set her face gladly towards her new home. They had sunshine and showers, pleasant talk, love and cheerfulness. They recognised the cottages, houses and little valleys as they went along, pointing out to Mary the way they had come to her, three months earlier, and the places on the turf by the roadside where they had sat down to rest, as they went by Helmsley and Rievaulx. Later they went through Wensleydale, on the road which William and his sister had first travelled, when they went to make Dove Cottage their own. It was charming to show all these familiar places to Mary, who had been so little from home.

They reached the dear cottage on the third night after the wedding. Old Molly was overjoyed to see them and welcomed them as eagerly as when she had seen them first. They went by candlelight into the garden and were astonished to see the growth of the brooms and laurels since they had been away. Next day, they unpacked the boxes and she and Mary walked upon the hillside, in John's Grove and in all the old places. It was dull autumn weather. The lake was a mirror for the grey skies and the golden woods were quiet in their own tranquillity, stately and beautiful in their decaying; the ash-trees cast a reflection upon the water like a painter's sunshine, and the birch-trees looked like golden flowers. All the colours were melted together in a soft autumnal confusion, where green was gold and gold was green. Dorothy waited from day to day in a strange dead stupor, expecting to wake to agony whenever she saw William looking at his wife with that mild glow in his eyes, or Mary raising her head to give him her gentle smile. She held herself still when they climbed the staircase at night together, or when she heard their voices talking quietly overhead. At first she was too exhausted to care what they did or said, she went about like a woman walking in her sleep; and then, quite suddenly, she found that she had got beyond all that. She did not mind about William's marriage any more. It was going to make no difference.

Mary was just the same as ever, moving quietly about the cottage, taking most of the work off Dorothy's shoulders, releasing her to William. He had not changed, except that he was happier and easier to manage. His sister had never seen him in a better humour. He still sat working or reading upstairs for long hours by himself, he walked alone in the orchard, humming out his verses, and always called for Dorothy when he wanted a poem written down. He and she still took their great walks together, in rain and snow and wind; Mary could not come with them, for almost at once she had begun to carry William's child. She sent them out and welcomed them cheerfully home again; in the evenings they three sat together by the fireside as they had so often done before. William read aloud in his sing-song accents, or argued with Dorothy about poetry, while Mary smiled and sewed, rocked her chair and appeared lost in the enjoyment of her own meditations. They three were perfectly happy together, it was like being inside a magic circle, sheltered from time and trouble.

Their friend Coleridge was away from Keswick for most of the autumn. On William's wedding day he had published an *Ode to Dejection*, in the *Morning Post*, a most miserable poem. It had been first begun as verses to Sara Hutchinson, and continued after their morning in the orchard; then was finished as an address to William, who was much distressed by it. After that Coleridge had gone off to Wales, with Tom Wedgwood as his travelling companion. There was much talk of the pair of them going to Sicily for the winter, at Tom Wedgwood's charges; meanwhile they were walking about in the Welsh mountains and complaining of much bad weather. Their friend had cut down his opium to not more than half a gram in a day, less than an eighth part of what he had been taking at Keswick, but he was experimenting with hashish instead. He had heard that it was the nepenthe of the ancients and was drunk by criminals in Barbary, condemned to suffer amputation, but it did not cure his neuralgia. His friends had no word of him and did not guess how dangerously he was passing his time.

In his absence they did not greatly care to journey over the Raise to Keswick, where Mrs. Coleridge was very near her time with her fourth child and wanted no company; but she was glad enough to be rid of her eldest boy, Hartley, for a few weeks, and he was sent first to the Clarksons and then to the Wordsworths on a visit. The baby philosopher of Nether Stowey had grown into an enchanted child, dark-eyed and dark-haired, strangely like his father in his talk. He had inherited a taste for metaphysics and his proud parent was full of tales about the wonderful things he said. A year back, when Hartley was carried to the window at Greta Hall and bidden to look out, he had fixed his eyes steadily and for some time on the prospect and had then demanded, "Will yon mountains *always* be?" and had struggled most convulsively to understand the difference between the landscape and its image in a mirror. When he heard some older person say, of some event, "It is not now, but is to be"; he delighted his father by objecting, in his fluting babyish voice, "But if it is to be, it is." When his father called him and he did not wish to come, he asked cunningly, "Which Hartley do you want? There is a deal of Hartleys; there is Picture Hartley, and Shadow Hartley and there's Echo Hartley; and then there's Catch-me-Fast Hartley," seizing his own arm very eagerly.

Yes, he was wonderful for six years' old; of course his father was proud of him. Dorothy never wearied of listening to his rambling stories. He had a head as full of fancies as an egg is full of meat. He had lately invented an imaginary country called Ejuxria, which was to delight him for many years to come. It was to be situated on the banks of a stream called Jug-Force, which he said would break forth in the fields at the back of Greta Hall, and he was hard at work inventing a people who were to live on its banks. He used to tell Dorothy all about their history and customs and religious worship. He had inherited his father's interest in such matters and said of himself with some pride, "I'm a boy of a very religious turn." He liked to invent fantastic long prayers and have a chapter of the Bible read to him every night, but this last was partly because he was very much afraid of the dark. He was always terrifying himself with his own inventions. He woke up crying one night at Dove Cottage because he had made up an animal with its skeleton outside its skin and then had fancied that it was lying under his bed; and he always insisted upon a candle, "to keep away the *Seems*." Mary and Dorothy asked him tenderly, "What do you mean, my love?" and he repeated, half-laughing, half-crying, "The *Seems*; what *seems* to be and is not, men and faces and I don't know what. They are sometimes ugly and sometimes pretty, but they all turn ugly in the end. They *Seem* when my eyes are open and worse when they are shut; and the candle cures the *Seems*." So they both kissed him, left a night-light in a basin and the door on the crack, and listened outside until he was breathing quietly. Dorothy used to go in later on tiptoe and hang over him enraptured. He seemed to her like a changeling, a fairy creature, she thought that he would do something very wonderful when he was older. In her heart she imagined that his father must have been just such another when he too was six years old. Perhaps that was why she yearned over Hartley with so much tenderness; but William drew down his long upper lip and shook his head, saying, "I think of him with many fears. I doubt he is too much like his father. I do not know what will become of him."

The second boy, Derwent, was a fat roly-poly creature, scrambling about everywhere and not yet able to talk plainly; he was nicknamed Pipos, and Stumpy Canary, because of a yellow coat that he wore. Mrs. Coleridge's last child was born that December, a girl so frail and small and waxen that it seemed a wonder she lived. She was called Sara, after her mother. When Dorothy heard of this child's birth she felt the terrible envy of a barren woman who sees the years passing and the laws of her being unfulfilled; but she hid the feeling in her own heart, and would not let it cloud Mary's and William's first Christmas together. That year, when the fiddlers came, it was Mary who opened the door to them and they drank to her and the hopes of the coming year.

In the spring their friend Coleridge went to London, to stay with the Lambs in Mitre Court Buildings, a sad visit, for he came in time to see poor Mary taken away to the madhouse. He told them about it in a letter home, which his wife showed to them. "On the Thursday before last she met at Rickman's a Mr. Babb, an old friend and admirer of her mother's. The next day she smiled in an ominous way; on Sunday she told her brother that she was getting bad, with great agony. On Tuesday morning she laid hold of me with great agitation and talked wildly. I told Charles there was not a moment to lose; and I did not lose a moment, but went for a hackney-coach and took her to the private madhouse at Hoxton. She was quite calm and said that it was the best to do so. But she wept bitterly two or three times, yet all in a quiet way; Charles is cut to the heart." Dorothy could have wept herself when she heard the story. She could not bear to think of the sad brother left alone in his dejection and it frightened her to imagine the quiet woman whom she had seen sitting by her own fireside, now raving or moping in the madhouse, beset by her own distracted fancies. It seemed to her the most dreadful fate possible. She felt as if a cold finger of foreboding touched her when she thought of it and she burst out passionately to William, "I had rather die than go out of my mind."

As the months went on and the spring returned she had more and more of William's old companionship. Mary had come with them at first, and they had spent a great deal of time on a mountain terrace which William had discovered, on the Langdale side of Helm Crag. Here the two women sat with their work on the hillside while the poet walked to and fro on the smooth green mountain turf, humming out his verses to himself, very busy with the jog-trot rhythm of *The Prelude*. Later, when she could not get so far, Mary walked in the orchard or sat under the blossoming apple-trees, waiting for her time to come. War was declared again with France and the whole nation was anxious, but in Grasmere they heard little of such matters. The blue sky arched over the warm green valley, it was as safe as a nest; there seemed to be no place beyond. And in May the swallows came back and took possession of the old nest over Dorothy's window. She stood with Mary on the path below, looked up and saw them sitting side by side, with their small sweet faces peeping over the rim of the nest. When she heard them sing their own low twittering song to one another she squeezed Mary's fingers and whispered, "Perhaps they are the very same two who came last year." The cuckoo sang all day for William and Dorothy found a place high up on Loughrigg from which she could hear the bird answering its own echo from the mountains, with a soft mechanical persistence which delighted her. Mary's time was fulfilled and on a midsummer morning, at dawn, in the middle of June, after a clear and starlit night of watching, with the birds singing in the orchard, the young swallows chirping in the nest, the roses in full bloom and the sun shining on the mountains, William's son was born. His sister had not known how much she loved Mary until she saw her with William's child in her arms.

He was a wonderful creature, of course, the most beautiful baby that any one had ever seen; a noble boy with great unfathomable staring blue eyes, a long nose like all the Wordsworths and an astonishing likeness to his father. He thrived and flourished from the first; he was a fat fair baby, cooing and gurgling, with the most engaging creases in his thick dimpled sunburnt arms and legs. He slept all day long in the orchard with a meat basket for his cradle, he never cried at all; while he was still very young he was floated across the lake, like Moses, in his cradle at the bottom of the boat and made one of a dinner party on the island. They called him John, after his sailor uncle, and Coleridge, brother Richard and Dorothy were his godparents. He should have been named after his father, but there could hardly be another William in that household yet.

2

Mary recovered rapidly; the placid creature was made for motherhood. Sitting in the midsummer sun, with her baby in her arms, she smiled happily upon her world and did not make the least objection when William, with a detachment all his own, suggested that this would be the moment for Dorothy and himself to go on a walking-tour with their friend into Scotland. The plan had been talked over earlier in the year and half-agreed upon, but Dorothy had expected her brother to change his mind about going when it came to leaving his wife and his young son. Their friend, however, was wild to go; when he came over to the christening, in the middle of July, he could talk of nothing else and he fired William. It was Dorothy who found herself hanging back, urging Mary doubtfully, "Shall you not mind being alone? I do not think I ought to leave you." Mary, however, with her heavenly smile, insisted, "I shall not mind being left while I have my baby. Sara or Joanna can come to be with me, you know, they are both wild to see him and they are very sensible girls; besides, I am really so well that there is no need for you to miss your holiday. Do not stay for me, my dear;

William would like to have you to himself again, as he did before we were married." She was perfectly cheerful and sensible about it all. Mary never chose to feel herself affronted by any show of neglect, there was something very noble in her simplicity. Dorothy kissed her and thanked her and fell in with the Scottish plan. They were to go in an Irish jaunting-car; she and her poets were to drive or lead the horse by turns, they would lodge where they could and make no plans of where to spend the night. It would be a beautiful wander and they were to stay away as long as they liked, if it were five or six weeks. They were not to come home until they had perfectly explored the Western Highlands.

Meanwhile William went over all by himself to Keswick, where he was to meet some new friends of the Coleridges', Sir George and Lady Beaumont, then staying at Greta Hall. They were a rich and childless couple, fine society people, very grand and cultured, who patronised the arts. Sir George, the seventh baronet, had a seat at Coleorton, in Leicestershire and another near Dunmow, where his mother kept her dowager state, besides a fine town house at the corner of North Audley Street and Grosvenor Square. He had a famous collection of pictures and painted himself a little, in a mild gentlemanly fashion. Lady Beaumost was a trembling sensitive enthusiastic creature, who sketched in water-colour and read a great deal of poetry; she was a grand-daughter of Lord Chief Justice Willes. She and her husband had made the grand tour and travelled in France and Italy. Coleridge wrote that they were both wild to meet William. He had given William's poems to Lady Beaumont to read and she had said that if their author had chanced to come in, while she was reading *Point Rash-Judgment*, she believed that she would have fallen at his feet. Dorothy found this extreme sensibility exaggerated and a little distasteful and she was surprised to find that it did not affect her brother in the same way. He seemed absurdly gratified and she had to remind herself that the poor fellow had received very little praise or encouragement as yet outside his own circle. If it would cheer him to be given two fingers to shake by a baronet, or be gushed over by a fine London lady, all smelling-salts and swooning fits, she must not stand in his way. She and Mary were sufficiently occupied with their lovely Johnny. So William tramped off over the yellow bogs of Dunmail Raise and did not come back for a week.

When he reappeared he was full of his Beaumonts. Sir George was affable, condescending and courteous; his lady all sensibility and culture. Coleridge had declared that he thought her much like Dorothy, in her quick enthusiastic feelings, though of course she had not Dorothy's intellectual powers. She was most anxious to meet the poet's sister and felt convinced that they would be great friends. William reported all this with a rather fatuous smile and was to find his sister not particularly disappointed by the news that the Beaumonts were just going back to Coleorton. She said quite calmly that she supposed she could meet them some other time. William was glad to reassure her on this point. The Beaumonts were enchanted by the Lake District, which satisfied all their notions of the picturesque. They were coming back again next summer, quite certainly; there was even talk of their building a small house for themselves on the banks of Loughrigg Tarn, which had reminded the travelled pair of Diana's Mirror at Nemi. Meanwhile Sir George had made an even more charming plan; he had bought a parcel of ground at Applethwaite under Skiddaw and he was going to give it to William, so that the Wordsworths might go and live within walking distance of their friend at Greta Hall.

When Dorothy heard this she began to feel that she had been unjust to the Beaumonts in her thoughts. Sir George must have a most generous spirit. She and William and Mary all went over for a few days early in August, just before the Scottish tour, to look at Applethwaite and it was truly enchanting; a wooded ghyll most sweetly sheltered in the flank of Skiddaw, loud with the noise of murmuring pines and falling water. There was a tiny sunny green meadow in it, just above the stream, where a cottage could stand, looking westward up the lake to the mountains encamped about the head of Borrowdale. If they must needs leave Dove Cottage there could not be a better place to build a new nest; but William for some reason was tepid about the plan. You never knew how he would take a favour, he hated to have his own arrangements interfered with, or indeed to receive guidance in any way. He would not even write to thank Sir George. He said that he could not properly give his mind to it until he came back home from Scotland. The truth was that William hated writing letters and could never be got to answer them promptly. He said that whenever he took pen in hand he was oppressed by a dreadful choking sensation in his chest and broke out into a perspiration all over. He was the laziest and most sluggish correspondent in the world; although his letters began well and legibly, they always fell off into a slovenly scribble as he wearied of his task. So Sir George had to wait for his thanks and Lady Beaumont for Dorothy's acquaintance.

3

The three friends began their Scottish tour in the middle of August. They went up through the border country to Carlisle, a queer party to look at, gaunt William with a flapping straw hat to keep the sun from his weak eyes, she herself little and sunburnt in her plain cotton gown and old cloak, their friend mooning along, untidy and unbuttoned, a flabby indoor figure, wandering from one side of the road to the other, with his eyes on the ground. She and William struggled with the horse as it jibbed and backed, and found themselves out of practice with their driving. As for their friend, when it was his turn to drive, he preferred to lead the animal by the bridle. However, the day was fair and the empty stone wall country was cheered by the endless singing of the larks in the summer sky overhead. Carlisle when they came to it was all in a bustle from the Assizes. They were trying Hatfield the forger, the same man who had betrayed the pretty maid of the Fish Inn at Buttermere. It had been a great local scandal, and Mary Lamb afterwards saw it made into a play at Sadler's Well's, with mountains like haycocks for scenery, and a lake like nothing at all. The Carlisle crowd was wild to see Hatfield hang and a man in the street made Dorothy's two poets smile by warning them that this should teach them not to meddle with pen and ink.

They crossed the Solway and went up through the Border country. It took them a week to get to Lanark, because William must go by Dumfries to visit Robbie Burns' grave and reflect there upon mighty poets in their misery dead. At first they travelled among poor barren fields, in a simple naked land where the air was cold and the wind strong; later they climbed up over the high moors, beyond Nithsdale, where there were only sheep feeding and clouds moving, and the haystacks were tied down to keep them from blowing away. Dorothy could always walk over a moor with a light foot and she trudged along cheerfully in the wind and the sun. They met few people on the road, and hardly ever a carriage or a coach; only a shepherd sitting reading, with a book on his knees, screened from the wind by his plaid, while his flock pastured near him among the coarse grass and rushes; or a woman sitting motionless in the middle of a great yellow field, near a ruined cottage in a ring of blasted trees near Crawfordjohn; or a couple of bare-legged boys, with fishing rods in their hands and honeysuckle wreathed about their hats; what bower had it come from in those naked hills? Once they saw an old man in a Highland bonnet, walking with a staff at a very slow pace by the edge of one of the moorland cornfields; he wore a grey plaid and a dog was by his side. There was a scriptural solemnity, a sober simplicity about him which caught her fancy and she went on thinking about him long after she had passed him by. The women on the road reminded her of

French peasants, with their clean white caps and bright dark eyes. In Lanark, on the Sabbath, she saw them going to church in red cloaks. It made her think of the women of Goslar, as they used to go to prayers in their gold and silver caps, with their long cloaks, black or coloured. When she was in a new country she woke up and noticed a hundred such little things, it delighted her to store them in her memory for her own pleasure.

It was not very easy travelling in Scotland in those days. They had to sleep at dirty inns, with tables unwiped and chairs in disorder, unwashed floors and a stink of spilt liquor. There were sluttish servants and grudging landladies who would not give them fires. The cooking was bad; even William, who did not much care what he ate, grumbled at singed sheep's head, barley broth and oatcake as hard as a board. It rained a good deal and then they got damp sheets and smoky fires when they came in after a day's soaking; their poor friend complained mournfully about headaches, toothaches and pains in his joints. However, they got down into the Clyde valley, and saw the Falls in a fire-red sunset, with the Duke of Hamilton's fine house and formal gardens, though William was very angry because the porter would not let them into the picture gallery.

In Glasgow it rained dreadfully. Everybody laughed at their car from one end of the ugly town to the other, and dirty children ran hooting after them. They were glad to get away to Dumbarton, where they climbed up to the high top of the Rock, deeply stained by wind and weather and set in the very eye of the storms. They stood on the topmost platform and gazed up and down the great river. There were clouds on the cold and gloomy mountains whither they were going. They came down again and sat among the seaweed on the rocks, out of the tearing wind. They looked up at the sheep and the scarlet-coated sentinel on the Rock, walking up and down against the sky.

Next day they set out by the banks of Loch Lomond, in

chill melancholy weather. They seemed to have left the summer behind them in the south. The waters looked wide, the hills many and dark and far off. They were glad to get to shelter in the inn at Luss, though the landlady was the most cruel and hateful-looking woman they had ever seen, overgrown with fat and sitting with her feet and legs in a tub of water for the dropsy. It was probably brought on, said William gloomily, by whisky-drinking. She grudged them a fire and gave the two poets a couple of bad beds in a garret, where they were disturbed at midnight by a drunken man. They all spent a wretched night and wished themselves at home.

However, next morning was clear, rain-washed and glittering. The lights and shadows were vivid and distinct on the hills, and changing at every moment; the mountains seemed alive. The three travellers climbed the hillside to a point from which they could look down upon the lake, scattered all over with islands, without beginning and without end, under travelling fields of light and dark shadow from rainy clouds. William said that he would like to have a cottage on one of the islands, where he could row himself over with twenty strokes of the oars and be safe from all intruders. He was wild to go to an island with a ruined chapel, or some such matter, plain upon it; so they went down and hired a boat and were rowed over and walked about there. The boatman told them in his sing-song Highland voice that the ruin had been a stronghold for a robber, who lived there apart from his kind. Nobody could ever lay hands on him, he was such a good swimmer, "but at last," said the boatman, grinning, "they caught him in a net." It pricked her strangely to the heart when she heard her friend repeat these words, in his mournful and melodious voice, dwelling upon them, as if they made him think of his own case. She beheld him struggling in the net of his own follies, the strong swimmer, already doomed and sinking, with the water in his throat. The tears stung her eyelids and pained her throat; she turned away distractedly, stammering that the weather was bad and the boatman impatient to be gone. So they went back and on up to Tarbet, where the people of the inn stared at them and could not understand their English talk. There was nothing but salt meat and eggs for dinner, not even potatoes to be got and the whole house smelt strong of the herrings that were drying over the kitchen fire.

Next morning they asked the way to Loch Katrine and were told that it was a long way and the road bad, with no putting-up for the likes of them. However, William had his heart set upon it, so they took a pair of roasted fowls with them, leaving the car in Tarbet and were ferried across the lake to Inversneyde in a leaky boat. At the landing William dropped the bundle of food in the water. The fowls were no worse, but the sugar and coffee and gingerbread were all spoilt; it was a very typical thing for William to do, and his sister blamed herself for letting him carry the parcel. They visited Rob Roy's cave and afterwards wandered for a long time over the desolate moor till they came upon the shore of Loch Katrine. The whole lake seemed a solitude, neither boats, islands nor houses to be seen and they did not then know that if they made a smoky fire for a signal the ferry-boat would come over and get them. Coleridge and she were faint with hunger and could go no further till they had refreshed themselves, so they sat down, ate up one of their chickens and drank of the water of the lake. She was troubled about her friend, for she began to see that he had neither the strength nor the spirits for such a journey, they ought never to have brought him. She persuaded him to sit with her in the heather while William ranged the shore of the lake. Presently a Highlander came by in plaid and bonnet upon a careful-going horse; this figure enchanted her. The man had a little English and could direct them to a sheep farm, where they might get a night's lodging. The people were out harvesting in the field before the door and made the travellers very welcome, though a smile was on every face when William said that they had come to see the Trossachs; no doubt these people thought that they had better have stayed in their own homes.

Dorothy dried her wet feet before the kitchen fire and the good housewife lent her a pair of stockings; then carried in the tea-things and set cheese and butter before them, with fresh barley-cakes, soft and leathery. She made up a bed for the tired girl with blankets fresh from the *fauld*, and wakened her in the morning with a bowl of fresh whey, "for," said she, "we make very good whey in this country." They all breakfasted with the farm-folk in the kitchen and heard stories of Rob Roy, who had lived nearby and had been dead only about eighty years. They said his bones were buried in a pinfold on the next farm. He was as famous in these parts as ever Robin Hood was in the Forest of Sherwood; the cottagers loved to tell how he could run and fight, how his arms were so long that he could garter his stockings below his knee without stooping, and how he robbed from the rich to give to his poor neighbours. All this talk was very merry and at parting the farm-wife gave Dorothy an eagle's feather.

That day they hired a boat at the ferry and she and William were rowed down to the foot of Loch Katrine and back again, but their friend walked down by the shore, for he was afraid of taking cold if he sat still in the boat. The wind had dropped, but it rained almost the whole day long. The mirror of the lake looked black, deep and calm, there was no sound even of falling water. William wrapped himself up in the boatman's plaid and lay at the bottom of the boat; but his sister sat upright, with her hands clasped in her lap, gazing at the misty rocks, the birchwoods and deep heather, as the oars dipped and the boat glided from one bay to another, beneath the precipices, among the huge and solitary mountains. They did not get back until after dark and she was wet through and almost sick with cold, but the woman at the ferry-hut set them by a good fire. She had coffee ready and she brought out the whisky bottle for them. Afterwards they asked her for sugar, butter, barley, bread and milk and with a smile and a stare more of kindness than wonder she replied, "Hoo, ye'll get that," bringing each thing separately out of her cupboard in the spence. Whenever they asked her for anything it seemed a fresh pleasure to her that she had it for them. The man of the house would not draw near the fire, nor suffer his wife to get him dry clothes until she had served them.

The fire soon scorched them into comfortable feelings and they caroused their cups of coffee together, laughing like children, though their eyes smarted in the clouds of peat smoke. It puffed down the chimney and spread above their heads under the roof, where the hens were roosting on beams so crusted over and varnished by the smoke of many winters that they were as glossy as black rocks on a sunny day, cased in ice. Her two poets slept that night on straw in the barn, and slept well; but Dorothy was given a chaff mattress in the inner room and she lay long awake, watching the firelight and moonlight mingle among the varnished beams and rafters, till the light of the fire faded away and the man and his wife and child had crept into their bed at the other end of the room. Between sleeping and waking she heard the waves beating against the shore of the lake all night long, the rain falling and a little brook running; and when she sat up in her bed she could see the lake through an open window place at the bed's head. She knew that she would remember that night all the rest of her life.

Next day they walked back through bad weather and pouring rain. They were all soaked to the skin when they reached the ferry-house at Inversneyde, to go back over Loch Lomond. It was Sunday and they had to wait a long time in the leaky mud-floored hut until the ferry-boat returned from taking all good folk to church. There were two pretty barelegged girls in the hut, in long grey plaids falling to their feet. They were as beauteous and as wild as squirrels and they stared at the strangers with an innocent look of wonder; they only had a few words of English, which they pronounced slowly and with difficulty, but most sweetly. They lent Dorothy a sprigged cotton gown and a blue linsey petticoat to put on while her own gown was dried, and laughed and chattered to each other continually as they dressed her, repeating half a dozen times with gleeful merriment, "You never had on the like of that before." William warmed his feet meanwhile in the ashes on the hearthstone, gaped at the pretty creatures and took them into his mind; afterwards he wrote a poem about the elder one and made her the spirit of the Highland scene. Presently the boat came over the placid lake, laden down to the gunwale with a coloured cargo, perhaps twenty people coming from church, the men in their tartan plaids, the women with scarlet cloaks and green umbrellas, all reflected in the water, as pretty a sight as Dorothy had ever seen on a rainy Sunday.

They crossed back over the lake and walked to Tarbet, through the gathering twilight, hearing a child calling the cattle home in a strange tongue, through mist and falling darkness, with torrents roaring upon the mountains and no house in sight; the child's voice affected her strangely. That night she was very tired and glad to lay up her legs and loll in indolence before the fire. Their friend seemed wearied out and even William was subdued, but a good night's rest restored his iron frame and he talked eagerly of going on to the west. At that their friend burst out suddenly upon them, swearing that he had had enough of this journey. He was very unwell, he said, all his bones ached continually with the bad weather, he could not sleep in hard beds, nor eat wretched food; he would die of these hardships. He talked in the strangest way, accusing them furiously of dragging him up to Scotland to kill him and then he fairly burst out crying and stamping like a child, saying that he must go home. Dorothy did her best to comfort and encourage him, while William sat silent and staring. There was nothing he disliked more than having to alter his own plans for other people and he was never very compassionate towards his friend's troubles. Dorothy induced their companion to drive as far as Arrochar, where there was said to be a comfortable inn; but when they found it full and were told to go on to Cairndow, over the pass called Rest-and-Be-Thankful, their friend would go no further. He scrambled out of the cart and said sulkily that he preferred to turn back and go to Edinburgh. So they parted out the contents of their common purse by the dirty edge of the sea-loch, among the broken shells and yellow seaweed, where the gulls were flying and the noise of falling torrents mingled with the sound of breaking waves. It was a sad parting, like so many that he had forced upon them; they watched him going back along the shore, a stout shambling figure with downbent head and uncertain steps, among the inhospitable hills.

When they had lost sight of him they drove on heavily. In looking over the map of Scotland, when she was in her own home, she had often thought how pleasant it would be to follow the long windings of the sea into the inner solitudes of the mountains, but now all that was spoilt for her. The stillness of the mountains, the motion of the waves, the streaming torrents, the seabirds, the fishing boats, all were melancholy; for her thoughts were full of her friend. She pictured him travelling mournfully home alone, with no one to look after him. He was so dreadfully helpless, worse than William. She had always been the one to find their night's lodging, as well as see the horse fed and littered. She was sure that he could never get on without them and burst out to William, "We ought not to have brought him here, he cannot do what we do. We should have taken him to some warmer place, we should have known that he was unfit for such a journey." She continued to lament their friend's departure until William, who was always harsh when he was disappointed and hated to have her thinking of any one but him, said jealously, "Well, he will be able to buy those cursed drops of his in Edinburgh. I suppose that is what he has been missing while he has been with us." This silenced her completely and they drove on together in their car by a road which seemed to wind into the very heart of the mountains, a pensive solitude where nothing was to be seen but floating mists, scattered stones and herds of black cattle. They climbed over the pass into Glen Kinglass, in a wonderful wild red sunset, coloured like her own bleeding heart, came by moonlight to the inn at Cairndow and slept there.

4

After that she and William had to make the best of Scotland by themselves. They went up through the long lonely glens by stony trackways, they had wild adventures at bridges and ferries, sometimes they lost their way, or were benighted and refused shelter. William said it was the most romantic country that he had ever seen and he was perfectly happy striding along in silence, hour after hour, with his burning look of solemn exaltation, a gaunt comical figure under the steep wet precipices, among the black peat mosses. They went up by the shores of Loch Awe, gliding like a river of salt water under shining cliffs, and past Kilchurn Castle to the ferry over Loch Etive. There the tide rushing under the boat terrified their horse so much that they thought he would sink the boat with his stamping and plunging, or throw himself overboard. Further on the road, next day, among the long hills of Appin, the poor brute was frightened by the sound of the waves beating on the shore and by the upright shafts of a roller sticking up over a wall. William pulled, whipped and struggled in vain; they both leapt upon the ground and the horse dragged the cart after him down the bank of the loch and overturned it in the water. Dorothy gave up everything when she saw the frightful sight of the horse lying struggling in the harness, she thought that he would lame himself and that cart be broken in pieces; and then how would they get home? But a man came up in the same moment and assisted William in extricating the horse. After an hour's delay, with the help of strings and pocket handkerchiefs, they mended the harness and set forward anew. William led the poor animal all the way, for the regular beating of the waves frightened him and any little gushing streams that crossed the road would have set him off again.

After that they turned their backs on the green islands and the glassy water and went up through rainbow showers into Glencoe, where William was glad to hire a Highland driver to take them through the wrinkled and puckered windings of the naked mountains. They stayed a night at the famous inn called the King's House, but found it as dirty as a house after a sale on a rainy day, and crowded with drovers and carriers. She had never seen such a wretched place. They sat shivering for more than an hour in an unheated room before they could get fire or food, and then it was only a shoulder of mutton so hard that it was impossible to chew the little flesh that might be scraped off the bones, and some sorry soup made of barley and water, for it had no other taste. There was no hay or bedding for the tired horse and they sat up half the night trying to dry the wet sheets of their beds before the smouldering peat fire. They looked out of the window and saw the moonlight in the empty glen, they felt as if they had come a very long way from home.

After that they turned eastward and encountered better weather and a more civilised country. At Tyndrum they were astonished and hurt to get news of their friend Coleridge. The incalculable man had apparently turned back and come north again by another way, almost as if he had planned to avoid them; he had slept at the King's House, or rather lain awake, sick and tired, with the noise of the drunken folk in his ears, only four days before they went there. It seemed as if he had turned aside on purpose to be out of their way, for the people at the inn said that he had gone back to Edinburgh. She forced herself to say lightly to William, "Then he is better and perhaps will join us later"; but she was cut to the heart.

In the fourth week of their journey they went by Loch Tay to Blair Atholl, but up there folks were inhospitable. They had to go through the Pass of Killicrankie by moonlight, with their tired horse, seeing only a black chasm and hearing the roaring of the river, because an uncivil woman would not take them in and give them beds, "for no reason," said Dorothy, "but that *she would not.*" However, though they missed the way to Loch Rannoch, they did see the Falls of Tummel in full spate, and the Duke of Atholl's fine castle, with an absurd summerhouse, lined with mirrors, reflecting the waterfalls. Then they turned south again; they came back by Ossian's Grave in the Narrow Glen, where William wrote a sonnet, and by Strathearn and the roaring Falls of Leny to Callender. Here nothing would please William and her but to go up again and have one more look at Loch Katrine in the fine weather. So they went back and slept another night in the ferryman's hut. Walking by the lake that night they met two women and one of them said to Dorothy, in a friendly soft tone of voice, "What, are you stepping westward?" In that remote place, under the glowing sunset sky, the words enchanted her and her brother; stepping westward seemed to be a kind of heavenly destiny. But all along the way the people had been friendly and charming, save for a grudging innkeeper or landlady here and there. The wandering pair did puzzle the country folk a little; they were often taken for husband and wife, or asked if either were married. When one woman was told that William had both wife and child at home she said, as if surprised, "And the man's a decent man, too." Another seemed astonished that Dorothy was not his wife, but then recollected herself and said, with pious gravity and perfect simplicity, "To be sure there is great promise for virgins in Heaven," and she related a long story of her own married misfortunes to her amused guest, while she kneaded out the oatcake which was proving such a trial to Dorothy's aching teeth. Going east from Callender by Stirling to Falkirk a drover remembered seeing them in Glencoe and came up to ask how they had fared since; so friendly were the people and so astonished to be visited.

The brother and sister came to Edinburgh in bad weather. A cloud of black smoke and rain together hung over the crooked gables of the Old Town, till it looked like a city in a vision; the empty new classic squares glistened in the wet and the country all about it was blotted out. When they climbed Arthur's Seat for a view of the Forth they saw nothing. They slept at Roslin and next morning were up early to walk through the glen by Hawthornden to Lasswade. William had some correspondence about ballad-poetry with a young Edinburgh advocate, named Walter Scott, who was spending the summer in a cottage at Lasswade with his bride; and had been invited to call upon this gentleman if ever he came north. So he and Dorothy descended upon the young couple before they were out of bed. They waited some time in the parlour; then their host came clumping down on his lame foot, a stout, broad-shouldered, fresh-coloured gentleman in his early thirties, with a rosy face and a kindly blue eye. He looked more like a Border farmer than a lawyer, was dressed in a green shooting-coat, corduroy breeches, grey knitted stockings and heavy shoes, had a homely Scots burr in his voice and came in with a great bull-terrier lollopping after him, hanging out its pink tongue and grinning amiably. William could never abide dogs, but Dorothy and old Camp took to each other immediately.

His master gave them both a great welcome. He was a man with so much genial fire in him that it warmed all who came near him. He called down his young wife, a lively brown-skinned dark-eyed creature with French blood in her and a bright foreign vivacity, who made Dorothy think of a younger, prettier, more ladylike and elegant Annette. They were swept in to a country breakfast, the most memorable of the tour, ate porridge and cream with silver-mounted horn spoons out of wooden basins, and had their plates piled with salmon and home-cured ham, oatcake and honey. Afterwards they stayed at the cottage for the whole morning; their host took them into his study and read his border ballads to them, *Johnny Armstrong's Good-night*, and *Thomas the Rhymer* and the *Wife of Usher's Well.* He was a sensible humorous talker, not witty but wise; his laugh was like a cock crowing, but when he talked of poetry his quick glancing grey-blue eyes became fixed in a solemn brooding gaze and his mouth looked sad and earnest, while his whole face glowed with feeling. She liked him immensely and so did William. They felt as if they had known him always; they met as if they had not been strangers and they parted friends.

He went back with them to Roslin and directed them to Melrose, where he promised to meet them two days later; he would have liked to have gone all the way with them. They journeyed south through the Sabbath quiet of the autumn country, beside the bonny water of Tweed. It murmured through unfenced pastures full of bleating sheep and they were charmed by the soft pastoral landscape. Dorothy wanted to turn aside and go up the Water of Yarrow, which she fancied must be as sweet and lovely as the ballad made it, but William said that they must keep Yarrow for another time. It was a sad disappointment to her, she had a strange foreboding that she would never came back there again. However, she and William went on to Melrose and there, on the Monday morning, Mr. Scott met them and showed them all round the Abbey ruins. He was on his own ground here, travelling to the assizes at Jedburgh, for he was at that time Sheriff of Selkirk; when they had visited Dryburgh they found him again at Jedburgh and saw him limping through the rain, in the judges' procession. There was no vacant room in the inn, except the judges' sitting-room, where Dorothy dried her clothes at the fire until the court rose; but on hearing Mr. Scott's name a brisk old body found them a lodging at her house and in the evening the Sheriff dined with them, drank a bottle of port and read them a part of his new poem, the *Lay of the Last Minstrel.*

Next day he drove with them up by Teviotdale through the soft yellow-green fields in the early morning to Hawick. They scarcely passed a house for which he had not some story. They wished that he could have gone with them into some of the remote dales of the Border country, for he was friends with all the tinkers and drovers, ale-wives, ministers and dominies, pedlars and shepherds. In every house he could find a home and a hearty welcome; but he had to go back and put his nose to the grindstone in Edinburgh and after breakfast they were obliged to part with him, which they did with great regret. They looked at Branxholm Hall with interest, for his sake and for the sake of his Lay, recalling his bright glancing eye and glowing cheek as he had recited it in their Jedburgh lodging. They talked much of him as they journeyed home by Eskdale and saw their own mountains rising before them, a dark blue wall against the declining sun. Two days later they arrived home between eight and nine o'clock, where they found Mary in perfect health and Joanna Hutchinson with her and little John asleep in the clothes-basket by the fire.

5

When they got home again there seemed to be a great many changes. All sorts of things had happened since they went away and the saddest was that the Clarksons had left the neighbourhood. Dorothy had said good-bye to them before she went to Scotland, with many regrets, but poor pretty Catherine had suffered so much with rheumatism since she came to live in the Lakes that it had affected her heart and the doctors had told her that she must go to the south of England, at any rate for a change and treatment. It was melancholy to think of the dear white house at Eusemere shut up and empty. The whole countryside was in a great ferment, the war was going badly and everybody thought that the French were coming over to invade the country. The dalesmen were all drilling and forming themselves into volunteer regiments. Even William caught the martial fever and would go over three days a week to Ambleside to march and shoulder a musket; only tough old Thomas Wilkinson, at Yanwath, stuck to his Quaker principles and let his carts and horses be distrained upon, rather than pay the rate which was levied to maintain a cavalry regiment.

The vale looked lovely in its autumn colours when they went over to Keswick. The October woods were rich with all the hues of decaying fern, the colour of the unripe lime, of the ripe lemon, of the bright orange or its dried peel. Little woolpacks of bright vapour rested upon the mountains and slanting pillars of light travelled across Derwentwater. Greta Hall was more crowded than before; two new people had come there while the Wordsworths were in Scotland, Robert Southey and his wife Edith, who was Mrs. Coleridge's sister. They had lately lost their only child, a little snub-nosed grey-eyed girl named Margaret, who had died of meningitis and they could not bear to go on living at Bristol, where this had happened.

They came to stay at Greta Hall, not guessing that they would spend the rest of their lives under its flat slate roof, and Edith Southey was devoting herself passionately to her baby niece Sara, grafting her into the wound in her heart while it was still fresh. So said Robert Southey, who had himself been almost inconsolable for the loss of his daughter. Dorothy pitied them both and was glad to gather from Mrs. Coleridge's nods and winks that they hoped for another child, the most natural consolation in their case. She liked Robert better now than she had done when she met him that time in London, and he patronised William's playwriting. He was still somewhat formal in his manner and disparaged the scenery of the Lake district with travelled condescension, saying that it compared unfavourably with the great barren mountain ranges of Spain and Portugal, where he had spent much time since his marriage; but he was on the whole a pleasant, interesting talker and a great reader of old poetry and chronicles, especially Spanish and Portuguese. He had established himself and a considerable library in the great study upstairs, with the French-grey merino curtains and the view up the lake. He had already covered half the walls with shelving for his books, in which he was, he said, a great coxcomb. He was in obvious agonies when he had to watch William turning down the leaves into dog's ears and making fingermarks on the treasured pages. William was never to be trusted with a valuable book. He really did not care much for actual paper and print and it was a family joke against him that he would cut the pages of a new volume with the butter knife.

When they had seen Southey's study they went and sat with their friend Coleridge in the organ-room, where he was crouching over a small fire, looking cold and wretched. His eyes and his whole face were swollen up, he was sipping his red laudanum-grog and full of his miseries. Dorothy said, "I am afraid you are not well," sat down beside him and listened patiently to his story of his ailments. He groaned, "This body of mine and rainy weather never can agree together. I have been taking violent medicines to bring on a fit of the gout, if that might help me; I have walked one hundred and sixty-three miles in eight days to the same end, but all to no purpose. I ache in all my bones. Every night at five o'clock I suffer agonies of neuralgia, all down the right side of my face, as if a giant were striking me great blows with a hammer. I have tried everything, but I cannot deaden the pain."

He turned his glass of the stupefying liquor about in his hands and sipped from it, while William fidgetted about the room and stared out of the window. He thought their friend too much in love with his own ill-health. "I struggle to keep myself awake with writing and reading," groaned the sick man. "I dare not sleep now, for if I doze off I wake in a hour or so screaming with fear. My dreams are an agony to me, filled with guilt and rage and unworthy desires. I cannot remember them after I am awake again, but I know they are all horrible." He turned his light-filled, dreadful eyes upon her, wide and staring, and murmured, "These whispers that come to me, just as I have fallen asleep, what are they and whence?" and shuddered with the fear which lay upon him. "I lie sick and sore from want of sleep," he told her. "I listen to the rain falling; and the night wind pipes a thin doleful note, like a child lost in the storm, crying aloud, half in grief, half in hope to be heard by its mother. But last night there was no wind. Everything was still as I woke at midnight and heard the voice of the river. It seemed to grow like a flower on the water, beyond the bridge. I lit my candle, stirred up my fire and closed my window to shut out the noise of the Greta; then I was able to work on at my books till cockcrow. There was no sound in the room except the ticking of my watch and the noise of the fire, the low voice of quiet change and destruction. But when I opened my window again at daybreak I heard the cocks crowing in the town and after they had ceased the river going on for ever. I suppose it will sound so after you and I and all of us are gone."

He was very wretched, and she could not get him to talk of anything else but his troubles. She left him with William and went down again and had tea with Mrs. Coleridge and her sister. They had nothing good to tell of him. Mrs. Coleridge said, "It is a pity he ever went to Scotland with you. It seems to have upset him very much. To be sure, you were not very long together, were you? I cannot understand how you came to miss each other so often at all those outlandish places in the Highlands, but he says it was your fault, or your brother's, I forget which." She and Mrs. Southey had made themselves very comfortable in the parlour, eating muffins with their skirts turned back to a good fire. Mrs. Southey shivered and said, "To my mind it is a very disagreeable climate that you have all chosen to live in. I tell my brother-in-law that he should go to Spain or Portugal for the winter. I am sure the sun would do him all the good in the world." Mrs. Coleridge retorted, "I am sick of hearing him talk about warm climates.

He could be very well looked after here, if he would but take a little care of himself, not go out wet, and change his clothes when I tell him; but he has got it into his head that he must be travelling again. First it was the West Indies; then last spring he wanted Captain Wordsworth to take him on the China voyage, and now it is to be Malta, or Madeira, or Sicily, I don't rightly know which."

She sniffed a little and said pointedly to Dorothy, who was looking grave, "Of course I understand he wants to get away from me and from the children. He has been upsetting himself about that Miss Hutchinson again. All the time you were away, after he had left you in Scotland, he kept going over to see her at Grasmere. He pretended that he was going to inquire for Mrs. Wordsworth and the baby, but they tell me he used to spend whole days sitting with Miss Sara in the orchard. I do not think it is very pretty of your sister to encourage him in such nonsense, for nonsense it is. Why, where would be the sense of his fancying himself in love with her?" Dorothy was so startled and angry that she could scarcely stammer out an indignant defence, "M-Mary would n-never do anything to hurt you." Mrs. Coleridge tossed her head and shrugged her shoulders. She said, "To be sure my husband is old enough to know better, but he has always been ready enough to make a fool of himself over any silly young woman who will read books with him and listen to his poetry." And she gave Dorothy the old married woman's look which had always kept its power to wound and insult her. Dorothy was thirty-three years old, and life had done something to tame her, but there was still a fire in her heart and it burst into a roaring flame of anger when she saw the two sisters nodding their heads together and looking at her spitefully. She cried out, "It is not true . . . it is not true," got to her feet and pushed back her chair; but Mrs. Coleridge only persisted, "Oh! it is true enough and so you will soon find out. You do not know all that has been going on while you were away. He has been in and out of Miss Sara Hutchinson's pocket now for long enough and the last news is that she is to come and live near us after Easter."

Dorothy retorted furiously, "You know that is nothing new. It was all settled before we went to Scotland. The owner of Gallow Hill gave Tom Hutchinson notice at Michaelmas, because he had made so many improvements to the farm that she took a fancy to live in it herself. Tom had to turn out, he could not help himself. He has taken this house at Dacre so as to be near us all. Of course Sara and Joanna are coming with him, they have always made their home together. It is only natural that they should want to be near Mary."

Mrs. Coleridge said, "Very natural, I dare say"; in a sceptical fashion and Mrs. Southey made sympathetic noises. Dorothy saw that it was hopeless to talk to the pair of them and she sat defeated, beginning to wonder a little herself whether she was quite so delighted as she had been about having the whole Hutchinson family within a day's walk or ride over Kirkstone. It was an even easier and shorter journey, she reflected, from Park House at Dacre to Keswick; their friend could ride it any morning that he chose. While she pondered this consideration Mrs. Coleridge began to weep a little; her blue eyes grew shiny and her plump face reddened.

She burst out, "I dare say it would be a good thing if my husband were to go abroad this winter. At least he would not be visiting her every two or three days. If he were in foreign parts he might forget all about her and I am sure we could all get on very well without him." Then she fairly burst out crying, "But he will pine away and die, all among those nasty foreigners, without any one to tend him and I shall be left a widow." Mrs. Southey petted and stroked her sister while the poor woman wept, "Oh! he has been a bad husband to me. You do not know what I have suffered. Robert has always been so good to you. I wish I had married somebody like Robert."

Dorothy left them both at it, the frilled mob-cap and the turban, nodding and weeping together by the fire and went back to the organ-room, where she found her poets sitting silently together. Coleridge had just told William that he had indeed made up his mind to go to Malta for the winter. Dr. John Stoddart, the advocate-general of the island, was a friend of the Lambs and might employ him as his secretary, but he was determined to go in any case, if not to Malta, then to Sicily. He suggested, with a cheerful disregard of all the possibilities, that the Wordsworth family might come with him. He thought that he might be away about two years. She could not think how they would get on without him.

6

While they were in Keswick, that October, they met another old friend, the young man Hazlitt who had paid them a visit at Alfoxden. It seemed as if it had been a very long time ago. Dorothy did not like him as well as she had done then; he had changed from the fervent and admiring boy into a harsh critical aggressive young man, with a set of sceptical judgments picked up in Paris. He had been there to study the masterpieces of the Louvre and now fancied himself destined to be a painter instead of a writer. He had come north while they were all in Scotland and had been out and about Keswick vale sketching clouds, rocks and waterfalls in the manner of Claude Lorraine, not very successfully as yet, but although he was impatient and irritable in everyday life, nothing was too much trouble to young Hazlitt when he was at work. The moment that he took a brush in his hand he was perfectly happy and at peace with all the world. He had toiled with astonishing patience at a portrait of Coleridge, a sad failure, with the expression of the face quite dolorous and funereal, but he laid it aside when William came, and clamoured to sketch those gaunt and striking features. William at first affected an air of indifference and threw himself into a slovenly and awkward posture, but gradually recovered himself, assumed an attitude and called up his best looks. He made repeated fidgetty inquiries about the progress of the likeness and was very much disappointed when he was allowed to look at it, complaining, "I knew I was not handsome, but I did not think I was as ugly as that." The sketch was not in fact extremely like him and after a couple of sittings the artist lost patience with it and tore it up.

After this incident William drew down his long upper lip and decided that young Hazlitt had changed for the worse since he went over to Paris; apparently he had long forgotten another young man who came back from France with a set of opinions which shocked his elders. The artist was certainly full of flippancy and irreverence; he could take nothing seriously, it appeared, except the flesh tints of a Titian or the exquisite hands of a Correggio. He was uncommonly quarrelsome and very ready to take offence. Coleridge said of him that he was like a lump of phosphorus in a bottle, you had only to take out the stopper to get a burst of flame. He was certainly a fiery creature, but he burnt with a very smoky lustre. He could not agree with any one for long. He was particularly disagreeable to the women of the household. Kind Mrs. Southey and foolish Mrs. Coleridge were at one in thinking him a most disagreeable young man. Apparently it had come to their ears that he had said, with a toss of his unkempt black head, "The wives of poets are for the most part pieces of furniture in the room," and this judgment, which had only made Mary Wordsworth smile, had annoyed the two Fricker sisters greatly.

Evidently poor William Hazlitt had some personal reason for thinking ill of women. He declared that they were all hypocrites, with their downcast eyes and soft enchanting airs, and was forever railing against their folly. "It is not easy to keep up a conversation when the women are in the room," said he, not caring who heard him. "It is thought a piece of rudeness to differ from them, but it is hardly fair to ask them a reason for any foolish thing they say. In France, to be sure, the ladies are subtle and witty, they can talk of things in general and reason as well as the men do here; but in England, the women leave the room as soon as any interesting subject is started, or they attend to something else. I have no patience with the silly creatures." All this violence amused Dorothy, who imagined that he was smarting under some piece of feminine unkindness, and it only made her smile when she heard that he had been having his fling at her, saying, "I have an utter aversion to blue stockings; I do not care a fig for any woman that even knows what the word 'author' means." She did not mind his snarling, but even she was vexed when he began one day to criticise their friend, saying, with his cool sneer, "If Mr. Coleridge had not been the finest talker of his age he would have probably been the greatest writer, but he lays down his pen to make sure of an auditor. He is very eloquent, to be sure, but he is very tiresome with his eloquence; he does not care a brass farthing whether people understand him or not, he only wishes to be admired. Everything that he says is far-fetched, irrelevant, and laboured. He tries to make something more out of his subject than it is worth; he rambles on with a great flow of confused and cloudy speech, but he comes to no conclusion in the end and the least interruption puts him out."

This he said to Dorothy at the end of a long dissertation on philosophy, to which he had been forced to listen, without getting in a word himself edgeways. He vexed her greatly with his cynical sneer and his air of irritable condescension. She retorted sharply, "You did not think so poorly of his talk at Alfoxden. You asked nothing better then than to sit at his feet and hear him discourse." He shrugged his shoulders and excused himself. "That was five years ago. I have my eyes open now, I am no longer wrapped in cotton wool." Decidedly he had changed for the worse, she thought, since those days; but all the same it startled her when he flung out, with an astonishing air of authority, "Our friend has done his best work. He will flirt with all the Muses in turn, I dare say, but he will never write another poem like the *Ancient Mariner*."

She dismissed this as perverse folly; in that circle they still thought the poem a trifle, a few verses strung together on an impulse, to pay for the wander to Lynton. She said, "I am sure you are wrong," very warmly and he sulkily persisted, "I am sure I am right." He had great confidence in his own opinions, had young Mr. Hazlitt, and soon managed to offend every one in Keswick. He would not flatter the local gentry and indeed preferred rougher company than theirs, he said that he would not make himself a martyr to the society of a country town. He ended by making love to a village girl and being ducked in a horse-pond for it by some farm lads; after that he tired of Cumberland and went back to London. He painted Charles Lamb in the habit of a Venetian senator, an admirable portrait; later he deserted the brush for the pen again and took to writing critical essays, a task for which nature had well fitted him. Keswick was glad to see the last of him. The people there all said that he was a very disagreeable quarrelsome person and would come to some bad end.

7

Just before Christmas their friend Coleridge came to Dove Cottage, bringing little Derwent with him and intending to stay only a few days on his way to the south; but he had caught a chill on the journey and lay sick at the cottage over Christmas. When the fiddlers came they had to be sent away for fear they should disturb him. His illness made a great deal of trouble in that little house, for Mary had a bad cold most of the time, old Molly the maid was sick, and with Derwent and the liveliest of Johnnys underfoot the women were busy enough; but they nursed the sick man devotedly and ungrudgingly. When he was at his most feverish one night he raved about his Asra, clutched at Mary's white apron, and rambled about his two beloved women. Mary laid her hand on his burning forehead and he caught it, clung to it and seemed to recognise her, for he moaned, "She will forget me . . . she will forget me." Mary soothed him and told him, "Asra does not forget so easily." Dorothy gave her a long indignant jealous glance across the bed and turned away, but afterwards she knew that she had been unjust and tried to speak steadily to Mary of her sister. Mary said, with her calm a little troubled for once, "It is best that he should go away. When he is in Malta he will forget all about her." Dorothy said bitterly, "Men forget more easily than we do," and Mary sighed, "Poor Asra, she will think of him for longer than he thinks of her. Unfaithfulness is not in her nature."

In the middle of January the sick man was sufficiently recovered to leave them, which he did with a hundred pounds of William's in his pocket. He spent some time in London, then went to stay with Sir George and Lady Beaumont at Dunmow, where he was richly entertained. He did not actually start for Malta until late in the spring. Meanwhile they were all hard at work at the cottage, making fair copies of all William's manuscript poems for him to take with him on his journey. William had just then put aside everything else in order to work upon the poem on his own early life, which he afterwards called *The Prelude*. That spring he composed between two and three thousand lines of it. He walked out every morning by himself, in the pleasant mild rainy weather, taking his green umbrella with him. The women used to look out and see him standing stock-still by himself under it, during many a rainy half-hour, in the middle of a road or field, lost to all about him. He was already in the seventh book of his poem, which had turned out far longer than he ever expected. "It seems a frightful deal to say about myself," he admitted to Dorothy, with his rueful grin. "I do not think it should be published in my own lifetime, or not at least until other work has been written and published of sufficient importance to warrant my giving my own history to the world." He did, however, seem to be sailing along with a fair wind behind him, pouring out his inexhaustible recollections of his own youth. Meanwhile the two women were continually writing out and recopying his earlier manuscripts, which were in a wretched confusion and almost illegible. Coleridge had asked for copies to take abroad with him. Dorothy wearied herself to death, sitting long hours at her desk, toiling over the work, with head and back and hand aching, till she felt ready to sink under a sense of painful unrest and confusion. She did not think that the copying would ever be finished in time and lay awake at night worrying about it; but at last all was done and the packet made up. It was despatched to Grosvenor Square with a loving letter and many messages to kind Lady Beaumont for her hospitality to their friend. He sailed on the ninth of April, 1804, in the *Speedwell*, from Portsmouth, bound to Malta, and they did not see him again for over two years.

After he had gone there was a sad quiet feeling for a long time in her heart. She busied herself with the house and with little Johnny, who had grown into a rosy-cheeked fellow, very strong and as happy as a bird in the open air. He delighted in every sound he heard, the crows high up in the sky, the wind in the trees, the little brooks by the roadside. He liked to play at his aunt's feet and would riot through the tape and thread and oddments in her work-basket like a little pussy-cat. It filled her heart top-full with pleasure to see him look up at her so sensibly as he sat on the grass. She thought that he would very soon learn to walk, or at least to raise himself up from the ground, for when she did not go to him the moment he wanted her he would make the most astonishing efforts to lift himself. He was certainly an uncommonly vigorous and splendid child. She thought him just like his father and adored him. Mary was at work again all that summer and in August she bore a daughter, a little lovely creature who was christened Dorothy after her aunt. Dorothy did not like any child to be saddled with such a name for her sake, but Mary and William insisted.

Lady Beaumont was allowed to be godmother. She kept up a regular correspondence with Dorothy and by this time ranked as quite an old friend, though no one but William had yet seen her. Johnny was a little jealous and would sometimes hit his sister and make her cry, but every one else adored her. She was a very pretty baby and her father's darling. The Coleridge children came over with their mother and were enchanted by the little creature. It was a busy happy summer and autumn.

William and Dorothy had a lovely wander together over Whinlatter Pass and through the Vale of Lorton. They visited the great yew trees in which William delighted, and when they came home again began to make a round hut in the orchard for him to sit and write in, lined with moss like a wren's nest. Also the Hutchinsons had settled into their new home, at Park House, near Dacre and had to be visited. It was a rather bleak white hilltop farm, across the lake from the Clarksons' old home at Eusemere but it had a charming little castle near it, set in a green meadow, where Dorothy fancied that William's children, when they were older, would like to play at Border raids. Mary was very happy to have her brothers and sisters within twenty miles of her, though it was a stiff climb up over Kirkstone Pass and down again and a long way round by Keswick. They all went over to Park House by the Kirkstone on New Year's Day, though Grasmere Water was frozen hard enough for skating. Dorothy carried her baby niece in her arms, and William carried Johnny. The children were none the worse but the women both caught bad colds, because William was afraid of being benighted and hurried them up the hill so fast that they were overheated with the bright sun and the bad going. Worst of all, William himself caught a dreadful cold in his eyes, from the wind on the top of the Pass, which troubled him for the rest of his life, so that he could not bear any strong light, or indeed read print for long together. His wife and sister thought often afterwards that it was a pity they had not stayed by their own fireside on that fatal New Year's Day, but the thing was forgotten at the time in something much worse which came upon them within six weeks afterwards.

Brother John had been on the high seas all that autumn, returning from his voyage to Macao and up the Pearl River to Canton, for silk, tea and opium. They had been very anxious lest his ship should fall in with a French enemy squadron on the way, but he came safe home to London and they begged him to spend that wartime Christmas with them. It was a sad disappointment when he wrote back that he had no time to come north; the *Earl of Abergavenny* must put to sea again at the end of January and her captain was too busy to leave her. He wrote to them cheerfully from Portsmouth, full of hope and just on the point of sailing, in great spirits, trusting to "make a good voyage of it, if not a very great one." Twelve days later, when they thought John already at Madeira, Sara Hutchinson walked in with a letter in her hand. It came from their brother Richard and it told them that John's ship had been wrecked. She had struck upon the shoal called the Shambles in Weymouth Bay and John and most of the poor folk on board her had been drowned.

8

Dorothy could not believe it at all at first; she sat there as if she were dead and then she burst out into a great storm of weeping. She cried out, "Oh! no; oh! no, it cannot be true. Why must it happen so? He always laughed at us for being afraid of shipwreck, he said that ships were only lost by mismanagement and that we need not fear that with him. There must be some mistake, it is not John's ship; it is some other." William gave a great sigh as if his heart would break; he said, "John always had a great fear of pilots; do you not remember how he used to say, It is a joyful hour for us when we get rid of them? It was the pilot that put her on the sands and ruined John." He groaned, "What poor blind creatures we are! We were all hoping and struggling to get him the command of this ship, he was so proud when he heard that he had obtained it, he hoped to do so well out this fatal voyage; and now he is drowned." He said, "When we used to stand on the tops of the hills by Racedown and look over the sea towards the south, we never thought that we were looking towards John's grave." Then his face worked and he covered it with his hands and said, "God keep the rest of us together; the set is broken." Mary cried too and tried to comfort the forlorn brother and sister; but the tears ran down her face as she lamented, "John was so good and kind and true. He loved this place and everything that we did, he looked forward continually to coming here and making his home with us when he had done with the sea. This was the place where he hoped to end his days, but now he will never see it again"; and then she burst out crying, "He never saw the children. Oh! I wish so much that he had come here at Christmas and seen the children." That was what Mary minded most.

William said, "What will poor Coleridge do when he hears this? He loved John and he knew how we loved him. It will break his heart," and Dorothy lamented, "Every one who knew John will be heart-broken. I keep on thinking of his lovely happy ways, how he used to wander alone in these hills, or go up to the tarn fishing, or sit by the fireside . . . how he helped us to furnish the cottage and to make the garden . . . how he would call me out in the evening, many a time, to look at the moon or stars, or a cloudy sky, or this vale in the quiet moonlight. The stars and the moon were his chief delight." Her voice broke; and she leaned her head on her hand and sobbed, "I cannot speak of him as he was. I must have done."

The worst of this trouble was that they could get no more news for many days to comfort them. They could only read Richard's one short letter over and over again and question and wonder. There were dreadful accounts in some newspapers which were brought to them. It was said that the ship had struck upon the sands an hour or more before any signals of distress were fired, that the boats had not been lowered in time, that everything had been in utter confusion and that John had made no effort to save himself. William refused stubbornly to believe anything that he saw in the papers, he persisted that John would have done all that could be done. He wrote off at once to Richard for more news, but the strange fellow was too busy, or too stupid to realise what distress they were in. He did not answer for three weeks, though they wrote again imploring news, persuading themselves that he must be ill, or that their letters had gone astray in the post. It was kind Charles Lamb who satisfied them in the end, from his desk in the East India House. He had seen and questioned the survivors, and he pieced the whole story together for them with great sorrow.

John had not been to blame in any way. The pilot had still been in charge of the great East Indiaman when, at five o'clock on a dark and stormy February evening, as she was nearing the east end of the Shambles, the wind died away suddenly and the strong tide of Portland Race swept her into the breakers, where she struck. John cried out, so that many men heard him, "Pilot, you have ruined me," but afterwards he was very calm and cool. He ordered the topsails to be set, to lift her off the shoal, and gave orders for signals of distress to be fired. These were not heard by the other vessels in the bay, because the night was so stormy. At about half-past seven they got her off and set all sail, hoping to beach her, but she had taken in so much water that she was water-logged. The chief mate told Captain Wordsworth that the carpenter could not stop the leak and he answered, "It cannot be helped, God's will be done." He was then standing upon the hen-coop on the bridge. A few minutes later the ship went down, before all the boats could be launched. The bay where she sank was so shallow that her topmasts stuck out of the water; and some survivors climbed into the shrouds, fighting each other like drowning rats, and clung there among the waves till they could be rescued. John was swept overboard when she sank and was seen struggling for a time, having laid hold of a rope, but there was a heavy sea running and the night was very cold. He was a strong swimmer, but he must soon have been exhausted. Between two and three hundred persons were drowned in this shipwreck. John's body was later cast up on Weymouth Beach and he was buried at Wyke church in Dorset, with other victims of the disaster. He was just thirty-three years old.

All the household at Dove Cottage went about their work with dismal hearts. Dear John had known the place and loved it well. Everything that they saw reminded them of him, and when Dorothy walked out in the green vale she saw nothing that he would not have loved and enjoyed. There had been still weather for some days together after they heard the dreadful news and it seemed to mock their grief with its melancholy. Dorothy had even a feeling of joy when she first heard the wind again as she lay in her bed. She felt that she would never again have a perfect joy in the world and she knew that William felt that too. She kept constantly employed and tried to be cheerful for his sake, but it was heavy work. At first she could not bear to speak of John, but later, as she grew stronger, she found that it did her good to remember him. She turned to the melancholy garden and put it in order; she played and walked with Johnny and the baby, she and Mary cleaned the house and they all three worked to finish the moss-hut in the garden, so that William might have some place to write in, out of earshot of the joyous children. Even on rainy mornings it became a warm shelter and the wrens often alighted on the roof and sang their low song there. She and William found it the sweetest place on earth and they sat there very often, for the two clung together more than ever since the loss of their brother. She had begun to write down her recollections of their tour in Scotland, before John's death, thinking that he might like to read it when he was at sea and now William urged her to finish it. At first she found the task a very painful one, but afterwards it grew to be a comfort to her. In June all was done and William finished *The Prelude*.

He had been almost seven years writing it and when he had done with it he fell into a great melancholy. The reality seemed to him to fall so far short of his expectation; he was disappointed in the finished work and had many sad and heavy thoughts of his dead brother. He said to Dorothy, "I worked to show John that he had not placed a false confidence in me. I never wrote a line without thinking that it might give him pleasure, but now he will never read it." Dorothy and Mary could not bear to hear him talk so. It was a most unusual mood in him, for he was in general satisfied with his own work once it was done. They persuaded him to take a holiday and after making some difficulties he consented to go over and fish in Patterdale for a few days. Mary and Dorothy walked with him as far as the top of Grisedale and parted from him beside the tarn where she and William had bidden John farewell for the last time. She had visited it twice since John's death; the first time had been agony, but now it was another feeling. She had learnt to rejoice in his memory, and the tarn had become a holy place to them all. The three sat down by the water and had some sweet talk of their lost brother. Then William went from them more cheerfully down the stony path, with his fishing rod over his shoulder and the two women went home.

X

I

THERE WAS a great deal of coming and going at the cottage all that summer. Walter Scott came to visit them, with his wife; he was just the same as ever. He dined with them in the parlour, sitting and talking while Mary and Dorothy dressed the leg of mutton at the fire. Little Johnny adored him. William took him up Helvellyn, and his friend Humphry Davy with him, to see the place where the young man Gough had lately fallen down the black precipice under Swirrel Edge. Gough's dog had watched his bones faithfully in that lonely place for three months together, until some shepherd heard it barking; it was so scared from dwelling in that solitude that it would let no man near it, till in the end the sheep dogs brought it close enough to be fed and caught. All the people in the vale knew this story and the two poets each wrote a copy of verses upon it; "*A barking sound the shepherd hears,*" and so forth. Walter Scott was in great spirits. He had lately published his *Lay of the Last Minstrel*, the same poem of which they had heard the beginning in the lodgings at Jedburgh. It had been very well received and was likely to start a new fashion for ruins, armour and forsaken knights and ladies.

After the Scotts had gone away Aunt Threlkeld came over from Halifax. The good woman, who had brought Dorothy up, thought her much changed and aged by that sad year, but Dorothy, laughing and sighing a little, complained, "Dear aunt, I am thirty-three and I have lost half my teeth, my cheeks are quite sunk. You must not expect me to be a beauty nowadays." She knew that she had grown very thin and haggard, but she felt that her heart was as young as ever when she played with the children, and she could still walk over the hills with a light foot whenever William invited her to a wander. She found that summer a strangely happy one. Brother Richard came to stay and was more pleasant than usual. When he went away he gave her a pony to ride and a side-saddle, so that she and William might get about the country more easily; this was to prove a great delight to her. Catherine Clarkson came upon a long visit. She took lodgings at Robert Newton's in the village and though she had become a great invalid, crippled with rheumatism and unable to walk much because of her weak heart, yet she was cheerful and merry. It was a joy to see her every day. She was charmed by her godson Johnny. He was a dear lively little boy, whose first word had been "Happy," which he used to chant as he wandered from room to room. He loved to visit Mrs. Clarkson, scramble up on her bed and be petted. Her maid, Susan, made him his first pair of blue breeches; he was very proud of them and of a little pocket to hang at his belt, which Susan made him.

All this summer and autumn they heard little of their friend Coleridge. He was at no time a good letter-writer and the posts were terribly uncertain, with war by sea and land. He had soon quarrelled with John Stoddart, the advocate-general, a stiff lawyer, upright and precise, who could not put up with the poet's shambling ways; but he had found another patron in Sir Alexander Ball, the governor of Malta and one of Nelson's sea captains. He had spent the hottest part of his first summer in Sicily, had returned to Malta the previous winter and had been lucky enough to get a temporary appointment in the Treasury; but now he lost it again and left the yellow island. They did not know where he was. There had been talk of his spending the winter in Naples, or in Rome.

The times were very dangerous, nobody knew what the Emperor would do next. His troops over-ran Austria, Poland and Germany; the Czar's army could not stand against him. It was said that he was going to invade Italy again, he seemed invincible. The news was all so dismal that they quite dreaded the arrival of the papers There was the wildest excitement in

Penrith and Ambleside that year when, in the middle of October, the bells were rung for the victory of Trafalgar. William and Dorothy heard the news at Patterdale, where they were spending a few days with friends. The maid-servant opened the door, poked in her head and with an uncouth stare and a grin of pleasure told them that there had been a great victory and Lord Nelson was shot. Dorothy burst into tears and William would not believe it at first, but they soon heard enough to leave them without a doubt. The news worked upon William's mind very powerfully and that autumn he wrote a poem which he called the *Happy Warrior.* He intended it as a memorial to the great admiral and to his own dead brother. He worked very hard all that winter, for starlight walks and winter winds were his delight and his mind was often more fertile in that season than in any other. He began to write *The Excursion*, a poem about his daily life in the valley, finished his great *Ode upon the Intimations of Immortality in Childhood*, and composed an *Ode to Duty*, with which he was very well pleased.

At Christmas he and Mary went over to Park House for a time and Dorothy had the cottage and the children to herself, to her great pleasure. It was her thirty-fourth birthday and it was a very happy day for her, though she could not but cast her mind back to the previous year, when John, dear John, was in London, with all his heart set upon the accomplishment of his fatal voyage. The Christmas before that her friend Coleridge had been under their roof. She thought much of him. When the wind, rain and snow drove down the vale and the chimney roared as if it would come down upon the cottage, her heart fluttered and ached to think how dreadful such weather was for a sea voyage and she wished him somewhere safe upon land. But she could not have much leisure to brood upon these fears and sorrows with the children tumbling about at her feet, little Dorothy laughing and Johnny all alive at the thought of two plum-puddings rumbling in the pot and a sirloin of beef smoking before the fire. Old Molly and John Fisher were in the kitchen; when dinner was ready they came upstairs and partook with her and the children.

Afterwards the fiddlers came to play and all the children of the neighbouring cottages were assembled in the kitchen to dance. There were half a dozen of them, boys and girls, they made a pleasant pattering sound with their feet upon the stone floor. Johnny had long talked of the time when the fiddler was to come, but he was too shy to dance with any one but his aunt, and when she was out of breath he stood by the wall, as grave as an old man; little Dorothy was in ecstasy. It was the sixth Christmas that her aunt had spent in Grasmere and she thought it the pleasantest yet. When the fiddlers had gone she undressed the children and put them to bed. In ten minutes after all was stillness and perfect rest. She sat in the parlour, with the door open to the bedroom, so that she tiptoed across now and then to peep in at the two of them upon their pillows. There was no sound except the ticking of the family watch, which hung in its pocket over the chimney-piece, the nibblings of a mouse in the wainscot and the beating of one single irregular flame in the wood fire. She sat and dreamed for a sweet hour, then wrote her Christmas letters to her friends, and to Catherine Clarkson, who best could understand her meaning, she said that the last six years had been the happiest of her life.

2

After Christmas, when Mary and William came home again, they brought Sara Hutchinson with them. She was to be with Mary and help her, through the spring and summer, for Mary was already carrying her third child; in the end it was decided that she should make her home with the Wordsworths for the rest of her life. Tom Hutchinson had his little sister Joanna to keep house for him over at Dacre. The laughing tomboy had grown into a sensible solid farmer's sister, a great hand with lambs and chickens. Sara had always been the bookish one of that family, she would be happier where she could hear talk of such matters, and Mary had always been her favourite sister. She was glad to help with the children and was not bad company in the house. She had a pleasant dry humour and did not put herself forward. Between her and Dorothy there would always be the undercurrent of hidden feeling concerning their absent friend, but while he was still lost somewhere in Italy, sending no word of his plans, the two women could do well enough together.

Early in the year William and Dorothy went over to Keswick, to see if they could get any more news of the wanderer, but even his wife did not know where he might be, and his children seemed almost to have forgotten him. Dorothy asked Robert Southey, who now seemed to be the head of the household, whether Hartley, who should have remembered him best, did not ever ask for his father, but Robert took snuff, and shook his head doubtfully. He said, "Hartley will never speak of him. He is an odd boy and like his father in this; he has plenty of affection for those who are with him, but none to spare for those who are away. It is out of sight, out of mind, with Hartley." She could not speak for the moment, because he brought back so much past trouble by that reflection; and Robert continued, "When our old housekeeper Wilson was so ill last year the boy never showed the slightest concern about her, though you know how good she has been to him and how much he seems to love her. He would not even go near her, lest it should give him pain. He put her out of his mind and did his best to forget her, or so it seemed to me. I was very anxious about his behaviour." He gave her an owlish look which was very characteristic of him, peering up over imaginary spectacles, for he had ruined his sight with too much bookwork. He said, "Hartley is a most unnatural child."

She could not help laughing at his gravity and said affectionately, "You must not worry yourself over him. Children are all unnatural little wretches at that age. I am sure Hartley loves his father very dearly, and his old Nurse Wilsey too"; but Robert would not be comforted. He persisted, "I cannot understand the boy at all. I fear he is too much like his father. He has a most prodigious and unnatural intellect, but he is in danger of dreaming away his life. You would think he had two left hands, he is so clumsy; when he puts his food into his mouth he forgets to swallow it. He is the oddest of God's creatures and becomes quainter every day. Have you heard him talk about this imaginary island of his, this Ejuxria, as he calls it?" She said, "Oh! dear me, yes; he talks about it by the hour. He is very amusing about it"; but Robert Southey did not think there was anything humorous in the matter. He gazed at her lumpishly and lamented, "The boy thinks of nothing else. He has drawn a map of the place, with all the towns and rivers and mountains, and the other day he was stumping about dictating to his mother a long history about a certain Saint Malo, who lived there. He will not admit the existence of any other world. I verily believe he thinks he lives in Ejuxria." She said, smiling, "Why, it is only that the boy is a poet. You should know what that means, you are a poet yourself. Did you never make up such fancies when you were his age?" He shook his dark handsome head and looked utterly blank and stupid, protesting, "I hope I never had any such nonsense in my mind." She sighed and despaired of his ever understanding Hartley; it was odd that, for a man who earned his living by writing poetry, Robert Southey should have so little imagination. That, of course, was his trouble; the kind sensible hard-working creature had not a spark of the divine fire in him. He kept on toiling away at enormous epics. *Thalaba* had been his first and he had lately published a most dreary poem, called *Madoc*, about a legendary Welsh chieftain and his exploits. William thought it insipid and contemptible and had been quite jealous of its success. She got up and left Robert in his great study, at his fine writing-table, still peering doubtfully up at her as if he were looking over spectacles. His farewell words floated after her, "That boy will waste his powers as his father did before him. He lives in a world of his own, he will never do any good in this life."

She went downstairs and peeped into the yellow-white parlour, which the Coleridge family called *Peter*. Hartley was lying on his face on the hearthrug, trying to read a book by the flickering light of the wood fire. She went in and sat by him on the striped yellow silk couch with the scroll-end, asking him pleasantly, "What news from Ejuxria, Hartley?" and he informed her very solemnly, "I have had letters and papers from there this morning." She said that she hoped his news was good; but Hartley shook his dark head and said, with his lip drooping, "No, no; things are going very badly there. My people are too fond of war. I have just made an eloquent speech in the senate, which has not made any impression on them, and to war they will go." She sighed to think how fatally children in their play would imitate the follies and miseries of the world into which they had been born; and to distract him from his fancies asked him over what book he was wearing out his dark eyes. He said, "It is *Robinson Crusoe* and my uncle gave it to me. I read it very often"; but when she asked him whether he liked it he said, with a strange unchildlike passion, "It is well enough while he is on the island, but I will not read the end. I do not care about what happened afterwards. Nobody shall make me read that. I never will know." She protested, "Should not the poor man go back to all the people who loved him," but he only stuck out his under lip with the obstinacy of seven years old and maintained, "If I had been Robinson Crusoe, I would have stayed on the island for ever." He seemed to be a little mad upon the subject of islands; many people are, of course. Dorothy would have laughed at his solemnity if it had not suddenly struck her that his kind dull uncle was perfectly right about him. The boy did not wish to grow up and take his place in the stupid everyday world, he wanted to go on amusing himself all his life in the islands of his imagination.

She did not know what was to become of him. He was a changeling, and there was nobody in that house who could manage him or understand him. She wished with all her heart that his father would come back.

3

That spring, 1806, the French armies came to Naples, to make the Emperor's brother Joseph king of it, and their friend Coleridge did actually begin to be in some danger of arrest. It seemed that he had written some articles in the *Morning Post* when he was working for them, denouncing the Corsican tyrant, and the French secret police had a black mark against his name in their books; or so he imagined. He escaped out of Rome in May, and went to Leghorn, where he got a passage to England on an American ship. They say that she was chased by a French cruiser in the Bay of Biscay and that he threw all his manuscripts overboard; whatever he did by the way, he did not get home until the middle of August. Meanwhile his friends in Grasmere had no notion where he was and were very anxious about him.

William went to London in March for six weeks, the first time that he had been south since he married Mary. He stayed with the kind Beaumonts in Grosvenor Square, where everything was very rich and magnificent. He also visited brother Kit and his wife Priscilla and their small boys in Lambeth, for the clever young don had given up his Cambridge fellowship for a Kentish rectory and the office of domestic chaplain to the Archbishop of Canterbury. One of these days, the family decided, Kit would be a dean, or perhaps even a bishop. William visited Basil Montagu and all his old friends, including the Lambs, whom he found hard at work, in Mitre Court Buildings, writing at opposite ends of the same table, like a literary Darby and Joan, they said, she taking snuff and he groaning all the while and saying he could make nothing of their task. They were writing a children's book, *Tales from Shakespeare*, for they said there were no good children's books to be got, only moral tales. Charles was doing the six tragedies, *Lear, Macbeth, Hamlet, Timon, Othello, and Romeo and Juliet*; while Mary was getting on capitally with the comedies, only she complained of having to set forth so many female characters in boys' clothes. Charles declared that she thought Shakespeare must have wanted imagination; he was still as great a tease as ever, but she did not mind him. They two seemed uncommonly happy together. Mary had been out of her wits for a time, from the shock of hearing of John Wordsworth's drowning, but she had quite recovered again and was placid and composed. She sent loving messages to Dorothy and promised that Johnny should have a copy of the *Tales from Shakespeare* when they were finished.

William was dreadfully missed while he was away, it seemed strange to be a household of women and children only, but there was at least more room to turn round without him. They were crammed in their little nest edge full and often talked of moving to some larger house, where they could keep two young servants, so that William might have a place to work in away from the children and they could have a bed for a friend; but they could not decide anything until Coleridge came home, for he had said that he would never live through another winter in Cumberland and they hoped to settle somewhere near him, if that were possible. William came back from London in May with a charming suggestion from Lady Beaumont, that they should all spend the following winter in the home-farm on Sir George's estate, at Coleorton in Leicestershire; but they did not know what to say until they heard from their friend.

In the middle of June William's third child was born, another boy this time, almost three years after Johnny's own birthday and on just such another exquisite June morning; it seemed to Dorothy like the same thing happening over again when she held the little warm creature in her arms.

He was called Thomas, after Mary's favourite brother and perhaps a little too for Tom Poole at Nether Stowey, and for Thomas Clarkson; it was a name with many friendly associations in that household. His sister Dorothy, whom they now called Sissy, and sometimes Dora, to distinguish her from her aunt, was in ecstasy whenever she saw her baby brother. She had grown into the sweetest chatterer ever seen and she talked about little Tom not only the day through, but in her dreams at night, repeating, "Baby, baby," till they smiled to hear her. She was her father's favourite, never happy when in his sight if she was out of his arms.

As soon as Mary was strong enough to be left, William and Dorothy took the little girl over Kirkstone Pass to Park House. Johnny had been sent there some weeks earlier, for fear he should catch whooping-cough, for all the village children had it in Grasmere. It was a fine journey for Dora, her father carried her on his back over the mountains and then they all went down Ullswater in a boat. Dora was the sweetest companion that ever travellers had; she noticed the crags, the streams, and everything that they saw, and when they passed by any living creatures, sheep or cows, she began to sing her baby songs, *Baa, baa, black sheep* and *Cushy, cow, bonny*, which her aunt had taught her. She was not even frightened in the boat, though for half an hour she cried dreadfully, wanting to be out and in the water. That was all the trouble they had with her on the journey and afterwards she fell asleep and did not wake till they landed. She and Johnny loved their holiday at Park House, where there were fluffy yellow ducks and chickens, a pet lamb in the orchard, a family of kittens in a manger with stiff upright tails, very soft and wild, scrambling about in the straw and a great turkey-cock who frightened Johnny. Dorothy was very happy there too, sitting on the green grass with Joanna, outside the little castle in the valley, while the children tumbled about them in the summer sun: she was quite sorry to go home again

In August they heard the happy news that their friend Coleridge was home again. His ship was lying in quarantine off Portsmouth. They supposed that they might look for him within a week or two, and when they had another short letter, dated from the Lambs' rooms in the Temple, they were sure of it. They had not seen him for two years and a half, Johnny and little Dora could not even remember him. Their aunt tried to tell them what he looked like, the father of their Keswick playmates, Hartley, Derwent and Sara, but she found that she could not remember him clearly, as he had been when he went away, pale, sick and distracted. In her mind he had reverted to what he once was, a young man with light eyes and a broad shining forehead, for ever talking in his beautiful voice. She told them that when he came home he would be the most splendid person they had ever seen.

William was gravely delighted, he went about humming tunelessly to himself, repressing the contented grin which threatened to stretch his lantern jaws; he too had forgotten a little what their friend might be like. Mary watched her husband, smiling at his evident pleasure, but she became a little doubtful when the days stretched themselves into weeks and still their friend neither came nor wrote. She said, anxiously, "My dear, we really must be making our plans for the winter. We cannot keep Lady Beaumont waiting much longer. She has written again and again to know whether we will take the farm or no. She will think us most ungrateful and inconsiderate. We cannot go on like this. Do, pray, write to your friend again and ask him what is to be done. I do not want to make that long journey with the children after the weather gets cold. You know baby's cough is very troublesome and Dora gets croup so easily." The children had all taken the whooping-cough in the end, in spite of going to Park House to be out of the way of infection, and all through that long hot September they were coughing and whooping miserably; you could hear them all over the cottage. Mary was very much worried about the baby Tom, who had it worst.

She sat up half the night nursing him and rocking him in her arms and grew very fidgetty about him. Mary was usually as placid as a cow in a field, the most contented object in nature, but when the children were ill a cow that has lost its calf was not more distracted than she.

By the middle of September they had all made up their minds that something was wrong, though they would not admit it to each other. Then one day the postman, trudging over White Moss in the thundery heat, had a letter for them in the box at his back and it was from Mary Lamb. The good creature wrote in her crabbed ill-formed hand, in much distress, to say that Coleridge had left them and gone to a lodging at the *Courier* newspaper office, in the Strand. He was ill and wretched and could not bring his mind to anything, but he swore that nothing should persuade him to come back to his wife. He would never live with her again.

Mary and William looked at each other. Dorothy turned away her head for fear either of them should see the jealous satisfaction which leapt up in her at the news that her friend's unhappy marriage, after all these years, had come to an end. William sighed, "I never thought he would go back to her" and Mary burst out, with her warm eager maternal look, "But these three poor children; what is to become of them? The boys are wild to have him back, they have been counting the days till they could see their father again; even poor little Sara, who cannot remember what he looks like, is always talking of him. Mrs. Coleridge said that he would be here in the last week of September without fail; she told me that she had had a letter from him. She asked me with tears in her eyes whether I thought she had changed much, or lost her looks since he went away; then she looked at herself in the glass, cried and wrung her hands and said that if he would but come back she would try and make him a good wife." William shook his head and said, "God knows they were never fit for one another." Dorothy flashed out the shooting lights of her wild eyes at the married pair, and exclaimed, "She does not deserve to have him back; she has never deserved him."

Mary looked at her with astonishment and pity. William gave her a glance less tender than severe, then said to his wife, doubtfully, "Your sister will know more of this than we do, I suppose." Mary agreed, "Yes, he will surely have written to Sara. We may hear something when she comes home." Sara was then at Park House for a few days, for she had wanted to spend a little time with Tom and Joanna before going to Coleorton for the winter. Dorothy had not realised that the pale girl might have a finger in the pie still and burst out in her ignorance, "What has all this to do with Sara?" The married pair exchanged a glance of intimacy and knowledge which bewildered her, they had an understanding from which she was shut out. She began to stammer very much, as she always did when she was agitated, choking and struggling with her words as she protested, "B-but t-that's all over. That must be all over." They said nothing and her resentment flooded every corner of her mind with a ninth wave of barren bitterness. She exclaimed, "Perhaps he loved her before he went away, but he has been gone more than two years. You could not expect him to be faithful to any one for as long a time as that." She stopped and panted for breath, looking from one to the other.

William's face was set in its heaviest lines, he looked as he did when he fixed his brow against the wind and open sky. He groaned, "This will be a wretched business." Mary laid her hand on his shoulder as she stood beside him, and said confidently to him, "You can trust Sara. She will be able to manage him, she will not try to come between him and his children." Dorothy stared at her as she bent over William, calm and wholesome and strong. He covered his wife's hand with his own, as it lay on his shoulder, and turned his face to her; and Dorothy thought, "These Hutchinson women take everything away from me." But her mind itself stammered and refused to find words for the secret hope which Mary had just calmly laid in ruins. For a moment or two nobody spoke; then William said, "Well, I must see him and speak to him. I will write to him and tell him that if he does not come immediately I must insist on seeing him somewhere. If he appoints London I shall go." And he concluded with simplicity and earnest kindness, "I believe if anything good is to be done for him it must be done by me." His words were some comfort to his sister's sore heart.

4

September, however, slipped into October, the trees turned yellow and the mornings grew frosty, without a word from their friend. He did not answer William's letter or come on the day that his wife expected him. William did not dare to start for London, lest they should pass each other on the way. Lady Beaumont wrote that she and her husband would soon be going back to London, could not the Wordsworths come down and settle in the home-farm before she left? Naturally she did not understand why the journey should be so long delayed. Mary was beginning to fidget again about the children catching cold by the way, even William lost patience. Dorothy felt that she could not bear to go away without seeing their friend, but the decision did not lie with her; so on the third Sunday in October, 1806, they drove down by the side of Windermere to Kendal, where they were to pick up Sara Hutchinson. When they drove into the inn-yard she came out to meet them, trembling and in great distress, crying and holding out a letter from Coleridge. He had just missed her by half an hour at Penrith, she had left on the south-bound coach and must have passed the London coach which brought him down. He wrote that he could not bear to come to Kendal, just to see them and then part again; the lines were shaken and ill-written and blotted in part by her tears.

It was dreadful to miss him so nearly. They all looked

blankly upon one another and the tired frightened children, who could not tell what was happening, burst out crying. Mary looked distracted between them and Dorothy could hardly soothe them. William, however, said calmly that they would all wait in Kendal one more day. He went into the inn to order rooms for them and sent off a messenger with a letter to Keswick, for he naturally supposed that Coleridge had gone there to see his wife and children. This they all believed; but before seven o'clock in the evening, as the women were putting the three children to bed together in a great four-poster with green serge curtains, William knocked at the door of the bedroom and said that Coleridge had come to Kendal. He was staying at another inn and was waiting to see them. So they left the children in charge of a friendly chambermaid, with a piece of Kendal mint-cake to keep them quiet, put on their cloaks and went out with William.

It was very dark in the long cobbled street. Mary and her sister both stumbled and hung upon William's arm, but Dorothy walked by herself and folded her arms beneath her old grey duffel cloak against the frost of the October night. She could see neither moon nor stars, but she heard the roaring of the river down at the foot of the hill, grinding the stones in its bed and complaining aloud. The air was thin and cold in her nostrils and her heart was beating so fast that she could not speak. Presently they saw the red light shining through the curtains of the tavern where their friend was. They went in and found him sitting in a little dirty parlour by himself, sunk in a broken leather arm-chair, half-asleep, staring at a fire of glowing peat and sipping at a steaming glass. The room reeked of spirits and peat-smoke together, it was insufferably hot. When the door opened he turned his head and gaped as if he did not know them, then he got slowly and clumsily to his feet. Dorothy had never felt such a shock as she did then at first sight of his face. It was bloated and swollen, dead white, and like the flesh of a person in dropsy, his eyes were lost in fat. He was utterly changed and extinguished, all the strength and plumage of his youth were gone for ever. She would not have known him.

She could not go forward or speak to him, she leant against the wall and her knees gave way beneath her. William went in and took Coleridge's hand in his own strong clasp, even Mary was able to smile at him faintly, but she could not. She could only stand there trembling and fighting down her emotion, while Sara Hutchinson flung back the hood of her black cloak and stretched out both her hands to the returning wanderer. He took them in his and gazed long at the pale girl, while he shook his head and mumbled, "You should not have made me come here. I did not mean to see you. I did not mean you to know how I am changed." He turned away from them all, sank down again in the shabby chair and buried his face in his hands. He had not spoken to Dorothy and she felt as if her world had come to an end.

William was magnificent, even his sister had not known that he could be so kind and strong. He sat down by the trembling man, laid his hand on his knee and spoke to him with the utmost affection and forbearance, even with cheerfulness, as if nothing had changed between them. He spoke of common things, of plans for the journey and the winter, of his friend's travels and of the household at Keswick; Mary talked timidly but eagerly of the Coleridge children. Nobody mentioned Mrs. Coleridge. Sara Hutchinson hardly opened her mouth. She sat with her black hood still lying about her shoulders, her plain pale face and smooth hair rose from its folds with a strange distracted look. She clasped her hands on her knee and sat as still as a statue, but her eyes never moved from the broken creature in the chair. She looked him over and over, as if her eyes could never have enough of him. Dorothy knew too well the enchantment under which the girl laboured, but she herself had gone far beyond all that. She stood still, leaning against the wall, trying to think what could now be done to save her friend, and searching that white bloated countenance for some gleam or shadow of its old divine expression, but never saw it as it used to be.

There was at times some faint light of interest in his drugged eye, when William questioned him cheerily about his journey and roused him to some travellers' recollections. He spoke with a certain dreary pleasure of the lion-tawny island where he had dwelt, of the noisy crowds thronging up and down the staircases of precipitous streets; of the marble pavement in the cathedral, all inlaid with the armorial bearings of the Knights of St. John; of ships coming and going in the blue harbour of Valetta; and of the mimic pomp and parade of the governor's court. He seemed perversely glad to chatter of routs at the palace, of red carpets and suits of armour, and the trains and feathers of the ladies, of uniforms and naval scandal; but whenever the talk turned upon his own family affairs his eye glazed and his face became vacant. He sank together in his chair, turned the glass of grog about in his fingers till the sugar melted in the laudanum, sipped, shivered and yawned as if he had forgotten the presence of his friends. They could do nothing with him that night and at last, long after midnight, they forced themselves to leave him.

5

They laboured with him all next day, but could get little from him. He was sunk in a dreadful stupor, sodden with liquor and opium together, tormented by frightful irresolution. He rambled from one thing to another and was hardly able to keep his eyes open. They could not persuade him to any one course of action and when they pressed him too hard he would burst out into wild accusations against them. "You are all in a tale together, you want to drive me back to my wife, but I will never go to her. I am resolved to part from her or die." He blubbered, "You none of you care what becomes of me. I have wearied you out with my ill-behaviour.

You can none of you endure me now, except Sara here, and she does not understand what I am like. I want no one but her, you may all leave me; she is gentle and kind, she forgives me. Let her stay with me. She is my only hope." He snatched at the girl's cold hand, mumbled it with his unsteady lips and implored her not to leave him, while her sister Mary sat by with a set look and William shook his grave head. Sara Hutchinson looked at them all defiantly; then she drew his shamed head to her breast and comforted and caressed him, speaking to him in a low brooding murmur, while Dorothy turned her back on the pair of them. She felt as if she had been stabbed to the heart when she heard the sick man mutter, "It won't be for long, I can't live in the state I'm in; if there is no other way for you all to be rid of me then I will destroy myself. I have suffered enough. Hell is here and I am in it, I cannot endure any more misery." And he looked round at them all with a dreadful sly cunning, to see whether he had moved them by his empty threats. She was sick at heart for his folly and the dreadful change in him, his fire was out and choked with ashes.

She could hardly bear to listen to him, but William treated him with the most scrupulous and delicate patience. He was like a careful old sheepdog trying to pen a silly wether with the rest of the flock. Time and again he worked round to the same point; time and again his victim broke away with a flurry and a scramble and all was to do afresh. Should they alter their own plans? offered William; should they go back and spend yet another winter in Dove Cottage, or take a house in Hawkshead where he could live with them? Would he come with them next day to Coleorton? Their friend said violently that he would never survive another winter in the cold north, then more vaguely believed that now he was so near her he would go as far as Keswick and thrash out the whole question of their future with his wife. William agreed; "She has a right to see you. She does not understand that you are turned so much against her, she should hear it from your own lips. You must tell her what you mean to do for her and how you will provide for her and the children. Are they to have the Wedgwood pension? and if so what are you to live upon? At least the boys must be properly educated." Mary, with the rich colour mounting in her cheeks, urged him warmly, "You must see the children. You do not know how often they have talked of your coming home. Hartley is grown into a wonderful boy, so brilliant and clever, he is a son for any father to be proud of; Derwent is so handsome and healthy and your little girl is like a fairy or a snowdrop, so pale and delicate. She does not even know what you are like, she is always asking us to tell her about her father. Surely you could not go away again without seeing them."

He muttered ungraciously that if he went to Keswick he would be caught and tied down, like a bird on a twig sticky with bird-lime. They could all see that he dreaded his wife's tears and lamentations unbearably, but William urged him to it, saying, "You will never have any peace in yourself till that is over and done with." At last it was so arranged. He was to go to Keswick, arrange matters there and come to them at Coleorton in a month's time. If he could get them away he was to bring his boys with him. Early on the Tuesday morning Mary and Dorothy packed into a post-chaise with the nursemaid and the three children and drove away. William and Sara were to stay another day, make certain that Coleridge did start for Keswick and then follow by the coach. They were left standing at the inn door, with Coleridge between them like a prisoner. He looked as if he did not know where he was and he never gave his departing friends a look or gesture of farewell. It was the bitterest moment of Dorothy's life when he was left behind.

6

The three days' journey south was a tiring business for all of them. Johnny and Dora were lively enough to begin with, bobbing up and down, drumming on the windows of the chaise, calling to the postboy to crack his whip and gallop up hill and down dale, waving to drovers on the roads and shepherds in the fields as they went by them. They were excited by the cheerful bustle at the inns, and by the changing of horses after each stage, for they had never been further than twenty miles from home; but long before night they were weary of the confinement and whined for Grasmere and old friends. Baby Tom's cough was very bad. Mary thought that he had caught cold in the inn at Kendal. He lay flushed and choking in her arms and she was very worried about him. However, they travelled down into the midlands by easy stages, so that William and Sara overtook them. They all reached Coleorton on the last day of October and immediately everything seemed to get better.

The great house stood in a park full of oak-trees, with a view towards Charnwood Forest, which the smoke of the collieries would spoil for the next generation, but it still seemed romantic in those days. The hall was a fine old place, though Sir George was rebuilding it to suit the modern taste and the farm where they were to spend the winter was very snug, a flat-fronted three-storied house built of the claret-red bricks of the midlands, facing to the south, warm and sunny. They arrived on a sharp frosted evening, with the smell of autumn bonfires in the village and Sir George's pheasants calling in the covers, wanting nothing but coal fires and warm beds, which they found prepared for them. Lady Beaumont came down to call upon them the very next morning, before they were half unpacked. Johnny rushed in to tell his mother that there was such a pretty lady at the gate, and when they looked out there was Lady Beaumont, a slender dark-eyed gushing creature, in a dove-grey quilted silk pelisse and an ermine scarf and muff, with a lap-dog in her arms and a tall footman waiting upon her. She came in with a waft of perfume, dropping the yapping little dog to take them all by both hands one after the other and sigh out a fluting welcome. "Here you are at last! I began to think that I should never see you. I know I ought not to come while you are still so busy with your boxes, but I could not wait to welcome you. We have been such friends on paper these two years." This was to Dorothy's address; for she and Lady Beaumont had carried on a steady correspondence ever since the time when the Beaumonts had taken such care of Coleridge, in their Grosvenor Square house, when he fell sick there on his way to Malta.

Lady Beaumont sank on to the sofa and gazed appealingly at them, as if she begged them to like her, while she murmured, "Where is your dear, delightful brother? Am I not to see him?" William was dug out of his own parlour, where he was unpacking his papers. He made himself more agreeable than might have been expected, bending over the lady's hand with surprising affability for him, while she begged him and Mary to come to dinner that evening. "You must come, you must all come," she urged them, clasping her hands as if she feared they might break her heart by a refusal. "You know Sir George and I must positively go to London to-morrow or the next day at latest and I cannot be happy unless you will dine with us first. Oh! why could you not come sooner? I had promised myself so many evenings in your company!" She was so anxious to please that you could not crush her by refusing to like her and Dorothy did like her very well, once she had accustomed herself to the Grosvenor Square manner. It was like the sweet subtle clinging perfume which the lady spread about her from her silken skirts; at first it worried you, then you liked it and afterwards you missed it when it was gone. She sat on the sofa for twenty minutes, chattering away, while the women smiled at her and William bowed and smirked at her clumsily. Dora played with this charming godmother's filigree smelling-salts and secretly stroked her ermine scarf; the child was enchanted by the black tails upon it, which she took for kittens' tails. Dora always had a passion for kittens. Johnny could not take his eyes off the pretty lady; he sat and stared at her like an owl until she rose and pinched his round cheek and floated away.

William was much gratified by this immediate attention from his patrons. Sara was a little flustered by the thought of dining at the Hall. She doubted that her best gown would not be good enough for the occasion and spent the rest of the day ironing it and freshening it up with pink silk bows, a little too bright for her pinched and sallow face. Mary was chiefly anxious about leaving the children alone in a strange place for a whole evening, but fortunately they seemed to have taken to the maid at the farm; as for Dorothy, she never cared what she looked like and was anxious to meet Sir George. So they dressed themselves in their best and crossed the corner of the park in cloaks and pattens, under a rosy frosty sunset, all hungrier than usual, for the Beaumonts were so fashionable that they did not dine till five, even in the country.

The Hall was not looking its best, for Sir George had got the workmen in; he was adding a picture gallery and remodelling the saloons in the neo-Gothic style. It would all be very cold and forbidding when it was done, but at present there were planks and heaps of lime in the drive and scaffolding all over the house. Lady Beaumont's green drawing-room, however, had not yet been interfered with, though it had to be approached through an unfinished octagonal stone hall like a chapter-house. It was charming still with its flower-wreathed carpet, its elegant gold and white furniture, its bird-cages, flower-paintings and tinkling glass lustres; a very feminine room, much like its owner. Lady Beaumont swam to meet them, very elegant in India muslin, her gown cut as low as a ball-dress, with rose-coloured kid sandals on her feet and seed-pearl flowers wreathed about her neck and slender arms. Sir George stood majestically upon the white fur hearthrug, warming the tails of his fine plum-coloured coat and fingering the bunch of antique seals dangling at his fob; he was a handsome rosy courteous gentleman, rather pompous in his manners, with a big Roman head and a good leg for a silk stocking. He made himself very gracious, but Sara was terrified of him.

The dinner was the finest meal that the women had any of them eaten, though Lady Beaumont apologised for everything being out of order, because they were on the point of leaving. They ate turtle soup and a haunch of venison, pheasants from Sir George's covers, and pineapples and grapes from his hothouses; menservants in livery waited upon them. Sara hardly dared to open her mouth. Mary was calm, handsome and silent, as she always was in company. Dorothy found Sir George an interesting talker and got on well with him, but she was a little disturbed by the anxious servility with which William deferred to his host and hostess. She had never seen him behave like that before since he was quite a young man and she did not like it; even when he was a shy and awkward boy he had not betrayed quite that eagerness to agree with his betters and his compliments to Lady Beaumont were delivered with so awkward a smirk and grin that his sister was quite ashamed of him. She thought to herself, as she had once thought with a shock when she saw him walking at a distance, "Can that be William? How very mean he looks!"

But after they had left the gentlemen to their wine it was better. Lady Beaumont was charming to them in the drawing-room. She quite won Dorothy to her side by her transparent admiration of William; and charmed Mary by praising her children, saying with a nervous flutter of her thin hands and a mist in her dark eyes, "You do not know how I envy you the three of them." She had no child of her own, poor lady. Presently the gentlemen came in and an enormous silver tea-equipage appeared, and was set out by two footmen. Lady Beaumont sat down at her harp and sang in a little voice like a pure thread of silver and afterwards she begged William to read aloud to them out of her own copy of the *Lyrical Ballads.*

The room was hushed to silence while he did it. Sir George sat with his eyes closed and his finger-tips pressed together, handsome and half-asleep, as if he were in church. Lady Beaumont had her hands clasped and her eyes fixed on the reader, the women of his household sat quiet while the familiar words ran over their minds. William's harsh chanting voice rose and fell, it filled the room with its own solemn music and Dorothy, relaxing slowly from all her doubts and miseries, said to herself with renewed faith and fervour, "There is nobody like William."

7

She and William went up next morning to see some of Sir George's books and pictures, though the best, he said, were packed away, ready for London, including the great Claude, the landscape which this rich conoisseur took everywhere with him. On the following morning he and his lady set off for Grosvenor Square, in their new travelling carriage, while their servants followed in the old family coach, with a mountain of trunks, band-boxes and bonnet-boxes. The Wordsworths were left to pass the winter at the home-farm. They were certainly very snug there, with great fires out of Sir George's coal-pits, game from his covers and eggs, butter and cream from his farm, as much as they chose; there was room for them all in the farm-house and a kind maid to help with the children. Dorothy was depressed at first by the rank smell of the wet turnip fields, the muddy lanes and weeping skies of the midlands and pined for the mountains, but she scolded herself for her ingratitude and tried to like Coleorton.

Their friend was continually in all their thoughts. He remained at Keswick through November and part of December, struggling through the long difficulties of the separation from his wife. He wrote that she wept and argued and broke out into outrageous passions, urging continually the one argument which had any effect on her mind, that this person and that person, and everybody would talk. The stupid affectionate creature clung despairingly to her home and to her settled position, trying all her foolish useless little arts in turn upon her exhausted husband; she could not imagine what was to become of her if he left her, for she had no power to make any life for herself except the one which she had always known. It was astonishing how steadily her husband did hold out against this tempest of distressed bewilderment and against the well-meant ineffective counsels of the Southeys. Edith, to be sure, made matters worse by her vigorous defence of her sister; while kind Robert Southey struggled in vain against his old instinctive distrust of his brilliant brother-in-law. He was profuse in advice to which none of the family listened. He knew well enough that the burden of the Coleridge family would certainly settle down in the end on his own broad uncomplaining shoulders. There would be four more hungry mouths to be fed out of his one inkstand and he was most anxious that the matter should be patched up if possible. William wrote to urge that the Coleridge boys should spend the winter at Coleorton and at last they heard that a separation had been arranged. Coleridge himself supposed that it was to be permanent; he was to take the boys and arrange for their schooling, their mother was to keep the little girl and have the boys for the holidays.

Just before Christmas, as they were putting up the holly and ivy in the parlour, Hartley arrived with his father. Dorothy had never been more happy in her life than when they had had him for an hour by the fireside, for his looks were like his old self; and although they only talked of common things, and of their friends, she perceived that he was contented in his mind and had settled things at Keswick to his satisfaction. Hartley was rosy and excited from the journey. His father said that he had been the most enchanting companion, chattering in his own sweet friendly fashion to all their fellow-travellers, though he had been quite beyond his father's control, wandering off and losing himself whenever the coach stopped. He was then just ten years old, a dark-haired, dark-eyed exquisite boy, with a full drooping mouth and a fluting voice. He had a terrifying resemblance to his unhappy father, the same sad look of morbid intelligence, the same arched delicate brows and rough dark curly hair. She could see that his father must have looked just like that at ten years old, with all his troubles still before him, and her heart ached for Hartley. He was the boy she would have wished to have, his father's eldest son, who might have been her own if everything had been different. She hung over the child and could refuse him nothing; but everybody spoiled Hartley. It was impossible to resist his sad confiding look, his stealing hand and wistful smile. He was dreadfully plausible with his excuses and singularly helpless and infantile. He left his books and toys everywhere as he tired of them, it was impossible to train him in any sort of method or order, scolding only bewildered him and he drifted about in a world of his own. She dared not think what would become of him.

In her inmost heart she no longer thought of her Christmas birthday as a day for jollity, and they all had much that year to trouble them, but they tried to be gay for the four children. They brought in holly and mistletoe and a great Yule log from the Hall woods, they played hunt the slipper and blind man's buff, snapdragon and spillikins, charades and riddles; children always love dressing-up. Their friend seemed less wretched than she had feared. He made a great and evident effort to cut down his drinking, took to ale instead of brandy, and for a time reduced his doses of opium; she was deceived into thinking that the renewal of their old pleasant companionship might yet cure him. He could not take the great walks that she and William did, but he strolled under the leafless oaks of the park with Sara beside him and in the evenings they all sat round the fire, after the children were in bed. The women sewed or knitted and William read aloud, in his strong chanting voice, evening by evening, the long rolling cantos of *The Prelude*, the poem which he had planned years ago in the woods of Alfoxden and begun in his cold lodgings at Goslar, the fruit of seven years' toil and recollection. The firelight painted the circle of familiar faces, night after night, as William recited the exaltations and agonies of his youth, all over and done with and laid away in verse for ever; but their friend sat with his hand shading his ravaged face. Dorothy could not see the ivory brow, but only the dark hair already going grey above it. On the last night, when William had done and laid his poem down, Coleridge rose, pressed the hand of his friend and seemed about to speak, but in the end he could not find words. He turned away and muttered something to himself. She thought he said, "God help me."

XI

I

FOR A TIME their friend did seem lifted out of himself, but as the grey Midland winter slipped by he relapsed, grew moody and jealous and took to his opiates again. He said that he could not sleep at night without them, nor get through the day without brandy. He turned sour, fretful and sullen and talked of his discomforts with a dreadful whining self-pity which sickened Dorothy. Sara Hutchinson encouraged him in his complaints by waiting on him hand and foot; he had but to burst out in his maudlin voice that something ailed him and she would come running, crying, "What is the matter? Let me help you." She lavished upon him an extravagant and indiscriminating pity which only ministered to his dejection. He could no longer force his diseased will to any sustained effort. He did no work, for he said that he could not settle to it while he was in such uncertainty about his private affairs. His wife had begun to pester him again with more of her silly letters. She seemed incapable of understanding that their separation was to be permanent and she kept on imploring him to relent and come back to her. He called Dorothy into his room upstairs one morning to read one of these blotted scrawls and it was like having the poor silly creature in the room, crying and wringing her hands over her lost happiness. She folded the page and gave it back to him, ashamed of having read it; then said, slowly, "The poor soul is half-frantic. I cannot but pity her."

He was vexed at that immediately, and protested, "It is nothing but wounded pride and fear of what people will say of us. She does not love me, we are nothing to each other now. We could never come together again. She is only trying to make a fair show before the world." Dorothy knew that this was for the most part true, yet Mrs. Coleridge's letter stuck in her mind; she said reluctantly, "I cannot bear to hear you talk of her so. You two were happy together once." He burst out angrily, "No, never, never; I was forced to marry her, I did not want her. I hate the sight of her"; and at Dorothy's shocked look continued harshly, "Oh, you are all against me now. You take her side, you want to part me from the only woman who could save me. You think the blame is all mine, you are trying to get rid of me. You are all tired of me . . . you despise me. . . ." He was half-crying, half-raging like a child, his voice rose to a shrill scolding note, she could not bear to listen to him. She thought of the blind and hopeless love for him which had been a fire in her own heart all these years and said passionately, "That is not true; you know it is not! It is you who have turned against us. William feels it and I feel it; you will not let us help you. It seems as if you will not let us love you. We made you happy once, but we cannot do it now. You have been wretched since you came here."

She faced him undaunted, trembling with generous indignation, and he could not withstand her; after a moment he turned away and sank into his chair. He covered his face with his hands and groaned out, "Can you wonder if I am wretched? Do you think I do not suffer when I compare William and myself? We two have changed places a little in these nine years, have we not? I was able to set him on his road once, but now he had gone plodding past me and I am left behind. I have thrown away all my chance, I have ruined myself; William may look down on me if he chooses." Something mean and bitter in his accents made her say with reproach, "I did not think you would ever be jealous of William." He persisted sullenly, "Well, I have cause to be jealous. He is loved and happy, he has a great future still before him, but I am a lost man. I have murdered myself." He sat there in obstinate self-pity, sunk in his chair and huddled together.

She did not know what to do for him. She stood dumb with tears in her eyes, and had a sudden agonising recollection of him as he leapt over the gate at Racedown and came bounding down the field into their lives. She had not guessed then all that he would do to make her wretched.

The door opened and Sara Hutchinson came in, with a kitchen apron tied over her gown and a basin of broth in her hand, steaming hot, with marigold petals floating for seasoning on the top. The two women looked at each other with a silent enmity; then Sara shut the door and came in. She put down the basin upon the table; then, as if they two were alone, she knelt down by the sick man and began petting him and coaxing him as if he were a child, filling the spoon and putting it to his lips. Dorothy turned on her heel and walked out of the room, defeated. As she went down the stairs she found her knees shaking under her with a jealous frenzy which she could not control. She had to stop and hold by the newel-post while she told herself over and over, "He is ill, he does not know what he is saying. Sara likes to have him in this state, because it gives her power over him. He will never get well while he is in her hands." It was not all true, but there was more than a grain of truth in it somewhere. She could not bear to see him so degraded.

2

At the end of February Coleridge's restlessness overcame him and he insisted on going up to London, where he had a chance of giving a course of lectures. William was very doubtful about this; he said, "It is the wrong work for him. He will drink to keep himself cheerful while he is in company, or to give himself strength to lecture and afterwards he will drug himself quiet to get a night's sleep. He will be flattered and encouraged to exert himself on amusing others; he will spend more than he gets and at the end of the winter he will have nothing to show for it." But go the sick man would and he insisted that Hartley should go with him. Dorothy thought that very bad; she lamented, "Hartley will be petted and spoilt by idle foolish people, he will copy his father's shiftless ways and get his head turned; at least let Hartley stay here with our children," but Hartley wept at the suggestion. He was bored with the little Wordsworths, who were all much younger than he was, and he did not want to go to the village school. He adored his brilliant father, who took him for walks and talked to him about chemistry and philosophy as if they were the same age; he wanted to go to London, to see Lady Beaumont's fine house in Grosvenor Square and have his quaint sayings repeated and laughed over by grown-up people. Dorothy was much distressed, she burst out to Mary, "If Coleridge will not listen to William or to me cannot your sister persuade him to see reason?" but Mary only sighed and said, "I fear his father is determined to take him."

So off went Hartley with his father in the coach to London, where he saw all the sights and was much petted by every one. He wrote a puppet-play and a poem to a young ass, which much amused his father's friends. He was painted by a young artist called David Wilkie, a *protégé* of Sir George's, he enjoyed himself greatly and did no lessons, it was an *annus mirabilis* for him. Coleorton semed very quiet with those two gone.

The spring came in gently, with primroses and violets in the hedges, and the rooks were very busy in Sir George's elms. William wrote a poem about the Shepherd Lord of Brougham Castle, beating it out in his mind as he paced to and fro between the farm and the Hall. He also devised a number of inscriptions in verse for urns, seats and grottoes, which Sir George meant to have engraved and set up here and there about the grounds; such trifles were then the fashion. William and Dorothy also prepared a new edition of his poems, in two volumes; it was as much Dorothy's book as his, for it contained all those lyrics which she had found and written down for him, when they two were living together at Dove

Cottage before he married. She did not think that he would ever write like that again. William was like the cuckoo, in the old rhyme which she taught the children that spring; in May he had sung all day, but in June he was changing his tune. His first sweet singing time had passed away, he fluted now with a sadder, more monotonous note, and Dorothy had little part in his singing.

When the sheets of the book had been sent away they amused themselves with another occupation. William planned and laid out a winter garden for Lady Beaumont. He and she had talked it over before she went off to Grosvenor Square and exchanged interminable letters about it. They planned a warm and sheltered corner, hedged about by firs and laurels, in a neglected part of the grounds. There was to be a long border under the terrace wall, with a south aspect, full of late-growing Michaelmas daisies and autumn roses and gay with flowering bulbs in the spring; the old quarry beyond was to be tapestried with trailing coloured berries and to have a pool in it which would reflect the church spire. A gold and a silver fish were to swim there and close at hand there should be a grotto with fossils in the walls and a mosaic of coloured pebbles in the floor.

Lady Beaumont had got the notion from a paper in the *Spectator*. She thought that it would be charming to wrap herself in her Indian shawl and stroll up and down the green mossy walks, between the clipped hedges of laurel and holly, in the winter sunshine, watching the birds; but Mr. Craig, the Scottish head-gardener, shook his head over these amateur notions. He thought fountains, bowers and grottoes quite out of fashion and said that the water would freeze and the fish die. He shook his grizzled head and muttered, "Losh," and "Heard ye ever the like?" and "Her leddyship kens naething aboot gardening. There's mony ane wad hae thocht themselves affronted . . . but it disna signify . . . folk maun do muckle they hae little will to do, in this warld . . ." and so forth. The truth was that he did not want William coming into his garden for two hours every day and telling him how to set about his work; but they made friends with him in the end. He set up a bench on the sunny side of a holly bush for William. The poet composed there frequently, or in the grove, pacing up and down between the young lime-trees which had been planted to look like the aisle of a cathedral; and Dorothy and the children had great fun sticking cockle-shells into the wet plaster of the grotto under the terrace steps. Their handiwork is there to this day.

3

In April, when the songs of spring were in the grove, William and Mary went up to London to stay with Basil Montagu in Soho, and took Sara with them. The pale girl had never been to London and it was natural that Mary should like to take her sister with her; Dorothy would not admit the jealous pang which she endured because Sara was going to see their friend. She herself stayed quietly at Coleorton with the children. It seemed dull when the others were gone, but the children were very sweet to her. Johnny had begun to go to the village school that winter, stumping off proudly every day with his dinner in a satchel and a bottle of milk in his pocket. Dora, they said, was just like her Aunt Dorothy at the same age, rosy, lively, wild and quick-tempered. She and Johnny had great battles, in which he was quite dangerous from his exceeding strength, for when he was disposed to quarrel with Dora he would snatch up whatever was nearest, a stool, a chair, a stick or even the poker. Their aunt had to be continually on the watch over the lively pair. Baby Tom was still thin and delicate after the whooping-cough. He was a sweet quiet child, with large blue eyes full of light and a curious pointing movement of his tongue when he smiled, which had made his father call him the Serpent-tongued.

Poor William came back from London in low spirits. His poems had fallen very flat and the critics seemed not to care for them at all. Dorothy was very much vexed and Lady Beaumont was indignant; she had boasted of her poet everywhere and it was her first experience of a disappointment with which the Wordsworths were already only too familiar. William's poetry seemed fated to be admired by no one but his friends. Lady Beaumont dashed off an angry letter, full of sympathy, which followed her poet to Coleorton, but William snubbed her for it. He would never admit a wound and he wrote back coldly, declaring that nineteen out of twenty of her fashionable friends could not be expected to appreciate his work. Such people, in the senseless hurry of their lives, did not read books, they merely glanced at them in order to talk about them and he would be stone-deaf to their buzzing.

The poor fellow was in fact very sore over his reviews and quite jealous of any author who succeeded better than he did. He was not at all pleased to hear that Mr. Clarkson's long history of the Quaker movement had gone into three editions and was even a little sour about the great success of the Lambs' *Tales from Shakespeare*. He and Mary had seen the dear creatures in London and found them well and cheerful, though the popularity of their book had not altogether consoled them for the sad failure of Charles Lamb's play, *Mr. H.*, which had been hissed off the stage at Dury Lane that winter; but literary folk must endure these reverses. Walter Scott came back with William from London and spent a few days with them on his way north. He at least could not complain of his public. He had set a new fashion with his *Lay of the Last Minstrel.* Every fine lady and gentleman now chattered of keeps and dungeons, escutcheons, wimples and morions. Mr. Scott could go on writing romantic mediæval poetry for as long as he chose. He was planning a poem called *Marmion* and had half a dozen other such subjects in his head. Poor William rubbed his nose gloomily and began to wonder whether he might not try something of the same kind himself.

They stayed at Coleorton till June, then they all packed up and went slowly back to Grasmere. They spent a fortnight in Halifax and Dorothy had great pleasure in revisiting the places which she had loved as a child. Aunt Threlkeld had long married Mr. Rawson, who owned a mill in the Ryburn valley, up above Sowerby Bridge; they stayed with her and heard great talk of changes in the West Riding. The mill owners had not yet come to putting in machinery, though within five years there would be rioting on that account, but all the different processes of cloth-working were being gathered into the mills now instead of being carried on in the cottages, as before. The place seemed larger and much more busy, for a clothing town always flourishes in war-time. Dorothy went down with Uncle William Threlkeld to look at the Piece Hall and it was noisier than ever, with great lengths of cloth hanging down from all the balconies and the square in the middle crowded with carts and horses. Even the chapel where she used to sit under Mr. Ralph on Sundays had been enlarged and her old seat was there no longer; but all her old friends were as kind and cheerful as ever. The girls she had been at school with, Jane Marshall and the rest, were most of them married now, with children growing up, and she liked to take William's children to visit them.

After Mary and the family had gone on home to Grasmere she and William had one of their old wanders together. They spent a day at Bolton Abbey, crossed the stepping-stones and sat in the ruins and went up to look at the Strid. William planned to write a ballad on the place, or perhaps something longer yet; he did not see why he should not embroider a piece of mediæval tapestry as well as Walter Scott could do, if he had a mind to it. Afterwards they two went up through the country round Ingleborough, a new landscape for her, where limestone bastions and escarpments fortified the long slopes of the hills. They rested under the white cliffs of Gordale, and drank the cold water of the Aire welling up full-grown out of Malham Cove; they passed a waterfall dropping down into a bottomless pothole on a brown moor, and leaned over the mouth of a black cavern to hear slow water running out of darkness into darkness. William said it was a haunted country, but it made Dorothy think of going with their friend to the Mendips, to visit his sacred river, long, long ago, when they were all young together. She wondered where he was and what he was doing. He had gone down that July to visit Tom Poole at Nether Stowey, taking Hartley with him, and his wife was at Bristol with her mother and the younger children; she pursued him constantly with letters and messages. No doubt they two would meet before the summer was over and perhaps in those familiar places he might weaken again to her entreaties. It all seemed sad and hopeless. Thinking of him, Dorothy lagged a little on the hot July moors, among the flowering heather, and William said, "You do not walk as well as you used to do."

When they got home again there seemed to be great changes in the valley. Their first walk in the evening was very melancholy, and their spirits sank, for everything seemed to have altered. Men and trees had fallen; old Mr. Sympson was dead and his son, too, and young George Dawson, the finest young man in the vale; all the trees at Bainriggs were cut down, the giant sycamore near the parsonage house was gone and all the finest fir trees that overtopped the church steeple. Even their dear cottage seemed a poor crowded wretched place after the fine rooms and comfort of Coleorton. It soon grew plain that they would never fit into it again with comfort, and they began to look about for a larger house, but did not find one easily.

The only place to suit them was an ugly new villa called Allan Bank and they all hated the sight of it. When you came over the White Moss from Rydal the first thing that you saw was this ugly square yellow building, with its two flat gables, staring you in the face from the hill behind the church steeple. It had quite spoilt the view of the lake from their moss-hut in the orchard. It was being put up to his own taste by a rich, common fellow from Liverpool, Mr. Crump, who intended to live there when he retired from business; but meanwhile he was not sorry to let it to the Wordsworths, once the workmen were out of it.

Mary and Dorothy went to look at it and were forced to admit that it would suit. It stood high and from the amber-green rocky pasture before it you could look out upon an amphitheatre of mountains, from the ridge of Fairfield to the smooth head of Seat Sandal. From her own window Dorothy would be able to see the clouds boiling up over the nick in the skyline where the pass went over into Patterdale, the way by which John had left them for ever. There would be plenty of good rooms in the house when the workmen had done with it; William would at last be able to have a study of his own, instead of pacing up and down the orchard, or trying to write in the parlour on his knee with the children playing about him. They could each have a bedroom of their own and there was another great room which could be kept for a study for their friend Coleridge. They expected him to spend much of his time with them and they were ready to take in his two boys and send them to school in Ambleside. All this they wrote off to him eagerly, but as usual got no reply. The Southeys said that he had been expected at old Mrs. Fricker's in Bristol, but had never appeared. They did not know whether he might be at Nether Stowey, or in Bridgwater, where he had spent some time, or whether he might not have gone back to London for the winter; so the Wordsworths had to come to terms with Mr. Crump without him. It was arranged that they should move into Allan Bank at the New Year, if possible; or, if the walls were not dried out, then at Easter.

4

Dorothy was sitting in the moss-hut, on a mild afternoon in the first week of November, when she heard a tumult in the house and Mary shouted. She was alarmed and ran down the garden slope with her heart beating fast. When she got indoors there was Hartley Coleridge, skipping about the panelled parlour in his own elf-like fashion, for joy at being in the north again. She looked through the window after she had kissed him and saw a post-chaise and two steaming horses; then in came Mrs. Coleridge, with Derwent and Sara, one in each hand. She was stout, red-faced and beaming, all out of breath and full of explanations. She had on one of the new poke-bonnets, high in the crown and plumed with feathers and a long green cloth pelisse, trimmed with cheap fur and buttoned all the way down the front with a row of buttons as big as crowns. She looked very well and was in great spirits, gushing and friendly, quite certain of her welcome. She babbled, "Well, here we are, all but my husband. He is gone to London to lecture to all the fine folk and I am sure we could never have got him into the chaise. We were so crammed together that you would have died of laughing if you had seen us. We have come all the way from Bristol by way of Liverpool. I do not know how many days we were on the journey, but I thought we should never get here. I cannot tell how we should have managed it if Mr. de Quincey had not been with us. He has been so kind and helpful and the children are all so fond of him, I declare they mind him better than they do me."

Dorothy became aware of another presence against the light of the open door, a slender dreamy youth, shy, small and modest, with a delicate profile, long eyelashes, curling light-brown hair and a pouting girlish mouth. He seemed terrified out of his wits and the hectic red and white came and went in his thin cheeks as Mrs. Coleridge dragged him forward, exclaiming, "This is Mr. de Quincey. He is so anxious to meet Mr. Wordsworth; he has read all his poems and has been writing him letters about them these two years from Oxford, so he says." The young gentleman clung to Mary's kind hand, as if it were a spar in the ocean where he was drowning. He gazed into her soft brown eyes, with their slight fascinating cast, while Mrs. Coleridge teased him, "Just imagine, the poor fellow has been as far as Coniston twice in the last three years, hoping to meet Mr. Wordsworth. Once he even walked as far as Hammerscar to look down upon the roof of your house, but then he ran away in a fright. I do not think he would be here now if I had not taken him under my wing."

Mr. de Quincey wavered forward and turned his bright and dreamy eyes on Dorothy, who had just come forward to greet him with the shy stammer which still plagued her as badly as ever when she had to meet a stranger. She fancied that he hardly knew where he was. He turned from her to stare at the door with intense expectation, which was presently explained when William came in, quite uninterested in his timid admirer and chiefly preoccupied with paying off the postboy. The young man seemed dreadfully agitated by the presence of his idol. Death on a pale horse, as he confided to Dorothy later, could not have alarmed him more. William was certainly very stiff with him. He had not yet learnt how to take such enthusiasm gracefully and this girlish youth had been plaguing him with admiring letters from Oxford for over three years. Dorothy wondered how the boy had ever had the courage to do it. She herself thought him remarkable and very interesting, she pitied him for his tongue-tied shyness and it gave her pleasure that William should have attracted such a promising disciple. She was ready to be kind to Mr. de Quincey; but all that she could do for him at the moment was to leave him with his deity in the parlour, while she and Mary chivied the children out into the garden to play in the moss-hut and then set themselves to entertain Mrs. Coleridge, a touchy guest who required all their attention for herself.

They took her into the bedroom next door and there she plumped herself down upon the edge of Mary's high-piled feather bed four-poster, took off her great bonnet with a sigh of relief and began to dust its nodding plumes with her handkerchief; saying anxiously, "I do not think it has taken any harm from the journey. I never like to wear my best bonnet when I am travelling, but if you do not there is no knowing who you may meet. There was a gentleman in the inn at Gloucester was looking at us all very hard and afterwards he asked the chambermaid who were the lady and gentleman with the handsome children. I suppose he imagined Mr. de Quincey was my husband, as we were travelling together"; and she gave her foolish laugh and ran on, "I do hope you will neither of you say anything to the young gentleman that might make him suppose things had gone wrong between my husband and me. I would not for the world have people talking. I think it is a great disgrace when a man will not live with his wife and children and I would not mention it to a living soul. I never have done so and never will; and I shall take it very ill if you gossip about our affairs to Mr. de Quincey."

Mary said in her calm voice, "Of course we will not speak of it, if you do not wish it." Dorothy, who was vexed by the word gossip, exclaimed with scorn, "What does it matter what Mr. de Quincey thinks, or what any one thinks? It is for you two to settle between yourselves whether you will endure each other's company any longer or no. There is no disgrace in parting." She stared with contempt at the shining red face of the fat flustered woman who sat on the edge of the bed, fanning herself with her crumpled handkerchief. Mrs. Coleridge opened her mouth two or three times like a gasping fish; then she protested, "But it *is* a disgrace, everybody thinks so. I am sure all my friends are laughing and sneering at me by this time." Mary said in her soothing way, "Nobody would be so unkind," but Dorothy said sharply, "Where is the use of staying together if you do not love each other any longer?" Her voice broke into its old wretched stammer on the word, "L-Love!" Mrs. Coleridge gave her a sharp unfriendly glance, turned a deeper red, snorted, blew out her lips and exclaimed, "Oh! love; that is all you poets think about. Love and dove, ring and spring; there never was much love lost between us two and now it's all over. We do not need to trouble about such nonsense." Dorothy and she looked at each other and hated each other; Dorothy thought, "If he had met me first I could have made him love me and marry me, but this silly woman came and caught his eye. She took him from me before he knew that I existed. We were meant for each other. I should not have deserted him, whatever he did, with me he would have been happy and safe. She had ruined him with her folly."

Mary was trying to soothe the offended woman, murmuring in her dovelike way, "But if you declare openly that you are separated, I do not see how any disgrace can follow from that, my dear. It is much worse, surely, to go on as you have been, tormenting each other; it is dreadful for the children to be brought up in such a house. Why do you not speak out? why do you not tell every one that you have agreed to part? There might be a buzz at first, but soon all the talk would be over, whereas now folk will go on hinting and gossiping to the end of the chapter. They will make the whole business out much worse than it really is. They will say that your poor husband has deserted his wife and children and left them to be provided for by other people and you know that is not true."

Mrs. Coleridge only repeated bitterly, "Well, he may stay away if he likes. I care nothing about it, so long as he will not talk," She seemed obsessed by this fear of scandal. She mopped her great blue eyes, stared at them like a lost bewildered child and began again about disgrace and neglect, sobbing, "How can you say it would be better for the children if their father and I were to separate? Why, I do not know how I am ever to bring them up if that happens. It is just because of the children that he ought to stay with me." Mary petted her and consoled her. "You must stay the night with us. It is too late for you to drive on all the way over Dunmail Raise. We shall manage somehow, you know we can always contrive a bed over the way at a pinch. We will fit you in. Dorothy shall go down now, draw the curtains and brighten the fire; she will tell Sally Green to put on the kettle and set out the tea-table. I am sure you are all hungry and thirsty after that long drive." Dorothy caught her oblique brown glance and was only too glad to steal away, leaving the married women together. She had no patience with Mrs. Coleridge.

She went downstairs planning how to stretch their hospitality for such a large party. It was a pity they had not yet moved to Allan Bank, it would be a very tight fit on this occasion. William and Mary would have to take Dora's cot into their bedroom and she would have to give up her own room to Mrs. Coleridge and little Sara, and sleep on the parlour couch. The two Coleridge boys could go across the road to Peggy Ashburner's attic and there was no help for Mr. de Quincey, he would have to share the back bedroom with Johnny. She hoped that he would not mind being waked at dawn by Johnny reciting the Apostle's Creed, a recent accomplishment which he inflicted on all visitors; but in any case she had worse troubles to think about than the discomfort of Mr. de Quincey's night's lodging.

5

He proved the most amenable of all her guests. He was a singularly amiable young man and what was good enough for the Wordsworths was quite good enough for him. Dove Cottage was a shrine to him and all their candid shifts and discomforts merely roused his veneration. He followed her about as the children did, getting in her way a good deal, but very anxious to be helpful, and when they all crowded into the parlour for tea he sat himself down next to her, as far as he could from William. He was very shy and silent, less at his ease with men than with women and unable to open his mouth at first in strange company; but the children apparently already adored him and had discovered that at heart he was still one of themselves. Johnny blushed with pride and pleasure when he was allowed to sit next the young man. This won Aunt Dorothy's heart and she was very ready to lend her ear while Mr. de Quincey talked about himself. He for his part found her sympathy as quick and inevitable as the pulses of light itself and presently under cover of the family chatter about them he was pouring out to her the strangest farrago of childish hopes and fears, in a mild quiet whispering voice most inappropriate to the experiences which he related. She very soon came to the conclusion that you could not believe half the things he said. He told her the most fantastic adventures, as far-fetched and incredible as Hartley Coleridge's legends of Ejuxria.

He seemed to have had a most unhappy childhood, alternately spoilt and neglected by a domineering mother. He had run away from Manchester Grammar School, with Euripides in one pocket and William's poems in the other, if you could believe him; he had wandered aimlessly about the country and starved in London for months, for no reason that she could discover, since his family were rich and not ill-disposed towards him. He had had the most peculiar adventures in the house of a moneylender in Greek Street, Soho; he had lived for weeks upon the charity of a young street-walker whom he called Ann, and never knew by any other name. He said that she had found him in a swoon in Oxford Street, one winter's night, had taken pity upon him and fed and sheltered him for weeks by her earnings, but after that she had disappeared and he had not been able to find out what had become of her. His eyes as he related these stories were not less limpid than those of fat Derwent Coleridge opposite, above the rim of his mug of milk. She glanced from her new guest to William, at the bottom of the table, with his stooping shoulders hunched up to his ears, stolidly munching Grasmere gingerbread and honey with a rocklike indifference to the nursery chatter about him; and smiled to think what an odd thing a young poet could be. She thought with amusement that perhaps she had lived a little too long in Grasmere.

She was, however, pleased and relieved to hear that Mr. de Quincey had now made terms with his family and was pursuing his studies at the University of Oxford. She thought that this must suit him excellently; and was surprised to hear him lisping his intellectual disdain of the dons and undergraduates at Worcester. He maintained that there was no scholarship to be found there, and she said hurriedly, "William always tells us that the undergraduates at St. John's in his day were all very frantic and dissolute. They did no work, but spent their time cock-fighting and horse racing. I suppose it is the same nowadays at Oxford." Mr. de Quincey replied with his nervous stare, "I have no notion what they do. I work night and day; in two years I do not suppose I have exchanged two hundred words with a fellow-creature." This she thought most pitiable; she could not bear to think of the poor young man sitting alone in his rooms, with his barrier of books before him, cramming his aching head with knowledge and shutting himself up from his fellows.

To put the picture out of her head she began to question him about his recent visit to Nether Stowey. He told her that he had visited her dear old friend Tom Poole, who seemed to be just as rude and uncouth as ever. He had been inside the cottage where the Coleridges used to live, once upon a time, and had even walked through the woods to Alfoxden, now quite shut up. She blushed like a girl in spite of her thirty-six years as she burst out, "And are there still donkeys in the holly wood?" but Mr. de Quincey assured her gravely that there were still a great many. She excused herself, laughing, "My brother and I were always very fond of the donkeys. He wrote a poem about them called *Peter Bell*; he has never ventured to publish it yet, but one of these days I hope he will bring it into the light"; and then she asked him, with a slight timid stammer, whether he had seen Coleridge that summer. She had a feeling that this young man would tell her, far more truly than his own wife could, on what shore that doomed mariner was now stranded. She murmured "We are all so very anxious about him."

He said, in his mild quiet whispering voice, "Yes, I was determined to find him out. I hired a horse and rode over to Bridgwater to see him: he was living at Bridgwater then, you know, and not at Nether Stowey. I rode up the street and saw him standing in the doorway, looking like a lost man. I knew him from his large soft eyes and the strange dreamy haze which clouded their light. He looked at me steadfastly for a minute or more and it struck me that he did not see me, or anything else about him. When I spoke to him he started and muttered some nonsense, nothing to do with me. I knew at once that we were fellow-victims, he and I." She glanced at the young man, quite startled, and he said composedly, "Yes, we are both opium-eaters. Such slaves always recognise each other when they meet." He uttered this with a strange mixture of neurotic horror and shrinking vanity which made her blood run cold; she hardly heard him as he rambled on, telling her of the poet's kindly welcome, his great swelling tide of eloquent talk and the hours that they two had spent together. He said, with a child's innocent satisfaction, "We talked together of religion and philospphy for about two hours. Once *she* came in and interrupted us, but that did not stop him. He just introduced us and then went on talking and she had to go away." He gave a wicked sidelong blue glance like a naughty schoolboy at Mrs. Coleridge, talking away beside William, eating hard and thoroughly pleased with herself. Evidently he thought Mrs. Coleridge funny. Dorothy could not help laughing herself and after that they were fast friends.

In the end the young man from Oxford stayed nearly a week in those parts. Fortunately for himself he was a good walker, otherwise William would never have put up with him. They took him all their favourite walks. Mary took him into Easedale and Dorothy to visit the Lloyds at Brathay; and on the day after William walked him round the two lakes in the rain. On the Saturday they all made the great climb over the Kirkstone Pass and down to Patterdale. The women and Johnny rode in a cart and the men walked beside it. Dorothy knew and greeted all the country folk as they passed. At Patterdale a horse was found for the young man and he and William rode on through the moonlight glades of Gowbarrow

Park, where the boy's tired and excited fancy created Moorish windows and temples of the Hindoos among the leafless branches, all as fantastic, unreal and shadowy as the broad gleams of moonshine from the midnight lake. He remembered that ride all his life. They stayed that night at Eusemere with their good Clarksons, who had come north for a few weeks and next day, which was Sunday, they evaded the Quaker meeting and walked together through Lord Lowther's woods, William repeating to his disciple long fragments of a romantic mediæval poem which he had been composing since Dorothy took him to Bolton Abbey for a wander. It was called the *White Doe of Rylstone* and young Mr. de Quincey at least was in a mood to think it beautiful.

On the Monday he was packed off, rather nervous, by himself, along the valley by Threlkeld to see the Southeys and Mrs. Coleridge at Greta Hall. He found Robert civil but alarming, was welcomed kindly by Mrs. Southey and uproariously by the Coleridge children. Robert Southey had by this time settled down into very regular habits. He was the breadwinner and the house revolved round him, the Coleridges were only visitors. Poor Robert took himself very seriously, as well he might, with so many mouths to feed out of one inkstand. Mrs. Southey was already at work producing what would in the end be a long family; and now he had all the Coleridges on his back for he did not know how long, besides another widowed sister of his wife's, Aunt Lovel. The great house was crowded already, but nothing was allowed to interfere with Robert's time-table.

He worked every morning until two in the study upstairs, then he dined and afterwards walked out to do his measured three miles in all weathers, with his clogs on his feet and a book under his arm. He allowed himself tea and an hour's talk in the parlour at six, then he must read his London paper and answer his letters, which he always did on the day of their arrival. None of this was perhaps very inspiring, but he did get through a great deal of work. He had just begun to write regularly on literary subjects for the *Quarterly*, he did an astonishing amount of translation, criticism and reviewing and he was toiling patiently away at a long poem called *The Curse of Kehama*, all about Hindoo gods and goddesses, which was supposed to be going to be his masterpiece.

Everyone liked and respected Robert, but he was not very interesting to a young man who valued originality above all things; and Mr. de Quincey soon found out that Southey and Wordsworth had more respect than affection for each other. They were guardedly polite and still quite distant, for all their long acquaintance. The two households had not much in common. The visitor was amused by the contrast between the neat and sunny breakfast-room at Greta Hall, where the host waited courteously upon every one; and the little crowded parlour at Dove Cottage, with the kettle boiling unregarded on the hob and the children squalling, while William sat untidy and buttonless, his wife sugared his tea for him and Dorothy left her porridge to take down some verse which had just occurred to him. For all that, however, Dove Cottage was the more inspiring place of the two. The young gentleman from Oxford returned thither with delight, related all his wanderings to Dorothy, said good-bye to her at ten o'clock at night at the Ambleside inn and drove off post to catch the south-bound coach at Kendal.

They had all liked him immensely. Even William said in his grudging judicial fashion, "There is certainly something unusual about that young man"; but when Dorothy burst out, "He admires you immensely, he longs to have you for his friend," William drew back and said with his usual chilly dignity, "My friendship is not in my power to give." He went on to develop one of his sententious parallels between friendship and a flower, saying that a sound and healthy friendship was the growth of time and circumstance, and that where these were unfavourable it was vain to look for it. Dorothy agreed vaguely, "Yes, I know you are a busy man, William; I dare say you have not time to make a friend of him," but she thought that the chance-sown flower had already sprung up, between herself and Mr. de Quincey. She fancied that time and care might bring it into blossom and she was glad to think that William had invited his admirer to come back in the following winter, when they were settled at Allan Bank. In that great house there would be plenty of room for any chance visitor.

6

That winter was a very hard one for poor folk. The roads were blocked with snow for weeks together, avenues had to be cut in the drifts, in some places half a mile long, and the farmers lost many sheep on the fells. The trees were covered for days together with sparkling frosted snow and the ice on the lake was so thick that it would bear all the village skating upon it. Mary had gone to Stockton and did not dare come back until William went to fetch her, they only just got home in time to spend Christmas with the children. There was no chance of moving into Allan Bank, the workmen could not finish it. Poor William had to go on struggling to compose the *White Doe of Rylstone* in the one room now common to the family, into which visitors were admitted, with the children frequently playing beside him when the snow was too deep for them to go outside. She could not but admire the fortitude with which he endured this turmoil, but the poem did not get on as rapidly or as pleasantly as usual; perhaps it was the noise in the parlour or possibly the mediæval style really did not suit poor William.

A sad thing happened in the Vale that spring, 1808, for two poor folk were frozen to death in a snowstorm on the fells. Dorothy knew them quite well, they were George and Sarah Green, the parents of their own little nurse-girl Sally, a decent couple who had lived long in Far Easedale. These people had a cottage and a patch of garden-ground, and they were hard-working and honest, but terribly poor. The village folk said that the Greens had but one fault, they were too stiff at receiving favours and they kept so much to themselves that nobody guessed how near they were to starving. They dwelt in solitude and poverty, in a hovel of grey stone beside a brawling brook; it looked as if it had grown out of the mountain, like the boulders which were scattered all about it. The parents climbed over the fells, one cold March morning, to go to a sale of furniture at a farm in Langdale and about midday it started to snow, not heavily, but enough to whiten the ground. They started home about six o'clock and must have been bewildered by the mist and snow, for they were never seen again alive, though about midnight some folk in a lonely cottage fancied that they heard crying and calling; but they took it to be noises in the wind.

The six unsuspecting young children were left alone in the cottage in Far Easedale, for two whole days, from Saturday morning to Monday noon. Nobody went that way, but they waited patiently and without fear, because they supposed that their parents were snowbound over in Langdale. Jane, the eldest girl, kept them all quiet. She nursed the baby and rocked it on her knees, she kept the fire in, wound the clock, and milked the cow night and morning as her mother had told her to do; but on the Monday afternoon as it grew dark she became very anxious. She went through the snow to a farm on the other side of the valley and asked timidly to borrow a cloak, that she might go and seek her parents. The alarm was then given and all the men in the vale went out with lanterns to search the fells. The women ran to the cottage and found the ragged orphans crying together, the fire out at last and only the baby asleep in the cradle. Their food was almost run out, there was nothing in the house but two boilings of potatoes, a little meal and bread and a few pieces of lean dried mutton. The men searched for two days before they found the bodies lying together in a snowdrift, the woman near a wall and her husband a little above her.

Dorothy and Mary went to help and they both went to the

funeral, with all the decent folk of Grasmere Vale. The mourners sat beside the two coffins in the parlour and the children gathered round the kitchen fire, half-frightened, half-amused to see so many strangers. Young Jane sat on a little stool by the chimney corner, nursing the baby quietly on her knees, for it would go to none but her. The village women cast looks of sorrow on this innocent pair. A threepenny loaf was dealt out to each of the guests, an ancient custom, even then falling into disuse. Dorothy and Mary did not like to rob the orphans by taking theirs, but found that they would give offence if they did not do so. They followed the coffins down the solitary valley, through the melting spring snow, and stood in the clear pure air by the churchyard gate. The men uncovered their heads whilst a psalm was sung; then husband and wife were laid in one grave. The next day the furniture was all sold and the cottage was left empty.

Dorothy was one of six ladies who collected money for the orphans and found homes for them in the vale, where they could be boarded out for half a crown a week. They must be well housed and well fed, the boys taught to read and write and the girls to cook and sew. She wrote an account of the tragedy which was sent round to bring in subscriptions and she had a fine fight over the arrangements with Mrs. North of Liverpool, a rich new-comer, much disliked in the vale, who had come to live at Rydal Mount and wanted to manage all her neighbours. Dorothy won the battle and took the children away from Mrs. North's nominee, a dirty lazy old woman, quite unfitted to manage them. She and Mary took immense trouble to find the children better homes and it warmed her heart to discover how much kindness there was in the vale.

It had been declared with one voice that the baby and her sister Jane were not to be parted, so they went to the blacksmith and his wife, a kind childless couple. The Wordsworths would have liked to have Jane as a nurse-girl themselves, but they felt that they could not cast off Sally, though she was a stupid and careless girl, and as it later turned out, not to be trusted with young children. The two little boys in petticoats Dorothy took herself to the farm where they were to live. They cried at being left in a strange place, but a slice of bread and butter comforted them and the kind looks of the farmer's wife, who had lately lost her eldest son and had no child at home. Her husband had yielded to her desire of taking the two orphans, in the hope that they might divert her brooding thoughts, and indeed at the next visit Dorothy found her more cheerful than she had been for a long time. The children, poor things, were perfectly contented. They were too young to fret long and one of them was overheard saying to the other, as they played together, quite happily, "My Daddy and Mammy's dead, but we'll never go away from this house."

The seven year old boy went to John Fleming, the kind shepherd, who patted the lad's weeping head as lovingly as if he had been his father and said in his broad hill speech, "Never fear, mun. Thou shalt go upon the hills after the sheep. Tha kens my sheep and I'll give thee a fleece a year to spin thy stockings." Then lifting up his old head he said to Dorothy, "This little lad and his brothers and sisters used always to come to our clippings and they were the quietest bairns that ever I saw, we never had any disturbance amongst them." All through that spring she used to meet the pair of them in her walks, the old man feeble and paralytic, creeping at a slow pace and with tottering steps, with his dog and his staff, peering about the fields after his sheep; and the boy running here and there, as sportive as a mountain lamb, wandering at will after his own fancies, yet always coming back to look up into the old man's face. He had quite settled down in his new home and when he was taken to the field which had been his father's, in the green floor of Far Easedale, he looked about him quite cheerfully and only said, "My mother's ewe has got a fine lamb." Dorothy could have wished herself a child again, to forget trouble so easily.

7

William was in London while all this was going on. He had gone up to try to find a publisher for his long poem, the *White Doe of Rylstone*, but unfortunately he showed the manuscript first to Coleridge and to Charles Lamb, and they both told him that it would never please the public. Longmans would have taken it, but William was always too easily discouraged and decided to keep the poem by him. He had no pleasure in publishing; indeed he detested the ordeal and always said that if he were a rich man he would keep all his poetry in manuscript, not to be seen until after his death. His devoted and uncritical household were much disappointed. They thought it a beautiful poem, though perhaps not quite equal to his best and they had counted upon Longman's hundred guineas to cover the move into the new house and their increased expenses there. Without it they would have to pinch and scrape and work their fingers to the bones, and so Dorothy told William when he came home again in April, but she could not move him.

He had a sad homecoming, for a week or so earlier Sara Hutchinson had given them all a great fright. The pale girl had grown thinner and paler all that winter, as if she were pining for something she could not get. She coughed a great deal and complained of a sharp pain in her side, which frightened Mary, because their sister Peggy had died of consumption and she knew the symptoms too well. Then one March evening Sara, who had been languid and feverish all day, rose up out of her chair, caught her breath and fell into a dreadful fit of coughing. She gazed at them with a terrified surprise, holding her handkerchief to her mouth, and they both saw blood runing out of one side of her crooked mouth. They ran to her and held her up; then got her to bed in the warm room downstairs and took turns to sit with her, Mary hung over her, stroking her cold damp hand, nobody dared to think of how her sister had died.

By the time William came back Sara was up again, dragging herself about the cottage, gasping for breath after any exertion and holding her side. She whispered valiantly that she was better, and would soon mend when the fine weather came, but they were still most anxious about her; and to crown all, William had not been an hour in the house before Johnny fell sick. This child, admired by all for his beauty, strength and sweetness, continued very ill for a week, tossing in a high fever and complaining continually, "My head . . . my head. . . ." Young Mr. Scambler, the apothecary, rode up from Ambleside every day and talked of water on the brain. They all thought that they must lose Johnny; however, after blistering and bleeding he slowly recovered. He had grown very thin and his features seemed enlarged. His face had an unearthly beauty which terrified Mary, there seemed nothing left of him but his great mournful eyes and his big Wordsworth nose.

With all this sickness in the house Dorothy was half-distracted, for the burden of their daily life all fell on her. She was the only active one, for Mary was expecting another child and could not do much, especially as she fell over some planks which the workmen had left behind up at Allan Bank, and sprained her right wrist just before the move. Dorothy spent her days making covers and curtains, sorting papers, linen and books, altering carpets to fit the new rooms, and running up and down the hill to the draughty new house to hurry the workmen, while the children tumbled after, or played at houses with the slates and stones which the builders had left in the garden. William was not expected to do anything, indeed, she could have wished him elsewhere, for when he was in the house they had to cook regular meals, whereas if they had been alone they could have done very well with eggs, bread and porridge, as women do in a move. She did not know how she could ever have got through the work without the help of Mary's sailor brother, Henry Hutchinson, who was staying at Park House and came over to help her when he found what straits she was in. He was the handiest creature in the world, could sew, cook, wash up dishes and put up beds. He was delighted to sit cross-legged for hours upon the floor at Allan Bank, sewing her carpets together with a sail-maker's thimble and spinning yarns to her of his adventures, how he had been shipwrecked and had yellow fever and been cast into prison in foreign ports. She loved him for his kindness; and all the more because once or twice he reminded her by some sea-lingo of her dear brother John, and how he had helped them, eight years back, when they were settling into Dove Cottage.

In all this trouble she had hardly leisure to regret the dear home, in which she and William had once planned to spend their whole lives. She tried to put it out of her mind, as she rushed up and down the hill with her bundles to the ugly new yellow house, or knelt to stretch and nail down carpets, climbed the steps to hang curtains at the great windows, or pushed the meagre furniture about and tried to make it fill the big square rooms. They had not got half what they wanted. She and William would have to go round to all the farmhouse sales and pick up more, when they could afford it, but she did not suppose that Allan Bank would ever look so homelike as the old Dove and Olive Bough.

They moved in May. There was a bad moment at the last when the cart had gone up the hill, with Mary riding on the top on a feather bed and William solemnly trudging in the dust beside the wheel. The children had ridden up earlier in charge of Sally Green. Dorothy was left to go through the low dark empty rooms and lock up the door for the last time. She could not but think of how the cottage had seemed to welcome her when she came there first with William. She had thought then that it was for ever, but those days were over. William had found his happiness elsewhere and she did not grudge it to him; only she knew, quite suddenly, that her own youth was over. She was leaving it behind at Dove Cottage, in the dark rooms where the mice would run undisturbed over the boards, but find no food; in the orchard where the birds would nest without fear in the overgrown tangle of trees; in the moss-hut which a winter's storm might now pull down. She had been a girl when she came there, but it was a troubled woman who went away. She lingered a moment on the doorstep before she turned the key on those last eight years; perhaps she thought of her friend, perhaps only of William. Then she locked the hospitable door and went away with her rapid ungraceful walk, across the vale and up the hill to her new home.

XII

I

Mr. de Quincey left Oxford that summer, without a degree, poor fellow, for he got into a needless panic in the middle of his Schools, and ran away on the night before his vivâ. He went to London for some months and wrote Dorothy a most melancholy description of their friend Coleridge, how he lived over the office of the *Courier* newspaper in the Strand, stupefied by the hum of the printing presses and the noise of the street. There he sat drinking laudanum, his head enveloped in night-caps and surmounted by handkerchiefs endorsed upon handkerchiefs to keep off any draught which might revive his neuralgic pains. He had given a course of lectures that spring at the Royal Institution, but had often felt so ill that he could not rise from his bed when two o'clock came. At first all Albemarle Street was blocked with fashionable carriages and many people were turned away, but after a time the audiences dwindled. People would not come every week only to find closed doors, or a lecturer almost too ill to stand, mumbling fragments from a bundle of notes all in confusion, and dropping his papers while he gulped down water to freshen his cracked and fevered lips. It made Dorothy's heart ache to think of it. William had told the same tale when he came back from London in March. She longed for Coleridge to come north again and she knew that Sara Hutchinson pined for him too, but he did not come, and did not answer letters.

They had some news through the Lambs in May of another old friend, which amused them. William Hazlitt, that quarrelsome, woman-hating young man, had married a friend of the Lambs, and a most unhappy marriage it was to prove. The bride was Miss Sara Stoddart, the sister of Dr. John Stoddart, the Advocate-General, who had taken Coleridge out to Malta. Mary Lamb had been a bridesmaid at the wedding, in a gown of white China silk; Charles had made a pun and been almost thrown out by the verger of St. Clement Dane's, or so he said. The Lambs had moved into a new set of chambers in Middle Temple Lane, where they had much more room than they had had in Mitre Court Buildings, but not such a pleasant view; they could no longer see the river, only the three trees in Hare Court and the pump there, from which Charles remembered drinking when he was six years old. Mary Lamb was out of her wits for a time after the fatigues of this move, a sad relapse, but only to be expected; that was all the news that summer from London, but there was bad news from Spain. The King had abdicated and the French had invaded the country, to put the Emperor's brother on the throne; it was said that the English would soon be fighting in the Peninsula. William thought very badly of the foreign situation.

The Wordsworths had a new neighbour that summer, a bold lordly Scot named John Wilson. He was just down from Oxford, a tall handsome ruddy young man, like King David, with a loud musical voice, long straggling fair hair, a great Homeric laugh and a pair of blue eyes as bright as sapphires. There was plenty of fire in him, but whether it was the fire of youth and vitality, or the fire of genius, time had yet to show. He was the son of a Paisley manufacturer, now dead, and had brought his mother and sister to live with him in his cottage at Elleray, on Windermere. He had bought a piece of ground there, with a noble view of the islands, and planned to build himself a great house on the site. He was exceedingly rich and eligible; Mrs. Coleridge said in her plaintive way, "I suppose all the girls will be setting their caps at him. Well, he is certainly worth catching, he is a pretty fellow and they say he has a fine fortune. I think he is a little taken with your cousin, Miss Mary Marshall. She must not let him slip through her fingers, or Miss Jane Penny will get him." These were the two local beauties.

Dorothy Wordsworth, at close on forty, was still romantic enough to be angry with Mrs. Coleridge. She could not bear that way of talking about love and marriage; but Mary Marshall only laughed, she did not mind being teased about her young men, of whom she had plenty. All the girls of the neighbourhood were in fact wild about Mr. Wilson. He was uncommonly fond of society, as a rich young man should be, and proved a godsend to the county; he was forever making up picnic parties, to eat cold ham and chicken on the islands and frighten the sheep. He would dance all night and be up at four next morning for a tramp over the hills. He had a passion for sailing, kept seven yachts on Windermere, besides a ten-oared barge and several small row-boats, dressed himself by preference in white ducks and a blue sailor's blouse and liked to be called the Admiral of the Lake. He could not do anything quite as other people did it, there was an eccentric flavour about all his feats. If he walked, it must be for a great distance; they said that he had once tramped over the mountains, praying aloud, for sixteen hours on end. He was a great practical joker, liked to fire his gun up a chimney and startle people by the cloud of soot he brought down, would wrestle, run or jump against any man, loved fishing and cock-fighting or indeed any sport; once he turned a bull loose and chased it on horseback for miles with his friends, all armed with long poles in the Spanish fashion.

This tremendous fellow had conceived a passionate admiration for William and for his whole family. He was forever inviting them to jaunts and picnics and once actually dragged William off for a week's camping and fishing in Wastdale. William was flattered at first, but later he drew back a little; he had grown retired and silent of late, hated to have his hours of work interrupted and found John Wilson almost too exuberant for his melancholic temperament. Mary, unexpectedly, liked Mr. Wilson exceedingly. You might have thought him too noisy for her, but apparently he pleased her; however, Mary liked everybody. She could not go on all his excursions because of her state of health, but she always seemed pleased to have him burst into the garden at Allan Bank, fling himself down at her feet on the grass, and rattle away to her about his exploits. They treated each other as if he were her schoolboy son and she his indulgent mother; that was Mary's way with men. Sara Hutchinson did not like him, for his roving attention passed her by. He was all for pretty young women, and she resented this; besides she was still too much of an invalid to stand the noise he made. Dorothy was in two minds about him; he amused and excited her, but she felt some flaw in the cracked bell of his gaiety, he seemed to be always forcing himself on to some new display and she agreed with William in doubting whether there was much behind it.

2

Mary's fourth child was born that September, a queer, bald-headed flat-faced creature with bright blue Chinese eyes which turned up at the outer corner; they called her Catherine after her godmother, Catherine Clarkson. As soon as Mary's trouble was over Coleridge turned up expectedly, bringing his two boys with him and young Mr. De Quinecy followed soon after, like his slender shadow. That autumn there were thirteen people in the house, if you counted the two maids from the village, besides Hartley and Derwent, who went to school in Ambleside, but came there for Saturdays and Sundays. It was an unlucky number for Dorothy, and she soon wished herself back in Dove Cottage, or anywhere but in the great costly house, where nothing was ever comfortable. Mary recovered slowly after Catherine's birth and Sara was still languid and wretched; besides, she spent most of her time shut up with Coleridge in his study, taking down and copying out what he wrote. There was little help to be got from her with the house or the children, and this made far too much work for the two servants, what with washing and cooking and baking to be done at home and a cow and two pigs to look after. The new house had been ill-built and badly dried-out, it was so damp that the water ran down the walls and so close under Silverhow that all the chimneys smoked continually.

The masons were in and out all that autumn, tinkering with the chimneys and the wet walls. The work of the house was doubled by the smoke. Dishes were no sooner washed and set into the pantry than they were covered with smuts; chairs, carpets and painted ledges needed endless cleaning and were never clean. They all stumbled about with smarting eyes and choking throats, there was no end to scouring and scrubbing, all the new paint was ruined. On stormy days they could have no fire in the kitchen and were obliged to cook in William's study. Once even that chimney smoked so badly that Dorothy, with a candle in her hand, stumbled over a chair because she could not see it and Mary had to go to bed with the baby in the middle of the day to keep it warm. William's eyes were troubling him again, no doubt because of the smoke.

He did not want to write any more poetry; instead he tried his hand at a political pamphlet on foreign affairs. He was very angry with the government for not supporting the heroic Spanish peasantry more vigorously in their struggle against foreign invaders. Many a time he went from Allan Bank to the top of the Raise, as late as two in the morning, to meet the carrier bringing the newspaper and hear the latest news of Sir John Moore's retreat upon Coruña or the terms which the government had made with the French. He toiled away at his pamphlet, in hopes of rousing public opinion, but it was not work for which he had much aptitude and he said gloomily that he would be put in Newgate when it came out. He gave himself dreadful headaches by working so long in the smoky study and Dorothy was distressed about him; she thought that he would do no good with journalism, though indeed it would be pleasant if he could write anything for which there might be a brisk sale, for they were dreadfully short of money. Coleridge hurt her feelings exceedingly by telling her, when she urged William to print the *White Doe* without any more fidgetting revision, that her anxiety about money matters was spoiling her literary judgment, but then he never cared how bills were to be paid, or indeed whether they were to be paid at all. That was not in his nature.

Altogether, it was a most uncomfortable winter. Their friend had come down from London full of a great project for bringing out a new weekly review. He was to edit it, and it was to be the crown and vindication of his life. William and Robert Southey and all the rest of his circle were to be contributors; it was to be called *The Friend* and it would make all their fortunes. He spent most of his time, all through November and December, shut up with Sara in the smoky study, drawing up a flaming prospectus and writing letters to all his friends begging for their subscriptions; he had madly promised that the first number should come out in January. Nobody but himself would have ventured to send out such a prospectus, before he had written one essay, or even made any printing arrangements; but William and Dorothy agreed, though doubtfully, that perhaps it was the only way for him. If he felt himself bound by his promises he might get something done. They were very anxious about him, for though he had cut down his doses of opium to a sixth of what he had been taking in London, and was more lively and cheerful than he had been for a long time, yet he was often obliged to lie in bed half the day and sometimes felt so poorly that he was unable to do any work whatever.

There was a fine muddle over the printing arrangements. At first he had tried to get Mr. Clarkson, for old friendship's sake, to take charge of them for him in London; but his rambling and contradictory letters so irritated the methodical Quaker that he withdrew from the undertaking, much to Catherine Clarkson's disappointment, for she still had faith in Coleridge.

So the first number had to be postponed from January to March. Then there was a plan to employ old Mr. Pennington, the bookseller and printer in Kendal, and after he went out of business some wild talk of setting up their own printing press in Grasmere, which diverted the children greatly. Finally their friend heard of a printer in Penrith who would undertake the work, if they would buy him a new machine and some fresh type. It seemed absurd to choose a man at such an inconvenient place, a day's journey from them, with the Kirkstone Pass in between, it would be very difficult to keep in touch with him; however, their friend had grown so restless and impatient that, one wild March morning, he disappeared out of the house, went to Penrith, and did not come back for weeks.

He sent no word of what he was doing and they grew very anxious about him. William, who seemed very irritable and depressed, burst out one day to Dorothy that he had given up all hope of Coleridge ever doing anything of importance to benefit himself, his family, or mankind; all those great gifts of his had been spoiled and wasted by the weakness of his character. Dorothy greatly feared that he was right. She tried to hope against hope but her spirits had fallen very low during that sad winter. She had to admit to herself that it was a relief to have the sick man out of the house, but she fretted very much over what he might be doing in Penrith. It was possible that he was ill and certain that he was drinking and drugging as he could not do while he was with them. She and William wrote to their old friend, Thomas Wilkinson, the Quaker of Yanwath, to ask him if he could do anything to help the truant.

3

All through that winter the children were her chief consolation. Johnny, the noble boy, grew more like his father every day; she loved his shy looks of gladness and his beautiful blushes when anything pleased him. Dora was a wild clever creature, with golden curls and quick hands and feet, as lively as a kitten. When she and Johnny ran about the garden of Allan Bank together they made Dorothy think of herself and William, chasing butterflies and hunting nests, in the garden at Cockermouth, more than thirty years back. Tom was a great chatterer by this time, a simple, innocent and very loving child, but rather greedy. He spent so much time in the kitchen, among the pots and pans with the cook, that he was nicknamed Potiphar, a typical bad family joke which greatly vexed his infant dignity. The little bald baby Catherine, as she began to look about her, made them all laugh with her comical face and her crooked Chinese blue eyes. Mr. De Quincey, who was with them all that winter, was sweet with the children. He was perfectly content to moon about, read and play with them; he shared a room with Johnny. It was like having another child in the house, he was no more trouble than that. Dorothy enjoyed having him sit beside her, turning over the pages of a Greek book, while she sewed for the children. Johnny and he were great friends and allies, but Catherine was his favourite and he made them promise that when she was old enough to read he should be her sole tutor. They all agreed that Catherine would be a very learned lady, for Mr. De Quincey was a great scholar.

He was greatly missed when he went back to London in February, taking William's Cintra pamphlet with him, for he had promised to see it through the press. The elder children were always clamouring to know when Mr. De Quincey would come back again, and Dorothy's letters to the young man usually carried some message from them. She wrote to him a good deal that spring, for she was putting Dove Cottage in order for him. He was to come back in the autumn and he had taken the cottage from them for seven years. She thought this a charming plan. He had given his orders for its renovation with a young man's extravagance. The rooms were to be painted and whitewashed, the village carpenter was making furniture and putting up yards of shelving, for where William had had three hundred books Mr. De Quincey had three thousand. Dorothy made him curtains and covers and had the garden set in order for him. It delighted her to go down there and pace the orchard again on a fine spring morning, or sit for half an hour in the moss-hut and think of old times, as she listened to the cuckoo calling. She fancied that the little birds, her old companions there, were glad that she should come back again, for they had never seemed so joyous among the bare branches of the gnarled apple-trees. The woodman's axe had been sadly busy in the vale that year and all the trees on Nab Scar had been cut down, but she liked to think that for the next seven years the orchard at Dove Cottage would be a safe covert for the birds.

She was less happy about the two Coleridge boys than she was about their own brood. Mary's and William's children all seemed healthy and happy, they had a magic circle of warmth and safety about them, in which they could grow up undisturbed. It saddened her to watch the contrast between these contented creatures and the young Coleridges. Now that she had the children of that unhappy marriage continually under her own eye she began to understand how hardly the dissensions of their parents had pressed upon them. Black-browed, sweet-tempered Hartley had been sadly spoilt by his winter with his father in London, which had confirmed him in all his precocious and unstable ways. He knew perfectly well that he was cleverer than any of the other boys at Mr. Dawes' school in Ambleside, though backward in book-learning for want of proper teaching; and he presumed on it, putting his head on one side in his own caressing fashion when at a loss for an answer and coming out with something so droll and original that the schoolmaster had to laugh.

Mr. Dawes hardly knew how to deal with this phœnix among sparrows, who got through his work so quickly and easily and was such a lazy dreamer. The other boys liked him well enough, though they thought him very odd. He won favour among them because he could tell such marvellous stories in the dormitory at night, but they bullied him a little, as was natural, because he was small and timid. Nobody realised at the time how frightened Hartley was of the bigger, rougher boys at the school, or how he dreamed of their faces at night and woke up, screaming. Poor fat Derwent, dull, handsome and healthy like all his mother's family, seemed like a dunce beside his elder brother, though he worked twice as hard. He said mournfully to Dorothy, "Mr. Dawes doesn't love me because I cry when I am scolded and I ain't such a genius as Hartley." His full red lower lip drooped and he looked for the moment exactly like his mother as he complained, in just her fretful voice, "All the others are punished, but Mr. Dawes only looks at Hartley and never scolds him at all, though he has done just the same thing. It is because he is a genius. All the boys think it very unfair." He was, however, devoted to his brilliant unstable brother and added, with mournful justice, "Of course Hartley *is* a genius." He did not betray a touch of envy for those Coleridge qualities which he himself so singularly lacked. He had a very generous nature. Dorothy's heart smote her and she hugged Derwent remorsefully, but he only looked bewildered. The stolid little boy was unused to such demonstrations from the brown-faced, sharp-tongued lady whom he called Aunt Dorothy. She was often impatient with his slowness and he understood perfectly well that Hartley was her darling and her favourite. It was because Hartley was so like his father.

Little Sara Coleridge, her father's only daughter, hardly ever came to Allan Bank at that time, for her mother thought that the rough Wordsworth children might spoil her darling's beautiful old-fashioned manners. When the small creature did once visit them she proved dreadfully shy and strange, a pale patient girl, with long smooth hands and hair like floss-silk, who looked as if a breath of wind might blow her away. Her mother had taught her to keep her long white muslin frocks clean and her pink sashes uncrushed; she stared and shrank back when she saw her father romping with Dora Wordsworth. He used to tease Dora and call her his wild cat of the wilderness, and she always answered with a squall, inviting him to some fresh skirmish. He made a great pet of her. His own daughter was jealous of Dora's quick tongue and yellow curls and when her father asked her, to tease her, whether she did not think his wild cat had grown very pretty, she shrank away, frowned and burst out with an angry, "No," as she turned her shoulder on him.

He was hurt to find that his own child had become so much estranged from him in his absence and did his rueful best to make friends with her again, taking her on his knee and telling her long fantastic German fairy stories, about witches and dwarfs and enchanted princesses. He even let her sit on a stool at his feet in the study when he was working there with the other Sara, Sara Hutchinson. Little Tom Wordsworth loved to do this and was quite happy if he could but touch the big man in the chair now and then and be looked at; but his own child seemed to have no wish for it. Her mother must have poured into her ears long poisoned complaints, half-understood, against the pale girl who had taken first place in her father's wandering fancy, for little Sara Coleridge would not make friends with Miss Hutchinson on any account. Sara Hutchinson had not the art of making friends easily with children, as Dorothy had. She was kind, but cold, and though she was very gentle with the Wordsworth children when they were ill, she had not the vitality to romp with them or amuse them. They none of them cared for her much. Little Sara Coleridge pined openly for her mother. She had never been away from home before alone and when Mrs. Coleridge drove over from Keswick to spy out how her darling was getting on the prim child rushed at her, imploring to be taken back to Greta Hall.

It was a tragic scene to Dorothy. Mrs. Coleridge soothed and caressed the weeping child who clung to her full black skirts, sobbing, "I want to go home . . . I want to go home

. . . I don't like it here." She lifted up her daughter's flushed face, and dried her tears, assuring her, "Mother won't leave you, Mother will let you drive back with her." Then she stared round at them all with a triumphant sparkling air of indignation and declared, "I must say you don't seem to have made her at all happy among you." Her husband said bitterly, "The child has been taught not to love me," and turned away.

He did not see how white his daughter turned when she heard him say it, or how she stared from her father to her mother with her great bewildered eyes. The pale taper of beauty burning in her face was quite put out by her tears, she looked wretched and ashamed, and glanced from one face to another, trying helplessly to understand what they wanted her to do or say next. Dorothy's heart bled for her. The boys rushed in at that moment from school, Hartley gay and charming as ever, Derwent clumsy and cheerful like a puppy; both flung themselves at their mother. Their father lifted his finger to the other Sara, and went off with her to his study, moving heavily and clumsily, as he always did nowadays; you might have thought that his feet did not belong to him. Mrs. Coleridge hardly noticed his departure. She had her three children about her, all devoted to her, and with that she seemed satisfied enough. She went home next day and took her daughter with her. William wrote to his old friend, Tom Poole, at Nether Stowey, that spring, urging him to come to Grasmere for a visit, and saying that they two must make some plan together about the future of the Coleridge children, for their father, he feared, would never be any more good to his family.

4

It was March when Coleridge left them for Penrith, but April and May went by without any signs of the wanderer. Dorothy was wildly delighted when, on the first of June, the opening number of the new magazine arrived by post from

Penrith, but there was no word from Coleridge in it and when she had read the thing through she was quite disappointed. After so much excitement and so many preparations it seemed to her extravagant and unevenly bad; there was too much about himself in it, and the second number, though it arrived punctually a week later, was not much better. However, the editor himself appeared a week after that, walking in at ten in the morning, very much pleased with himself. He had got up at five, he boasted, and come over the Grisedale pass from Ullswater, through the dews and vapours and bird-song of the June morning. He had something of his old godlike look for a few moments as he sat there laughing and applauding his own exertions, while William drew down his heavy brows and gazed at him in troubled silence.

It seemed that he had been rescued from the Penrith taverns by that sturdy old Quaker, Thomas Wilkinson. From Coleridge's lies, contradictions and exaggerations they made out that Tom and his sister had taken the sick man into their cottage at Yanwath, cured him and set him to work. In their simple Quaker household he had risen and gone to bed early, lived frugally, drunk only water, been led to his desk at regular hours and the pen put into his hand. In the reaction after a prolonged debauch the opium-eater had yielded meekly and now fancied himself a reformed character. He sat among his friends, talking away with something of his old brilliance, waving his fine hands about as he used to do and sketching out impossible plans for the future. Dorothy did not dare to hope that he would carry them out, though she could only smile in pity when he knocked at her door next morning at six o'clock. He had come to take baby Catherine from her instead of the nursemaid and was as proud as a child of his early rising. She felt that such virtue would not long endure.

His improvement, however, did last through the early summer. He was full of hope and of good resolutions, with which he tried to pave the bottomless pit of his destiny. He worked by fits and starts, either doing a great deal or nothing at all, as was his way, but he could compose with an astonishing rapidity when he was in the mood. More than once he wrote a whole number of *The Friend* in two days. He seldom took pen in hand himself. His ideas had always flowed more freely in conversation and he would dictate for hours at a time to the pale and weary Sara Hutchinson. She never complained, however hard he worked her. Mary was worried about her pallor and wasting and her constant dry little cough, but you could not make her rest. All the Hutchinson sisters were as obstinate as mules about having their own way, though they were so soft and gentle with it that you did not realise how stubborn they could be. Sara was the most determined of them all, she would not budge an inch unless she chose. She had trained herself so carefully to study all Coleridge's fancies and habits that now he would have nobody near him but her. He never asked for Dorothy's help nowadays ; he left her to employ herself with the housekeeping and the children, while he shut himself up in the study with Sara. When Dorothy went past that closed door she could sometime hear the great tide of his eloquence rolling on like a river, as it used to do, but more often there was silence, or his dreadful whining voice, half-crying, half-bullying, complaining that he was being killed with work. Sometimes he would stamp and throw things about like an angry child. She did not think that he was drinking, but after a time she was sure that he was taking opium again, as heavily as before. Sara could not keep him from it when he cried for it and said that he would die if he could not get his dose. She had some power over him, but not where his enchantment was concerned; in that she could not help him.

She flagged very much as the hot summer wore on. They could not make her rest or walk out, or even sit in the sun, unless she was certain that Coleridge did not want her to work for him; and he kept himself shut up in the study all through that long lovely summer. The children came home for the holidays, Hartley and Derwent from Ambleside, Dora from

Miss Weir's boarding-school at Appleby, and Johnny from the village day-school. There were picnics on the lake with John Wilson and his "merry men," bathing, fishing and moonlit walks; but Coleridge would not stir from the garden, though he would sometimes drag his gross flesh out and sit sunning himself on the lawn, with his hands folded in his lap, staring through half-closed eyes at the grass and trees, or the mountains shimmering in the August haze. Dorothy could not bear to see him so, or think what he once had been.

In October Mr. De Quincey came back, and there was all the fun of helping him settle himself, his fine mahogany furniture, and his nineteen cases of books into Dove Cottage. The children were enchanted to have him back again. The two elder ones were always begging Aunt Dorothy to take them down to the cottage, and little Catherine, who could not walk yet, but was a fine crawler, would always make a straight line for Mr. De Quincey when she was set down on the floor, with her comical eyes intent upon him and her little bald pate foremost. He would play with Catherine by the hour, he said that she reminded him of a little sister of his own who had died young.

The Friend came out regularly all through the summer, and less regularly through the autumn, but it was not proving a great success. The weekly commentary by the editor on public affairs, which had sounded so well in the prospectus, never seemed to get written in time; the numbers had to be filled up with old poetry and German legends. Coleridge used anything that he had by him, his own letters home from Hamburg, that autumn when they all went to Germany, his reflections upon Sir Alexander Ball's administration in Malta, any old stuff that would cram a column. All his friends had to help. John Wilson wrote him an article. William dragged himself away from his poem, *The Recluse*, to write several more, and translated some sonnets from the Italian; Southey gave his brother-in-law some good advice, which was not followed. Even old Tom Poole was asked to write down that tragic story of the hanging of John Walford, the charcoal-burner, which he had told them so long ago, under the gibbet above Nether Stowey; and very well and simply he did it in his own words, but it was never printed. The magazine died first.

Payments had come in very slowly, and a good many people gave up their subscriptions after the twentieth number. Coleridge wearied of the whole affair and often threatened to give it up. They all urged him to continue, but with little hope; even Sara, who had the greatest interest with him now, could not do any more with him and after Christmas she seemed to lose heart. It was another winter like the last, with storms, wet walls and smoky chimneys to add to their misery. Coleridge did less and less work, he lay in bed always till after twelve o'clock, sometimes much later. He never walked out. They saw very little of him, for he did not leave his own parlour, except at dinner and tea, and sometimes supper, and he always seemed impatient to get back to his solitude. He went the moment that his food was swallowed. Sometimes he did not speak a word all through the meal and he did not listen to what the others were saying. When his boys came home at the week-end he would rouse himself a little to talk to them, especially to Hartley, but he never seemed to care how they were getting on at school, or ask them about what they did there. He was always buried in his books. He read enormously and continually, or sat hour after hour, sunk in his own gross helpless body, drugged and staring at the candle-flame.

He made a great deal of extra work in that overburdened household. There was always his parlour to clean, or his fire to light, or his bed to be made at some unreasonable time. They had to tempt his capricious invalid appetite with gruel and eggs, or toast and water, and there were many other little services which all told upon the women of the house, who could not leave him to the raw village servants. They would not have grudged all this sick-nursing if they had felt that they were helping or pleasing him, but he had grown terribly irritable with the progress of his intoxication. He complained of everything and could not even be patient with Sara. When she urged him to exert himself he would turn on her and rage at her, because she would not leave him in peace, and then fall into a childish weeping because he said that she was driving him to his death. Dorothy was torn in pieces between hatred of Sara and pity for her, Mary was distracted. They all thought that Sara would go into a decline like her sister.

5

Passing one morning by the door of the study, Dorothy heard raised voices and Sara sobbing and crying. She could not bear it any longer; she knocked and when she got no answer boldly opened the door and went in. It was a lovely April day, with flying gleams of windy light and shadow on the green mountains, and she had been playing battledore and shuttlecock with the children in the orchard. She came in fresh and dishevelled from the sweet spring weather, but these two were shut up together in their morbid solitude, with the curtains half-drawn and a great fire burning. Coleridge was sitting beside it like an old man, wrapped about with two or three shabby coats and waistcoats, with a cotton nightcap on his head and a handkerchief bound grotesquely about his neuralgic jaws. He had William's grey shepherd's plaid round his knees, but he was sitting shivering, as if he could never more be warm, holding out his unsteady hands in turn to the blaze and nursing his laundanum glass against him. The room had a sour stuffy smell, like a sick-room where a man has long been bedridden.

When Dorothy came in he turned his sodden white face towards her, slowly and with difficulty, and gazed at her with a steadfast dreamy look. His expression was quite blank and it did not change for her; his mouth sagged a little open, his pupils were so contracted that she thought he could hardly see out of them. He looked as if he were burning and wasted with fever. His lips were blackened and cracked with a thirst which could not be assuaged. After he had stared at her without recognition for a moment or two he lifted the glass carefully to those parched lips and drank from it greedily. His clothes were all spotted with the food which he had dropped upon them and there was a rim of black round his nails.

When he had drunk he dragged himself closer to the fire and muttered, "He's cold, very cold." He had lately fallen into this trick of speaking of himself in the third person, like a child wanting to be pitied. Dorothy could not bear to listen to him. She turned from his dreadful abject figure and went quickly to Sara, who was crying with her head on the little mahogany desk at which she always wrote. She said, "Dear Sara, what is the matter?" and put her hand on the other woman's shaking shoulder, but was quite startled to find how sharp its bones were under her hand. She raised Sara's head and dried her tears, put her arm about her and discovered how thin she had grown. Sara choked and sobbed again, then fell into a paroxysm of wet and strangled coughing. When she took her handkerchief away from her mouth there was a bright stain of fresh blood upon it.

Dorothy was dreadfully shocked. She exclaimed, "But you are ill, you must not sit here. Come away, come upstairs with me; you should be in bed, you have no right to be working. You are killing yourself." Sara gasped for breath, as she always did nowadays after any exertion; she leaned her exhausted head on her hand and confessed, in a voice like a thread, "Yes, he is killing me. I can do no more. I must leave him." At that the sick man by the fire began to mutter sulkily, "Well, let her go, let her go; I don't want to keep her. She is tired of me, and does not care what becomes of me, she only thinks of herself. I'm ill too, but nobody minds that. You're all in a tale together, setting her against me. If she goes it will be the end of me. I can't work any longer, I'm dying. She has murdered me, you have all murdered me here amongst you." It was the way that he always talked now, when any one crossed him. He let the glass of laudanum fall from his nerveless hand and it tinkled and smashed upon the hearthstone. Then he got up and stumbled out, trailing the plaid shawl behind him. He left the door ajar and the two women heard him go shuffling away from them down the passage, muttering to himself as he went.

Sara lifted her head and listened. There was a fixed red spot in either cheek, her eyes stared from their wasted sockets and her dry lips trembled. She said, "I shall go away from here. I cannot bear this torment any longer. I must be out of the sight of his face and the sound of his voice. I will go back and live with Tom. He was always a kind brother to me, he will be glad enough to have me. I will stay with him till I am better. It is a long way from here." Tom and Joanna had left Park House, a year before this, and gone to a new farm, Hindwell, in the Welsh Marches, under the bare shoulder of Radnor Forest, a warm western brookland, muffled with oak-woods and loud with running streams. Sara moaned, "If I am at Hindwell he will never think of me, he forgets any one who goes away. It is out of sight, out of mind with him and better so. There is nothing left now that I can do for him and I am not wanted here any longer." She was racked and torn by her dreadful harsh cough and she wiped the blood from her lips again.

Dorothy was much distressed. She remembered that this was the little Sara Hutchinson who had once been so young and eager, who had been ready to love her dearly before life came between them. Her arm tightened about the thin shoulders and she stroked and kissed the pale cheek as she said, "You are always welcome here and you know it, but you shall go to Tom for a little while if you choose. You have a right to go and we will all help you." Sara leant her head on Dorothy's shoulder. Her pale brown hair clung to her damp forehead, her eyes were terrified and dark with fever, her hand was dry and burning. She said, "I can do no more for him," and her voice was very dreary.

Dorothy said, "You have done enough. He is finished. I have no hope of him now. I say it unwillingly enough, God knows, but we shall never cure him. If he were not here with us, under our roof, he would be drinking and drugging himself continually; even here he is deceiving us all the time and deceiving himself." Her voice was sharp with tragic indignation; she burst out, "It is all hollowness and emptiness now and we know it. He will tell me that he is writing, that he has already written half a *Friend*, when I know that he has not written a single line. He speaks of the paper as if it could go on, but that is all lies. He is tired out and you have no more power to drive him on. He is past helping. You must not stay with him, or he will destroy you."

Sara moved and sobbed against her shoulder, but she continued earnestly, "Do not think that it is his love for you which has stopped him in his work. Do not believe it. His love for you is no more than a fanciful dream, otherwise he would prove it by trying to make you happy. No, he likes to have you about him and devoted to him, but when you stand in the way of his self-indulgence he has no more use for you. Forgive me for saying it, but he will be happier without you. There will be nobody then to drive him on, he will sink down into his folly and be at peace." Her face was drawn and set, for the moment she looked like her inflexible brother. Sara wept like a child, "He has broken my heart in this last year," but Dorothy only said, with a dreadful look of smiling despair, "Hearts do not break as quickly as that. I have lived a long time since I saw him first."

She kissed Sara, a thing which she had not done for a very long time and said to her as cheerfully as if she had been one of the children, "You shall go away to Hindwell. Tom and Joanna will be glad to have you with them. It will be warm down there by this time, the ditches will be full of primroses and there will be lambs in the fields. You shall sit in the sun and be well looked after, they will make you fat again on good butter and cream and Herefordshire cider. William will arrange about the journey. Now you must come upstairs with me and get into a warm bed, you must not cry any longer." She put her strong arm round Sara and lifted her to her feet; it was like lifting a child, because she was so thin and so weak. They went upstairs together.

William was very kind about it all, but quite firm; he said, "Certainly she must go. It is the best thing she can do. I wish she had come to it sooner. I have no more hope of him." His face was set in its heaviest lines as he declared, "It is a shipwreck. He had greater gifts than any of us, but he has wasted them all for want of resolution. He is a lost man." And while Mary wept for her sister he summed all up, "We must think what is to be done for his children."

Sara was nursed up and sent away to Hindwell, and the paper came to an end, for Coleridge did no more work after she went. He wandered about the house in a restless way for a little and then said that he would go to his wife. Mary was to have another child in May and he wanted to be out of the bustle. He could not bear to be in a household of which he was not the centre. So off he went over Dunmail Raise, and Dorothy sighed to see him go. She did not guess that she would not see him again for ten weary years.

XIII

I

THEY HAD hardly leisure to miss their friend, they were so distracted that spring by nursery troubles. Their little Chinese maiden suddenly fell ill. Careless Sally Green, the nurse-girl, had let her stuff herself with the balls of raw carrot which Johnny and Dora had been making for their popguns and after being very sick she fell into an attack of convulsions. They did all that they could for her, put her into a hot bath, dosed her and sent for Mr. Scambler, who bled her after the fashion of the time; but she fell from one fit into another and then into a drowsy stupor. Next morning they found that she was paralysed all down her right side. The apothecary said that she must have ruptured a blood-vessel in the brain and could not tell how long she might not take to recover. William was dreadfully troubled, Mary distracted and quite unlike herself, she was very near her time and could do little for the child. Most of the nursing fell upon Dorothy and she spent a long time every day massaging the little girl's arm and leg, which were as weak as those of a new-born child.

Mary bore her last son early in May, a boy called William after his father, and while she was laid aside Dorothy had everything to do in the house. Catherine grew stronger as the days grew longer. They used to put her out naked in the sun and she began to crawl again and help herself along by chairs and tables, but still she could not stand. She dragged her right leg heavily, as if it did not belong to her, she could not control its movements, or straighten out the contracted knee. Dorothy had most charge of her and came to love the queer crippled thing more passionately than any of the others, as if she had been her own; but the child's sickness was a great grief to them all and Mr. De Quincey, down at the cottage, was distracted by the change in her.

This trouble made the weeks slip by uncounted and they had little time to miss their friend. He was at Keswick, apparently, all that summer, with his wife and children, no longer a host but a guest in the house which Robert Southey had now bought for his own, out of the money he got for the *Curse of Kehama*. The household at Allan Bank heard nothing from Coleridge, but they were used to that and expected no better treatment. Dorothy had grown so pale and worn with nursing that in July William took her south for a holiday, her first for a very long time. They stayed a month at Coleorton, not in the farmhouse this time, with all its memories of her friend, but up at the Hall, where the kind Beaumonts made much of her. It was delightful to see how well the winter garden had grown up in three years. Then William went off to Wales, to Hindwell, and Dorothy visited the Clarksons. She had an adventurous night and day journey, cross-country, on the top of the coach with dogs and servants, by Leicester and Stamford to Cambridge. They stopped at the gateway of William's old college, St. John's, to set down the Professor of Arabic, who very strangely was a Cockermouth man. She could not but think, between smiles and tears, of William clambering down from the top of his coach, more than twenty years earlier, a gawky country fellow from the north, gaping about at caps and gowns and envying his elders, a raw boy with all his troubles still before him. For his sake she rose at a quarter before eight next morning, went to Trinity Chapel and stood in silence while the organ played for many minutes before the statue of Newton, looking at the silent marble face of which William had written. She walked through the courts and groves of St. John's and stood to gaze up at the window of his old rooms over the college kitchen. It was August and there were not many people about; she crossed the river and hunted out the ash-tree, clothed in ivy, under which her brother used to stand, on winter nights, foot-bound beneath a frosty moon, gazing at its lovely branches, a homesick, resentful captive far from his native mountains. For his sake she picked a leaf from the tree and wrote to William that it was still standing.

Mr. Clarkson met her and took her to Bury St. Edmunds. Catherine was just as sweet as ever, though very fragile. They kept her for six weeks in the little red-brick town. It had a pleasant society and Catherine Clarkson had been brought up there and knew every one. Dorothy met many people, among them a lively relative of Catherine's, Henry Crabb Robinson, who was to become a great friend. He had been in Germany when they were, and in Coruña during the retreat, as foreign correspondent to *The Times*; he knew the Lambs and admired William's poems. He went with her to London, where she was to stay with the Lambs in Middle Temple Lane, and while she was there he used to forget that he was reading for the Bar and would come and take her sight-seeing every morning. The Lambs took her to the theatre and altogether it was a most charming holiday. Dorothy, who did not much like London, and usually found it noisy and tiring, had never enjoyed herself so well; only the visit had a sad end, for after she had gone Mary Lamb fell ill and had to be taken away to Hoxton. Dorothy blamed herself sorely for not discovering that the kind woman had tired herself out with too much excitement.

The homecoming to Grasmere was not a happy one. She cut short her time to hurry back, because William wrote that the children were ill and when she got home she was horrified to find poor little sweet Catherine wasted to a skeleton, hardly recognisable. She reproached herself bitterly for leaving Mary so long alone, while she enjoyed herself in the south and vowed that she would not go away again for a long time. They all went for a change of air to a cottage at Hackett, on the south side of the mountain, overlooking Langdale. An old servant of theirs lived up there and the children always loved to go and run wild among the crags. It was certainly a pleasanter place than Allan Bank and when Dorothy got home again to the great empty half-furnished rooms and smoky chimneys of the eastward-facing house under the hill the cold seemed to cut her through and through. When Dora woke her morning after morning with a shout, of, "Aunt, it is a *blasty* morning, it does *blast* so," or "Aunt, it hails so hard that you cannot see Fairfield"; then Dorothy felt that she could hardly bear to throw off the blankets, get out on the cold floor and dress herself. She was thankful to remember that their lease of Allan Bank would be up at Easter. In May they planned to move down to the old Parsonage by the church. William was up and down all winter, seeing to the workmen who were renovating the place, but the parson was so old and ill that they did not like to hurry and disturb him.

2

All winter they heard nothing from their friend. William had told Dorothy when she first came home, that she had missed him by a day or so, another reason to make her regret the length of her holiday. Coleridge had passed through the village and actually stayed a night in Allan Bank. He was travelling with their old acquaintance, Basil Montagu, the father of the little boy who had stayed with them at Racedown and Alfoxden. This gentleman was now a barrister in good practice, a delicate, handsome charming creature; he had married again, and Coleridge and Hartley had stayed with him in London three years earlier. He now offered to entertain their friend in his house in Frith Street, Soho, for the winter.

William thought this would be undesirable and was determined to put a stop to it. "I took Montagu aside," said he to Dorothy, "and told him that he would be a fool to lodge our friend under his own roof. He had better put him in lodgings nearby, if he is determined to befriend him. Poor

Montagu is the most industrious fellow in the world, and his practice is now very heavy. His health is by no means good and his wife tells me that he needs rest of body and mind when he comes home at night. He is the last man to stomach what we have all endured in this house. He would not listen to me at first. He was sure that he would have enough influence over Coleridge to keep him at work and was resolved to take him in and do all that could be done to save him. On that I spoke out and told him what our friend's habits were while he lived here."

Dorothy was much alarmed; she knew how tactless and outspoken William could be when he was not watched and exclaimed, "I do hope you did not say anything that could make trouble if it were repeated. You know Mr. Montagu is very indiscreet, he cannot hold his tongue even about his own affairs." William replied gloomily, "I am sure I told him no more than he would find out for himself in two days. I said, The man has rotted out his guts with drinking and ruined his brains with that cursed Kendal Black Drop. He is not fit to live in your house."

Dorothy was very much distressed to hear him speak so harshly, she stammered, "Oh! William, if that should ever be repeated to Coleridge it would break his heart," but William only drew down his long lip and repeated stubbornly, "Well, it is not fit that he should go into houses where he is not already known. I could not help but warn the Montagus." He had put on his most self-righteous and obstinate look, but she fancied that he was himself a little uncomfortable, for he continued to justify himself at some length. "You need not trouble yourself about it. Montagu did not need to quote me, to get out of his offer of hospitality. He saw enough of Coleridge's habits upon the road, I fancy, to make him repent of it. After Coleridge had been in their house two days it came to a quarrel and Montagu turned him out. He is gone to his friends, the Morgans, at Hammersmith. I suppose they are not so particular."

She breathed, "Oh! dear, if only nothing was repeated. I wish you had not used those words"; but William would not admit himself in the wrong. That was always impossible to him. He persisted, "It is no more than I have told our friend to his face, time and again. I have never minced matters to him." She sighed, "But to say it to a third person, that was the trouble," and William got quite angry with her. He said, "To my mind the Montagus are very well rid of him." You could never do anything with William when he had got into such a frame of mind, he would go on arguing in his own favour for ever. She let him be, and after a few days the matter slipped out of her conscious mind, in her anxiety about Catherine.

The child slept with her at night and was often sick and feverish; she needed a great deal of rubbing and nursing by day and now cried for Aunt Dorothy oftener even than for her mother. With this tie and the work of the other children hanging over her Dorothy hardly had time to write a letter or open a book. Their friend did not write himself, but was heard of through the Lambs in November; Charles wrote affectionately, "He has powdered his head and looks like Bacchus, Bacchus ever sleek and young. He is going to turn sober, but his clock has not struck yet." Her new crony, Henry Crabb Robinson, also wrote of meeting the great man at a party, where he had looked well and talked with much eloquence. All this sounded reassuring and Dorothy did not worry about Coleridge at first, but when she wrote to him on important business and got no answer, only a message through Charles Lamb asking rather curtly for a return of some manuscripts, she did feel grave misgiving.

His family had not heard from him either. Even Mrs. Coleridge was very worried, and it would have pitied anybody's heart to see Hartley's hopeless look as he inquired of Dorothy every week, when he came in, whether there was any news of his father. The boy was growing up fast and the family troubles weighed on him more than they did on the younger two. In March there was a rambling letter from Mary Lamb, saying that she feared there was a coolness between William and Coleridge; but the poor soul was on the brink of one of her mad fits and was taken away a few days later, so that Dorothy never got any answer to a letter which she sent off at once in reply begging for some explanation. She had begun to suspect that Basil Montagu had made mischief somewhere, but she did not yet realise how serious the matter was; they had had so much neglect and coldness at various times from their friend. It was a dreadful shock to her when, at the beginning of May, Mrs. Coleridge sent over from Keswick a long rambling letter, from her husband, full of wild charges and slanders against William. Her brother called Dorothy into his study to show her the thing, sheet after sheet of crossed and illegible writing, and she struggled in vain to make it out, but she was quite bewildered by its tale of unprovoked and incomprehensible wrongs. She laid it down when she came to a place where her friend declared that he had been driven to madness by William's cruelty and injustice, and faltered, "But William, what has happened? What are you supposed to have done to him? You have always treated him with so much forbearance."

William avoided her eye and confessed, "I suppose it is the old business. I fear Montagu repeated what I said to him in confidence. Coleridge talks of many injuries, but I can think of nothing else." They stood together in silence. Dorothy could not reproach her brother when she looked at him. He seemed to have grown quite old and shrunken in a moment, since reading that dreadful letter. She picked it up again and turned over the crumpled sheets. Lunatic phrases jumped out at her, here and there, "unprovoked sufferings" was one, and "cruel and unjust conduct" and "atrocious treachery." She felt a great wave of indignation slowly rising and gathering force in her brain as she studied this farrago of insincere and exaggerated emotion. William groaned, "I wish to God I had held my tongue," but she hardly heard him. She burst out angrily, "Why, this is base ingratitude, after all that you have done for him, and are still doing. We have stuck to him through thick and thin, we have suffered untold injuries from him and now he is putting it about London that you have driven him to madness by your treatment of him." William's fine worn face twitched at that, as if she had pierced him, and she said passionately, "Why, you are paying for his son's schooling while he is slandering you all over London! It is intolerable. It must be stopped. You must write and tell him to hold his tongue."

She had not been so angry since she was a hot-tempered child, raging against the unkindness of grown-up people who treated her with an injustice which could not be explained. She was shaking all over with rage. William said heavily, "If he asks for an explanation I shall give it, but I will not defend myself against mere tale-bearing. I cannot stop his mouth, if he believes these fancies of his no argument will change him. I shall not answer this letter." He added slowly, "Sometimes I think the man is mad."

She did not contradict that, but when she was a little calmer she urged him, "At least write and defend yourself to Mrs. Coleridge. She is a poor fool, I know, but she is more loyal than I used to think her; she might do something." After much reluctance William consented to give an account of the matter from his point of view and sent it over to Greta Hall, but Mrs. Coleridge only answered, in her silly frightened way, that she dared not forward any such letter to her husband. He had not desired her to show them his complaint, and if she transcribed William's letter and sent it on he would think they were in a plot together and would not open her letters in future. So they were no further on. Mary hoped that their friend's sick fancy might die away of itself in time. She said, "He is only trying to blame somebody else for troubles which are due to his own fault"; but Dorothy said, "We have hoped against experience and against reason, till I have no hope left. Time itself cannot change him now." Mary grieved that he should treat William so, after all his kindness, but Dorothy, though she was still very sore on that point, could say proudly, "I hope I am not angry with him for any personal reason. If he had not blamed William for his downfall I suppose he must have blamed some other person. He will never admit that the fault is in himself. I only grieve for the waste of his genius and his good qualities." She added in a lower tone, "But I do grieve whenever I think of him."

3

That same month they moved down to the Parsonage. Dorothy had no regrets for Allan Bank. It had been an unhappy house in many ways, what with their friend's long sickness and estrangement, Sara's illness and Catherine's; nothing had ever gone right there, the place was "curst." She was glad to shut the door upon its great cold echoing rooms and go down to the village. The Parsonage reminded her a little of Dove Cottage, grown larger and more comfortable; it was low-browed and yellow-washed, with black oak floors and beamed ceilings. It had two nice parlours downstairs and a cabin of a study for William, where he could have his books about him and hang up the picture of Coleorton, which Sir George Beaumont himself had painted and given him. The house was just across the road from Grasmere church, beside the bridge. The clear Rotha flowed down that way over a pavement of red and grey stones and there were always small trout feeding under the churchyard wall. The children loved to hang over the bridge and fish for them with bent pins and bread, though they never caught any, and William liked to poke about the church, in a cool smell of damp walls and mouldy hassocks, looking at the inscriptions on the monuments, or wander among the grassy mounds under the yew-trees in the graveyard; he always had a great taste for epitaphs, had William.

They had had a very wet spring and it was bad weather

all through the move. Veils of rain swept down the valley continually, and the low field in which the Parsonage stood was poached into a morass. The children ran in and out all day long, leaving their wet and muddy footmarks on the carpets and the workmen who were putting in the new fire-places seemed to take a pleasure in treading lime and dirt into the floors. William's books were stacked in the barn at first, but the rain came through the roof and soaked the packing-cases; so all his precious volumes had to be carried into the house and dumped in stacks on the floors until the shelves were ready; they were dreadfully in everybody's way. The workmen were all behindhand with the bad weather, which continued right on into June and July. Little Catherine was cross and feverish with the damp; and poor Tom, who had always been weak in his chest since that winter journey to Coleorton after the whooping-cough, cried and coughed and grew very thin. Mary was very much worried about the two of them, she went about saying that the Parsonage would never suit the children. Johnny and Dora, however, thrived exceedingly that summer and thought it much more amusing to live in the village than up at Allan Bank. They regarded the church as part of the house, ran in and out and spelt over the inscriptions in imitation of their father. Johnny thought he had enough Latin now to try it out on any tombstone he could find.

They also became great church-goers, a duty which the family had not hitherto performed very regularly. Mary took the troop in the morning and Dorothy in the afternoon, they made a very proper show in the Rectory pew. Dorothy had not been much to church of late years, for one reason and another, though when she was a wild thoughtless girl and lived with her uncle, Canon Cookson, in Norfolk, she had been twice every Sunday and even taught in the Sunday School. Now she sat through the prayers and sermon, with a child on each side of her, dressed in its best Sunday clothes and leaning sleepily against her. She looked at the leaves moving outside the windows, the damp patches on the walls and the naked rafters intricately crossed above her, like the branches in a wood, with sometimes a swallow twisting and turning among them before it darted out again with a shrill twitter into the sunshine; the children loved it when a swallow got into the church in sermon time, and so did she. At first she felt like a wild bird herself, strayed into a place which was like a dark prison, but after a time the quiet and holy peace of the church came to lie like a charm upon her troubled spirit and she found comfort in going there.

The war news was very exciting all that spring and summer, Lord Wellesley seemed to be doing great things in the Peninsula against the Emperor's troops. The children played Spanish wars in the orchard all through the holidays. After that Dora went away to Appleby to the boarding school, and Mary and William took the two delicate ones, Tom and Catherine, to the sea coast. It was bleak and treeless there, but they could see the sunsets over the Isle of Man and ships hanging in the air. William walked on the shore daily and came back strong and cheerful, but Catherine did not get as much benefit from the sea-bathing as the doctors had hoped. The autumn was not so pleasant as the summer in Grasmere; the Parsonage seemed as damp as a well, the water ran down the walls and green mould grew upon everything. The chimneys smoked as badly as they had done at Allan Bank, the parlour was so smoky that they had to give up using it and all crowded into poor William's little study. Sara Hutchinson came back again to live with them; she was much better but still very delicate and the women and children often sat in her bedroom by her fire for comfort. At that time it was not yet recognised that consumption might be given from one person to another and nobody saw any danger to the children in going near her.

Dora came back from her boarding school at Christmas, much improved in her manners and wildly delighted to be back again at home. It was fine glittering weather, with snow on the mountains. Dorothy and William took a great walk together while the others went to church, and later in the day they all played cards with the children. The fiddlers came round the village and everything was gay. When Dora heard the fiddles tuning up she rushed madly to the kitchen and jigged and danced wildly, with her golden ringlets floating; but the fiddlers played the old tune, "Oh! the days when we were young," and Dorothy found that the tears had started into her eyes, thinking of her friend.

4

He had not been in the north all that summer, but they heard that he was coming to Keswick in February. He had been lecturing in London through the autumn of 1811 and people had crowded to hear him. He was all the fashion, even Lord Byron admired him and had been to one of his lectures. Apparently he had not yet forgiven William, or any of them, for they got no word from him, but Dorothy still kept in her heart a rag of belief that when he and William met again the quarrel would somehow be patched up. She had tried to kill this hope, but it still survived, obstinate and bleeding, ready to spring up again at a word. It was the most dreadful shock to her, and to all of them, when Coleridge passed by their turning in February and did not stop to see them. He had his boys with him in the post-chaise, for he had picked them up at Mr. Dawes' schoolhouse as he drove through Ambleside. They stretched out their arms and pointed to the village, but their father only turned his head the other way and the postilion cracked his whip and drove on like the wind.

The Wordsworth family could hardly believe their ears when they heard this in the village. Mary cried and said, "I could not have believed he would do such a thing to us." Sara sat like a wooden image, staring at the fire; then she said with her dry strangled cough, "He has done worse," but Mary, drying her eyes, sighed, "Never worse than this. Poor boys, what will they make of it?" Dorothy was broken-hearted, but William, when she spoke to him of it, was as cold as a stone. He said that he would neither write nor go to Keswick after that, everything should be over between them. He looked as stubborn as an old mountain ram in a gap, with its head down; his sister knew that she could never move him. He had been like that ever since he was a little boy, there was a point beyond which he was inflexible, you might cut him in pieces but he would not budge. She hoped against hope that some word might yet come from Greta Hall, and when all was silence she wrote and wrote again herself to her old enemy, Mrs. Coleridge, sending messages to their friend, imploring him not to leave the country without seeing either herself or William. She was past dignity or petty resentment, half out of her mind with generous indignation and longing; she wrote stiffly at first, then more and more wildly, until she no longer dared look back at what she had said. She took her letters to the post herself secretly from William, but she got no answer to her appeals, nothing but the insult of total neglect. At the end of six weeks they heard by a side-wind that Coleridge had gone back to London.

In April Catherine Clarkson wrote from London, in her pretty shaken hand, that he was more bitter against them than ever. Perhaps more mischief had been made at Keswick, or perhaps he was seeking to justify himself for his neglect of them while he was there, for he had set all literary London by the ears with his version of the quarrel. Mrs. Clarkson was full of concern and indignation; she had heard dreadful things said and had contradicted what she could, but she felt certain that there had been deliberate lying somewhere and inventions against the Wordsworths. She implored William to come up to town and confront Coleridge and Montagu with the whole vile business. At first he utterly refused and said it made him sick to think of meeting them, but Mary, always a peace-maker, persuaded him to go and Dorothy was hot to have him defend himself. She wished now that he had done it at the very beginning of the quarrel, eighteen months earlier. In the end it was decided that he and Mary should take little Tom with them and go to her brother at Hindwell. William could leave his wife and his delicate little boy there for a change of air, which they both sadly needed, for Mary had grown dreadfully thin that winter and never rested when she was at home with the children; while he himself could go on to London. The Beaumonts were always asking him to come and stay with them in Grosvenor Square. There was no difficulty about that, and when he had got to the bottom of the whole matter he could arrange a meeting with Coleridge, through the Lambs, or the Clarksons or Crabb Robinson. So the three of them went away, while Dorothy and Sara were left to mind Catherine and spoilt little Willy, the only two children left at the Parsonage. It was a strange thing for Dorothy to look back and remember how bitterly she had once hated Sara Hutchinson. Now the two spinster aunts were perfectly happy together, sitting out in the spring sun, with the children tumbling about them, sewing and reading and talking of old times.

William got to London at the beginning of May and wrote to Dorothy as often as he could, telling her all that was happening. He was very comfortable with the Beaumonts. Lady Beaumont was much occupied with dinners and balls, the Opera, and driving in the Park, but she was very kind to him and arranged for him to meet people who could help him; it would have been a delightful visit if it had not been for the trouble with Coleridge. That dreary business dragged on lifelessly, there was no heart or passion in it, only endless recriminations and explanations. Everybody seemed to be taking a hand in it. Charles Lamb tried to act as intermediary, without much confidence, but Coleridge would not meet Montagu, or listen to his patron Wedgwood. William would not read letters which Coleridge had written to other people, or meet him alone, for fear of some dreadful hysterical scene. He was stiff, cold and disgusted by the whole business. Coleridge ranted to everybody about fancied wrongs which only existed in his own diseased imagination. It was most difficult to get any plain statement out of Basil Montagu; but it did in the end emerge that he had not only repeated William's fatal phrase, but had said that William had asked him to repeat it.

That was as much as any of the three would now admit, or perhaps could clearly remember, of how the quarrel had started. Crabb Robinson ran from one to another, a friendly cheerful busybody, softening down the things they said to him; eventually he got the two men into one room. They met, touched hands, exchanged some formal explanations and parted with relief on both sides. The fire of friendship was out, they would never warm their hands at it again; that was all over. When Dorothy got the letters about the business she showed them to Sara and they both shed some tears. It was odd to think how long they had been secret enemies over the man who had done them both so much injury. Dorothy knew that she was weeping not for the gross broken sodden creature who had slandered them all, but for a young man who had jumped over a gate, or walked in a holly wood and listened with her to the nightingales, years and years ago. That man had long been dead to her and to himself, but she could not stop weeping for him. Sara Hutchinson laid the pages of the letter together carefully and said, "He will never come back to us."

5

Mrs. Coleridge came to stay at the Parsonage for a few days, while William was still in London over this business. She had been asked out of family politeness to come over and use Mary's empty bedroom. She brought her own little Sara and Robert Southey's young daughter, Edith May, so that there were now three Saras in the house, but Miss Hutchinson kept to her own room a good deal while Mrs. Coleridge was there; they two would never be very friendly. Dorothy had dreaded the visit, under such circumstances, but found it oddly more agreeable than she had expected. Mrs. Coleridge was just the same as ever, full of her own troubles, all bustle and complaints, but nothing seemed to worry her for long. She had a blessedly short memory or perhaps time had taught her to make the best of what could not be altered. Dorothy found her quite a pleasant companion. Times change and we change with them; she herself had discovered how much cause Mrs. Coleridge had to complain of her husband, and no longer blamed the wife alone for the failure of that disastrous marriage.

It was really very pleasant to sit under the churchyard wall in the shadow of the flowering hawthorn which grew there, watching the children run races with the lambs in the meadow and talking sadly and idly of old times. Mrs. Coleridge could be quite good company when she chose and she remembered things that even Mary did not know, silly things about the donkeys in the holly wood behind Alfoxden, the way the tan-pits used to stink when you sat in Tom Poole's jasmine arbour, and the time when the village thought that William and his friend were foreign spies. She also liked to dwell upon the days when they were young together and did not know what life was going to do to them. She was the only one of them who still wrote regularly to Tom Poole, faithful quarterly letters crossed with family news.

They avoided the subject of the quarrel, after one outburst from Mrs. Coleridge, who tossed her head in her old flighty way and said of her husband, "Well, I hope he has learnt now who are his best friends. I hear your brother was no more patient with his ways than I have been all these years, and spoke out much more roundly to him than I have ever dared to do." At that Dorothy got up and would have walked out of the parlour where they were sitting, but the poor fat foolish woman burst into tears and sobbed, "You must not mind what I say, you must not listen to me. I do not want to offend you.

I am so wretched that I hardly know what I am talking about. Heaven knows what is to become of us!"

Dorothy sat down again out of sheer pity and listened while Mrs. Coleridge poured out her anxieties about her children. "Hartley is such a queer boy. I suppose he is very clever, but he is so strange and difficult, I do not understand him at all. I cannot do anything with him. Of course I love the dear fellow, but I cannot make head or tail of half the things he says. He can never do the right thing at the time. I am afraid he is going to be another of these geniuses, though I am sure there was never anything of that kind in my side of the family; but he is the living image of Mr. Coleridge." And she laid her hand on Dorothy's knee and said, with tears in her eyes, "Oh! my dear, sometimes he is so like his father that it makes me tremble."

Dorothy comforted her as best she could, saying, "They are both dear boys. I hope they may be a comfort to you"; and Mrs. Coleridge cheered up a little as she reflected, "Derwent takes after me, thank Heaven! He is a real Fricker. The dear good fellow does everything that he is told. I shall never have any worry with him, I am sure. But they cannot help but suffer from all these troubles, they both have such tender hearts. Why! it is dreadful how they felt it, poor boys! when their father drove through Grasmere last February and would not let them stop to see you." At this Dorothy fixed her eyes on the other woman's face and trembled very much as she asked, "Did they speak of it to you?"

Mrs. Coleridge rambled on in her simple fashion, "Oh! yes, to be sure, my dear; they told me all about it as soon as they got to Greta Hall. They bring everything to their mother. It was dreadful for them, because nobody had told them that your brother and my husband had had such a quarrel. Why, Hartley was so astonished that he could not say one word as the chaise passed your turning and Derwent could not keep from crying, but their father only turned away his head. He left it to me to do the explaining and I could not tell what to say." And she added in her plaintive way, "Poor Hartley turned as white as lime when I told him that Mr. Wordsworth had a little vexed his father by something he said to Mr. Montagu."

Dorothy had never heard the whole of this story before and was much upset; she sighed, "Indeed, Hartley is old enough now to feel such things." Mrs. Coleridge retorted, "They are all old enough now to understand that their father will never come back. Hartley feels it as a grown person would and Derwent cries because the boys at school tease him about it. Even my little Sara puts her hand on my knee and asks me why her father does not live at home like other fathers, and I cannot tell her." She cried again and protested, "Indeed, indeed, I have tried to be a good wife to him all along, but he would not help me. And now I suppose you are all very angry with him, and he will not even come here to stay with you. It was something to have him as near to me as Grasmere, even if he would not live in Keswick; I knew you all looked after him as well as you were able. I could trust you to be good to him. And sometimes I was able to come over and see him. But now you will all hate him, because he has quarrelled with your brother and spread such stories about you." She wiped her eyes, blew her nose and said, "I am sure I do not blame you."

Dorothy stammered so much that she could hardly speak. She said, "We have always l-loved him and we l-love him still; but I d-do not think that he will ever come under our roof again. I do not believe it can be hoped for." Mrs. Coleridge cried, kissed her expansively and said, in her childish fashion, which you could not take amiss, "Well, my dear, I used not to like you at all, but now I like you better than I did, very well indeed, much better than that Miss Hutchinson. I cannot abide her and the children will not make friends with her either, though we all like your sister-in-law very much. And of course I know my husband ought to have married somebody like you. I was never good enough for him, though he did love me once, when I was young and pretty and he knew no better." She said it with a pathetic humility, mopping her blowsed face and looking fat and plain. Dorothy thought, "Yes, he loved this woman once, but he never loved me, though I have had my heart on fire for him all my life"; but she did not say it aloud.

6

Then just after Mrs. Coleridge had gone home, while William was still in London about the reconciliation, and poor Mary in Wales, where nobody could get at her, the most dreadful thing happened. Their delicate Catherine fell sick again and died in a few hours. She had been playing under the hawthorn tree by the churchyard wall, as cheerful as ever, and jogged up and down on Dorothy's knee, playing her old game of "riding to London to see Mr. de Quincey" which always delighted the queer Chinese maid. When bedtime came she had run upstairs quite gleefully, striving to get before Willy and proud that she was to have the treat of sleeping in her mother's bedroom. In the evening Johnny looked into the bedroom and found her lying with her eyes fixed. He was alarmed and called his Aunt Dorothy. She knew what was going to happen as soon as she looked at the child and called out for Sara Hutchinson in a fright; they sent for Mr. Scambler and both did what they could, but all to no purpose, before midnight she had a dead child in her arms.

It was the most tragic business, she blamed herself for she knew not what, the child had seemed as well as ever. She had never seen death strike before and she lived over and over again in her mind the moment when the little thing shuddered, sighed, and turned limp and heavy in her arms. She did not know what she would have done without Sara. She herself was so heart-broken that she could not bestir herself to action, but Sara did everything that must be done until Mary and William came hurrying home again and they could try to comfort each other.

Catherine was buried under the hawthorn tree in the churchyard across the way, beside the river, where she had so often played. The children would see the green hillock over her whenever they went to church. They all missed the crippled girl dreadfully, by her very weakness she had won her way into their hearts. Only Dora seemed at first, when she came home from school, quite happy and unaffected, though she had loved Catherine dearly; but when Aunt Dorothy told her that she must not put Catherine's name into her prayers any longer she fell into an agony of tears, went weeping to bed and would not be comforted, as if for the first time she had understood what death meant. Young Mr. de Quincey wrote the most distracted letters from London, recalling how Catherine used to sleep and lock her little arms round his neck, half-dreaming. He talked wildly of his own sister, who had died young, neglected and ill-treated by some unkind nurse, and tormented himself with a fancy that Catherine had also called for him in her delirium and been unanswered. It was an extravagant and morbid grief which alarmed Dorothy. When he came back to Dove Cottage he was still talking very queerly about the child. They had given him her red shoes and a lock of her hair. He told Dorothy solemnly that several times, when he was lying on the grass of her grave, as he often did, he had seen his little love coming towards him, in her blue bed-gown and black skirt, looking just as she used to see.

That summer, 1812, they were all very sober. The picnics and parties were not so pleasant as usual and Mary stayed at home when they went up to Hackett, for she could not bear to go back to the cottage where Catherine had always been so well and happy. The war news was frightening. The Duke of Wellington was winning his battles in the Peninsula, but the Emperor had gone to Moscow with a great army, intending to conquer Russia; nobody knew how that business would end. Coleridge was in London, but all his family were at Keswick. When the Wordsworths went over they did not hear him much spoken of. The Southeys had a tribe of children now growing up with the young Coleridges. Little girls in white muslin gowns and pink or blue sashes, with square fringes and long curls on their shoulders, handsome boys in coloured jackets and long white trousers, rioted all over Greta Hall in the holidays. It was a happy house for children. Poor Uncle Robert worked dreadfully hard, going like clockwork from history to poetry, from criticism to biography; it was all task-work with him now. He was a manufacturer and the library was his workshop, but he was always ready, in his prescribed intervals of leisure, to go with the children on a donkey-riding picnic, or make up a water-party on the lake. There was a place called Mutton-Pie Bay where they used to have splendid picnics at least once a week. Mrs. Coleridge thought that there was almost too much junketing for her delicate and excitable brood.

Quite a number of people came to Greta Hall nowadays, as a literary pilgrimage; the names of Coleridge, Southey and Wordsworth were recognised as forming a school, people began to talk about the Lake Poets. That summer, 1812, there appeared in Keswick, among other such pilgrims, a childish couple come from the south on what appeared to be a protracted honeymoon. The bridegroom was an exceedingly wild and handsome youth, as red and white as a girl, a bright fiery being with storm-tossed curls and an open Byronic collar. He was Percy Bysshe Shelley, the son of a baronet, heir to six thousand a year and a wild atheist and revolutionary. His little bride Harriet was a blooming young creature of seventeen or so, the daughter of a publican. They said that he had run away with her, the summer before, out of an academy for young ladies on Clapham Common.

This childlike pair were living in a furnished cottage at an absurd rent. They ran about the garden like mad things. The young poet did chemical experiments and let off fireworks at night in the garden, floated paper boats on the Greta and ran whooping down the bank after them; his neighbours thought him quite mad. The Southeys pitied the inexperienced couple.

Kind Mrs. Southey lent them sheets and tablecloths, with which Chestnut Cottage was ill-provided, and gave Harriet much good advice about housekeeping, which went in at one ear and out at the other. Poor Robert Southey said to Dorothy ruefully, "There is a man here who seems to me like the ghost of myself. He is just what I was in seventeen ninety-four. He is heir to an immense property and seems as much troubled by the notion that he will have six thousand a year as I used to be at his age by the knowledge that I had not a penny. Naturally he disapproves of me and thinks my notions and principles very old-fashioned. I tell him that all the difference between us is, he is nineteen and I am thirty-seven. I try to convince him that he may yet do a great deal of good with six thousand a year." They laughed together and Robert added with one of his heavy sighs, "God help us! the world wants mending, but these young men do not set about it in the right way." She thought what a good creature Robert was, when all was said and done.

This young couple presently left Keswick, having found their great man too reactionary for their taste. They went to Ireland and later to London, where they quarrelled and parted company. Little Harriet took to bad courses and killed herself; the young husband ran away with a blue-stocking, married her and went to live in Italy, where he was drowned sailing a boat in the Mediterranean. The story was long and sad and in Keswick they thought it very scandalous. For years people pointed out Chestnut Cottage as the place where the mad poet Shelley spent his honeymoon.

That autumn there was a wedding in the Wordsworth family too. Mary's brother, Tom Hutchinson, came up from Hindwell to marry his pretty cousin, Mary Monkhouse, the girl whom Mrs. Coleridge had teased about not catching John Wilson. They were much inclined to marry cousins in that family, it had happened several times over. So now there was another Mary Hutchinson again, and Dorothy and all of them were glad to have the dear name revived; but within a month of this gay November wedding Mary and William had another load of trouble to carry. Little Thomas, the gentle and innocent boy, the one for whom William himself had the greatest affection, caught the measles and died after a week's illness.

Dorothy was over at Watermillock, on Ullswater, staying with Jane Marshall who had been her schoolfellow, when he first fell sick. She got a letter from Sara Hutchinson which frightened her, for the delicate little fellow had already been ill for three or four days, and they were always worried about his chest. He was supposed to have had measles already and his Aunt Dorothy could not get it out of her mind that this must be something more serious. However the Marshalls all tried to cheer her up and next morning her fears seemed foolish. She set out quite cheerfully in Mr. Marshall's carriage to Penruddock, where she got on to the Keswick coach, for she could not go over the Kirkstone alone on foot in December. If there were better news for her when she got to her journey's end she meant to stay for a few days with the Calverts at Windy Brow, and see the folk at Greta Hall, before she went back to Grasmere. But when she got to Threlkeld, there was William, leaning against the inn wall, wrapped in his old volunteer cloak against the bleak winter wind, and she knew from his closed haggard face that something dreadful had happened to him. She climbed down off the top of the coach, flew to him as she used to do in her girlhood and seized him by the arm. He turned his fixed and distracted look upon her and gave a long sigh as if his heart would break. He said, "Tom is dead," and she burst into a passion of tears, but she felt as if she had known his news before he spoke.

After she had come to herself a little she was told that the Grasmere cart was going home and she could either be conveyed in it or send for a chaise. As always, she had little money in her knitted silk purse so she chose the cart and lay at the bottom upon some straw. William sat beside her for part of the way and told her of his little boy's illness, how he had gone on well for nearly a week, but then there was a sudden change and he was dead in two hours; in his heart-broken voice he said, "Tom was too good for us." Part of the way he walked by the cart in silence, through the grey December afternoon, with his eyes on the road, never raising his head to look at the black sides of the mountains, or the bog-grass blowing in the wind on top of the Raise. Dorothy herself lay in a stupor of misery, and was only roused from it when, after dark, they reached home and the candlelight shone from the open door. Mary received her with the calmness of an angel. She was ashamed of her own weakness and reproached herself bitterly that she could not bear the sorrow as that stricken mother did. Mary had lost two children in one year, yet she could smile and comfort others; she had a divine strength.

After the boy was buried, however, Mary gave way and wept bitterly. Tom had been a child of a heavenly disposition, meek, simple, innocent, unoffending, with a celestial sweetness in his face impossible to forget. He had been a dovelike creature, the most like herself of all her children, the one who caused her the least pain and gave her the purest delight. The poor woman had scarcely yet recovered from the shock of Catherine's death, but had been dejected and feeble all that summer and now she sank into a dreadful melancholy. William, too, was very wretched. It had been a cruel stroke for him, he had loved the dead boy passionately and grieved continually for his little gentle son. His sister thought that he looked ten years older since the death of Thomas. He hardly spoke to any one, but shut himself up with his books. Everything about the vale now reminded these sorrowing parents of their lost children and William began to talk at last of removing out of Grasmere.

There was a vacant house called Rydal Mount, over the hill on the way to Ambleside, in a most beautiful situation between the fells and the reedy mere, the very place which they had longed for in happier years. They would see the Grasmere hills from its garden and be within a walk of the churchyard where the children were buried, but all their daily walks and ways would be changed and this they fancied might cure Mary of her sorrow in time. The house belonged to that bad-tempered Mrs. North from Liverpool, who had had such a great quarrel with Dorothy and Mary about the Green children. She was very disobliging over all the arrangements for the move; however they got away from the sad Parsonage in May and all drove over the White Moss to their new home. William had just been made Distributor of Stamps for the County of Westmoreland, a post which Lord Lonsdale had obtained for him. A clerk could be engaged to do the work and William would be richer by four hundred a year. This made a great difference to all their plans and they wished it had come sooner, but had no heart to rejoice over their windfall yet. They were all wearied out with troubles and fatigue. Mary was so low that it made your heart ache to see her.

Dorothy was the last one to leave the Parsonage. In the rich yellow evening light it seemed as quiet as the grave, there was nothing left within its walls but desolation, gloom, and cheerless silence. She was glad to shut the door upon that empty house. Her last look was for the two small graves by the churchyard wall. The hawthorn tree, in whose shadow Catherine used to play, was in white again although she slept beneath it; under those flowering branches it was possible to think of hope and immortality.

XIV

I

It was May, 1813, when they moved into Rydal Mount for the rest of their lives. That was the year that the Emperor came back defeated from Russia and the Duke of Wellington drove the French back over the Pyrenees and carried the war into France, the year that Robert Southey brought out his *Life of Nelson* and was made Poet Laureate. William looked down his long nose over this appointment, but the Court would not have Lord Byron, and Walter Scott had refused the appointment, so Robert Southey got it. The little Southey girls were charmed and twined Papa a laurel wreath when he came back from London. The year after that William published his own long poem, *The Excursion*, in a fine two guinea quarto edition. It was a sad failure, for so expensive a book would only sell to rich people who bought what was fashionable and William, alas! was not yet the fashion. Every one was still reading Lord Byron's poems. William had miserable reviews; Jeffrey cut up the book in the *Edinburgh Review*, and Hazlitt paid off some old grudges by two spiteful articles in the *Examiner*. Charles Lamb wrote a defence of it in the *Quarterly*, but the editor lopped the article about so ruthlessly that William was quite angry with its author for treating him so shabbily. The whole family were dreadfully disappointed by the failure of William's great poem. He had been working on it so long, parts of it had even been written as far back as Racedown and it had all his Grasmere life in it. Dorothy could not bear to think that so much patient thought and toil were to be wasted. She had begun to fear that William's poems would never sell in his lifetime, but still she clung to the hope that his work would become immortal when he and she and all their petty cares were forgotten.

In that spring of 1814 the allies marched into Paris, the Emperor was deposed and the war came to an end. It was like some strange dream to have peace in a moment, prisoners let loose, and France a country which English people might once more visit after twenty-two years. She and William could go and see Annette and Caroline if they chose. Caroline was going to be married quite soon to a young man called Baudouin, whose brother had actually been a prisoner of war in England and was known to the Wordsworths. Dorothy thought that it would be a real delight to go to her niece's wedding, though she could hardly imagine the small dancing chatterer of Calais sands grown husband-high already. England and France had been at war together for the whole of that child's life. If there had been peace between the two countries William might have married her mother and Dorothy been robbed of all that dear companionship with him which had made her history. It was strange to think of that, but stranger still to imagine herself robbed of her dear companionship with Mary, who had been more than a sister to her these twelve years.

Dorothy smiled ruefully as she pictured herself aunt to a nestful of skinny yellow imps with Annette's black eyes and shrill laughter, in place of their own dear brood. She wondered whether William's French daughter had grown up like him. At Calais she had often shown a look of him, about the nose and mouth especially, but she had been too young for any one to tell whether she had his poetic fire. Among his lawful children, only Dora showed the spark. She was a lively quick affectionate creature, sometimes most wilful and difficult to handle, there was certainly something unusual about her, though she was little more than a tree-climbing tomboy as yet. Dorothy wondered constantly whether Caroline might not be a more interesting girl even than Dora, but when she tried to speculate on this William did not answer, and went away. Perhaps he did not want to be reminded of the follies and agonies of his youth, now that he was grown so grave and respectable, or possibly he really was not interested. It was all so very long ago, it might have happened in another world.

Mary was more sympathetic, but said with her divine smile, "I think children take after their aunts and uncles more than they do after their fathers and mothers. I know the old village women always say so and I believe it is true. Of course I did not know you when you were Dora's age, but William says she is exactly what you were then and I am sure my Johnny often reminds me of his Uncle John." Dorothy was struck by this reflection and admitted its truth. Johnny was very like the dead sailor, a dunce at his books, but noble, kindly and modest. He would develop late, but already they had begun to depend upon him in any family trouble. Dora was herself renewed, an awkward girl, wild, eager, vivid, born to suffer and enjoy. There seemed to be something in this theory about aunts and uncles. None of the brood, however, had Uncle Kit's academic brilliance; and it would be dreadful if Willy, a spoilt, vain, obstinate child, absurdly petted by his father, should take after Uncle Richard, who had muddled the family affairs all his life and had just distressed them all by marrying his cook. She ended by kissing Mary and saying, "Your children should try to be as much like their mother as they can, they could not do better."

The younger generation was growing up fast around her now. She wished that she could have felt as happy about the Coleridge children as she did about William's surviving three. Derwent to be sure was an anxiety to nobody, and young Sara was growing into quite a learned girl, studying French, Latin and music and making great progress in Italian. She would be able to earn her living some day by teaching, if she could outgrow her delicate teens; but Hartley was the one about whom Dorothy felt frightened, she could not say why. He went up to Oxford in the autumn. Uncle Robert had coached him at home for a year, after he had learnt all that Mr. Dawes could teach him, and had Greek enough for a whole college, but he was still the same brilliant incalculable creature, with far too much confidence in his own powers and a perilous habit of finding excuses for anything he wanted to do. He was a marvellously eloquent talker, like his father, when he was in the right mood and company; but his shyness made him formal and sometimes a little affected with strangers. He had awkward manners by nature, and his mother complained that he made no attempt to improve them. His appearance was as odd as his manners, for he was still not more than five feet tall, with remarkably strong features, some of the thickest and blackest eyebrows ever seen and at that time of his life a beard which a Turk might envy. One young lady in Keswick had shaken her ringlets and declared with a titter that he looked like a Portuguese Jew. He was always very shy with strange young women, and they found him alarming, though they all understood that he was very clever and was going to do great things in the world.

There was no getting any answer out of his father about his Oxford fees. Coleridge had done well out of his London lectures and that old play of his, *Remorse*, which he had brought to Racedown, had been furbished up and put upon the stage two winters back, by Lord Byron's influence. It was well noticed and ran for twenty nights. He made some money out of that, and hoped to put on another, but it all melted away again with his way of living. He was taking anything up to a pint of laudanum a day nowadays, and once drank a quart in twenty-four hours. In the end all the old friends had to club together and arrange for Hartley's fees so that he might take up the postmastership which he had won at Merton.

Uncle Robert and William were very active in the matter, Tom Poole paid up like a man, Basil Montagu helped, so did the kind Beaumonts and Cottle, his father's old publisher, and his Coleridge relations at Ottery St. Mary. They were all proud of Hartley and wanted to give him his chance, for his own sake and his father's. So the money was scraped together and Hartley went off to Oxford in great spirits, with a vast deal of parting advice from his uncle and from William about not wasting his time, or shirking the prescribed books, but keeping regular hours of study and trying to behave like other people.

2

All that winter William and Dorothy were planning and hesitating about the visit to France for Caroline's Easter wedding, but they need not have troubled, for on the first of March, 1815, the Emperor landed again from Elba and marched to Paris. It was the worst news that had come overseas for a very long time; Dora said, "Why did they not kill him while they had him?" and there were many people who felt the same. Dorothy was exceedingly distressed for poor Annette and Caroline. She could not but think with what bitter anguish Annette, who had worked all these years for the Royalist cause, must have lighted her candles for the illuminations when the Emperor returned. It was a summer of many private and public anxieties, the last only dispelled when the Ambleside coach came down at the end of June, dressed with flowers and oak leaves, and the horses decked with ribbons, bringing news of the victory at Waterloo and the abdication of the Emperor. That was like the end of a bad dream to every one, though Dorothy had no patience with the tinkling of the Ambleside bells, when she thought of so many brave men dead in battle.

The joy of victory seemed to her to be an awful thing, but every one else made merry. They had a great bonfire on the top of Skiddaw for Waterloo, roasted beef and boiled plum puddings, sang 'God Save the King' round the most furious body of blazing tar barrels that ever were seen, drank a huge wooden bowl of punch, fired toy cannon at every health with three times three, and kicked large blazing balls of tow and turpentine down the sides of the mountain. William went up, and Mary and Dorothy, they took Johnny with them and all the Southeys. William wrapped himself up in Edith Southey's red cloak and looked very noble, only he managed in the dark to kick over the kettle of water, and as there was no more to be got up there the rest of the company became very drunk on neat rum.

They formed a huge circle and danced round hand in hand while behind them hovered an immeasurable arch of the most intense darkness, for the light of their bonfire quite put out the moon. Then there was a procession downhill. All the torches were lit at once by the mad fellows who had got at the rum and the way downhill was marked by a track of fire from flambeaux dropping their pitch and tarred rope. One fellow was so drunk that his companions placed him upon a horse with his face to the tail to bring him down safely, they were just sober enough to guide him and hold him on. However, down they all safely got by midnight, and nobody the worse for the toil of the day, though they were eight hours from the time they set out to the time they got home. Such were the rejoicings of victory. Derwent and Sara Coleridge were not allowed to go up the mountain, but they watched the procession from the windows of Greta Hall with their mother. They saw the fire-balloon go up and the fireworks climb and flower over the lake. Only Hartley was away. He had gone to spend his vacation with his father at Calne, in Wiltshire. It had been arranged that he should divide his time between his father and mother. He had just finished his first year at Oxford.

The year after he tried for the Newdigate Prize, with a copy of verses on *The Horses of Lysippus*, but another scholar succeeded. It was a dreadful disappointment to Hartley, who had made sure of this distinction. He was quite stupefied. He would not admit how shaken his own faith in himself was; he sang, he danced, he whistled, he leapt, he ran from room to room announcing the tidings of his rival's success, but it was all bare sands with him next day. He had a sudden strange conviction that all his aims and hopes were doomed to disappointment and he consoled himself with a bout of heavy drinking. This was the first time that he gave way to a consolation which would one day ruin him. They did not know how he had taken his defeat at home, and were only surprised and sorry that any one should have written a better prize-poem than Hartley.

That summer of 1816 his father went into voluntary restraint, at the house of a doctor named Gillman, to be cured, by force if necessary, of his opium-eating. He told Mr. Gillman with tears that he could not keep from the drug now for more than sixty hours and begged for the strictest discipline. Mr. Gillman and his wife agreed to the undertaking and he came to their house in Highgate, with the proof-sheets of *Christabel* in his hand. The first few weeks were an agony, but his resolution held; they cured him in the end and he made his home with them for the rest of his life.

3

That same summer there was an unpleasant village scandal about Mr. de Quincey. There had been a break in his friendship with the Wordsworths, for John Wilson had carried him off to Edinburgh, where he himself was now a professor in the University, and Mr. de Quincey had spent a year there, writing for the papers. Now he was back at Dove Cottage, but the better class of people would not have much to do with him, for they said he drank, and drugged and kept low company. All that spring he had been hanging about after a farmer's daughter, Peggy Sympson, a tall handsome silent girl, with a broad Lakeland accent, but very little to say for herself, whom Dorothy remembered as the dunce of Grasmere school. Peggy had a father alive and several brothers, a rough lot, all violent politicians and great speech-makers at election time against the clergy and gentry, but she herself was a gentle ignorant silent creature. The Sympsons all thought Mr. de Quincey a very wonderful person. They lived at a farmhouse called the

Nab, on the shore of Rydal Water, a long low house with pointed church windows, wreathed in roses and honeysuckle all summer long. Mr. de Quincey used to visit his Peggy there every evening, when the bats were flickering about the eaves and the owls hooting across the lake. People gossiped about the way they walked in the garden, or sat in the arbour together. Dorothy herself could not help but see them several times as she came home from Ambleside in the long June evenings; but the little poet and the great motherly girl must have been lovers long before, for by mid-summer she was in full fruit and the scandal plain to all the women of the neighbourhood. It was an uncomfortable business for the Wordsworths, who all kept away from Dove Cottage, and William was very much annoyed about it.

Peggy Sympson bore a son to her poet in November. Sara Hutchinson, who had never greatly cared for him, came in one snowy afternoon, knelt down to warm her bony hands by the fire and said to William and Dorothy, "Your precious Mr. de Quincey will have to marry Peggy Sympson after all." She blinked her sharp green eyes, screwed up her thin face, all pinched and dry with the cold, and said with an old maid's spiteful relish, "The girl has presented him with a son, I hear; a great bouncing child, quite unlike his father, though I suppose it is his. I heard the tale just now as I came from Ambleside. They all say he is delighted and means to marry her, but old Sympson and the boys would break every bone in his body if he did not. I suppose they think him a good catch, though he drinks like a fish, fuddles himself with opium, and tries in every way to be as great a gun as Mr. Wilson." Poor Sara had no longer any sympathy with romance.

Dorothy was bewildered by the fire of jealous and illogical resentment which swept through her. She was consumed by one of the hot flushes of irritation which had lately overtaken her whenever anything crossed her; she trembled in every limb and stammered very much as she burst out angrily, "How can he degrade himself so? He has no decent feeling if he can bring himself to marry that stupid heavy common girl. What can he see in her?" She was almost too vexed to know what she was saying. Sara gave a thin spiteful laugh and retorted, "Oh! He is in raptures about her beauty, her good sense and simplicity, and her angelic sweetness, as he calls it. He always seemed very shy with women, but no doubt she met him half-way." William concluded the discussion by saying, with extreme severity, "If he marries her he is ruined. The thing is inexcusable, in any case. I wish you all to have no more to do with him." He looked as grim as a judge, sitting between the two angry women. Dorothy had a strange puzzled recollection of Calais and Annette and William's own bastard daughter.

His Caroline had been married in Paris soon after the French king was restored to the throne by the Allies and was now about to bear her own first child. Dorothy experienced a sudden dim regret that time had done so much to change William. He had been generous and impulsive once, and so had she, but of late years she felt that the grass had withered and the flower faded for them both. William had grown self-centred, mean and self-righteous. He was dreadfully strict and reserved, he had withdrawn himself even from her. She felt wretchedly confused, bitterly envious of dull Peggy Sympson, who had attained the natural fulfilment which was now for ever denied to her. She heard herself say, with a bitter reluctance, "Yes, if he marries that creature I for one want to see no more of him," and she did not contradict William when he concluded with authority, "The man is no longer worthy of our friendship."

Mr. de Quincey did, however, marry the mother of his child soon after Christmas and took her to live with him in Dove Cottage. Dorothy could not bear to think of them inhabiting her own dear rooms, she would not walk past the cottage any longer if it could be helped. The two were shut up in it together and were hardly ever seen out of doors, except after dark. Mr. de Quincey had always loved long midnight walks and Peggy was ashamed to be seen by neighbours. He became quite nocturnal in his habits, like a bat or an owl. They said that he lay abed all day, groaning in misery at the frightful scenes and faces which he beheld in his opium-dreams, while his wife hung over him, crying in her soft bewildered country accents, "What is it that you see, dear? Oh! what is it that you see?" She nursed him most devotedly during those two first frightful years. She bore him another child, a daughter, and Dorothy, when she heard that, remembered how dearly he had loved their little Chinese maiden; he had always been fond of little girls. Afterwards he recovered a little and actually edited a local paper for a time. They met him and talked to him in the excitement of the Kendal elections, in 1818; but they never were friends again and they lost sight of him when he went away to Edinburgh first and afterwards to London. The chance-sown flower of friendship had withered.

4

People had thought, when the French wars came to an end, that everything would now be happy and prosperous, but it was not so. There was much rioting and discontent everywhere and when Dorothy went to spend some months in Halifax, in 1817, with her old cousins, she saw great poverty and distress. Cotton and worsted mills and steam engines, she wrote to William, were no better than encumbrances upon the ground, trade was so bad after the war. The rich manufacturers were keeping their mills going as best they could, to employ their workmen, but this could not last. The whole West Riding was in misery, though she did not see the worst of it, for she was in a large comfortable house with two rich old ladies and servants to wait upon her, but she missed the children's voices and her dear home. She was glad to get back again in time to play cards with the children on Christmas Day, and drink a toast in cowslip wine to William and Mary, who had gone up to London.

They were all richer now, they could travel about when they choose and visit friends without counting the cost. They had plenty of friends in London who could entertain them. The Lambs were in Great Russell Street now, near Covent Garden and the theatres. Mary's cousin Tom Monkhouse, the brother of pretty young Mary, had a fine house in Queen Anne Street, always at the Wordsworths' disposal; brother Kit was in the Rectory at Lambeth, a widower now, since his wife Priscilla had died in childbirth and glad enough to have his sister visit him. Dorothy spent the early summer of 1820 very happily at Lambeth, except that she had lost all her teeth and was having to pay many visits to her dentist. The old mad king had died that spring and the Prince Regent had succeeded him. London was all agog about the coming trial of Queen Caroline.

William and Mary came south in July and they all attended Tom Monkhouse's wedding and afterwards set out on a continental tour with the bride and bridegroom. Dorothy was to see the Alps at last. She had never been abroad since she went to Calais with William, eighteen years back, she who had once felt that she could walk round the world. They travelled in two carriages, went through Belgium and Germany, crossed the Alps into Italy and came home through France; it was the most wonderful journey. Only Dorothy was almost fifty now, a little thin brown-faced spinster, who tired more easily than she used to do. She was made ill by heat, queer foreign food, and shaking and jolting over hard roads; but she must see everything, for her greedy eyes were storing themselves with pictures against her old age.

She looked out for every place which William had seen in that undergraduate walking-tour of his, with Robert Jones, before the French Revolution, thirty years ago; and William loved to point them out to her. They had great adventures, with thunderstorms, fleas and hard beds and greedy cheating landlords; they all kept journals and Crabb Robinson, who met them and travelled part of the way with them, was quite shamed by the bareness of his own when he read how much Mary and Dorothy had written down afterwards. They stayed in Paris on the way home, saw Annette and the Baudouins, Caroline and her husband and daughter. William invited Annette to spend an afternoon at the Louvre with herself and Mary. The two women looked at the pictures and sideways at each other, each holding William by an arm. They did not know, either of them, a word of the other's language. William and Dorothy took the grand-daughter, who was now four years old, to see the wild beasts at the *Jardin des Plantes.* The little creature had been called Dorothée, after her aunt, in memory of Calais.

They were stranded on the homeward voyage on the sands of Boulogne, but on a falling tide and were rescued and got safe to England a week later. They stayed for a fortnight in London, saw all their old friends, dined with the Monkhouses in Gloucester Place, went to the play with the Lambs, and had William's youngest boy, spoilt stupid little Willy, out for half holidays from the Charterhouse, which had much improved his manners. Kit had left Lambeth, to become Master of Trinity College, Cambridge, so they missed him; but Dorothy did persuade William to do one thing on which she had long resolved and that was to visit their friend Coleridge in his lodgings at Highgate. William looked down his nose a little, but consented; he agreed that they ought to see their friend, for a very sad thing had happened that summer. Hartley had lost his fellowship and been obliged to leave Oxford in disgrace.

He had taken his degree and in the previous year had got a fellowship at Oriel, to his father's great pride. Little Willy Wordsworth came back from school that night and told his mother, "You never saw master in such a good humour in your life. As soon as he got the letter about Hartley he rose up, gave a shout and proclaimed a holiday; the boys all huzzaed and there was such an uproar, mother." That was charming news, and even Uncle Robert Southey, who had lost his own clever eldest son Herbert four years back, and never been the same man since, quite cheered up at this triumph of his old pupil. He never realised that Hartley had got his degree and his scholarship through his own brilliance, in spite of his oddity and the defects in his education. Everybody thought that the young man's future was now secure, but for one reason or another, the dons at Oriel dismissed him from his fellowship after a year. They said that he neglected his college duties, kept bad company and was always getting drunk.

It was difficult to get to the bottom of all the stories about him. His own friends vowed that he had been unjustly treated and misunderstood, but he did not stay for judgment. He ran away from Oxford, and for a long time nobody could find him. Dorothy had heard the beginning of this trouble in June, when she was at Lambeth and had cried out to Kit, "Oh! poor Hartley, this will break his father's heart," and so it almost had done. Coleridge was distracted to think that his son was ruined and went about muttering, "Why did he not come to me?" He wrote letters, offered money, sent his sensible second boy, Derwent, to find out what was happening, went to Oriel and saw Dr. Coplestone and the fellows himself; but all to no purpose. They offered Hartley three hundred pounds as compensation for the loss of his fellowship which satisfied nobody. His father advised him not to take it, lest it might seem an admission of guilt, but in the end, when there was no hope of Hartley's restoration, the money was taken and put by for him. He must bear his disgrace.

All this trouble had dragged on through the summer and autumn, while the Wordsworths were abroad Dorothy could not bear to think of what their friend must have suffered. As they went up the hill to Highgate she quite dreaded the meeting and would have turned back if she had been alone, but William strode on, as if they were on quite an everyday errand. It was not the same for him as it was for her. He had seen their friend from time to time since the great quarrel, but she had not laid eyes on him for ten years, not since he walked out of Allan Bank after Sara Hutchinson left him. She did not even know what he looked like nowadays, except that they said his hair had gone almost white, from his many illnesses, while she and William were only grizzled.

Highgate, in the autumn of 1820, was a village still, with a three-cornered green, a duck pond, a blacksmith's forge and a little inn, *The Flask*, beside the turnpike. It kept up a yearly fair, when young men and girls came out from London to dance under the trees. Mr. Gillman's house was the third on the green, facing the church, a roomy respectable brick dwelling, with a good garden. In front of the house was a grove of stately elms. Behind it the hill dropped away towards Hampstead, with crazy brick walls tumbling down the slope, ivied cottages, hidden gardens, steep lanes and flights of steps. In summer, when the gardens were leafy, and the set of the air was going southward, taking the smoke away, there would be a fine blue shimmering prospect over the green fields in the valley; but this was an autumn day to suit Dorothy's age and mood, a grey quiet afternoon with a bite in the air and a smell of burning leaves, and there was an olive-tinted haze over the city. Their friend had a room of his own, high up at the back of the house. While she waited for him in it with her brother she stared out through the branches of the cedar in Mr. Gillman's garden, thinking that he had chosen a pleasant place in which to end his days, but when she tried to say so cheerfully to William she could not because her lips trembled.

Presently he came in, and all her thoughts began to whirl about in her head, like dead leaves in a wind, because he looked so old and bent and bewildered. His hair was almost white, though he was not yet fifty, and his whole person was shrunk, shabby and irresolute. His great eyes had an air of mild bewilderment and pain, though his smile was as sweet as ever. He seemed very glad to see them and sighed, "This is good of you both . . . very good . . ." in a plaintive sing-song snuffle which quite startled her. His hand was flabby and soft, like an old man's, as he stood smiling and nodding at her. He was still the most astonishing talker; he and William sat down and discoursed on everything in heaven and earth, while she sat by tongue-tied, listening to that confused and meandering river of eloquence and thinking of the time when she had heard it first. He talked a good deal of himself and his sufferings, praised the faithful Gillmans and said that the doctor had saved his life. She saw a gleam of his old magnificent air as he said, "I owe a cock to Aesculapius, do I not?" but when he talked of his son he turned wretched and sat staring at the ground, mumbling that he feared Hartley had inherited no good from him. She burst out, "But he will outlive this, he will recover, we must all help him," and got a look which thanked her, but then the sad father shook his head and lamented, "It has been one of the four great sorrows of my life. I do not know what is to become of him." William was not much help, he had grown too stiff to console other people, all his sympathies seemed to have dried up in him. She wished that she had been alone with her friend. She thought that she might have said or done something to cheer him, but it was too late for that now.

They all went out into the garden and walked up and down a little on a sort of terrace there, beside a ropy wistaria. They talked of how green it would be in summer and Coleridge told them of his daily promenade under the elm-trees in the Grove and his walks upon the Heath. He said, "I met a young man last summer, in a lane near here, a loose, slack youth, not well dressed, a poet, it seems. He was walking with a surgeon from Guy's Hospital, a Mr. Green, a friend of Gillman's; he was introduced to me by the name of John Keats." William knew of this young man and said so. "A red-headed Cockney apothecary, I met him at an evening party, a year or two back. He read me some verses to Pan, a pretty piece of paganism and sent me a volume of his poems, but I have never cut the pages. I cannot be plagued with these beginners. I have too much trouble with my eyesight nowadays to read any verses except my own." He had assumed a sour disapproving look, it was a fact that he disliked to hear of any rising poet who might supplant him.

Their friend said, "Well, you will hear no more of him, poor wretch! His name will be writ in water, he says so himself. He has sailed for Italy. I hear he is far gone in consumption and will die there. I guessed as much when I met him. He ran back, after he had left me and said, 'Let me carry away the memory of having pressed Coleridge's hand.' When he was gone away again I said to my companion, 'There is death in that hand,' and now it seems I was right. We had walked at an alderman's after-dinner pace for two miles or so, and spoken of poetry and the meaning of dreams. At the last we talked of nightingales. He said that he was going to write an ode to a nightingale. They nest here in summer, you know, in Ken Wood and this young man had heard one singing its heart out in a plum-tree in the garden at Wentworth Place, where he was living. I told him to come back and see me, but he never did."

Dorothy looked about her at the garden, shivering in the autumn wind, and said to him suddenly, "Do you remember the nightingales at Alfoxden?" but he only shook his head drearily. He said, "Did we hear the nightingales there? I had forgotten that and yet I do remember I wrote a poem about them. I called them merry birds; why did I do that? I must have been in a merry mood myself. I know better now. A poet should die young, like John Keats, for when he grows old he loses the trick of singing."

She listened to him in a kind of despair, thinking, "Yes, he has forgotten our nightingales. We were all young together when we heard them sing, the sky was not tall enough for us to walk under; we had a fire in our hearts. It is ashes now, all over and done with, nothing left except a rhyme that we three wrote together, about an old sailor, in the careless days when we were young." The autumn wind seemed to chill her to the very heart. She stared about her with her wild eyes and thought distractedly, "My youth . . . my lovely youth, where has it gone? I shall never hear my nightingales again."

A proverb came into her head from nowhere, a Spanish by-word. Robert Southey had told it to her once and now she said it aloud, glancing at the naked trees, "There are no birds in last year's nest." The men looked at her as if startled by something in her wild look and tone, and William thought that his sister had been growing strange of late. She stood there in the empty garden, under the grey sky, and nodded her head up and down like an old witch, repeating to herself, as if it were a spell that had some meaning for her, "No birds . . . no birds in last year's nest."

XV

I

After that the years began to slip away faster and faster; the children grew up and prospered, but the older generation began to go quietly downhill. Mary and William lived on in their children, full of hopes and plans for them, but Dorothy had not quite the same comfort in them, though she loved them all dearly. John went to Sedbergh, and then to Oxford, after which he took orders; he remained a good sweet stupid creature, "laborious as an ass," said Hartley Coleridge, who did not think much of him. Little Willie was a horrid boy, spoilt, delicate and always troublesome. He went to Mr. Dawes because his father thought him not strong enough for a public school. Dora was the best of the bunch. She shot up into a bright enchanting creature, tall and graceful, with her mother's amiable smile and her father's marked serious features; she left school, did up her hair in a basketwork knot of light-brown plaits on her slender neck and ran about the house as lively as a lark. She and Sara Coleridge and Edith Southey were an inseparable triad, William wrote a poem about them. He adored his daughter and she him, they were inseparable.

The house at Rydal was always full of people and there were plenty of young men about for the girls to play with; they had dancing and picnics and went out on the lake. Dr. Christopher Wordsworth, the Master of Trinity, used to come every long vacation and bring his three clever sons with him to enjoy themselves with their cousins. William was very proud of Kit and always quoting "My brother the Dean," but was rather jealous in his heart, because Kit's boys were all so much cleverer than any child of his. He said gloomily to

Dorothy, "All my nephews will end as bishops or heads of colleges," and it did very nearly come true, for all that branch distinguished themselves as scholars, or in the Church. Dora was very fond of her three cousins and got on well with the Coleridge boys, who were often in and out of Rydal Mount.

Derwent was to be a parson, black-bearded Hartley had drifted back from journalism in London to teach in Mr. Dawes' school at Ambleside, Dorothy fancied, however, after a year or two, that her niece Dora did not take much interest in any of these young men. Perhaps it was because her father took up so much of her time. He did not get on with his great work as he should, but seemed content to rake out and publish old work, like *Peter Bell* and *The Waggoner*. His sister considered that he frittered away his time with sonnets, of which he produced a great many, but he had to have everything taken down and copied out by Dora, she had taken the place which used to be Dorothy's. William thought that every other claim should give way to his, and Dora never complained when she was kept behind from any party with her cousins, but her mother said to Dorothy that she feared Dora was less interested in the young men than in Mr. Quillinan.

This gentleman was a new neighbour, a widower, a retired army man, who wrote a little poetry himself and was a great admirer of William's. In 1821 he came to the Lakes, screwed up his courage and appeared at Rydal Mount with a letter of introduction from an Edinburgh friend. William received the heavy dragoon very coldly at first, twirled his chair about and made short and stiff remarks; Mr. Quillinan became indignant and thought him most disagreeable. Fortunately Dora came in at that moment, innocent and engaging, and provided a timely interruption; Sara Hutchinson followed and laughed William out of his frigidity. In the end Mr. Quillinan became a family friend.

He and his wife and two daughters came to settle nearby; they all liked him, and Dora was always in and out of his cottage. Later there was a tragic accident in that family.

Mrs. Quillinan swept her full short muslin skirt into the fire and was so terribly burnt that she died in a few days, in spite of Mary's and Dorothy's nursing. The heartbroken father left Rydal with his children, but after a time he drifted back again and seemed more than a little inclined to console himself with Dora, who sang about the house, did up her hair with a blue ribbon and seemed quite to have outgrown her earlier delicacy. However, nothing was said; the pair of them were in no hurry to settle their affairs and William at least never thought that his bright daughter might some day wish to leave him.

2

1825 was the gayest summer of all. Sir Walter Scott came in August and visited Professor Wilson, who came down from Edinburgh and opened up his house at Elleray on purpose to entertain him. There were great doings on Windermere, dinner-parties, tea-parties and a regatta on the lake. Mr. Canning, the Secretary of State, was there too, but the crowds thought Sir Walter much more interesting. He was the greatest literary figure they knew, now that Lord Byron was disgraced and dead. He had been the fashionable poet for ten years and the fashionable novelist for another ten, had been to court in London and at Holyrood, and refused the laureatship, which Robert Southey had taken thankfully after him. He had earned great sums of money and frittered them all away again, in printing and publishing ventures and in adding sham pepper-box turrets and baronial halls to his Gothic mock-castle at Abbotsford. Another year would see him bankrupt, the whole crazy system of his finances toppling to the ground, and he himself left to start all over again among the ruins of Constable's publishing business; but nobody guessed it yet. He seemed to be king of his world and everybody crowded to see him.

Dorothy thought him quite unchanged. She had not set

eyes on him since he came to Coleorton, eighteen years back, but his glancing eye was as bright as ever under the heavy eyebrows, though the long hair had gone back from his forehead and turned quite silvery above his rosy face. He shook her most affectionately by the hand and talked of old times. He had his youngest daughter with him, a comely black-eyed lass called Anne; also his son-in-law, young Mr. Lockhart, who had married his elder daughter Sophia. Mr. Lockhart was a handsome sardonic literary man, a dark Lowlander, who worked on *Blackwood* with John Wilson; he seemed inclined to quarrel with his entertainment. They three had just been over to Ireland, to visit Sir Walter's soldier son, whose regiment was quartered in Dublin. They had been to Killarney, and home through Wales, where they had visited the old ladies of Llangollen. In Dublin the mere news of Sir Walter's presence in the theatre had stopped the play, while the whole audience cheered him.

It was a great day at Elleray. The Professor entertained them all to a grand regatta; forty rowing-boats in procession moved round the islands during about three hours' time, with little cannons pluffing, flags and streamers flying in a fresh breeze, two execrable bands of music lilting different tunes, and the rapid splashing of innumerable oars. It was a charming sight and the shores were crowded with spectators. Next morning everybody came to breakfast at Rydal Mount. The lawns were thronged with lion-hunters, the ladies fluttering in full skirts, huge transparent muslin sleeves and hats plumed with every kind of feather, the men choking in high black stocks, tight full-skirted coats, long trousers and yellow gloves. Professor William devoured so huge a breakfast that he staggered every one. Mr. Lockhart looked down his nose at his fellow-guests and wrote to his wife that there was a large assembly of vulgar men and women; little Quillinan, the heavy dragoon, he thought the only *genteelish* figure, Miss Wordsworth was as yellow as a duck's foot. As for her brother, the poet, he thought him intolerable, always bowing and scraping and trying to be noticed. He lectured every one in an insufferable manner and talked of nothing but his own verses. Mr. Lockhart had no patience with the old gentleman and wished that he would drop his airs and his preaching. He seemed to think Canning and Scott together not worth his thumb.

Dorothy could see for herself, as she walked on the terrace with Sir Walter that William was being particularly aggressive; it was his way of assuring himself that he was as good as other folk. She knew that he was jealous of Sir Walter's success and it touched her exceedingly to hear the great man say, as he looked about him, "Yes, we have all gone up in the world; but I mind the time when my dear wife and I came to visit you in your little cottage at Grasmere, and you and Mrs. Wordsworth dressed the leg of mutton in the same room where it was to be eaten. Those were good days, I wish I were back in them." He leaned on his crutch, looked about him and sighed, "I envy your brother this quiet life of his."

She said, "I think it is William who may envy you," but he shrugged his shoulders and insisted, "He would not want such grinning honour as I have. There is nothing in it, save that in Scotland I must sit at the top of the table among the old ladies and carve, which I do very ill. I have learnt to strut for the lion-hunters and manage my mane and tail as I should, but it is all dearly bought." He shook his silvery head and complained, "I have too much on my shoulders, you do not know how hard I have to work. Folk will not leave me in peace; my publishers are like the bogle that cried, *Mair meat, mair meat* to King Jamie. In the end they will eat me up, hair and hide." She laughed ruefully and confessed, "The public has not much stomach for William, I fear." Sir Walter gave her his old kind look and told her, "That man's time will come when we three are all under the sod. Trust me, your brother will never be forgotten." He said it so seriously that he brought the tears into her faded eyes.

Next day was very hot. The Scott party rode over with

William and Dora to Keswick to visit the Southeys. William spouted his own poetry all the way and Scott quoted it to him very politely, but never got a word about his own writings in return. They admired the pretty tribe of the Poet Laureate's daughters. Edith in particular was strapping, tall and comely. Her mother and Mrs. Coleridge were a handsome pair of sisters still, but Mr. Lockhart considered that the young Sara Coleridge best repaid him for the long hot ride. She had grown into a lovely blue-stocking, with the finest pair of eyes that he had ever seen. She was very clever and accomplished, could read Latin, French and Italian, played the princess in exile and talked very enviously, poor thing, to Anne Scott, who cared little for such matters, about literary circles in Edinburgh. Mr. Lockhart thought that the beautiful pining creature was like a character in a novel and wondered much what would become of her. The Laureate was pale and sickly, but very civil to his distinguished guests; he regaled them with sherry and cake and then they rode back to Rydal, where there was a fresh party of what Mr. Lockhart called "abominables" to stare at the author of the *Waverley Novels.* On the day after they all climbed over Kirkstone to Ullswater and went sight-seeing to Lyulph's Tower and Aira Force, since Sir Walter liked romantic scenery. Finally the Scott party were driven away to Lowther Castle in Lord Lonsdale's four-horse barouche.

Sir Walter held Dorothy's hand at parting and said to her, very kindly, "When will the arrow of your inclination point north again? I think you have never seen the Water of Yarrow yet; will you not come and let me show it to you?" She said with regret, "I was in Scotland for a little while last summer with Mrs. Wordsworth's sister, Joanna, but we did not get so far. Another time I promise I will come to Abbotsford." He said, "Do not leave it too long, the years are slipping by faster than they did, I find." Something mournful in his look brought the quick tears to her eyes as she promised, "Indeed I will come"; and they loosed hands and parted. She did not know that she would never see Yarrow, or cross the Border again, did not guess that within a year Sir Walter's wife would be dead, his money all lost, his rainbow bubble of success burst for ever. She and William went home again and William said sourly that it had been a very tiring week of foolish entertainment.

3

That year Charles Lamb retired from the East India House. He had worked there for thirty-three years and declared that he felt as if he had grown fast to the wood of his desk. He wrote delighted letters to all his friends, vowing that he would not have served another seven years for seven hundred pounds and made innumerable plans for the disposal of his leisure. He and Mary had left Covent Garden two years before and found a charming cottage for themselves in Colebrooke Row, Islington, with the New River running before it and a spacious garden behind, full of fruit-trees and pot herbs. In this suburban solitude the brother and sister hoped to live out their quiet lives. Charles had been granted a pension which would secure them both from want, and he planned to continue writing his essays. He and his sister had adopted a pretty half-Italian girl, Emma Isola, whose father had taught William Italian long years before, at Cambridge, and this nutbrown maid of theirs was to cheer them by spending her holidays with them; but none of these pleasant plans turned out quite as they should.

Charles was not at all happy in his retirement and did not know how to employ himself. Mary Lamb's attacks of insanity were growing more frequent as the years went by, she could no longer bear the strain of company, or any excitement. Even housekeeping soon became too much for her and after the death of their faithful old servant she and her brother retired to lodgings at Enfield. William visited them there, on one of his visits to London, and brought back a sad report of his old friends. They had both grown melancholy and strange in their ways, and Mary had been sadly rambling and depressed. He thought that it could not be long before she went out of her mind altogether. Dorothy sighed to think of the devoted brother and sister in such straits, she could not think what Charles would do without Mary.

William was growing a very dull dog nowadays, less and less of a poet and more and more of the respected country gentleman. He wrote little poetry, though the whole household were wearied out by correcting the proofs of a collected edition of his works, which came out in the year after Scott's visit. They all had to help, to spare William's eyes, which were so often so troublesome nowadays that he could not read anything but the largest print. Dora was his constant aid and companion, he could go nowhere and do nothing without his bright daughter, the two were inseparable. He was terribly anxious when the girl began to cough and grow thin, just as her two aunts, Mary's sisters, had done in their youth. He talked frantically of sending Dora to Italy for a winter and in 1828 he took her for a holiday to Germany, with himself and Coleridge.

Dorothy did not go with them; she spent that whole summer in the Isle of Man. Her youngest nephew, Willie, had been ill, and she took him with her to stay with Joanna and Henry Hutchinson, who had gone to live in the island. She loved her two nephews dearly and when, a year later, Johnny, the eldest, took orders and went off to his first curacy, at Whitwick in Leicestershire, it seemed a charming plan for his Aunt Dorothy to go and keep house for the serious and quiet youth. Whitwick was not five miles from Coleorton and it was the interest of the Beaumonts which had got John his title. Sir George had died two years earlier and there was a new heir, a distant cousin, at the Hall; but Lady Beaumont was living there still, a fine lively old lady, trailing widow's weeds and plumed like a hearse. Dorothy often visited her.

Most of Sir George's pictures had been bequeathed to the National Gallery which he had founded, and the gallery at the Hall looked half-empty without them; but Hartley Coleridge's portrait by David Wilkie still hung there, mellow and melancholy, and many of Sir George's own landscapes, each with a brown tree and a green tree in the foreground, according to his rule. The new heir had bought fresh furniture and altered the house; but the lime-tree grove which old Sir George had ordered had already grown into a whispering colonnade and the cedar which he had planted in the lawn was only just beginning to grow tall, for a cedar has a longer life than a man. The winter garden which William had designed was now a warm sheltered corner where Dorothy and Lady Beaumont could walk up and down on sunny mornings and talk together about old times.

Dorothy was a great walker still; the country people got to know her well, for she was always striding about the muddy lanes, a thin restless little woman with a nutcracker brown face, chin and nose nearly meeting. She swung her arms about in an ungainly fashion as she hurried along and they heard her talking to herself continually. The women tapped their foreheads when they spoke of the curate's queer old aunt who kept house for him, but the village children loved her and followed her about.

It was the walking that made her fall ill. She had taken one of her long solitary tramps in pouring wet April weather and within a few hours was stricken with fever and a violent internal inflammation, which the medical science of those days could neither diagnose nor relieve. She lay half-conscious and delirious for days together, raving in a high cracked voice of times and people long forgotten. Her life was despaired of and they sent word to Rydal, to fetch her brother; but William could not come, though his sister had often called for him in her fevered dreams. He was almost blind with the old trouble in his eyes, sitting in the dark with leeches and blisters to his temples.

He had to be left in Dora's and Sara's charge while Mary came south to nurse her sister-in-law. When Dorothy awoke out of her fever it was Mary's gentle face that she saw bending above her; and beside Mary's shoulder was the long serious frightened face of Mary's and William's son, the noble boy whom Dorothy had first taken from his nurse's arms at Dove Cottage, on a summer's morning years ago, when the swallows were nesting at the window. They thought her out of her wits still when she said, with her wild sweet smile, "Are the swallows back yet? I fear their nest is broken down."

Mary nursed her most tenderly until she was fit to travel. She went first as far as Halifax, to old Aunt Rawson who had brought her up, and stayed for a time in the big house by Sowerby Bridge, while Mary went back to William. The town had grown enormously. The valleys were full of chimneys and clattering mills, the August sky was full of smoke and reddened at night by the glare of furnaces. Aunt Rawson was always complaining that nowadays she could not keep her curtains clean. In a few more years the grass itself would be dirty on the hills where Dorothy used to climb as a child. There was a black tree of industry growing here in these valleys to threaten the green pastoral England which had nurtured William and Dorothy. The invalid was distressed by so much grime and noise, she pined for the shelter of her own native mountains and said plaintively, "I shall never be well till I am at home in Rydal." So they got her back to her own valley, but she was in bed all through that winter, a hard captivity for one who had always been so active.

4

It was a quiet winter for them all, and a sad one. William still had a great deal of trouble with his eyes, which were often so bad that he could not read or write for weeks together. He found the long candlelight or firelight evenings distressing in the extreme. Dora and Mary took turns to read aloud to him till their voices grew hoarse, or till he nodded himself asleep. He was very patient, but not very obedient to his doctor, for he would persist in composing sonnets. He had been told not to fatigue his brain in any way, but he could not forgo the soothing mechanical occupation. He had written poetry for so long that he felt unemployed if he were deprived of it. They made him go out whenever his eyes and the weather allowed it; at sixty he flattered himself that he was still as good a walker and skater as most of the young men of twenty about him and not far inferior to himself at that age.

Sara Coleridge had married that summer, while Dorothy was away, Henry Nelson, one of the Ottery St. Mary cousins, a young barrister who afterwards became her father's biographer. The princess in exile had always resented living on her Uncle Robert's charity and it had been her dream to go and live with or near her father in London; this dream was now fulfilled by what turned out a very happy marriage. Mrs. Coleridge had gone away too; she was to end her days with Derwent, her sensible successful second boy, who was now in orders and had a school at Helston, in Cornwall. She found great comfort in Derwent for all that she had lost. She was now satisfied, they said, to be quiet, and did not fret or flurry as she used to do. If adversity is the best school Mrs. Coleridge had had plenty of it in her time. Dorothy was astonished to find how much they all missed the poor woman out of the country. They had seen little of her lately, but there were so few people left who could talk of old times as she could.

Only Hartley Coleridge now remained behind in the north and he had been a sad disappointment to his mother. His school at Ambleside had failed and he seemed to have lost all his ambitions. He wrote a few essays and sonnets, some of which were published, otherwise he was dependent upon his family. His mother sent him small gifts and clothes from time to time; but whenever he had any money he used to wander away from Grasmere and be heard of here and there about the country, tramping from place to place and drinking heavily till all was spent. He was a wonderful talker, like his father, and the country people would always give him drink to set him going, that was the pity of it. After a time he went away to Leeds and lived with his publisher, Mr. Bingley, who kept him sober and at work for a couple of years.

All that time Dorothy's health was growing worse. She was not strong enough to go to her nephew John's wedding, in 1831. That summer, when William set out for Abbotsford, in the pony-carriage driven by Dora, with a green veil over his weak eyes, his sister cried at parting with him and said, "Now I shall never see Yarrow." She made him promise that he would go there for her sake, so he did and wrote her a poem about it; but the visit was a sad one, for they found Sir Walter old and broken. He was going to Italy for the winter in hopes of recovery, but he fell sick there, was brought home and died the following summer. The time was approaching for the Wordsworths when old friends began to drop away from them, like leaves from an autumn tree.

Dorothy was very ill again in the spring of 1833. She did not leave her bed for five weeks and her life was a struggle from day to day; but with the warm weather she rallied again and though she could not walk more than twenty or thirty steps yet she was able to be wheeled about in a chair for an hour or so in the garden. Dora used to drive her about the summer roads in a little carriage drawn by Naso, the fat pony, who had dragged William all the way to Scotland. In this conveyance they could go some way, even as far as the top of the hill, where they could look down on Grasmere Vale, round and green like a wren's nest, embowered in summer foliage.

Hartley Coleridge was living quite close to Dove Cottage again, with village folk named Fleming, in Town End. They used to meet him about the roads, a queer little figure who still looked like a boy, in a dark blue round cloth jacket and white trousers, with a black silk handkerchief tied round his throat like a sailor and a wide straw hat crammed on the back of his black curly head. He would walk beside the carriage for a little and talk to them in his mournful musical voice; then suddenly he would run from them like a child at full speed down the road. At a distance they would see him pause, stop dead, wave his arms about and then run on again as his thoughts moved him, sometimes swinging his hat in the air, sometimes shouldering the great stick he carried as if it were a gun. Hartley, it seemed, would never grow up. He had had some success while he was in Leeds, with a volume of poetry and with his *Northern Worthies*, a series of lives of famous north-country folk; but after that his publisher had gone bankrupt and Hartley had come home again to Grasmere, where everybody knew him, loved him and was ready to take care of him. It seemed likely that he would end his days there.

5

That September, 1833, Dorothy sat for her portrait, perched up valiantly in a yellow shawl and her best red dress, with her spectacles on her nose and her pet poodle, Miss Belle, beside her. The likeness was not good, but the family had never had any other. It was her last exertion before winter shut her into her room again. She declared stoutly that her prison was the prettiest and most cheerful in England. She could look out from her windows across Rydal Water to the fells; she delighted in the books and news supplied by friends and neighbours who came to visit her, and in a little garden of pot-plants which she had in the window. She tamed a pet robin too, which would come in whenever the sash was raised, perch upon one of her pictures and warble softly; this was a great delight to her. She sent her dear love to Edith Southey, when the stately girl was married that winter, and questioned Dora, who had been bridesmaid, most eagerly about the wedding. Yet she pined sadly for fresh air and sunshine and when the east winds of April kept her still a prisoner the longing became an agony, though she chided herself for her impatience. She wept for joy when she was carried out at last on to the terrace, saw budding trees and flowers about her and heard the cuckoo calling among the hills. It was like a return from the grave.

She did not guess how sad a year lay before her, one friend slipping away after another, like birds going south to seek the sun. It was July when William came to sit beside her chair and told her that Coleridge was dead. That was news which they had long expected, yet it came as a shock and a loosening of the ties which bound her to earth. She had not seen that lost friend for fourteen years, not since the three of them stood in the garden at Highgate and she told herself, "There are no birds in last year's nest," but she had felt that there was a bond which still united them while he lived. Now it was as if a sudden gale had torn down the old empty nest and scattered it at her feet. She knew that William felt it too, for he sat with his white head bent, staring at the ground. She could not see his eyes because of the green spectacles with which he was always nowadays disfigured, but she saw the twitch of his thin lips and heard the pain in his voice as he said, "All these years I have felt that he was still present with us"; and then, after a long silence, "We must prepare to follow him."

He told her that their friend had not lain long a-dying; he who had suffered so many pains had in the end quitted the body of this death as quietly as a child. In his last days it seemed that his mind had gone back to his youth, for he had turned the pages of his own poems until he found the one which he had written at Nether Stowey, in the summer of her first visit, beginning *This lime-tree bower my prison.* He had composed it while he was sitting in the cottage garden, with his scalded foot propped on a chair, too lame to go with his guests to the top of the Quantock ridge. It had been addressed to Charles Lamb and in the margin the dying poet had now scribbled, "Ch. and Mary Lamb—dear to my heart, yea, as it were, my heart. Aet. 63, 1834. 1797-1834—37 years." Dorothy could work the same mornful addition only too easily as she sat in the rustling green shade of the Rydal Mount trees, a prisoner who would never again climb to the top of any mountain. She wondered if their friend had thought of her, or of William, as he lay a-dying, but that she would never know. She said to William, "Poor Hartley, he will grieve longest of any." William thought that she had taken the news very quietly and was glad of it, but she herself knew that something had broken in her when she heard it, which would never mend.

She slipped down quickly after that into her weakness. She complained of no pain, but seemed content to lie quiet for long hours together, without speech, though her bright smile was full of love and tenderness for all who came near her. Dora nursed her devotedly. The tall girl was pining sadly for Edward Quillinan, who had gone to Portugal for the winter; everybody knew, without discussion, that William would not favour his suit. Dora did not complain, but she coughed and grew thin again, shut up all day long with old folk and sick people, for her father was as good as blind again for weeks together and her aunt, Sara Hutchinson, had grown to look so worn and haggard that you would have taken her for ten years older than her sister Mary. It was a melancholy household that Christmas, and when the fiddlers came they were sent away, for the Wordsworths had just heard the news of Charles Lamb's death.

The little man had been very greatly shaken by the loss of Coleridge. He had been living down at Edmonton with his sister, already dead to him for many months out of each year, now violent, now rambling, and past knowledge of her surroundings. She had always prayed to die before her devoted brother, but it was he who left her, with little warning. He had stumbled and fallen on one of his tottering walks, grazing his face against a stone, then developed erysipelas and was dead within four days. All this William told his own sister, sitting beside her bed. She gazed at him with her wild eyes, grown stranger than ever and murmured, "She should have died first. In losing her brother she loses everything."

He said, "She is in no state to understand what has happened. She will bear his loss better than he could have borne hers. There is a merciful cloud upon her mind, she cannot tell what has become of her brother." Dorothy put her hand to her forehead and said vaguely, "Yes, the cloud . . . I feel it sometimes, here. It lies upon me with a weight like frost. I cannot move it." He was troubled by her wandering and distracted airs. The doctors had warned him that her mind was becoming weakened by the strain of her long illness. He and his wife feared that she might go the same way as Mary Lamb had gone and so it proved.

Mary Wordsworth, the gentle and uncomplaining, had a sad year of it in 1835. Troubles never come singly and she had everything upon her together. First it was her bright Dora who seemed to have pined into a decline, was supposed to have spinal trouble and had to lie on her back for months together; then the doctors threatened William with the loss of his eyesight and at midsummer her own sister Sara died, after five weeks' illness. She had long shrivelled into a brisk censorious spinster, shrewd, sharp, bustling and reliable, the mainstay of the household; Mary, who had loved her dearly, did not know how she would do without her. In life she had never rested, but in death she wore upon her face a heavenly expression of peace and silence, her fretful anxious look was quite smoothed out. You could see then how she had once looked, long ago, to the strange genius who had comforted himself with her devotion.

Her vanishing was a sad shattering of Dorothy's faculties, after Sara's death she went out of her wits and never recovered. The doctors told William that there was no prospect of her being other than a prisoner for the rest of her days, and so it proved. She became like a very clever spoilt tyrannical child; "Faculty-struck, poor thing," said the village folk who peered over the locked garden gate and saw the emaciated little figure being dragged round the terrace in her wheeled chair. She liked to be noticed and would call out to people like a child, pleased when they laughed at her queer cracked voice and comical sayings. Sometimes she was very difficult to manage; she would rub her head violently as if she felt some oppression there, sing or cry out with a strange bird-like scream, and make foolish noises. She could only be turned from this by getting her to recite verses, which she would do with great feeling and most pathetic emphasis. On her better days she was still capable of understanding what was said to her and could astonish William by finishing a quotation which he had made from some poem which they both loved.

He could do more with her than any one, when she was at her worst his presence would quiet her. He spent much time with her, though it was a great grief to him to see her so changed. He would come down from her room with tears in his eyes and say, "All I can do for her now is to heat her nightcap for her. I have done it twenty times within the last quarter of an hour. It seems to give her a moment's pleasure and that is some comfort." She took a childish pleasure in the sound of the cuckoo-clock, which hung on the stairs. She would often lift her finger in delight when she heard its liquid double note, as if it made her think of vanished springtimes; and at Christmas, when the fiddlers came their rounds, if she were awake she would ask to have the window set open that she might hear their music. For the most part she was tractable and quiet, seeming to have no pain or discomfort. The doctors said that she might live a long time yet, but could never recover her wits. She still had her dying to do, all else was finished.

6

Dorothy was sixty-four when this cloud descended upon her and she survived another twenty years, unconscious of the troubles of those about her. During that time William declined into a simple dreary old gentleman, white-haired, green-spectacled, harsh and unapproachable. The country folk who saw him wandering about the roads said that he had a face without a bit of pleasure in it; he looked as if he had never been young. "He was not a man as folk could crack with, nor yet a man as could crack with folks. He would pass you by on the road as if you were nobbut a stone. His poetry had never a bit of a laugh in it and he kept it over long in his head." So they complained of the sour self-centred old man, shut up in the prison of his own nature. He got some fame in his latter years; people began to read and even to admire his poetry, which like his character had been much softened by age.

He and Mary used to go to London every year. They say that Mary was very jealous of her husband's literary eminence and was always watching to see that he had the deference due to him; otherwise she had grown into a small puckered withered winking lady who seldom spoke. William's eyes troubled him greatly. He wore his green spectacles all the time and at parties would protect himself from the candle-light by a kind of portable shade which he carried about in his pocket and stuck up against other people's candles. The young Thomas Carlyle saw him once at a grand dinner, beautifully screened in the shadow of this vertical green circle, slowly and steadily eating raisins with a rock-like indifference to the rest of the company. In London he was on the defensive still, very anxious to appear a dignified figure, but in the Lake country he became a kind of rural prophet and laid down the law to every one. Mary used to say to any stranger who did not listen obediently, "Mr. Wordsworth is never interrupted."

Their bright daughter married her old suitor, Edward Quillinan, in the end, but only after long waiting, like her mother, for her father could not bear the thought of parting with her and resisted stubbornly for years. She and her husband lived close by Rydal Mount and so did the child-like Hartley, who had come to end his days in the Nab Cottage, at the foot of the hill. It was the same house where Mr. De Quincey had courted his Peggy, long years ago. Hartley now had a little dark parlour there, heaped with dusty books and papers, but he only sat in it at nights or in wet weather, for whenever he could be out of doors he ran about the roads, a little old man with long white hair down to his shoulders, who waved his arms as if he thought he were flying and seemed to need stones in his pockets to keep him on the ground. The country folk all thought that he was the true author of William's poetry, for he seemed to them much more like a poet than the stiff old Distributor of Stamps. Hartley knew the insides of all the cottages for miles round and was welcome everywhere; his head was mid-winter, but his heart was green as May. He would pour out his wandering eloquence to these poor folk, but avoided his own kind. Sometimes he was induced to attend an evening party and would come gliding in, noiseless and shy, neatly dressed in black, with a stiff slow bow and a deprecating air; but he was sadly ill at ease in formal company. He preferred the humble folk in cottages and taverns and ran away from any house where he might be watched or controlled.

The Wordsworths kept guard on him without his knowing it. There was nobody else left to look after him, for his mother was dead and his uncle, Robert Southey, had come to a sad end. Mrs. Southey died in 1837, after a long illness. Robert took her loss strangely and stupidly, hardly seeming to grieve for her; and married again almost immediately, to his family's great annoyance. His second choice was a Miss Caroline Bowles, an elderly poetess with whom he had long carried on a platonic literary correspondence. It soon appeared that his wits were failing him and he sank into a melancholy stupor, from which he never recovered. At his death, five years later, William was made Poet Laureate. He was embarrassed by this honour, which would once have enchanted and delighted his family, and would have refused it, protesting that his singing days were over, but the new Queen, Victoria, insisted and the laurel wreath descended upon his worn temples. Two years later, in 1847, he went to London and attended a ball at Buckingham Palace; the American Ambassadress shed tears, they say, when she saw the white-haired poet go down on his stiff knees in a borrowed velvet coat to kiss the young queen's hand.

That summer died Mary Lamb, a happy mindless old woman of eighty-two, long lost to her world; and the young Dora, William's beloved daughter, who had waited too long for her happiness. She and Edward Quillinan only had seven years together before consumption killed her; that was her father's fault. William grieved terribly for his daughter, repeating over and over, "She was such a bright creature." When his faithful servant James urged with great simplicity, "But do you not think, sir, that she is brighter now than ever," the old poet burst into a flood of tears. The only thing that would comfort him in his grief was to sit by his mad sister and this Mary encouraged him to do. Dorothy did not always know her brother, but it seemed to quiet her, just to have him beside her.

Dora had died at midsummer and the second Christmas after killed her old playmate Hartley Coleridge. He fell into a ditch coming home from a Christmas party, when the fiddlers were going about the roads playing their old tunes, and was not found till morning; so he caught the cold that killed him. He slipped out of life as easily as he had lived. Every one in the Vale loved him and grieved for him. William himself chose the place for Hartley's grave, in the churchyard by the river at Grasmere, a plot close beside the green mounds that covered his own three children. Hartley had stood in that place on the day that Dora was buried. William told the sexton this and begged that the ground should be kept for himself and his wife; he said, "We are old people and it cannot be for long."

It was not for long; he followed his daughter a year later. He had just passed his eightieth birthday; he died full of years and honours, a peaceful sage who had long outlived the ardours and agonies of his youth, a poet no longer. His sister survived him for five years. She had experienced a strange lightening at the time of his death, had seemed to understand why all around her were weeping and had shown herself most gentle and tractable, as if she wished to help them; but afterwards she relapsed again, became quite senile, had to be fed, cleansed and guarded like a child, slept continually and grew more and more feeble. When she approached her eighty-fourth birthday Mary was told that she could not live many weeks.

7

That was at Christmas time, when the fiddlers were going about the roads. Mary stood by the dying woman's bed, late at night, and saw in the light of the nurse's shaded candle a placid waxen face, from which all the lines had lately smoothed themselves away. Dorothy slept as lightly as a child and her breathing scarcely moved the sheet over her. Mary said in a low voice, "She is very quiet to-night," and the nurse replied in the same tone, "Ah! she's sleeping easy now, poor lady, but earlier on she was awake and very lively. I had quite a bit of trouble with her. She heard the Christmas fiddlers going down the road, playing and singing, and she wanted to have the window open and listen. I thought it no harm to humour her, mum, as it was such a mild fine starry night, so I raised the sash for a few minutes, just to let her hear the tune. She got quite excited then and wanted to get up and go downstairs. She fancied there were some children dancing in the kitchen. She gets mixed up all the time and doesn't rightly know where she is."

Mary said absently, "I suppose she thought she was back at Dove Cottage." The nurse, who was a decent thoughtful woman, but a stranger to the valley, replied, "I couldn't say about that, mum; I did hear her telling me some nonsense about a bird and a nest, but I'm sure I don't know what she meant. I told her I must shut the window then, because the fiddlers were all gone by. She made a bit of fuss at first and swore she could still hear them at it; but I had to be firm with her, because it wouldn't do to have her catching cold. So I shut down the sash. She was quite good then, as soon as she understood that she wasn't going to have her own way. She's like a child, she knows when she must behave. Only she's like one of these clever children, mum, that will pretend they're in the right, whatever you say. The last thing she told me, before she dropped off for the night, was that she could still hear the fiddlers, somewhere very far off. She would have it that music always went on, long after the men who made it had done with their playing and singing. She said it went right up to the stars."

THE END